I0628791

THE INVASION

Book 4 in The Union Series

T.H. HERNANDEZ

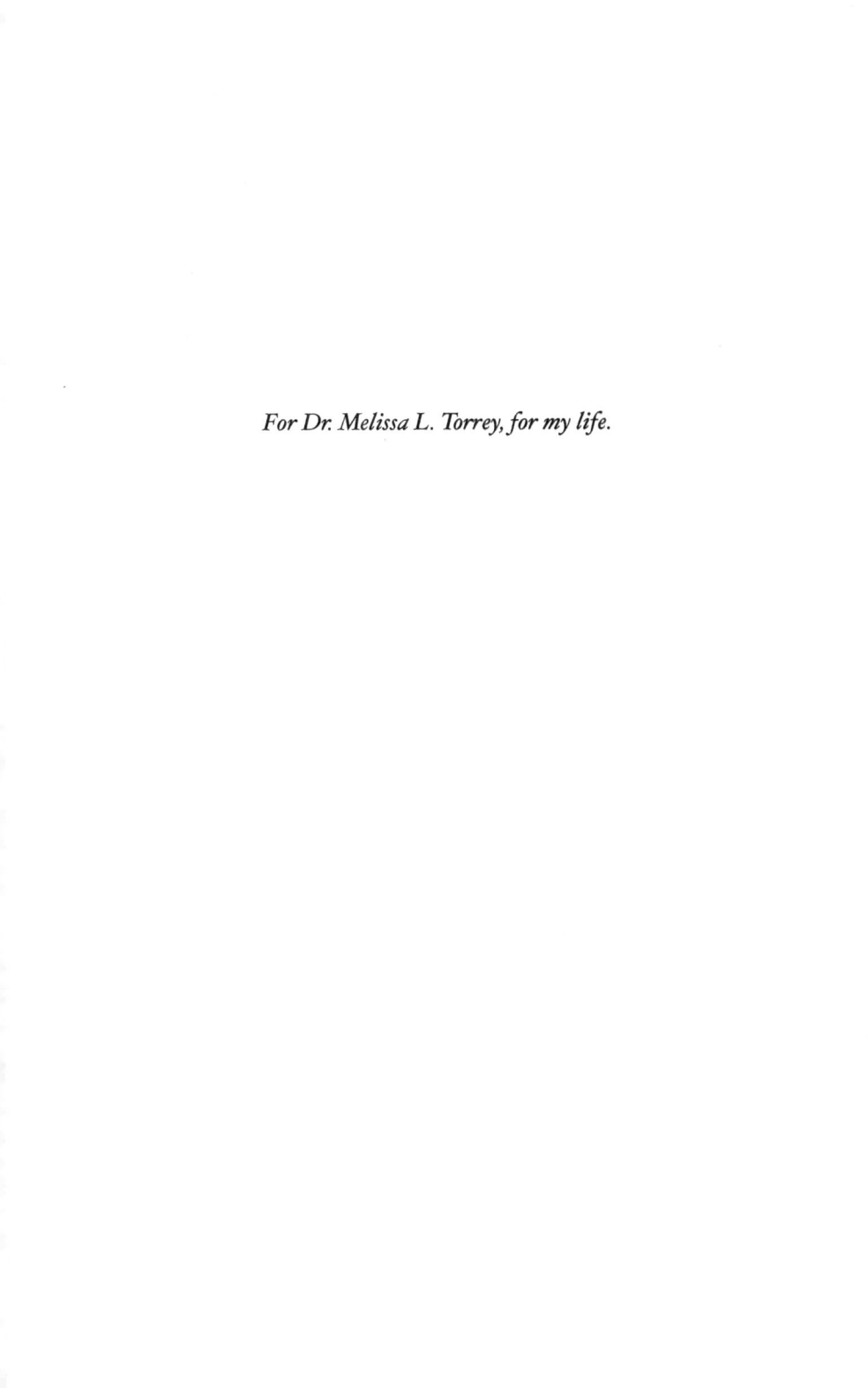

For Dr. Melissa L. Torrey, for my life.

COPYRIGHT

THE INVASION
© 2017 T.H. Hernandez

All rights reserved. No part of this publication may be reproduced, distributed, or transmitted in any form or by any means, including photocopying, recording, or other electronic or mechanical methods, without the prior written permission of the author, except in the case of brief quotations embodied in critical reviews and certain other noncommercial uses permitted by copyright law. For permission requests, contact the author by email with the subject line: "Permission Request" at the address below.

T.H. Hernandez
thhernandezauthor@gmail.com
http://thhernandez.com

This is a work of fiction. Names, characters, places, and incidents are a product of the author's imagination. Locales and public names are sometimes used for atmospheric purposes. Any resemblance to actual people, living or dead, or to businesses,

companies, events, institutions, or locales is completely
coincidental.

Cover Art © 2017 by Mark Sgarbossa (www.popgroovy.com)
Edited by Barbara Trageser and E.J. Hernandez

The Invasion / T.H. Hernandez. -- 1st ed.

ISBN 978-0-9908688-8-0 (Paperback)
978-1-5378803-5-8 (eBook)

BOOK 1 :: THE UPRISING

"The brave man is not he who does not feel afraid, but he who conquers that fear."
— Nelson Mandela

BOARDED

Evan

*T*he slowing of the A-Train pulls me from a deep, dreamless sleep. I sit up and twist, stretching out my neck, a smile overtaking my face as the events of the past day return to me. Bryce is alive. I left him sleeping in my hotel room while I hopped a train to go meet Tony. We're finally going to tell the world about the Ruins.

I glance out the window only to be greeted by darkness. There are no lights from the upcoming station. A murmur rises through the car as the other passengers voice my confusion aloud. Across from me a guy stares at his tablet, his eyes widening. His head pops up and his horrified gaze locks with mine, sending a chill through me.

"What's wrong?"

"We're being boarded."

"Boarded? What does that mean?"

"A bunch of people with guns, calling themselves the Uprising, are boarding the train."

The chill becomes ice, turning my blood to slush. Two words repeat in my head: *we failed.*

I get up and cross the aisle to look at the guy's tablet. He's reading a news story about A-Trains throughout the Union being taken over by soldiers. My breath stalls in my lungs. The murmur grows louder and someone begins to cry. Panic wells up from my core. Are they looking for me? Do they know I blew up their camps? I move toward the doors, driven by a burning need to escape before they find me.

"Where are you going?" tablet dude asks.

"I don't know, but this isn't good."

He studies me for a few beats with pale green eyes. "No, it's not. If the news stories are to be believed, anyway. We're not near a station. You know that right?"

I nod.

"And it's a long way down."

"Yep."

He shoves his tablet in his back pocket and grabs his backpack from the seat next to him, the corners of his mouth lifting in a wry grin. "Then let's go."

I lift a brow. "You're coming with me?"

He shrugs. "Like you said, this isn't good. I'd rather take my chances out there." He leads the way down the aisle to the side doors.

"What are you doing?" a woman screeches.

"Getting off this train," tablet guy says over his shoulder.

"Are you insane?" someone else calls.

"Maybe, but based on what I just read, staying isn't proof of sanity, either."

This guy is different from most Union guys, and yet, he doesn't speak like someone from the Ruins. He's missing the accent, for one, plus he lacks the roughness around the edges. While the other passengers are cowering in their seats, unsure what to do, he's ready to jump from the train with a total stranger.

He notices me staring and winks. "Are we doing this, Red?"

"It's Evan, and yeah."

"Chase." He nods before pulling the emergency release and pushing the door open.

The voices grow louder. "You're going to get us all killed," one of them yells. But to my surprise, several are lined up behind us.

I poke my head out the door and look at the ground far below. The interior lights spill out the windows and illuminate soft patches on the grass below. At least I think it's grass.

"How do we get down there?" A young girl, maybe fourteen, with wide brown eyes, asks.

My mind reverts to my Uprising training. "We need a rope of some kind."

Chase grins like an idiot at my side before moving back down the aisle and opening an overhead bin. He takes a handful of the small, personal-sized blankets they give passengers and returns, handing half of them to me. Between the two of us, we begin to build a blanket rope. Chase is using a regular overhand knot, which'll never hold.

"Tie it in a square knot, like this." I demonstrate the technique, showing him how it won't pull free.

"Got it."

Within minutes, we have a decent length, but not nearly enough. Chase grabs a few more blankets, and when we're done, we've got close to fifteen feet, but we're running out of time. The Uprising will be back here before long.

Chase reaches for my arm and turns me to face him. "You go down first."

"Why me?"

"'Cause I need you to help me get the others down."

The group planning on joining us has swelled to nearly a dozen. "Yeah, okay." Plus, if this brilliant plan doesn't work, I have more experience falling on my ass without breaking bones than probably anyone else here. "How do you want to do this?"

Chase scratches his neck and peers over the side. He ties one end of the makeshift rope to the handhold next to the door, tugging hard to make sure it's secure, before lowering the rest until it hangs about eight feet off the ground.

"Should we add another one?" I ask.

He glances toward the front. "No time."

Sucking in a breath, I grab hold of the blanket rope with both hands and back up, bracing my feet against the edge of the train. "You can do this," I whisper, refusing to look down. I close my eyes and wrap my ankles around the length below me, inching down the way the Uprising taught me. My hands sweat, but the moisture is quickly absorbed by the soft fabric. When I reach the bottom, I drop the remaining distance to the grass in a squat before giving Chase a thumbs-up.

The young girl with the wide brown eyes slides down next, her sniffling growing louder as she gets closer. She reaches the end and her shoes dangle in the air.

"Let go," I say. "I've got you.

She releases the rope and falls, limbs wild, her foot connecting with my jaw. I lose my balance and fall back, the girl landing on top of me.

"Sorry," she says with another sniffle.

I push up and give her a hand, pulling her to her feet. She wraps her arms around her torso to keep warm in the cool evening air. With so much adrenaline coursing through me, I can spare a layer, and pull off my hoodie, handing it to her.

"Thank you," she whispers.

The rest come down steadily, some more adept than others, before there is a long pause. Long enough that I begin to fear the Uprising has reached our train car. Before panic can set in, though, Chase begins his descent with smooth, practiced movements. He must be a rescue worker of some kind. He's far too well-prepared for what we just did than an average Unionite. So why didn't he know how to tie a proper knot?

Chase drops to the ground next to me, eyes wide, fixed on my back. *Shit.* I gave my hoodie to the girl not thinking about my tank top exposing my tattoo and the scar from where I was shot escaping the Uprising. Adding the inked U on my shoulder to the events of the past hour, Chase has every right to be suspicious of me. There's no way to explain it, either.

He shakes his head, as if he's clearing his mind. "Who *are* you?"

I open my mouth to tell Chase that I'm no one, but we just worked together to get ourselves and a dozen others off the train. He may have even saved my life. I owe him the truth. "It's a complicated story, but I'll tell you when we get someplace safe."

He presses his lips into a tight line and his gaze travels over me, head to toe and back again, but gone is the slight humor in his eyes from earlier. His muscular body is tense and distrust oozes from his pores. Between the soldiers and my rapid decision to jump from an elevated train, I can't blame him. Nothing about tonight has been normal, and now as far as he's concerned, neither am I.

I scan our surroundings to determine our next move. We need to get away from here. We're in a sparsely populated area somewhere in the South; beyond that, I'm clueless. Away from the train's lights, shadows prevail. I'm anxious to put as much distance between me and the Uprising as possible. The others can follow me or not.

Chase grabs my arm and spins me to face him. My gaze drops to his hand, and he loosens his grip but doesn't let go.

"My name really is Evan. Evan Taylor."

He studies me for a few seconds, likely struggling to place the name he's no doubt heard.

"I'm who you think I am, but what you don't know is —" A metallic click makes me freeze. A sound I'm only too familiar with — a rifle being cocked. My heartbeat pauses before taking off at a gallop.

A woman screaming draws my attention to the small group who escaped with us, corralled by a handful of soldiers with long, menacing guns pointed at them. I duck back further into the darkness, staying out of the sweep of their lights. Although I should run, I can't just leave these people. People who followed me down here.

"What the hell is going on?" Chase asks under his breath.

"I'm not sure, but my best guess is they want to see who bailed from the train."

"What do we do?"

I watch in horror as the soldiers push the group to their knees and make them place their hands on the backs of their heads. "I don't know, but if they capture me, they'll kill me."

His mouth falls open.

I don't have time to explain, but if I don't, he may try to stop me.

"Hey!"

My gaze shifts beyond Chase where a soldier is pointing at us.

"Two more over there."

Two soldiers remain behind to guard the other passengers while the rest march toward us. When they're close enough for me to make out their faces, I'm relieved not to recognize any of them. I angle myself in front of Chase to hide my tattoo. He seems to instinctively realize what I'm doing and moves closer, blocking their view of my back. I pull in deep breaths, trying to remain calm.

A narrow man with a sharp nose dressed in Uprising fatigues waves us forward with his long-fingered hand. "Over there with the rest of 'em."

Chase puts an arm around me, his large hand covering my ink. "What's going on?"

A girl not much older than me shoves Chase in the back with the butt of her rifle. "We ask the questions, not you. Over there with the others. Now."

Chase stumbles and his hand slips from my shoulder. He rights himself, draping his arm across my back again, but it's too late.

"Not another step," orders Sharp Nose.

I freeze, hoping they won't hurt Chase simply because he's with me, but the truth is they probably will.

My head drops and I turn toward him. "I'm so sorry, Chase."

Fingers laced, palms plastered to the back of our skulls, Chase and I tread across tall grass, overdue for a cutting, to where our fellow passengers are huddled.

"Everybody up," the girl soldier says.

Guns trained at our backs, we're marched across a grassy patch where a soft glow can be seen in the distance. As we near, I make out a couple of tents and a small fenced-in area. The lead soldier pulls open a gate and herds everyone inside.

He throws his arm out in front of Chase, stopping him. "Not you two." After securing the holding pen with a lock, he brushes past us. "Follow me."

We traipse after him toward a large tent. The girl smirks, seemingly pleased with herself. She probably thinks she caught a deserter, but she has no idea who she really has. Before they figure it out, I need to guarantee Chase's safety.

"He doesn't know me. We just met on the train."

"Quiet," she orders. The smirk falls from her face and she uses her angry face. If she wasn't holding a gun on us, I might laugh. She was not born to play the tough girl.

Chase narrows his eyes and stares at the ground.

"Chase," I whisper, "this has nothing to do with you, but they think you're with me."

The muzzle of the girl's rifle introduces itself to my stomach. "I said shut it."

Chase's face darkens and anger flashes in his eyes.

"Chase, there is nothing you can do for me," I wheeze out, catching my breath. "It's too late. Just...don't provoke them, okay?"

Something hard slams into the side of my face and stars dance across my vision before it goes black. The next thing I'm aware of is Chase pulling me to my feet. I blink, trying to orient myself, searing pain racing through my skull.

"Was that really necessary?" Chase growls.

"I said be quiet." She grinds the words out through clenched teeth, and I no longer find her humorous.

I run my fingertips gingerly over my cheekbone and wince. Lesson learned. Keep my mouth shut.

We wait what seems like ages before another soldier approaches, a beefy guy with close-cropped hair. "Follow me."

My stomach tightens as we turn and trail behind him, Chase in front of me. The girl jabs her gun barrel between my shoulder blades, reminding me she's still in charge. Buzz Cut stops at a smaller tent, opening the flap and holding it for us to enter. Solar lanterns illuminate the interior, giving it a warm, deceptively inviting glow. My eyes are immediately drawn to a group of soldiers in an animated conversation in the corner. Buzz Cut clears his throat, halting all talk as six heads turn our way.

My jaw hinges downward and for a few moments I can't move or even breathe. When my brain begins functioning again, I realize Draya is looking at me with the same expression of surprise mixed with horror.

She recovers first, rearranging her facial features into a mask of indifference. I inhale a deep breath and steel myself as she approaches. She pauses a foot away and crosses her arms, her gaze traveling over Chase first, then me.

She turns to Sharp Nose. "Where did you find these two?"

"On the ground. They jumped from one of the cars."

Draya's eyebrows lift along with the left corner of her mouth. "And why did you bring them here?"

Buzz Cut grabs my arm and spins me to display my tattoo. He releases me, and I turn back to face Draya. Her eyes are filled with shock and another emotion that doesn't make sense — hopelessness.

REGRETS

Cyrus

*T*aking a cleansing breath, I raise my knuckles to the door. It's early and I give a passing thought to getting coffee and coming back a little later, but the need to see Evan is more powerful than a desire not to wake her.

I knock and my teeth clench as I wait for a response. Rustling comes from the other side, but no footsteps, so I knock again. More rustling is followed by silence, then heavy footfalls approach the door. Not Evan. This must be the wrong room. I pull the paper Eddie gave me out of my pocket to read it again. Unless he made a mistake when he wrote it down, this is the right one.

The door opens and my eyes widen to the point I'm sure my eyeballs are going to escape their sockets. *Son of a bitch*. I blink to make sure I'm not hallucinating, and a huge smile splits my face. "Fuck, man, you're alive."

Bryce runs a hand over the top of his head and steps back from the door.

I take in the room, confusion replacing my initial shock. One rumpled bed. My attention returns to Bryce, wearing nothing but a pair of jeans, his T-shirt discarded on the floor.

My face is hot like I'm too close to a fire. I take a step back. No way would she sleep with him. Not again. Not when she knew I was coming back. My hands rake through my hair while I try to sort it all out. Eddie was weird when I showed up at his place. Did he know Bryce and Evan were holed up together in a hotel room? *Fuck.*

Dick turns and glances around the room, as if he's searching for something before turning back to me. "Look, she says you guys split up."

Bile rises in the back of my throat as I struggle against the building rage. My eyes lock onto his side where red, angry burns wrap around his torso. Before I can stop myself, my fist connects with his face with satisfying force, sending a sharp jolt up my arm that I relish.

He stumbles back, but doesn't fall, and I step forward to hit him again. My head throbs, on the verge of exploding. Douche braces himself for the next blow but doesn't move to defend himself. As I draw back, I notice the burns again and check myself.

He rubs his jaw and stares at me, anger flaring across his face.

I unload a few choice words, and his eyes widen in response, like my language offends him or some shit.

"Forget it," I spit, turning and storming down the hall. I slam my hand into the elevator button, but I can't wait for it to arrive, opting for the stairs instead.

White fury scorches through me and I punch the wall, feeling the crunch, the searing pain that temporarily distracts me from the storm raging in my chest.

The hum of activity in the station draws my attention away from my dark thoughts. No clue how I got here. The blood on my knuckle has dried and my fist throbs, although I'm considering putting it through another wall. A harried woman rushes past me on her way to the ticket machine, her destination most likely known. Mine on the other hand ... not so much.

I wander over to the elevators and push both buttons. Whichever one arrives first will decide my fate. Up will take me to the A-Train. Back to the Northwest before heading home. Down, means I'm staying. At least for now.

A bell chimes and the doors slide open, the down arrow illuminated. I step to the side as people pour out in a hurry to catch a ride to their final destinations. Stepping into the now empty car, I press the button for the lowest level and descend to the beach. Hours pass as I walk along the shore, going over everything in my head, anger surging in waves. Being pissed off may not be rational, but nothing about this is rational.

Hell, she disappeared into herself because she thought the asshat was dead, but he's alive and in her fucking bed. Morning gives way to afternoon and finally evening, and I've probably clocked twenty miles without eating.

Pivoting away from the water's edge, I trudge through the sand to the closest commuter station and hop a train to the back wall. I ride an elevator up, putting maximum distance between me and the ocean. As much as I love it, being there reminds me too much of her.

On the top level, I enter the first pub I find with every intent of getting piss-ass drunk. When I sober up, I'll head back out to the Ruins. Fuck fate, I'm done here. I shove my way through the crowd to an open stool at the bar.

A middle-aged bartender with a starched shirt and a crazy mustache that curls beyond his face flips a cocktail napkin onto the counter. "What'll it be?"

"Scotch."

Moments later he sets my drink in front of me, and I down it in one gulp. The alcohol burns my throat before warming my stomach on its way to my arms and legs, taking the edge off. When I catch the bartender's eye, I signal for another. Between sips, I stare at the ice cubes, forcing myself to think about the scotch, the scratches in the wood, anything but what I saw in that hotel room this morning. Soon the booze works its magic, leaving me pleasantly buzzed. Guzzling the last of the amber liquid, I set the glass down a little harder than necessary and order a third.

Bodies fill the large club, voices droning above the background music. A group of girls to my left are all wearing body-hugging outfits, an over-abundance of makeup, and screaming as they do shots. They're all very attractive, or at least they are in my alcohol-induced state.

One girl in particular is extraordinarily beautiful in an artificial way. She's tall and slender with dark silky hair and overly-made-up eyes that are so blue, they nearly look purple. She spots me checking her out and her bright pink lips pull into a smile, showing off straight, blinding white teeth.

She slinks over to me, her flowered dress hugging impressive curves, mesmerizing me with her moves. The knowing smile says she's aware of her effect on me. She reaches out and places a tan hand on my arm. "Whoever she is, she's a fool."

I throw her a smooth grin, the kind that always gets me into plenty of trouble. "Is it that obvious?"

"I've seen guys drink that much scotch for only one reason. She must have been an idiot to let you go."

Her voice is rich and velvety, and my body is responding even if my brain isn't engaged. Maybe what I need is a night of distraction. What could it hurt? I can catch the first train in the morning.

I signal the bartender and turn to the girl to find out what she wants. "I'm sorry, I don't know your name."

"Violet," she purrs.

The girl from the bar pushes her bedroom door closed and presses me against it, kissing me hard, desperate, wrong. She feels and tastes like a mistake. What the hell am I doing? I slam my fists back into the door and push her away.

"What's going on?" She gives me a sexy pout. "I thought you were into me."

"Look, uhh..." I can't remember her name. "I should go."

She crosses her arms over her chest and narrows her eyes. "You've *got* to be kidding me. Guys don't turn me down."

"I'm sure they don't. You're beautiful, but you deserve better than a drunk fuck."

The side of her mouth lifts in a confident smirk and her gaze roams down my body before rising back to meet mine. "I do, but I'll make an exception for you. One night, no regrets."

"That's a tempting offer, but I'm gonna pass."

"Are you for real?"

"It'd just be revenge on my part and...I can't do that to you. Or me." I reach back and fumble with the lock on her door.

She takes a step toward me, the heat from her too-close body overwhelming my senses.

I shut my eyes and push back against the scents and warmth and desire. This is wrong. "I gotta go." I fling open the door and head through the living room, bumping into the couch on my way out.

"You'll regret walking out on me," she yells.

Yeah, pretty sure I won't.

I wander the neighborhood, drowning in my dark thoughts and lingering traces of all the alcohol I consumed — a dangerous combination. With nothing better to do, I hop a train and ride south a couple of boroughs, not wanting to run into the girl or any of her friends.

The echo of live music trickles out of a nightclub not far from the station. Curious, I head in the direction of the sound and wander inside. This place is less crowded, with round wood tables spaced throughout, small groups of no more than four huddled around them. Two dudes play guitar on a raised stage as an older woman with long straight jet black hair streaked with gray sways and sings into a microphone with a haunting tone.

I signal the bartender and order a beer. He places it on my table, and I down it in one long pull before ordering another. Two sets and four beers later, I'm better than numb. Except when I stand to make my way toward the exit, my feet don't work right and I knock into the table. Paying closer attention, I do a decent job of navigating my way to the door, at least until my shoulder bumps a guy on his way in as I try to squeeze past.

"Hey, you okay, buddy?" the dude asks.

"Yeah," I mumble.

The cool air outside helps me shake off some of the brain fog, though I'm still a little unsteady. With a sudden urge to be on the beach, I stagger to the elevators and push the button, using the wall to steady me while I wait.

When the car arrives, I sway while the group inside exits before I stumble inside. The world spins around me as the elevator descends to the ground level. The doors slide open and I find the nearest terminal, hopping a train to the coast. Settling back in my seat, I rest my head against the window and shut my eyes.

HELL

Evan

*W*aiting is its own special kind of hell. One hour gives way to the next without anyone coming to see me, talk to me, or tell me anything. My brain is busy with so much free time, churning out every way they might kill me. If they were going to execute me, I think they would have done it by now, which means they know what I did. It's the only explanation for why I'm still alive. They want to know who else was involved.

Fear crawls through my veins like fire ants. Everything we did, every risk we took, was all for nothing. The Uprising invaded the Union anyway. Maybe this was the Uprising's strategy from the start. They were bringing people in here for months.

Jamming my palms into my eyes, frustration, anger, and fear war inside me until I'm being torn apart, one piece at a time. I slump to the ground and blow out a steady breath of defeat.

A rustling draws me from my thoughts and I turn to the opening where Draya stands flanked by two soldiers carrying folding chairs. Both guys could be distant relatives of Hercules. I swallow hard, trying to push back some of my anxiety, but all that does is make me choke.

Hercules One sets his chair in the middle of the space, and Draya takes the seat. The other guy drops the second one across from her. "Sit."

I eye the chair and weigh my options before reluctantly sitting and facing Draya. Unease hums across my skin as I raise my gaze to meet hers.

She turns her head and studies me for several long, uncomfortable moments. Staring into her piercing blue eyes, I'm transported back to the house in the Ruins where I first met her, the day I woke for the first time after they rescued me. She was wary of me even then.

"So, do you want to tell me how you got that tattoo?"

It's a stupid question. She knows how I got it. Same way everyone gets one, the same way she got hers.

"What camp did you train in?"

I stare back. There's nothing to be gained by answering.

"When did you desert?"

Stare.

"Were you responsible for the attacks on the camps in March?"

Stare.

She narrows her eyes and folds her arms over her chest. "Did you attack the supply trucks?"

Stare.

Draya stands and takes a few steps forward. I pop up, tensing. Her eyes never leave mine as she approaches, but she merely walks past, slamming her shoulder into me on her way out, her entourage grabbing the chairs and following.

"Hello," I yell for at least the tenth time. "I need to pee."

"Shut up in there," someone answers for at least the tenth time.

With a sigh, I walk to the corner of the tent to relieve myself before settling on a patch of grass far from my pee spot. I sit and hug my knees to my chest.

Draya hid the fact that she knew me, but also never asked my name. She might have convinced the others she didn't recognize me, but I saw the shock flicker across her face before she recovered. She didn't expect to see me, and she gave up too easily when I refused to answer her questions. Those two things are inconsistent.

I don't see any way out of this mess, which means my chances are better out there, where I have a fighting chance at survival. Laying on my belly, I lift the edge of the tent and peer under only to come face-to-face with soft black leather. Boots. Frustrated, I drop the canvas and roll to my back. I texted my mom not even a day ago that everything was going to be okay. This is not even a little okay.

I open my eyes to morning sun striking the exterior of the beige canvas, warming the inside and illuminating my surroundings. My stomach gurgles like marbles in any empty bowl. My muscles are tight from sleeping on the ground, and I get up slower than normal.

After a quick glance around verifies I'm alone, I crawl to the side and lift the bottom edge. No boots. I poke my head out and look both ways. This is it. My chance to escape.

"Get up!" comes a deep male voice from behind me.

Heart pounding in my throat, I scramble forward, toward freedom. A hand grabs my ankle and yanks me back hard, the joint popping. When I roll over, Hercules One and Two are standing over me, faces pinched with anger. Working in unison, they reach down and grab my arms, yanking me to my feet. A large hand shoves me forward, and I stumble before finding my footing. They flank me as I make my way outside, my eyes squinting as they adjust to the sudden harsh sunlight.

As they march me across an open field, I search for buildings, a place to hide if I can break free, but there aren't any. This strip of the Union is primarily for agriculture. Based on the pile I just stepped in, I'm guessing livestock. My head swivels, searching for Chase to no avail. In fact, the only other people I see are wearing Uprising fatigues. The rest of the passengers who escaped with us are nowhere to be seen.

They direct me under the elevated tracks, where the stalled train still sits, and approach the back wall. The ride down is silent, but when the doors open, a swarm of soldiers is humming about, some escorting other Unionites. I doubt any of them are sporting an Uprising tattoo, so they must have done something extreme to warrant an armed escort.

Hercules One grips my right elbow with his meaty hand and drags me into a narrow hall. His fingers dig in and I bite my lip to keep from reacting to the pain. He halts in front of a windowless door and pulls it open, shoving me inside. The room is empty. Four cinder-block walls are sandwiched between a concrete ceiling and floor with a single overhead light.

He pivots and takes a step toward the door, but before he leaves I croak, "Water?" My throat is so dry it hurts to swallow.

He pauses and glances over his shoulder before leaving and locking the door behind him. The door cracks open and a water bottle rolls toward me. I scramble across the floor to grab it, barely registering the door closing again. Twisting off the cap, I down half the contents before slowing down to save some. There's no way to know when I'll get more.

Sitting back against the wall, I take stock of my situation. Once again I'm locked in a small room with no apparent way out. I don't have too long to feel sorry for myself though. Hercules One and Two are back, with Draya this time.

Her two overly large protégés haul me to my feet, dragging me to the middle of the room. Draya stands opposite me, her eyes travelling over me, head to toe, as if she's appraising me. Yet she still doesn't let on that she knows who I am. Her eyes give nothing away, the same way Cyrus was able to mask his feelings from me after he became an Uprising commander.

Draya pushes off the door. "Let's try this again. Where did you train?"

We stare at each other for a few long moments.

"This will be better for you if you cooperate."

"How can this be better?" The words fall out of my mouth before I can stop them.

She presses her lips together, as if she's mulling over her response. "It will be...*less* painful."

To illustrate her point, Hercules Two wrenches my right arm up until my shoulder screams in pain, and I let out an unbidden, "Ung!"

Draya nods with an unreadable expression and H-2 lets go.

"Where did you train? Was it up in the Northwest?"

I reach up and rub my sore joint while I study her, wondering if she's planning on beating a response out of me. Draya might not be my biggest fan and may still blame me for Lucien's death, but I don't think she's capable of abject cruelty. At least I hope not.

Without taking her eyes off me, she lifts her chin and H-1 grabs both of my arms, pinning them behind my back. H-2 walks around in front of me, and for the first time I get the full impact of him. He's a massive block of muscle with bulging biceps that stretch the sleeves of his T-shirt. He balls up his fist and thrusts it into my midsection. A dull ache spreads out from my stomach, doubling me over.

My knees buckle and I gasp, desperate to refill my lungs. When I regain my breath, I lift my head to glare at Draya. "What the hell?" I wheeze.

For a split second, before she realizes I'm watching her, her face is twisted, like merely the act of looking at me is a painful reminder of everything she lost when Lucien died.

She quickly schools her features. "Where'd you get the tattoo?"

Even though I'm aware that not answering is going to bring more agony, I can't tell her. I won't put people I love in danger. My abs tense just before H-2's fist slams into me, and I immediately realize that was a mistake. Bile mixed with the water I drank climbs my throat before spewing forth all over his boots.

"What the fuck?" he yells, stepping back.

His dark eyes narrow into slits, his thin lips press into a tight line. His next blow is aimed at my face, and I turn my head in time to prevent a direct hit. His fist still connects with my jaw, sending mind-numbing pain through my head. Stars burst in my eyes, and if H-1 wasn't holding me up, I'd be on the ground. My vision clears and I stare at the man before me, wondering what kind of person hits a teenage girl half his size?

"That's enough for now," Draya orders, turning on her heel and opening the door.

I still don't know what game she's playing, but at least she's calling off the dogs. H-2 isn't done with me, though. He backhands me and pain explodes across my face before everything goes black.

INDEFINITELY

Cyrus

I open my eyes and immediately slam them shut. Something is beating on my skull with a hammer, and the smell of alcohol swamps me. With care, I pry my eyelids up, squinting against the harsh light. Confusion hits me hard, my brain is fuzzy as hell, and my mouth is as dry as the summer desert. My eyes regain focus, zeroing in on the lime green vinyl in front of me. I'm on a commuter train with no clue how I got here.

The reek of booze is evidently coming from my pores. I rub my hands over my face and slide out of my seat, heading for the doors. The floor slopes under me and my guts lurch, ready to expel their contents. I swallow and breathe through my nose until the urge passes. When we pull to a stop, I step out into a station and head for the closest map. I'm only a few stops away from the coast. Right, I was heading to the beach. Must've fallen asleep.

I could use a walk to clear my head, and opt for walking the rest of the way. The last thing I remember was going to a bar to get drunk. Apparently, I accomplished that.

In fact, I fucking nailed it.

A vision of a brunette comes into focus. Flirting, drinks, dancing, her body rubbing up and down mine before she led me back to her place. Before I ran from her like some emotional girl. I can't even do a revenge fuck properly.

The pain that started in my head is now rampaging through my body. I exit the tunnel as the sun slips above the horizon, casting a pink glow. The briny air hits my lungs and some of the tension erodes. Not a lot, but enough that maybe I can figure out my next move. I walk over to the boardwalk and kick off my shoes before sinking my toes into the sand. The pounding in my head subsides with each deep breath I take and each step closer to the ocean. When I reach the water's edge, I wade in and let the gentle surf lick my ankles. The cool water bites at my feet, allowing me to focus on something other than my hangover or the sight of a half-naked dickwad in my girlfriend's hotel room.

I still don't know what to do. Going back out to the Ruins and being back in that house without her might be too much. Maybe it's time to settle someplace new, somewhere I've never been. First I owe it to everyone to let them know what I'm doing.

My shoulders drop with the weight of my decision, and with a slow pivot, I head back toward dry sand.

The gaping hole in my chest grows until it devours my guts. My stomach rumbles. Right, I've been on a liquid diet for the past day and a half. Ducking into the first café I come to, I order a coffee and breakfast burrito.

The girl hands me my drink and I sip it, lulled by the murmur of conversation around me. When my food is ready, I grab it and head for the door, nearly bumping into a couple of girls on their way in. One girl sniffles. Shit, did I hurt her?

"Hey, sorry," I say, reaching for her arm.

She lifts her face, her red-rimmed eyes meeting mine. She gives me a small smile. "My fault. I'm just..." she waves her hand. "You know." She shrugs and her friend nods in agreement.

The sidewalk is thick with people, more than there should be this time of the morning. At least based on my experience in the Union. Maybe this is normal in the East, though. I eat my breakfast as I walk to the A-Train station two blocks away. At the top of the stairs, I bump into a gathering crowd hovering around a roped-off area. Several people in transit uniforms mill about on the other side of the ropes.

"Hey," I call out.

The closest guy pivots to face me. "We're closed."

"How long?"

"Indefinitely." He turns his back and resumes his conversation with his coworkers.

The big dude beside me leans forward, his shirt gaping between the buttons where it pulls over his extended belly. "Hey, asshole."

The transit worker walks over to us. "Haven't you heard?" His voice catches, betraying just how young he is. He can't be much more than sixteen.

The faces of those around me wear the same dumbfounded expression I do.

"Heard what?" the big guy asks, the anger lacing his words earlier replaced with confusion.

The kid merely shakes his head and moves further away from the rope.

While the group continues to shout questions, I go back downstairs, this time paying close attention to everyone I pass. An air of tension runs through the population, as if they're on edge, nervous. In all my time in the Union, the one constant has been consistency. Trains run on time, stores open as scheduled, Unis tend to be calm. And why the hell not? They live in Utopia. But this morning, something's off.

I enter the nearest pub and push my way through the throng to the monitors over the bar. The fact that a pub is this packed so early in the morning is yet another sign that today is anything but routine. The crowd between me and the displays is five deep, but I refuse to be deterred and squeeze my way through.

Someone elbows me in the ribs. "Hey!"

My eyes are fixed on the screens, my brain unable to comprehend what I'm seeing. The hair on my arms stands on end. A-Trains across the Union are swarming with Uprising soldiers, unloading cars at gunpoint. The volume is turned down, but words trail along the bottom. My basic reading skills only give me the gist of it.

I rake a hand through my hair as the sickening reality sinks in. Backing away from the bar, I find a table and slump into a chair. We didn't stop anything. *Fuck.* Despite the early hour, I order a beer when the waitress comes by. The crowd gathered around the monitors starts to dissipate, either leaving the pub, or finding seats at tables. My brew is delivered in a frosty mug, foam slipping over the rim and sliding down the side. I take a sip and lean back, watching the horror unfolding on the screen.

The same footage is shown over and over, with new details added from time to time. The Uprising captured or killed most of the Union's leaders, including the Prime Minister. If Evan's uncle is among them, she'll be devastated. Evan. Shit, she could be in danger simply by being related to a governor.

The need to do something crawls through me, making me restless. More than once I get up, ready to fight, but I always stop myself, unsure where to start. Running off without a plan won't fix anything. As the day progresses, new reports detail the Uprising moving further into the Union, rounding up police officers and other lower-tier officials, until they're in charge of all seven provinces, with a concentrated presence in the Southern Province. That must be ground zero for their operations. If I can get there, I may be able to infiltrate, convince them I'm still in the Uprising.

Eventually my own thoughts are interrupted by conversations around me, particularly one among a group of Unis at the next table.

"We should try to do something." The guy is around my age and for a second, reminds me of my brother, Lucien.

A pretty, dark-haired girl with large brown eyes leans forward. "What can *we* do, Dom?"

The dude next to her looks like he's allergic to dirt. And disorder. His pants are pressed with a crease running down the front, and not one of his blond hairs is out of place. "We can help somehow."

"Like how?" the girl asks.

The dark-haired guy, who I'm assuming is Dom, points at the screen. "We go there. I've seen a ton of war movies and there's always a central command. I'll bet that's it."

The girl scrunches up her nose. "The trains aren't even operating. How do we get there?"

Dom leans back in his chair, thoughtful. "The commuter trains are." Now they've really got my interest. "We can ride borough-by-borough till we get there."

Clean-cut dude nods toward me and the other two turn my way.

"Sorry, couldn't help overhearing," I say.

The girl throws a megawatt smile my way before glancing down at her drink, her dark eyelashes fanning bronzed cheeks.

"We can't sit around and do nothing," Dom says. "They attacked us, and maybe they're in charge now, but we can fight back."

They're so naive it's almost comical, but that kind of naivete will get them killed. I reach out a hand across the narrow gap between our tables. "Cyrus."

Dom shakes my hand. "Dominic. This is my sister, Valencia, and my buddy, Nate."

Nate and I shake hands and Valencia glances up with a small smile.

"You know we can't just show up there and attack them, right? They've got guns."

Dominic raises an eyebrow. "We?"

I huff out a short laugh, not even realizing I'd made the decision to go with them. "Guess so. Like you said, we can't just sit around doing nothing. Might as well go together. Plus, there's strength and safety in numbers."

"You watch a lot of war movies, too?" Nate asks.

I smirk. "Something like that."

Darkness settles across the Southeastern Province as we walk to the commuter station the next borough over. Traveling with Unis helps me blend in, but I don't necessarily trust them. I keep one eye on my surroundings and one on my traveling companions.

We've made good time over the past day. Dominic felt the upper levels would be safer, but I'm not convinced. The orderly efficiency of the Union is working to our advantage now, but anything can change. We're too boxed in up here.

We round a corner and hike up a flight of stairs to the platform to find Uprising soldiers headed in our direction. I drop my head, wishing I had a ballcap to obscure my face. Some of them could be troops I commanded or trained with, and I can't risk being recognized. Before they're close enough to make me, I duck into an open café, something rare this evening. The others follow me.

The place is nearly deserted since most Unis are holed up at home, hunkering down, scared shitless.

"What's wrong?" Dominic asks.

I can't tell him I used to be in the Uprising, so I settle on a partial truth. "Too many soldiers here. We should lie low until they clear out."

Nate runs a hand across his smooth jaw, and I wonder when was the last time he didn't shave. "Why?"

I raise an eyebrow at him. Was he not watching the same information I was all day?

He shakes his head. "They're not grabbing random citizens,

they're looking for government officials." He even talks like a starched shirt.

"Yesterday that might've been the case, but who knows what they're doing today."

Dominic nods. "Maybe you're right."

Outside, a soldier hauls a Uni down the sidewalk, hands bound behind him, reinforcing my point. The line we were fed during training was that the Uprising wanted access to the resources in here, fairness for the people of the Ruins. The only Ruins people I've seen so far are soldiers. And whatever they're up to, it's not making sure everyone in the Ruins has food, water, and medical care.

"What do you think they want?" Valencia asks.

"I don't know, but I'm sure they'll tell us when they're ready."

Nate shifts on his feet beside me. "Where are they from?"

I contemplate telling them about the Ruins, but that will only raise more questions I don't want to answer. "Your guess is as good as mine."

"You guys gonna order anything?" the guy behind the counter calls.

"Uh, coffee," I say.

We grab a table and spend the next several hours watching the activity outside. Hopped up on caffeine, I'm antsy and second-guessing my decision to hook up with these guys.

"What are you thinking?" Dominic asks.

I turn toward him, working to keep my face neutral. "I think it's too risky to go to the Southern Province now."

"Why?" Dom asks.

I lift an eyebrow and nod at the Uprising presence through the window.

Valencia swallows hard. "Oh. Maybe we should just go home."

Dom shakes his head, his fingers gripping tightly to his mug. "No way, Val. Then what? Wait for them to take over our apartment? Kill someone we love?"

"So, what then?" Nate asks, directing his question to me.

Except for Evan and her friends, most Unis seem happy letting someone else make the decisions and take the risks. They appear to genuinely want to do something, but dragging them into an Uprising camp, jumping into this without thinking it through, is beyond reckless. "We bide our time, regroup, and figure something out."

5

NOTHINGNESS

Evan

Total darkness greets me when I open my eyes. The stench of vomit invades my nostrils and I gag. I scoot back to get away from the odor and just that small movement is enough to make my head spin. Every inch of me screams in pain as I lay back down on the harsh concrete floor. Even my lungs hurt when I attempt to take a deeper breath.

With nothing but blackness surrounding me, it's easier to close my eyes and let the nothingness drag me back into oblivion.

Liquid fills my nose and mouth and I claw in front of me, searching for the surface. I gasp, choking on a combination of air and water and shove my drenched hair out of my face. Hercules One holds an empty bucket at his side, water still dripping from the rim.

Dizziness takes hold when I sit up, my body tilting. H-1 grabs my biceps, yanking me to my feet mere moments before my head would have conked on the concrete. Guess he wants the honor of doing the head conking himself.

Something about my face doesn't feel right. My fingers run over the planes of my face, hitting a tender spot on my cheek. Pain shoots through my jaw and into my head while stars dance across my vision until everything disappears.

Another blast of water hits my face and my eyes fly open to a pair of cold blue ones staring back at me. "Where did you train?" Draya asks.

My lips part to tell her off, but the words catch on their way out.

Hercules Two approaches me, and without warning his fist is in my stomach. A yell tears from my raw throat and I double over, screaming through my teeth.

"Where. Did. You. Train."

"In the Northwest," I gasp.

"Where in the Northwest? Which camp?"

The pain begins to ebb, allowing me to control my mouth. If I tell them what they want, they'll have no reason to keep me alive. I'm just not sure how much I can tolerate before I verbally vomit the truth along with the threatening bile. H-2 strikes the left side of my face with the back of his hand, sending blinding pain racing from my head into my spine.

"Northwest Seven," I scream. Shit, at this rate, I'll tell them everything and be dead within an hour.

Draya's eyes dim rather than brighten with the information. "Now we're getting somewhere. Who was with you?"

"Other recruits. There was a whole truckload of us, plus all the kids already there."

She narrows her gaze before turning on her heel and leaving the room, returning a few moments later with a tablet. "Several soldiers left that camp unauthorized, including the commander. Who was your commander, and where is he now?"

What the hell? First, I'm not telling her anything about Cyrus, even if she tortures me, but second... "Don't *you* know who the commander was?"

Her only response is an unblinking stare.

The open-palmed slap doesn't hurt any less as it rocks my head to the side. The stakes are too high now, and I manage to keep my mouth shut. "Answer the commander," H-2 snarls.

I bite my lips together and prepare for the next blow, another backhand across my face. In an instant, the face of the first girl I shot to save Marcus's life flashes before me. I close my eyes and do my best to stand a little straighter and take the next strike as penance for her. The fist in the gut is for the boy I killed, and I crumple to the floor. The boot to my ribs is for the kids blown up when the explosives went off. I hear the first crack, more than feel it. What they're doing to me pales in comparison to what I did. I can take this, I deserve it. But I can't prevent the small whimpers from escaping with each kick until the merciful darkness comes to take me again.

My shivering body drags me from peaceful oblivion back into the unbearable hell of consciousness. A puddle of frigid water spreads out across the concrete floor like an ink blot, cubes of ice scattered. I clamp my jaw shut to stop the chattering of my teeth.

A pair of brown leather boots comes into view. "We're wasting our time," comes a deep male voice I don't recognize. "She serves no purpose. Dispose of her."

Fear chills my insides to match my outsides.

"Wait!" Draya says.

The boots pivot and recede. Draya's voice is low and hushed, making it impossible to hear what she's saying.

"Fine," the deep voice says again. "You've got a day. If you don't get anything out of her by then, move on. We have bigger fish to fry."

Someone lifts me to standing, supporting me from behind,

which is good, since I'm not sure I can stand on my own. I let out an involuntary groan and silently curse myself. It's not like they can't tell by looking at me how messed up I am, but my ability to not react may be the only thing I'm in control of at the moment.

"Did you blow up the camps?" Draya asks.

Her face wavers, refusing to come into focus. My mouth moves but nothing comes out. A boot connects with my shin. This time, I keep my screams in my head.

Draya's next words are slurred, or maybe only to me. "Were you involved in what happened in the camps in March?"

I weigh my options. If I want to live, I need to give them something. Might as well cop to this. They can't kill me twice. I nod.

"Now we're getting somewhere." The satisfied smirk I can't see is evident in her voice. "You didn't do it alone. Who was with you?"

"No one," I croak, finding my voice.

"As much as I'm enjoying this, I really would rather not have to do it. It's taking too long. Just tell me who was with you."

"No one. It was only me."

A blow to my back knocks me forward and a sharp, blinding pain darkens my vision as I slump to the floor.

"How did you do it?" Draya's voice penetrates the darkness.

The cool concrete beneath my cheek is soothing, and I see no benefit in getting up. "I bought...explosives and a motorbike...in the Northern Territories." I drag in a painful breath. "It was easy to sneak in. The Uprising taught me everything I needed to know. It was easier than you might think."

"That's a nice story, but I don't believe you. You couldn't have been in multiple locations at once."

"I used timing devices." The silence that follows my statement is more unnerving than the beatings, but I don't dare open my eyes, instead curling inward to protect my vital organs.

"Where did you learn to do that? That's not covered in Uprising training."

Crap, I don't have an answer for that, and I let my body go

limp, trying to buy myself some time. The fact that I'm barely holding on to consciousness as it is may help me sell it. Ice water hits my face again, and I sputter, but stay on the floor.

"Where did you learn about explosives and timing devices?" Draya asks, her tone measured, as if she's working hard to remain clam.

I lick my lips. "From some people...in the Northern Territories."

"What people?"

"Just...people."

"What were you doing up there?" Genuine curiosity laces her voice.

"Looking for a way to bring down the Uprising."

"How did you escape?"

I've had some time to think about this answer. "I pretended to like one of the sentries and visited him when he was on duty. When I was ready to leave, I incapacitated him."

"I think we have everything we need," Hercules One says. "Loyolla will be happy."

"Not yet," Draya says, her words sharp. "Give me a second."

Warm breath tickles my skin and I crack an eye to find Draya's face next to mine. "We know who you are, Evan Taylor, we took your fingerprint. We also have a pretty good idea where you escaped from. The commander from that camp is missing, and I think you know where he is."

Dread ices my body more than any cold water could and my breath stalls in my lungs.

A satisfied smile pulls at the corners of her mouth. "She still has much to offer us, much more than Loyolla ever imagined."

———

Between sleeping, being interrogated, and staring at the ceiling, I manage to get through the days. I dole out snippets of information, stringing them along, buying myself enough time to figure out a way out of here. Two meals have passed since they asked me anything, although I'm not sure how many times a day they're feeding me.

My reprieve runs out when the door slams open, reverberating off the wall. Draya flips on the overhead lights. Pain enters through my eye sockets and zips through to the back of my skull. Draya's boots clop against the hard floor, echoing off the bare walls.

"Here."

I squint one eye open to find a proffered water bottle. Sitting up, I take it with a trembling hand. My fingers fumble with the cap, my ribs aching with every breath, until Draya huffs and grabs it from me. She opens it with one steady motion before shoving it back into my hands. Tilting my head back, I gulp the precious fluid, some of it dribbling down my chin. I wipe my mouth with the back of my arm and stare up at her piercing blue eyes.

Behind her are two different soldiers. Apparently, the Hercules twins have the day off. She uncrosses her arms and turns toward them. "Leave us."

They hold their ground, glancing at me briefly.

"That's an order."

They flick their gaze to me one more time before leaving and closing the door behind them. I try to stand, but dizziness kicks in. Instead, I sit a little straighter, fighting a wave of nausea.

Draya squats, resting her wrists on her knees. "Evan, you're even more stubborn than I thought. I expected some resistance, but not this much. What's done is done, and what happens next is all that matters. That's where you're going to help me."

"I'm not going to help you." My voice is only a hoarse whisper.

"Maybe not at first. But ultimately you will."

"What do you want from me?"

She tilts her head, the left side of her mouth lifting, and asks the one question that sends me into a spiral of panic. "Where is Cyrus?"

"What?"

"You heard me. Where's Cy?"

I cringe at the familiarity of the nickname. "I don't know."

"Funny, I don't believe you."

"I really don't." I study her face, trying to make sense of what's happening. "What do you want with him?"

She rocks back and sits on the ground, her knees bent. "Do you know what it's like to live every day of your life without the person you loved most in the world? Knowing you'll *never* see him again?"

Understanding dawns like chilled fingers, crawling up my spine. "No..." I whisper.

"I want you to know how it feels." Her tone is bitter and venomous.

"I don't know where he is, I swear."

"The others here," she says, waving her hand toward the door, "tend to be idiots, but I'm not. So, here's the thing, the only reason you're still alive is because I want you that way. I convinced them you still have a valuable piece of information — the whereabouts of one of our most prized commanders. There is no doubt in my mind that he helped you get out of camp."

"You just told me you want him dead, so even if I knew, I wouldn't tell you. But I don't. Whatever you think you know, you're wrong."

She pushes herself up and walks to the door, reaching for the handle. Her body goes rigid for a moment, then she glances back. "Oh, you'll tell me. We just need to find the right motivation." With a stiff yank, she opens the door and the two clowns from earlier are back, one of them is carrying a long silver tube.

Draya stops outside the room. "Find out where he is. Use whatever means necessary. If she dies, so do you."

The door closes behind her and I scoot away from them until my back bumps against the wall. My eyes take them in from top to bottom. The taller one is well over six feet, his closely-cropped hair is like a cap on his broad head. Wide-spaced brown eyes are topped with bushy eyebrows.

The other guy, the one holding the tube, is a couple inches shorter, but thicker through the chest, with over-developed biceps.

Deep lines crease the space between light blue eyes from years of scowling. A small white scar cuts across his square jaw that sits below thin, pursed lips.

They step toward me, Square Jaw bouncing that tube off the palm of his hand. They don't bother asking me anything. We all know there's only one question on the table. Bushy Brows reaches down and grabs my left arm, yanking me to my feet. He spins me around and lifts my shirt. Just as I'm convinced they're planning to rape me, something white-hot sears into my back. The intensity is focused at the point of contact, but somehow radiates out to every cell. A scream tears from my raw throat, sounding more like a strangled cry.

Gasping for air, I manage to sob out, "I don't know where he is."

The next one is higher up, between my shoulder blades, but the pain is just as blinding. My body bucks, but their grip on me is too strong. Tears stream down my face from squeezing my eyes shut so tightly it feels like I'm swallowing my eyeballs. "I don't know where he is, I swear." My breathing becomes rapid and I pant out my next words. "I... haven't... seen... him... in... two... months."

The bar makes contact with my lower left side, only inches above my kidney, and lasts longer than the other two.

"I don't know," my confession pours from me as a pathetic plea. "Please, I don't. I swear, please stop."

Bushy Brows lets go and I tumble to the ground. Two sets of footsteps move away from me before the lights go out and the door slams, leaving me in complete darkness.

I curl into a ball, pulling my knees to my chest and stuff my knuckle into my mouth, biting down hard. I need to feel pain somewhere other than in my back. I focus on the throbbing in my finger, the ache I control. My back burns like nothing I've ever experienced, and as time passes, instead of dulling, the agony intensifies.

For the first time since I was captured, I wonder if I'm strong enough to survive.

6

REGROUPING

Cyrus

"We close in five minutes," the guy behind the counter announces, giving us no choice but to leave the café.

After tossing down a healthy tip, I exit, keeping my head down, and lead the way past the soldiers down to the ground level where we hop a commuter to the beach.

Valencia takes the spot beside me. "Where're we going?"

"We can hang around the campground while we figure out our next move. I worked at one up in the Northwestern Province until last week. Maybe I can pick up some work in exchange for room and board."

My gaze shifts to Nate and Dominic sitting across from us. From what little I know about life here, they should all have some sort of job. "What experience do you have?"

Valencia scrunches up her nose. "With what?"

"Working?"

"Oh. I was a barista until the Invasion."

"I'm starting a teaching internship in the fall," Nate says. "Or at least I was."

Dominic sighs, scratching the back of his head. "I'm in my second year as a tech intern."

"Nothing's the same anymore," Valencia says with determination. "This is my home. I want to do something."

Nate glances at Valencia. "Me too."

Brow furrowed, Dominic leans back in his seat and nods.

We reach our destination without incident, and I allow myself to relax a bit. But only a fraction. I take a quick look around before slinging my bag over my shoulder and leading the way off the train. There's less of an Uprising presence here, but the people have a soberness to them —tightness of features, hunched shoulders, and bunched fists — I'm not used to in Unis. And yet so much of Union life is as it was before. Commuter trains run mostly on schedule, more businesses are open here than where we were before, and even a few kids are out walking their dogs.

A long line of people snakes from the check-in tent to the boardwalk.

"Stay here, I'll be back," I say.

Passing the throng of restless would-be campers, I approach the desk where a man is yelling at the harried clerk while two small children hang from his arms.

"We've been waiting hours. How hard can it be to check us in?"

I lean around the red-faced man and make eye contact with the girl. "Is the manager available?"

She shakes her head. "I don't know where she is right now, and I don't have time to find her."

"Hey, I was here first," the man snarls.

I ignore him. "Do you guys need help around here? I worked at a campground in the Northwestern Province."

Her face relaxes and a small smile tugs at the corner of her mouth. "Let me track her down." She returns her attention to the man whose wife is peeling one of the children off him. "I'll be right back, sir."

"Wait, what about my tent?"

"Please, sir. I promise I'm doing the best I can. I'll be *right* back."

The man huffs and turns to his wife. "Take them outside, for the love of god, Maddie!"

The woman eyes her husband before turning to her kids. "Let's go play in the sand." She glances at me, a harsh vertical line burrowing into the space between her eyebrows before taking her children by the hand and dragging them out.

A tall woman with darkly tanned skin and pale blond hair follows the clerk and approaches me. She thrusts out her hand. "Hi, I'm Selma. You're looking for work?" Her handshake is firm, her light blue eyes weary.

"Yeah. I've got some experience." I gesture outside the tent to where Dom, Nate, and Valencia are still in line. "And my friends can help, too."

"This is crazy. After the Invasion..." She shakes her head and blows out a breath. "So many displaced people. We just don't have enough room for everyone. We're putting up tents as fast as we can, but soldiers are tossing people out of their homes left and right."

I nod a response, unsure what else she expects me to say.

"Can you start now?" she asks.

"Yeah. Let me grab the others."

"You are a godsend! Meet me out back. We've got a lot to do before sunset."

———

I swing the ax, splitting the last piece of firewood and tossing it on the stack before wiping my brow with my forearm. The setting sun paints the horizon a deep hue of orange climbing into purple clouds that give way to a fading blue sky.

"So, what's next?" Dominic asks, appearing beside me.

I incline my head at the wood. "This needs to be hauled to the pile behind the supply tent."

He pulls on a pair of leather gloves. "I'm on it."

A grin splits my face. Unis may not be afraid of work, but they're terrified of a few calluses. Selma's been driving us hard, directing us to set up tents, haul bags for campers, clean and scrub every surface, and even mess duty. She's fair though, giving us room and board plus a small salary. Nothing like what I was earning before up in the Northwest, but with so many displaced people, not everyone can afford to pay for lodging. This being the Union, no one is turned away.

Most nights I struggle just to keep my eyes open past dinner, but after I help Dom move the firewood, we seek out Nate and Valencia and take up residence at one of the bonfires.

Nate's jaw practically unhinges with a splitting yawn. "Man, I'm so beat."

"I've never worked this hard in my life," Dom says.

Valencia leans forward and places her palms toward the fire, as if trying to warm them, despite the mild temperature. "What's the long-term plan? I mean, we're not going to hang out here and work forever are we? I thought we were going to try to do something."

Resting my forearms on my raised knees, I glance at their drawn faces, wondering if they have any idea what they're asking to get involved with. A well-organized resistance might succeed, but it won't be easy. "What are you up for?"

Valencia's drooping eyelids pop open. "What do you mean?"

"Armed soldiers are capturing and killing people. How far will you go to get the Union back? If you're not willing to fight, there's no point in doing anything, because that's the only way this can end."

"Why don't we wait to see what happens?" Nate asks.

I nod. "We can do that. We can wait and hope for the best, but they've brought down the entire government power structure, so I don't see this going anywhere but worse from here."

Dominic shakes his head, as if attempting to dislodge my words from his brain. "What can we do? We're only four people."

"You're right, the four of us alone can't do much, but how

happy do you think the rest of these people are with what's going on? There are far more of us than there are of them. We need enough people who want to fight back."

Nate's brows pull together. "Fight with what?"

I rub my hands across my face and look up at the sky. "That's one of many things I don't have an answer to. Yet."

Dominic went to bed not long after the abrupt end to our planning pow-wow. Nate stuck around a little while longer, watching Valencia more than anything else, but even he reached the point where his eyes wouldn't remain open and said goodnight a few minutes ago.

Now that we're alone, Valencia inches closer. I'd have to be blind not to notice the way she looks at me. She stares up at me with large, dark eyes fringed with thick black lashes. I wish I didn't give a shit, that I didn't need to do the right thing, be the good guy.

When she leans over and rests her head on my shoulder, the move is so achingly familiar that my body reacts, and I almost reach out to pull her to me.

Instead, I tense, draining the last of my beer and setting the empty bottle in the sand. "Valencia..."

She lifts her head, but remains close, her eyes searching my face. For both of our sakes, I should be honest with her.

"You're sweet and brave and a lot of other things I admire, but...I'm not over someone else."

"Oh." Her voice holds a hint of disappointment, but her eyes remain hopeful. Firelight dances across the dewy, hairless skin all Union girls seem to have.

"I don't want you to get hurt."

"I'll be careful."

I laugh for the first time since the morning everything went to shit. "I think Nate likes you."

She sighs and turns away. "Nate and I have known each other forever. He's almost as much like a brother to me as Dom is. It would be...weird."

"It hasn't been that long."

"I'm sorry." Her voice carries only genuine kindness.

Another group of campers approach and take spots around the fire. They've been drinking, and based on the volume of their conversation, it's a good bet they've been at it for a while. I take that as my cue and turn to Valencia. "I'll see you tomorrow."

"Goodnight, Cyrus."

The surf roars to my left as I walk to the staff sleeping quarters, my mind grinding away at memories. Talking with Valencia forced to the surface thoughts I'd been working hard to push down. Thoughts of a girl with hazel eyes and crazy red hair. God, I miss her. I miss her every hour of every day, even if I don't acknowledge it. I hate this ache in my chest, the hollow feeling in my gut. I climb into my bunk and punch my pillow, forcing myself to focus on other things, things I can control, like a plan for organizing a resistance.

Today was another grueling day. The flames from the bonfire lick the sky, spitting and snapping. I lean back against the log and stretch my tired back muscles.

Beside me, Dominic's eyes gleam with excitement. "I was thinking we could put together a citizens army or something. Like the Resistance who fought back against government regulations during the Second Civil War."

"They lost, in case you forgot, Einstein," Valencia says.

Nate scrubs his hand across his scruff. He appears uncomfortable with the beginnings of a beard, as if his face belongs to someone else. "If you look at history, though, you'll find examples of both successful and unsuccessful attempts. We only need to research them and see what worked and what didn't so we don't make the same mistakes."

I study Nate with fresh eyes. He's always come across as a bit of a pretentious tool, but he might actually have a brain in there.

"You might be on to something. The secret to success is to have more people fighting on your side than theirs, be better organized, and be ready to die for what you believe in. Without all those factors, we'll fail. This isn't something we can throw together overnight."

"Die?" Valencia asks.

"This isn't a game they're playing. It's war. People die in wars."

She swallows hard and turns away.

Dominic's gaze swings between me and Nate. "Shit...this is... this is like way more serious than I thought."

"War always is," Nate says. "It always seems like a good idea until it comes to getting your hands dirty. The First Civil War was romanticized. Before. After, it should have been a chilling reminder, but everyone was so excited to go to war again only two hundred years later."

Valencia lets out a long breath. "I don't know if I'm ready to die, but what they're doing is wrong." She shakes her head. "Soldiers are throwing more people out of their homes every day. The lines down here are only growing longer. Did you know some people are sleeping out on the sand? They're not even in tents."

These people have no clue what roughing it really is. "Things are only going to get worse from here. Remember that."

"Yeah, okay. So...what's next?" Dom asks.

"Getting our hands on weapons won't be easy, but I have some ideas. We may be able to recruit a lot of citizens from this camp. But again, this isn't an overnight thing and it'll be dangerous. If the Uprising gets wind of what we're doing, they won't bother asking questions." I pause, letting the full gravity of building a resistance sink in. "Are you still in?"

They're quiet for so long, I wonder if they're done. On some level, I'd love to just walk away from all of this. It's not my fight. Shit, I can't even convince myself of that. Even after everything, I'm still doing this for Evan more than anyone else. She may have destroyed me, but I can't just fucking abandon her. Even now.

7

BREAKING POINT

Evan

I wake to soft, stubbly kisses on my neck and let out a sigh before my eyes fly open in terror. "Cyrus! H-how... what are you doing here? You have to go. They're looking for you."

"I'm not leaving without you," he murmurs.

Against my better judgment, I pull him close, inhaling his scent of sunshine, soap, and something that is uniquely *him*. "How did you get in here?" If he got in, there must be a way out.

The door slams open before he can answer, and Draya strides in flanked by Bushy Brows and Square Jaw. Bushy grabs Cyrus, but Cy's too strong and pulls himself free. With one quick movement, he slugs Bush, sending him stumbling back, his head slamming into the wall with a satisfying crack.

Cyrus pounces on him. "Did you do that to her? I'll fucking kill you." His voice is low, calm, in control in that terrifying way he gets when he's protecting the people he loves.

Square Jaw grabs my biceps in his meaty grip and hauls me to my feet. He presses the muzzle of his weapon to my temple. "Stop! Now."

Cyrus spins, his gaze landing on the gun pointed at my head. His eyes widen and his arms go limp at his sides. My heart stutters as the fight goes out of him. Draya wants him dead, and if he just gives up, she's going to get her wish.

Bushy Brows rolls over and pushes up. He pulls back the slide on his handgun and aims at Cyrus. "On your knees."

Cyrus complies, placing his hands behind his head and lacing his fingers. Draya strides over to him and my pulse beats a staccato rhythm. She won't kill him herself, she can't, he looks too much like Lucien. That doesn't mean she won't order someone else do her dirty work. She stops before Cyrus, places the gun against his forehead, and pulls the trigger.

A silent scream tears from my throat, but no sound comes out because there is no oxygen. Anywhere. The room has been sucked into a vacuum and my insides are squeezed in a vise-like grip. My mouth remains open like one of those creepy clowns as my unblinking eyes stare in horror at the crimson liquid pooling around the boy I love. Square Jaw drops me and I hit the ground with a thud.

I crawl across the icy concrete floor as the first sob rips free, my arm draping across Cyrus's unmoving body. His blood seeps into and around me, wrapping me against him like a blanket, knitting us together as one. For the first time in days, I'm warm, and give in to the feeling, because no matter what else they do to me, nothing will be worse than this.

My eyes open and I'm alone in the room. I push up, my head swiveling, looking for Cyrus. My limbs shake with the adrenaline of my nightmare and overwhelming relief. Real tears chase my dream ones as I sob until my head aches.

The door opens and I lift my head to peer up at Draya through swollen eyes. Anger surges through me at Nightmare Draya's actions, and if I had the strength I'd kill her with my bare hands.

Draya makes her way across the floor and squats before me. "Are you ready to tell me?"

I hiccup and swallow hard, narrowing my gaze. "I told you, I don't know."

She studies me, pressing her lips together, then stands. "Perhaps not, but I'll bet you could come up with an idea of where he might be."

"Your guess would be as good as mine."

Something flickers in her blue eyes, something that doesn't make sense — fear. What is she afraid of?

Bushy Brows and Square Jaw return, Bushy carrying the same long slender torture device.

"Where do you think he is?" Draya asks.

"I don't know."

Draya swallows hard before turning to Bushy and nodding. "She knows something." Then sweeps out of the tent, leaving me with these two monsters.

The agony is worse this time and I'm ready to tell them everything, including where Cyrus is. Writhing, blinding pain turns my vision red, reminding me of my nightmare and Cyrus's blood. Instead, I tell them what I think they want to hear. "H-he said he was going to Mexico."

Bushy stops and glances at his meaty counterpart, giving him a brief nod. Before he leaves, he moves his device to a spot on my side between two ribs, searing me with excruciating savageness until everything goes mercifully black.

Time is hard to gauge, but I'm fairly certain days have passed since I was last burned or beaten. Staying awake for any length of time is impossible, but I'm terrified of sleeping. Sleep is filled with nightmares of torture and unbearable loss. In one dream, they capture and kill my uncle in front of me, in another my parents or Katie and Rachel. Sometimes Liam and Quinn, or Eddie, but mostly it's Cyrus. Every time I wake screaming until I'm hoarse and my skull is throbbing.

With slow, painful progress, I crawl to the door and grab the handle, pulling myself up until I can reach the light switch, flipping on the overhead bulb. The room floods with a harsh glare, illuminating the plate I licked clean from my last meal where it still sits on the floor. Sweat dripping from my brow, I drop back down and lean my head back, only able to suck in short, shallow breaths.

The lock clicks, and the door slams open. Draya enters with two different soldiers — a woman and a young boy, fifteen tops. Neither looks capable of threatening a puppy, which pretty much sums up how bad off I am.

I push myself to standing, and the room sways. Leaning against the wall sounds like a good plan. I cross my arms, attempting to cover my instability with indignation. Draya turns toward me and the room spins. Trying to focus on her face throws everything into chaos. I close my eyes and attempt to quiet the swirling inside me.

"You've proved useful, but I think you know even more."

I open my eyes and sigh with resignation. I can't take any more. No more pain, no more nightmares, no more anything. I'm ready to answer her questions.

The boy steps forward with a chair and unfolds it for Draya. She sits and snaps her fingers. The woman brings a second chair and sets it up for me. For the next few hours, I tell Draya what I think she wants to hear. Anything that will keep her from letting her goons abuse me. Death will be welcomed when we're done.

They have finally broken me.

My latest nightmares are less graphic than earlier ones. Maybe because the threat of torture has passed or the likelihood that they're searching for Cyrus in all the wrong places. Whatever the reason, I welcome the respite and allow myself to truly rest.

The door opens and lights flick on. Two sets of boots clunk across the concrete floor toward me. When I finally find the courage to glance up, two female soldiers are staring down at me, mouths drawn tight, noses scrunched.

"Get up," one of them orders. She's at least a dozen years older than me, her mousy brown hair pulled into a loose bun, wispy curls escaping and sticking to her sweaty face.

With a grunt, I push myself up, but within seconds the edges of my world go dark. The next thing I'm aware of, I'm on the floor, my knees bent, and my head pushed between my legs by a firm hand. A heavenly aroma makes its way through the brain fog and my mouth floods with saliva. A third soldier, the teen girl from the other day, places a tray of food in front of me. Hot food. Scrambled eggs, bacon, and some sort of fried potatoes.

My hand shoots out and grabs a fistful of eggs, and I inhale them straight from my palm as the girl's jaw drops. She thrusts a fork at me before sucking in her bottom lip and turning away.

The other two women remain, watching me eat. That would creep me out if I wasn't starving. The shorter one, shorter even than me, hands me a mug and my eyes close as the scent of fresh-brewed coffee reaches inside and hugs my brain. For a moment, warmth and gratitude envelope me. This is the kindest treatment anyone has shown me since the night of the Invasion. Wait, why are they being kind? Unless... Food catches in my throat and I can't swallow what is probably my last meal.

"If you're done, let's go," Mousy orders.

I take a swig of coffee to dislodge my breakfast and wash it down. Shorty grabs my upper arm, her long fingers curling around my withered biceps and yanks me up. She drags me toward the door, her white-blond hair swinging about her shoulders. My feet trip over each other, and I stumble a few times, but Mousy is behind me, shoving me between my shoulder blades to keep me moving forward. Once outside, they flank me, gripping my arms, and drag me through a corridor where several other soldiers are escorting other Unionites. My eyes are drawn to an older man, water dripping from his hair and gray-streaked beard. We lock eyes for a half second before we pass in opposite directions.

My captors halt in front of a utility room at the end of a narrow hall. Mousy drops my arm and reaches around, flipping on the lights. She shoves me inside where a showerhead juts out of the wall over a drain in the floor. There is no curtain, no privacy.

"Strip," she orders.

My fingers shake as I fumble with my belt and button of my jeans. Impatient, she unzips my fly for me before yanking my shirt over my head. I let out a groan, and she gasps as the full extent of my injuries becomes visible before taking a step back as if I'm contagious.

"Holy hell," Shorty says under her breath.

The atmosphere changes instantly, like the humanity fairy sprinkled them with compassion dust. Mousy turns on the shower, checking the temperature.

"We're going to clean you up," she says, her voice morphing from authoritarian to soothing. With a featherlight touch, she eases my pants off and helps me out of my bra and underwear.

My legs tremble as I make my way toward the stream. The water is only warm, but it pierces my tender skin like long, sharp needles, and I suck in a breath. I can't stop shivering even though I'm not cold. When I'm finished washing my body, I lean back to wet my hair.

"Here." Shorty holds out a bottle and squeezes shampoo into my hand.

Working up a lather, I attempt to purge days, or more likely weeks, worth of vomit, blood, saliva and god only knows what else from my curls. My fingers tangle with strands as I try to separate them before rinsing out the suds. Mousy shuts off the shower and drapes a towel around my shoulders. The rough cloth is like a cheese grater against my inflamed skin.

Shorty hands me clean underwear, a bra, fatigues, and an Uprising T-shirt. My movements are sluggish as I dress, and I wince each time clothing touches the raw spots on my back. Mousy sets a pair of socks and boots on the floor in front of me. I stare at them, working up the energy to put them on, but the effort of dressing wore me out. After a few moments, Mousy kneels before me and puts them on my feet.

Shorty takes my elbow with a light hand and eases me back down the hall. Instead of returning me to my cell, we turn the opposite way, stopping at a door in another hallway. Mousy scans her fingerprint and pushes open the door to a room that is similar to my old one but better in the best possible way.

This one isn't empty.

This one has people in it.

People I love.

8

POWER AND GREED

Cyrus

*M*y legs feel like they're filled with lead and I want nothing more than some quality time with my cot. After a quick dinner, I head back to the staff quarters to cash in on a night off.

Before I get far, Nate corners me. "Hey, we were thinking we could get together tonight. To talk."

I stifle a groan and glance longingly at the sleeping tent before turning to face him. "It's been a long day, Nate, can we meet tomorrow?"

"Look, we thought about what you said the other night. And we're in."

I spent the entire day worried about Evan and debating whether to go look for her. Where, I don't know, but not doing anything is making me stir crazy. If they're serious about this, though, a conversation might be worthwhile. With a nod, I follow Nate to the fire pit where the others are already gathered.

"We're willing to fight," Dom says. "To do whatever it takes.

This is our home and it's up to us to defend it. Like our ancestors did before us."

"Those are pretty words, but—"

"We get it, okay?" Nate says. "We know what we're agreeing to. If we're too afraid to fight for our freedom, we don't deserve it."

I notch up a brow with renewed respect for the uptight kid. "Alright then."

"They've moved on from kidnapping and killing officials to killing police officers," Valencia says, biting her bottom lip.

My stomach contracts around my dinner and I can't breathe. Bryce and Jack are cops, and as far as I know, Evan is still with Bryce. I finally find my breath and inhale a lungful. I'm only half paying attention as they talk, so Valencia startles me.

"Are you okay?"

"Yeah. Yeah, I have friends in law enforcement." Shit. I don't even know where she is, but it's taking everything I've got to not run off right now and scour the Union for her. There's got to be something I can do. Maybe the only thing I can do to protect her is what we've been discussing — bringing down the Uprising.

If we're going to do this, I've got to come clean with them. "Before we go any further, I need to tell you everything." They stop talking and turn to stare at me. This is going to be harder than I thought and words initially fail me. I clear my throat and get the hardest part out of the way. "I'm not from here. I was born in the Ruins."

Dom's jaw drops as he leans forward and Valencia's unusually large eyes get somehow even bigger. The next hour is spent telling them the real history, the one I know they've never heard. Evan said Unis don't even know anyone lives in the Ruins.

"Wait, are you saying..." Dom starts, but his words trail off.

Valencia shakes her head hard. "That's crazy. That can't possibly be true."

"Why not? Where do you think the soldiers came from?"

"So, you're saying the soldiers are from the Ruins?" Valencia asks.

"Yes, but it's not quite that simple." I give them a quick summary of the Mexican drug cartels and finish by explaining how the Union discovered the tunnels the cartels had dug under their walls and shut them down.

"So, it's about Mexico," Nate says

"It's about power and greed. How each side thinks things *should* be versus the reality of those caught in the middle. There's more." I spend the next couple of hours bringing them up to speed on the past ten months of my life. Midnight is approaching by the time I finish with my story and answer their questions the best I can. A long stretch of silence follows as they stare into the fire with unfocused eyes.

With a heavy sigh, Dom pushes up. "This is a lot to absorb, I think I'm done for tonight."

Nate glances at Valencia before pushing up, too. "Goodnight," he mumbles, shuffling back toward camp.

Valencia stares at me with wide-eyed awe. She thinks I'm someone I'm not. Without a word, she leans over and presses her lips to mine. While it's not completely unexpected, it catches me off guard. Her mouth is soft and warm, and I find myself responding for half a second before my eyes fly open and I place my hands on her shoulders to push her back. "I meant what I said, I'm not ready." With an awkward goodnight, I head back to the sleeping quarters, wondering if I'll ever be over Evan.

Nights by the fire pit are becoming routine as we meet to talk about building a resistance movement.

"For now, the camp can serve as our base of operations," I say. "We're here, we blend in with the other refugees, and we're earning money. I want to start training you along with anyone we can get to join us. Things like hand-to-hand combat, strength, and endurance. We can do some of that here, like running along the beach, squats, and pushups, but going forward, we need another place, somewhere more secure."

"Like what?" Valencia asks.

"I don't know yet, but I'm working on it. The other critical aspect is getting more people on board, so as you interact with others during the day, see if you can get a feel for who might be good to recruit. But keep in mind that anything we end up doing won't be quick or easy."

Dom leans back and stretches out his legs. "Like, how long are we talking?"

I shrug. "Unis are being kicked out of their homes, but they're hardly starving. Until they're forced to fight for their survival, they may not be willing to die for the cause. Things might have to get a lot worse before we'll have enough fighters."

Valencia pushes dark hair out of her face. "Things are already worse. Janel, this girl I met in the mess tent, said the Uprising is taking people and they never come back."

"Those are rumors and we shouldn't put too much stock in them." I rake a hand through my hair. "Still, there's usually some truth in most rumors. We should head up to a pub to catch the news."

Nate shrugs. "If they're even still airing the news."

"What should we tell them?" Dom ask. "The other campers, I mean. Do we say we're forming a resistance?"

I take a deep breath and blow it out between pursed lips. "Probably best to only approach people grumbling about the situation. Then just say some of us are talking about doing something, gauge their level of commitment before we tell them more."

The last thing we need is someone getting drunk and blabbing the wrong information to the wrong person.

In only a day, we managed to pull together a handful of potential resistance members. Most of them are other camp workers of various ages, both male and female, but at least one guy is a displaced resident camper.

The evening air has cooled significantly with sunset, making the fire inviting. The breeze blows in from the water bringing the briny scent of saltwater and sea life. Nate, Dominic, and Valencia park themselves on either side of me, ready to discuss details.

"I know where to get my hands on some weapons."

"Where?" Dom asks.

"When we came back in from the Ruins after attacking the Uprising camps, we had bags of guns and ammo. I stashed them in the Western Province."

Nate's eyes gleam with barely controlled delight in the firelight. "How many?"

"Several dozen handguns, couple thousand rounds of ammo, plus a little C-4. Not enough, but a start. I'll head out tomorrow to retrieve them."

Valencia twists toward me. "I'm coming with you."

"Bad idea."

Dom grabs his sister's arm and turns her to face him. "No way, Val."

"Look, I appreciate the offer, but it's safer if you stay here," I say.

"I'm turning in." Nate stands and inclines his head toward Valencia. "Can we talk?"

She glances at me, then pushes up and follows Nate as they walk out of earshot. Nate crosses his arms and Valencia gestures a lot.

Dom shakes his head. "Those two are so complicated. If she wasn't my sister, I'd push him to tell her how he feels and get it over with." He turns away from the arguing couple and studies me. "Although I think she's got a thing for someone else."

I put my hands up in defense. "I'm not interested if that's what you're getting at."

He shrugs. "She usually gets what she wants."

"Look, whatever she's up to, I'm not into her like that, but if you're referring to her coming with me, it's not gonna happen."

He takes a swig of his beer and sets his bottle down. "Okay." After a moment, he places his hands on his knees. "I'm beat. See you tomorrow."

He saunters up to Valencia and Nate, who are still arguing, and yanks Nate by the sleeve. Nate turns to glare at him, but after glancing between Valencia and Dom, sighs and follows his buddy.

Valencia watches them for a few beats before returning to the fire and dropping into the sand beside me. "You need someone to go with you, someone to watch your back. Why not me?"

"It's not safe."

"What *is* anymore?"

I let out a long breath. She's got a point.

"You weren't born here, Cyrus, which means I know how to get around the Union better than you do."

I raise an eyebrow. "I get around just fine."

"Maybe. But just fine might not be good enough. It's more than that, though. You're different. It's little things, but enough I noticed. I never would've guessed where you're from, but only because I didn't know it was a possibility. Uprising soldiers from the Ruins will notice those differences and figure it out. I can help you blend in."

"I blend."

She holds out her thumb, "The way you walk, like you've never been in a hurry in your life." She adds her index finger. "Your accent is subtle, but..." She turns away from the fire and gives me a pointed stare. "How long have you lived here?"

"Since February."

"Okay, well I've lived here for over seventeen years."

I mull over her arguments. I'd rather take Dom or even Nate, but neither of them offered. "Fine, I can use your help."

"Really?" she squeals.

"To be honest, it wouldn't hurt to have a second pair of eyes."

"Wow, that was easier than I thought."

I shake my head as Dom's words repeat in my head — *she usually gets what she wants*. "We leave first thing in the morning."

She squeals again and hops up, skipping across the sand like she won some damn prize instead of volunteering for a dangerous mission. No doubt this a ridiculously stupid idea, but I seem to be on a roll with those lately.

9

VIVID DREAMS

Evan

*M*y mind reels, terrified I'm only hallucinating. What I'm seeing can't be real. This must be another one of my vivid dreams.

"Evan!" Ally exclaims and rushes toward me.

Mousy draws her gun, and Ally halts, backing up until she bumps into Colin.

Will, Sonia, Marcus, Rainey, and Mateo are clustered in the corner. Their clothes are rumpled and dirty, but otherwise they all look good. Well fed. Unbeaten.

Shorty nudges me into the room, closing and locking the door behind her. Relief at seeing my friends gives way to dread. They shouldn't be here. My eyes sweep their faces, searching for any clue to make sense of this situation, before landing on Colin. His features are twisted, his brows drawn together, as if he's in pain. A knife spirals into my chest thinking of what they must've done to him.

Between the emotional storm of the past few minutes and the walk here, my head feels untethered from my body and the room sways. I take a step back, leaning against the wall for support. Mateo launches himself across the room and is at my side in seconds, catching me before I collapse. He grabs my waist to steady me, but I shriek and pull away when his hand grazes one of my burns. Colin swears under his breath while Ally begins to cry.

Mateo lowers me to the floor and lets go, but hovers nearby, as if he's unsure what to do. He finally settles beside me, putting his lips to my hair and making soft, shushing sounds. His features are embellished with emotions that are out of place on his normally stoic face. My gaze travels around the room again, taking in who is here, but more importantly who isn't. Certain we're being monitored, I lean up and whisper in Mateo's ear, "Where's Cyrus?"

His dark eyes search mine as he shakes his head.

What does that mean? Is Cyrus dead or does Mateo just not know? Maybe Draya has Cyrus. My nightmare flashes through my mind and tears flood my vision. I fist Mateo's shirt to steady myself as my body quakes.

Mateo leans down and whispers in my ear. "I don't know. We thought he was with you."

A slow sigh escapes. Maybe the Uprising doesn't have him, but he's not the only one missing. "What about the boys? And Simon?"

"The boys are with Ilona, Alexander, and Zak," Sonia says.

"They took Simon when we first got here," Marcus says. "We haven't seen him since, but they seemed to know him."

Makes sense. He was one of the people Bryce was investigating, the one who got Cyrus his Union credentials and probably some of the Uprising here now. He was with us when we took down the camps. I sure hope he's okay.

A strong odor assaults my senses — sweat and distinctly male. Mateo. I lift my head from his thigh, which I'm apparently using as a pillow. His eyes are closed, his hand resting on the floor next to him. I shift and move to the spot beside him.

Across the room, Ally is asleep on Colin's lap. His head is back, softly snoring. Will is lying on his back, mouth slack, and Sonia and Marcus are spooning, Sonia's head on Marcus's biceps. Rainey is the only other one awake. She's facing the wall, hands braced against it, head down.

Mateo shifts beside me. "Hey, Taylor." His voice is rough from sleep.

Rainey turns, narrowing her eyes, then makes her way toward us with careful movements, as if I'm an injured animal, ready to bite. She kneels in front of me and takes my face in her hands, rage boiling in her dark eyes. "What the hell did those assholes do to you?" She reaches for the hem of my shirt. "May I?"

I close my eyes and nod.

She lifts it enough, then drops her hand and steps back. "Holy fuck!"

Colin bolts up, dropping Ally to the floor. He scoots to my side and pulls up my shirt, staring at my torso. More foul words come out his mouth than I knew were in his vocabulary. The discoloration, a mixture of eggplant and bile, begins at my waistband and stops just below my armpit. Colin's face darkens, and he launches himself up, spinning and punching the wall. A stomach churning sound of bones cracking echoes off the concrete walls, and Colin pulls his hand back, yelling a few more choice words. Ally takes Colin's hand, and he winces, yanking it away from her.

Sonia settles beside me, her fingers shaking as she glides them over my bruises. "I—I need to check for broken bones. This is going to hurt, I'm sorry."

I squeeze my eyes shut. "Do it."

She presses hard and I can't contain my gasp when she hits a tender spot. "I'm so sorry."

I open my eyes in time to catch her exchanging a glance with Marcus, the one she has when someone is in bad shape. This time that someone is me.

My gaze travels around the room, my mouth full of so many questions. "Why are you here?"

Colin leans forward and rests his damaged hand on his knee. "We heard about the Invasion up north. We got here as fast as we could. Well, we went to Eddie's, but soldiers were waiting for us. They brought us here."

Dread fills my chest as concern for my friends makes me forget about my own pain for a second. "Did they beat you? Or burn you?"

"No. They didn't even ask us any questions. We've only been here a couple hours."

"I was on an A-Train when it was stopped. They saw my tattoo. They asked me about everything... about Cyrus."

Mateo strokes my hair with his big hand. "Shhh, it's going to be okay."

"It's not. You don't get it." I jerk out of his reach. "They're looking for him and won't stop until they kill him. They'll do whatever it takes to find him." I lean forward and ask Ally to lift the back of my shirt.

As soon as she reveals a few inches, she sucks in a breath and backs away. Colin lets out a steady string of profanity, Rainey joining in with a few words of her own.

Mateo cradles my face, forcing me to meet his dark gaze. "No one's *ever* gonna hurt you again. I promise."

I want to believe him, but the truth is I don't. If they find Cyrus, there's nothing anyone can do to protect me from the excruciating torment his death will cause.

A cry rips me from another nightmare, my throat still ravaged from all the torture-induced screaming I did. This time, instead of waking up isolated and terrified, a large hand cups my face, reassuring me I'm not alone. Not anymore.

Wiping tears from my eyes with my palms, I struggle to sit up. Colin sits near my feet, his hand wrapped around my ankle and reaches out to help me, but I wave him off, worried that any pulling, even in assistance, will only make things hurt worse. Loud groans and a few whimpers accompany my effort, but I make it to a seated position.

"I can tell by looking at you they don't feed you much," Colin says. "But they're eventually going to give us something to eat, right?"

I shake my head. "They're not big on feeding prisoners. But don't worry, you get used to it and it's not so bad after a while."

Ally studies him with a wary eye. She may be accustomed to his hunger outbursts, but I doubt she's witnessed how much fun he is when he's gone days without eating.

"So, what happened? After you got to the Union, I mean" My brain struggles to fill in the black spots of our earlier conversation. I'm not sure if it's from the beatings, lack of nutrition, or something else.

Marcus scoots over and sits before me, legs crossed, resting his forearms on his knees. "We came as fast as we could after we heard, but soldiers were waiting for us at Eddie's. Unfortunately we don't know much."

"Where's Eddie? Where's my dad?"

Colin shrugs. "I don't know. We never even made it to his front door. They grabbed us on the sidewalk."

A lump lodges in my throat. I need to find Cyrus and my family after we get out of here. *If* we get out of here.

The door opens and I slide over to avoid being hit by it. The sudden silence in the room sends a jolt of fear racing through me. Ally lets out a squeak and stares wide-eyed at the opening.

The door closes hard, shaking the wall I'm using for support, and Bryce drops to the floor next to me. "My god, Evan, what happened to you?"

"Bryce...Why are you here?"

He reaches out to me, but I shy away. His eyes cloud over, but before we can get into anything, the room erupts, everyone talking at once. He ignores them, his eyes sweeping over me, head-to-toe. "Evansville..."

"Bryce? What the *hell?*" Rainey marches across the room and shoves him in the shoulder. "We thought you were dead."

He glances up, pushing himself to standing and moves toward Rainey, pulling her into an embrace. "I'm sorry. I was going to come find you, but...then everything went down."

"I thought you died," Rainey whispers.

"I really am sorry." Then he shares the story he told me about a faulty timer igniting the C-4 before he cleared the tent. He lifts his shirt and shows them the burns crawling across his torso.

Rainey steps closer and glides her fingers across them. "I... dammit. Stop apologizing."

Bryce pulls her into a side hug, and she wraps an arm around his waist.

A smile splits Colin's face as he turns to me. "You knew?"

I nod. "He came to my hotel the night before I got on the train. I can't believe I forgot to tell you. I'm sorry." My eyes seek Rainey's, but she's still staring at Bryce.

Sonia takes a seat beside me. "I should wrap your ribs, Evan. I know you don't want me to, but..." Her gaze travels from Marcus to Colin before resting on Mateo. "Let me have your shirt."

Mateo's is the largest of the three of them. He doesn't hesitate, pulling it off with one hand, revealing the perfection that is his upper body. Ally's eyes lock on his chest as her lips part. I force myself to stifle a giggle at her reaction, because giggling would hurt like holy hell.

Sonia rips the T-shirt into strips then squats next to me. "Lie on your back."

I do as instructed, screwing my eyes shut. She lifts my shirt up.

"Sweet mother of—" The rest of Bryce's words choke off in his throat.

"It's not as bad as it looks—" Pain explodes behind my eyelids as Sonia presses against my ribs, turning my statement into a filthy lie.

A large hand grabs mine. "Squeeze if you need to," Mateo says.

I have a white-knuckle grip on him while Sonia continues her abuse, placing strips beneath me and wrapping them securely around my midsection.

Hushed tones buzz through the small space as Colin fills Bryce in on what happened to me. Bryce coughs hard then lets loose with a steady stream of profanity. Soon he's back by my side, brushing my hair from my face and gliding his thumb across my forehead.

A thin sheen of sweat covers my skin, and I'm fighting a bout of nausea by the time Sonia finishes. Bryce and Mateo help me get settled against the wall to recover. Bryce claims the spot beside me and places a gentle kiss on my head. I close my eyes, breathing shallowly, watching Sonia take the leftover scraps to wrap Colin's hand.

Rainey directs her dark stare at Bryce. "Why are you here?"

"I saw the boardings on the news and knew Evan was on a train. I was worried about her. The A-Trains weren't running, so I had to take a commuter. I hadn't been paying enough attention to the reports. I fell asleep in my seat and got nabbed while I was out. I didn't realize they were looking for me or I would've done a better job of keeping out of sight."

"Why were they after you?" Ally asks.

"Because I'm in law enforcement. They want to round up everyone who has the potential to oppose them."

"But how did you end up in here? With us, I mean," Rainey asks.

"This morning, they came in and grabbed me. I thought they were taking me out for execution, but they dumped me in here. Since I've been in custody, I've heard talk about officials being shot, although I think they've stopped that for now."

My eyes fly open and my breath stalls as the room spins. "My uncle?"

Bryce shakes his head. "I don't know."

The knowledge that my uncle might be dead is too much to cope with on top of everything else. How is this happening?

"Well isn't this sweet." Draya's voice rips me from sleep.

I push myself up from Bryce as Draya moves into the room accompanied by the Hercules twins.

Ally steps forward, her bottom lip trembling. "Draya? H-how? Wh-what's going on?"

Something else I forgot to tell them.

The testosterone brothers cock their rifles and point them at Ally. Her eyes widen in horror, and Draya throws up a hand, signaling them to lower their weapons.

Tears fill Ally's eyes. "Draya?"

Sonia's eyes narrow as she takes in Draya head to toe before crossing her arms. "Draya?"

Draya's mouth is set in a firm line as she glances around the room at the people who used to be her family. Sonia stares her down until she turns away, spotting Bryce. Grabbing her gun, she aims it at his head.

Fear squeezes my chest. "No..." I whisper, maneuvering myself between the muzzle and Bryce. "Please don't."

A satisfied smile crawls across her face, and she pulls back the slide to chamber a round.

Bryce shoves me behind him, and everything moves in slow motion, like I'm underwater. This is my nightmare except it's Bryce and not Cyrus. I can't let her kill him. Not after I already lost him once. "He has a baby on the way with a girl in the Ruins. You don't want that baby to grow up without a father." She saw how hard it was on Lucien growing up without parents.

The room goes eerily quiet, as if everyone is afraid to breathe.

Draya's eyes narrow on Bryce. "If you got a Ruins girl pregnant, what are you doing here?"

"I heard what happened and wanted to check in on my family, make sure they were okay." I forgot how easy it is for him to lie, the way it just falls effortlessly off his tongue.

Rainey stares at Bryce, her face dark, before she twists away.

Sonia approaches Draya, keeping an eye on H-1 and H-2. "What's going on? Talk to me. We're family."

Draya ignores Sonia and inclines her head in my direction. Her trained monsters grab my arms and yank me to my feet. My groan propels Mateo across the room, his fist connecting with the jaw of Hercules One with a thud, forcing him to drop my arm as he stumbles back.

H-2 points his weapon at Mateo, his finger on the trigger.

"Don't!" I yell, turning to Mateo. "It'll be okay." He promised to protect me and won't let me go without a fight, but they'll kill him. I look beyond Mateo to Colin, sending him a silent plea. He approaches Mateo and whispers something to him.

Mateo's body goes rigid, but he steps back, his fists clenched at his sides. His dark eyes lock onto mine as I'm steered toward the door. As I'm dragged out, a few younger soldiers enter with trays of food. My mouth waters as the aroma of roasted meat, potatoes, and salad parade past.

It's a short trek to my old room, where they deposit me. Unlike my friends, I don't get anything to eat. I take a spot on the floor and lean my head back against the wall, feeling more alone than ever. Maybe that's what that little visit was all about — to further demoralize me.

My fingers reach down and touch my ribs where Sonia bound them. It hurts more to have this stupid T-shirt wrapped around me, so I untie the knot and loosen the strips. Unwinding them, I pull them up to my face. They smell like Mateo. I close my eyes, inhaling deeply, and I don't feel quite so alone.

10

ORIGINAL PLANS

Cyrus

$\mathcal{V}$alencia arrives at my side as I'm stuffing the last of my breakfast burrito into my mouth. I wash it down with coffee and take in her outfit. She's dressed as if she's going out for an evening of entertainment rather than on a mission. Her jeans are so tight, I can't figure out how she moves in them and her sheer white top is see-through, revealing a black tank beneath. She gives me a smile before walking past and returning a few minutes later with a tray of food, taking the spot next to me.

I'm not sure if I'm supposed to comment on her appearance, but her heavily made up eyes and blood red lips are impossible to ignore. I swirl my cup and stick to safer topics. "I think we go back to our original plan. Take the commuter trains from borough to borough and work our way to the Western Province. We can't chance running into any soldiers who know me, so I can use your help keeping an eye out for them."

"I can do that."

"Did you tell your brother you're leaving?"

"Yeah." She drops her gaze to her food then turns toward me

with a forced smile. "I like the clean-shaven you. It's smooth and sexy."

I give her a quick nod of acknowledgment. "Figured it wouldn't hurt to change up my appearance a bit."

"I like that you left your hair long, too. That's the way Union guys wear it. Oh, wait, hang on." She dashes off and returns with a ballcap. "Here, this will shield your eyes some. No girl who's looked into those beauties will ever forget them."

"Thanks," I mumble and take the cap, pulling it on. "You ready?"

"Yup."

She grabs her tray and takes it over to the conveyor belt while I down the last of my coffee. After returning my dishes, I head over to the check-in tent to let Selma know we'll both be gone for a few days. She knew I was leaving, but not that Valencia was coming with me.

Selma gives me firm handshake. "Do what you need to do. I hope you find them. See you when you get back."

I lead the way to the commuter station with Valencia behind me. At least she's wearing sensible shoes. "What was that about back there?" she asks.

"I told her I was worried about family in the West and I want to go check in with them. It's not entirely untrue and it's a plausible reason why I'd need some time off."

"Ah."

We walk to the first train station in silence, boarding with others, blending in. Valencia's attire makes sense now. Most of the other girls on the trains are wearing makeup and dressier clothes. In between terminals, I watch the Union pass by outside. Sometimes it's tunnel walls, other times glimpses of boroughs. Eventually that becomes boring.

"So, where'd you grow up?" I ask her, to break up the tedium.

She tears her gaze away from the window to glance at me. "In the Eastern Province. Not far from where I met you."

"What about your family?"

She shrugs. "It's just me and Dom and our parents."

"Have you talked to them since the Invasion?"

"No." She returns her attention to the scenery.

"We can try to find them when we get back."

Her eyes remain fixed on the walls flying by. "No, that's okay. I mean, I'm sure they're fine."

"Valencia, you need to know they're safe."

She turns and pins me with an intense stare. "Tell me about *your* family."

I was looking to make small talk, not get into my tangled past, but I guess I opened this door. "I grew up with two brothers and a sister along with my mother and father. When I was fourteen, our town was hit by a tornado and my parents and younger siblings were killed. Me and my older brother, Lucien, packed up and moved further west with some friends. And then..." I blow out a puff of air, not wanting to go on, but Valencia stares at me with her huge dark eyes filled with expectation, until I find myself saying, "Last year...Lucien was killed. So, I'm on my own now."

She moves over and sits in the seat beside me, placing her hand on my arm. "Oh, wow, Cyrus. Gosh, I'm so sorry."

There's nothing else to say, and I turn and stare out the window, wondering why I decided to tell her that. Perhaps I just needed to tell someone. So, when she rests her head on my shoulder, I don't pull away.

———

Sleep is flooded with visions of a beautiful redhead with smooth skin and perfect lips. I may be able to block my thoughts during the day, but my subconscious won't let me get over her.

"Cyrus," Valencia whispers, shaking me. I open my eyes to find her brown eyes wide, jolting me fully awake. She inclines her head toward the front, and I spot two Uprising soldiers making their way down the aisle.

"Let's go. Now," I whisper and grab her hand, yanking her up.

Dragging her behind me, I move to the back of the car. The overhead display indicates we'll be leaving the station in ten seconds. I step into the stairwell and press the door button.

"Stop!"

Valencia hesitates, but the only way out of this is to pretend we didn't hear. I tug her along, and she stumbles out after me. The doors close and the train starts to pull out. I keep my eyes straight ahead and whisper for Valencia to do the same. My movements are slow and deliberate, as if this was always our stop. A swarm of travelers in the terminal allows us to be swallowed.

Once we're on the other side, I duck behind the ticket machine and check to make sure no one followed us.

"What was that about?" Valencia asks.

"They're looking for someone. Probably checking all the trains. We need to stay off them for now." I grip her hand and navigate the crowded Union pathways.

"What are we going to do?" This is more danger than she bargained for.

"I should put you on a train back east."

"Don't even think about it. I'm staying with you."

"Let's lay low for the night, figure out what's going on. We can find a camp and listen to the gossip. See if anyone knows who or what they're searching for. We'll go from there."

We head to ground level and stick to crowds while I scope out the commuter trains going to the coast. There's less of an Uprising presence down here. I lead the way to one of the cars and hop on just before it pulls out. We remain standing, ready to jump off if necessary. My eyes sweep our environment, assessing each passenger as I attempt to also keep my head down. The twenty-minute ride takes an eternity, and when we reach the other end, I'm on edge. I take Valencia's hand and she stumbles again, clearly not used to a life on the run. We make our way to the beach and stand in line to check in. The crowd swells beyond the check-in tent, consuming the sand all the way to the boardwalk. Two hours pass in the sweltering heat before we get to the front desk.

"Need a place for the night," I say to the overwhelmed clerk.

He swipes across his screen, glances between me and Valencia, and sighs. "I can arrange for you to share a tent with two other families. Will that work?"

"Yeah." I nod, feeling relief. I wasn't looking forward to spending the night alone with Valencia.

Ten minutes later, a teen girl escorts us to a canvas tent on the outskirts of camp. "I know it's crowded, but it beats sleeping outside." Sweat drips down her temple and into the collar of her white shirt. "The mosquitoes are wicked right now."

She pulls back the flap for us to enter, and I duck inside first. Two cots are pushed up against the side. The middle is lined with bed rolls and at least a dozen duffel bags. Evan said thefts in the Union are rare, but that was before the Invasion. After seeing where we're going to be sleeping, I hang on to our packs when we head to the mess tent for dinner.

We eat in silence and when we're finished we walk down to the water's edge where we can talk privately. With the level of danger we're both now in, I need to be more forthcoming with her. "I never should have let you come with me. I don't know what I was thinking. But now that you're here, I owe you full disclosure."

"Okay..."

"I met her out in the Ruins, but she's from here. I didn't know that at first. She was nearly dead of exposure when we found her in the desert. She's unlike anyone I've ever known — fierce, guarded, shy, aggressive. I fell for her almost instantly."

When minutes pass and I don't continue, Valencia asks, "How did she get out there?"

"She was kidnapped. Her boyfriend was a detective and investigating a smuggling operation. The smugglers took her as leverage. She escaped but almost died anyway. It took us awhile to piece everything together. I'd never met a less trusting person in my life. Once we figured out her story, we realized we might all be in danger."

"From the smugglers?"

"And the Union, but I didn't want her to leave. We came up with a plan for her to stay without risking anyone else. We were going to fake her death, but she wouldn't agree to it without seeing evidence that what we'd told her was true. I took her to a power plant the Union bombed, and while we were there, we overheard the plot to attack the Union. She wanted to go home and warn the Union. I was going to go with her, but before we left, the smugglers showed up to take her back and...my brother was killed."

"Oh, Cyrus. I'm so sorry." Valencia turns toward me and wraps her arms around my waist, laying her head on my chest.

She's trying to comfort me, but it's not something I want or need. Everything with Lucien and Evan is all wound up together. I don't return her hug and as soon as seems socially acceptable, I untangle myself from her embrace and start walking.

"I couldn't leave after that, and...she didn't want to go without me, but her friends came for her. Her Union friends. Her boyfriend...and she ended up going back with them." I take my cap off so I can run my hand through my hair. "When I couldn't get over her, I decided to come here to find her, but joined the Uprising first to learn what I could about their plans. Apparently they saw leadership skills in me and promoted me quickly through the ranks and I made commander in record time."

The rest of this sucks so bad, I need a minute to gather my thoughts.

"Okay..." Valencia urges me on with her hands.

With a hard swallow, I continue. "They sent me to a new camp, and she was there. Some shit went down and I had to get her out. We left together, but she was shot during the escape. I brought her to the Union to save her life. Once she recovered, we went back to the Ruins to try to stop the Uprising. Or so we thought."

Valencia is quiet for several moments, then turns and heads back toward camp. Her mouth twists as if she's trying to figure out how to phrase her next question. "So, then why aren't you together?"

That's not something I'm ready to share. "It's complicated and doesn't matter, but the reason I'm telling you all this is that we're heading to her father's house. That's where I stowed the weapons when we came back."

"Oh," she says, her tone flat.

"You can't come with me to the house, but you can wait nearby. Showing up there with you is going to raise questions I'm not in the mood to answer. Okay?"

"You're being ridiculous but it's your hang up, not mine."

"It's a..." I start to say it's a sign of respect for Eddie and the kids, that what happened is between me, Evan, and Bryce, but I already shared more than I'm comfortable with. Valencia's alright, easy to look at, but she's not easy to talk to. I'm always having to explain myself to her. She volunteered to come with me against everyone's advice. I don't owe her anything more.

We return to the tent in uncomfortable silence. Inside, our tentmates are in their cots and sleeping bags. I head to a vacant corner and lie down, Valencia following, but pulling her bed roll a little farther away from mine. For a long time after I hear her steady breathing next to me, I remain awake, trying to figure out our next move. Valencia and I spent so much time talking, I didn't have a chance to ask anyone in camp about the soldiers on the commuter trains. As I'm dozing off, I remember something Evan told me when she described her kidnapping and I know how we're going to get to the Western Province.

I wake first and nudge Valencia, putting a finger to my lips to keep her quiet. After a quick breakfast consumed in awkward silence, we duck out of camp and head away from the beach.

Once we're out of earshot of other campers, I tell her the plan. "We can't travel by commuter trains now. Not until we find out who they're looking for and why. When I left the Uprising, I was a commander. They don't just let commanders walk away. If someone recognizes me, I'm dead, and you could be considered guilty by association. Do you understand?"

She nods.

"Good, then let's go."

"Where?"

"Same place, but by cargo train instead."

"Oh."

Shit, I feel bad for being so harsh with her, but I don't think she gets the danger we're both in. I wouldn't be able to live with myself if anything happened to her. I utter a silent curse for agreeing to let her come along. She's turning into a bigger liability than I anticipated.

I risk one last commuter ride rather than wasting a day walking twenty-five miles to the back wall where the least observed cargo trains travel. Evan said that was how her kidnappers transported her. We're only on a couple of stops before soldiers board. I spot them immediately and yank my ballcap down. Valencia's fingers dig into my arm. It's too late to hop off before we pull out of the station.

They work their way back toward where we're sitting, asking everyone for their credentials. Mine are flawless, but I'm not sure if I've been flagged in the system. Maybe this has nothing to do with me, but they're searching for someone. Someone they believe is traveling by train.

A solider stops two rows ahead of us, and I stand, pulling Valencia with me. Moving casually, we ease to the door on the opposite side. I peek out from under the brim of my cap, relieved I don't recognize either of them. They're only one row away when we start to slow.

"Wait," one of them calls as the doors begin to open.

I push Valencia out and follow her off. The second her feet hit the ground, I yell, "Run!"

Taking her hand, I pull her through the populated terminal, the soldiers shouting after us. I pick up the pace, dragging Valencia and hoping like hell she can keep up. A shot rings out and she flinches, her lips pressing together to contain her scream. I turn and glance over my shoulder at the soldier who fired. His gun is pointed at the sky and not at us as his eyes scan the crowd.

"Duck," I say, and she follows me until we're surrounded by other commuters. For the moment, we're hidden.

A corridor comes into view and I dodge into it, pulling her along, her breath heaving in and out. Footsteps approach, but continue past. I wait until I'm sure they're not going to circle back before grabbing Valencia's hand and tugging her down the hall. We're still at least twenty miles from the back wall, but Evan said cargo trains travel throughout the Union. We just need to find the closest one for now.

Only a faint light helps guide us through the dim, empty tunnels. I'm not sure if the lack of human traffic is normal or a result of the Uprising's attack on the Union, but either way I'm grateful for it. We hike hours before we come across a slow-moving train. I push Valencia behind me and peek around the corner, making sure it's clear. There are several open boxcars that appear empty, and no sign of soldiers or Unis.

"We're going to have to hop on while it's moving. Are you up for it?"

Valencia nods, a slight grin pulling at her lips.

"I'll get on first then reach down for you. Okay?"

"Okay." She nods again and bounces on her feet.

I take off at a sprint and pace the train, reaching out and grabbing the handrail to pull myself in. Valencia is jogging next to the car when I twist around. "Take my hand."

She reaches out to me, and I latch on to her, but she starts to slip. If I adjust my grasp, I might drop her. A tunnel comes into view, taunting me with the fact that I don't have time to screw this up.

Holding tightly to her wrist with my left hand, I slide my right one down and grip her forearm, swinging her upward until she scrambles aboard only seconds before she would have been crushed.

Her eyes are enormous and her chest heaves. Shit, I nearly got her killed. She lies on her back, her knees bent, catching her breath. Then she begins to giggle, and before long it's all-out laughter.

My heart is still pummeling my rib cage, but soon I'm laughing along with her, a response to my overwhelming relief.

The day passes at an agonizingly slow pace. We take turns sleeping, keeping watch, and eating the snacks we brought with us. Any conversation we attempt is stilted.

Valencia stares at me for a long, uncomfortable moment before scooting closer. "Look, I'm sorry about what I said the other night."

"Apology accepted." I hope that ends the topic and we can go back to not being awkward around each other.

"It's just, well, I guess I was jealous."

No such luck. Why the hell do girls need to talk everything to death? "Of?"

"The girl who still so clearly has your heart." She places her hand behind my neck and pulls my face toward her. I inhale sharply as she takes my bottom lip between hers and kisses me tentatively. I don't push her away — it's nice. She presses closer against me, deepening the kiss and making her intent clear.

I pull away from her. "Valencia..."

"I'm a big girl. I know what I'm doing. I won't get hurt."

She grabs my T-shirt in her hands and lies back, pulling me with her. I try to push all thoughts of everything except this girl out of my mind. With the way she's touching and kissing me, it shouldn't be hard, but I just can't.

I push her away and sit up. "I know you say you know what you're getting into, but I'm not sure you do." The pain in Bridget's eyes when she realized I was still in love with someone else still haunts me.

She pushes up and shoves her hair out of her face. "I'm sorry. God, I'm always throwing myself at you. I'm..." She lets out a small laugh. "I'm not used to having to try this hard, and rejection is something I don't have much experience with. It won't happen again."

I should say something, but I don't know what the right thing is in a situation like this. All I can do is fuck things up even more. Instead, I lie back and close my eyes, begging sleep to take me.

BOOK 2 :: THE UNION

"A wise woman wishes to be no one's enemy; a wise woman refuses to be anyone's victim."
  – Maya Angelou

11

WESTERN PROVINCE

Cyrus

*C*argo trains cover territory faster than commuters for the simple reason they don't stop often. True to her word, Valencia hasn't flirted with me once since I rejected her. I think we're both pretending it never happened.

The miles roll on, and we make small talk. Once or twice an hour, I walk over to the opening to determine where we are. The locations are painted on the tunnel walls that rush by whenever we enter a new borough. Finally, we approach the southern end of the Western Province.

When the train begins to slow, I rub my hands together. "It's time. You ready?"

"Yup."

Taking a deep breath, I jump, stumbling a few steps across the concrete floor before righting myself. I spin to help Valencia, but she's already off and only a couple paces behind. We navigate the dark tunnels, dank and deserted, to the back wall where we take an elevator to the top level. There are fewer pedestrians up here than I'm used to, making me suspect a strong Uprising presence.

With one eye on our surroundings, I search for a map, which are posted every few blocks throughout the Union. I locate the clear glass board, hanging from a steel rod. After studying the illuminated display of the area, I realize we're only one borough south of Eddie's.

"We're not far," I tell Valencia. "But we'll have to walk."

She nods and falls in step. We hike the short distance, both of us on alert. The sun balances high overhead when we enter the park across from the apartment. This is the last place I felt truly happy. It's also where I was when my world began to collapse around me.

"Wait here," I say to Valencia. "Try to relax, or at least appear that way. I'll be back soon."

"Why can't I come with you?"

I pinch the bridge of my nose. "You know why. Just…stay here."

She collapses on a bench, crossing her legs with emphasis and folding her arms over her chest. Her furious expression conveys anything but relaxed.

With a heavy sigh I walk down the path. In front of me is a row of apartments stretching from north to south as far as I can see, openings every dozen units, providing access to the alley behind. Beyond the alley are the towers that support the elevated A-Trains, and past the rail is the back wall separating Unis from the Ruins. Behind me is nearly a mile of parks, gardens, trails, and businesses before the Union drops off to the level below, like giant steps leading to the ocean. In the distance, low clouds obscure the horizon.

I get no more than a dozen yards before I spot an Uprising soldier. She's not in uniform, but the edge of her tattoo is visible on either side of her tank top strap. A guy approaches her, his body loose, at ease. They exchange words and laughter before going inside Eddie's.

Shit. Not sure what to do, I start back toward Valencia to let her know there could be a delay when the front door opens. The girl and guy exit along with two uniformed soldiers, closing and locking the door before heading north up the pathway. I watch them disappear and weigh my options. This could be my only chance.

I move swiftly to the nearest arch and go around to the back of the building, counting off the number of units until I reach Eddie's. The yard is surrounded by a ten-foot tall stucco wall. My training is going to be fully tested scaling this without a rope.

Just like everything else in the Union, the alley is tidy. There's nothing for me to use as a step. Backing up, I take a running leap and grab the top of the wall. My palms scrape against the rough texture, and the muscles in my shoulders burn as I pull myself up, digging in with my toes.

My boots claw at the stucco and I inch up the side while pulling with my arms. I make it to a seated position before dropping to the grass below. The glass doors before me are off the living room, but the curtains are drawn, prohibiting me from seeing in, or anyone else from seeing out. I press my ear against it, listening, and when nothing but silence greets me, I test the sliding door. Surprisingly it's unlocked and glides open with ease.

Inside, pristine white walls enclose bold furniture of bright greens, oranges, and teals. The large display wall opposite the couch is dark. The first time I've seen that. Even when no one was watching any programming, Eddie always had it on, cycling through various scenes from around the Union, like a giant picture window.

I ease into the room and listen, keeping my eyes peeled for any signs of life. With soldiers staying here, though, it's safe to assume Eddie's been kicked out of his apartment. They seem to be taking the nicest ones first, and this place definitely falls into that category.

Trash, dirty dishes, and half-empty bottles of beer sit on every exposed surface. It reeks of fried food and sweat. The once spotless lime-green living room furniture is stained with some sort of spilled liquid. Breathing through my mouth, I step over a discarded pizza box on the floor.

I make my way upstairs and slip into Evan's room. My hand runs along the wall inside her closet until it finds the secret lever. A small door releases revealing a hidden compartment containing the weapons. I place the bags on Evan's bed and take inventory before loading one of the guns and chambering a round. After repacking, I shrug on the backpack and grab the two duffels before slipping over to the door and cracking it open.

Once again silence greets me, and I ease into the hall only seconds before the front door opens and the four soldiers I saw earlier enter, carrying bags of takeout.

I freeze then drop down and peer over the top of the half wall. My only advantage at this point is they don't know I'm here. With slow, cautious steps, I back up until I'm in Evan's room again, and silently close the door. Taking a seat on her bed, I plan my next move. While I'm fairly certain I can take out all of them before they figure out what's going on, I'd rather not have to.

Over my shoulder is the balcony where Evan would go on the nights she couldn't sleep, afraid her crying would keep me awake. There are similar balconies on both sides. For all the positives of life in the Union, I've always thought living so close to others is a big negative. Until now.

A four-foot wall surrounds the deck and a five-foot gap separates the neighbor's. I open the sliding door and step out. Leaning out, I throw the bags into the alley beyond the back fence before hopping onto the rail. I leap across the gap, landing on the deck in a crouch, then lower myself over the edge until I'm hanging by my fingertips.

The drop to the ground is farther than I calculated, but I manage to land easily. When I pop up, I come face-to-face with two young Uprising soldiers on the other side of the glass doors, eyes and mouths gaping open. I grab my gun and take two long strides toward the potted plant in the corner of the yard, using it as a step to launch myself up the wall. The first shot rings out as I slide over the top only seconds before another bullet chips the stucco inches from my head.

I scramble to my feet and sprint to the bags. There's no time to do anything but grab them and bolt. Another blast comes from behind, whizzing past my head as I twist, ready to return fire. The sound of children's laughter makes me stutter-step. A group of kids dash through the corridor between buildings and enter the alley.

Spinning away from them, I pick up the pace, desperate to lead the soldiers away from innocents. My lungs ache and my thighs burn as my boots pummel the pavement, the pursuing footfalls growing closer. A bullet pings the wall to my right and I dodge left. The end of the alley comes into view, and I round it into a busy pedestrian area, disappearing into the crowd.

I spot a stairwell up ahead and crouch-walk toward it at a steady pace. Once I'm in the stairway, I toss the bags over the railing and let them land three flights below before flying down the stairs two at a time. It won't take them long for them to figure out where I went.

My hand tightens around the canvas straps just as boots clomp on the metal risers above, heading in my direction. I rush down another flight before yanking open the steel door into a commuter terminal where passengers queue up to board an overcrowded train. On the far side of the line is a shelter, and I dash over, ducking behind it just in time. The door opens and soldiers flood through, guns drawn, their heads swiveling. I wait for the doors to begin to slide closed before sprinting the remaining distance to the car and boarding.

The soldiers gesture wildly outside the window as we pull out of the station. I thread my way through the standing-room-only car to the adjoining car and squeeze through.

The overhead display indicates we'll be in the next station in less than five minutes, where no doubt my welcoming committee is currently assembling. I have maybe thirty seconds to get off safely. Bodies are packed into the stairwell, forcing me to pry my way through them to the bottom step, my bags banging against legs and hips. Placing my hands on either side of the opening, I shove with all my weight until the doors give way.

"Hey, jackass, what are you doing?" someone says seconds before a woman yells, "You're an idiot."

She's not wrong.

Sucking in a full breath, I jump off, hitting the ground hard before rolling away from the track as the train goes careening around the corner. Taking quick stock of my surroundings, I spot a short service door to my left. It's locked, but a well-placed kick opens it and I slip inside. Once they reach the terminal, passengers will be eager to talk about the moron who jumped off a moving train.

My eyes adjust to the lack of light, and I quickly move to another door across the small room. I yank it open and stick my head out, surveilling the area before stepping into a corridor. Gun drawn, I inch my way down the hall, which leads to a series of maze-like passageways. The ventilation system pipes in a cool breeze, keeping me from overheating and the air from becoming too stale.

My next turn is a dead end, forcing me to backtrack. Except the Union doesn't create dead ends. Everything has a purpose. Turning around I head back and examine it closer until I find a concealed door and locate the release, just like the ones on the bottom level leading out to the Ruins. This one opens into another hallway next to the express elevators, offering me the ability to quickly go to any level I want.

I need to find Valencia, but they'll be looking for me. The only way to avoid putting her in danger is to wait until dark. I take the elevator down a dozen levels and blend in with everyone until the sun slips below the horizon.

Darkness provides some cover when I head back to the park hours later. My eyes shift constantly, surveying my surroundings, my hand never far from my concealed weapon. Valencia is pacing the grass between two light poles, her thumbnail between her teeth. When she reaches the puddle of light from one pole, she does a little kick and pivots, heading back in the other direction. Her shoulders are tense, her eyes fixed on the ground before her, utterly unaware of her surroundings. I sigh, but realize that alone may save her. She appears worried, but what Uni doesn't these days.

As long as she's illuminated I can't approach her. I duck behind a couple of shrubs and whistle. Her head jerks up and swings around, searching. She shakes her head and resumes her pacing. I maneuver closer, my boot catching a rock and sending it skittering toward her. Valencia spins, her eyes wide, tears brimming over the rims.

She runs toward me, yelling. "What were you thinking? You were gone for hours. How could you just go off like that without a plan if something went wrong?"

I put my hand up and glance around before grabbing her arm and tugging her along. "Shhh."

"Soldiers were here, looking for you," she whisper yells. "They scanned my fingerprint and cleared the park. I only came back here after it got dark. But what if I wasn't able to get back?"

"Keep making all that noise, and they'll be back here any second."

She follows me in silence for a few minutes before she starts going off on me again. Mostly, I tune her out, keeping my eyes on our surroundings, but she's just too damn loud. I yank her into an alcove and back her up to the wall. She stops mid-sentence, her large eyes even bigger.

"You're right, we didn't have a backup plan, but it will all be for nothing if they catch us now. Just...keep your voice down." I blow out an exasperated breath. She's driving me crazy. but we need to get along until we get back to camp. "I'm sorry. I didn't think about the possibility of you having to wait all day without word."

"Thank you." Her words come out on a sigh, as if me finally seeing things from her point of view is all she needed. This whole mission has been a massive fucked up mess.

I grab her arm and pull her back to the sidewalk, staying in the shadows as we move back to the express elevators.

"So, how are we getting back?" she asks.

"The same way we got here."

Her body relaxes beside me. "Okay, but from now on, we make detailed plans and you fill me in on exactly what's going on. Starting with what took you so long."

I clench my hands at my side, not used to people demanding information from me, but, after I put her in danger I guess she deserves some answers. "Fair enough."

We work our way into the cargo tunnels and hop a train heading east. As the hours drag by, I fill her in on what happened at Eddie's with the soldiers, and escaping, and why I had to wait until dark to return to the park. Her lack of questions and silent acceptance of my story confirms my belief she had no idea what she was getting into coming along with me.

When I finish, she yawns. "I'm tired." Without further conversation, she curls up in the corner.

I'm not sure what I'm supposed to do. On the one hand, I feel like I should comfort her, but I told her not to come and don't think I owe her that because *I* almost got killed. When boredom sets in, I lie on my back, cross my ankles and manage to doze off.

12

SOMEWHERE SAFE

Evan

*M*y empty oatmeal bowl still sits beside the plate that held overcooked broccoli. Weird food pairing, but at least they're feeding me. Based on the rotating meals and bottles of water, I calculate I've been alone for close to forty-eight hours. This latest treatment makes me feel like a non-entity, a fish in a tank who needs to be fed twice a day, but is otherwise ignored.

A strange scratching noise outside my cell grabs my attention. On hands and knees, I crawl over to the door. The sound gets louder and is accompanied by hushed voices. I press my ear against the door to make out the words, but something pushes up against it. Muffled clanging is followed by a sudden shuddering and I roll away just as the door is pulled away, the hinges removed.

Mateo strides in wearing a fresh Uprising-issued T-shirt. He scoops me up and dashes back out where the rest of my friends are waiting with a banged-up Draya. We follow Draya into an elevator. Her eyes are glued to the numbers above the doors as they count down to the bottom level. She doesn't join us when we exit, but I catch a glimpse of Sonia nodding goodbye over Mateo's shoulder.

Marcus takes the lead, but Bryce rushes up to him. They have a whispered conversation, and Bryce gestures in the opposite direction.

I curl into Mateo's chest as we walk, gripping his shirt in my fist. The air changes from dank and stale to dank and breezy as we move into the tunnels. I suck in my breath, trying to lessen the pain as Mateo picks his way across two sets of tracks toward an unmoving train.

Bryce hops into one of the cars and Mateo hands me up to him. Bryce lowers me to the floor before reaching down to help the others up. The car rocks as everyone moves about, finding spots. Mateo is the last on, and slides the door closed. Within moments, the train lurches forward.

"Where are we going?" I ask.

Sonia brushes the hair from my forehead. "Somewhere safe."

Soon the rhythmic rocking lulls me to sleep.

Groggy and disoriented, I glance around, taking in my surroundings. Train. Friends. Freedom. Well, as much freedom as can be had under present circumstances. Colin is beside me, his head resting on the wall.

"Where is this safe place we're going?" I ask him in my still tortured voice.

"The Southern Province."

"Why? What's there?"

"Someone we can trust." He leans down and kisses the top of my head. "EvTay, you're like a complete mess, I don't know if you know that."

"Oh, well that explains a lot."

He laughs and shakes his head.

We sit quietly for a few minutes and my mind drifts back to our escape. "What's the deal with Draya? Why'd she help us?"

Sonia lifts her head off her knees. "After they took you out of the room the other day, Draya came back in to talk to us."

Ally snorts. "Marcus, Rainey, and Will had to pull Mateo off her."

Colin grins. "It was like Chewbacca going after Lando in The Empire Strikes Back."

"She came in alone and unarmed, what the hell did she think we'd do after what she did to you?" Marcus asks.

"In all fairness, she didn't really do it herself."

Sonia shakes her head. "No, but she didn't stop it. She said she always planned to get you out. She was just waiting until the opportunity presented itself. Keeping you alive long enough was her biggest challenge."

"Nothing happened until tonight, though," Marcus says. "It had to look like we overpowered her. She'll take the heat for going into the room alone."

Mateo grins. "I had to rough her up to make it look legit." He cracks his knuckles. "That was fun."

"It must have worked," Colin says. "If it hadn't, the backup plan was for her to come with us."

"Why didn't she just come with us in the first place?" None of this makes sense.

"She wanted to remain behind to help cover our tracks," Sonia says.

Colin shakes his head. "I don't trust her."

"You don't know her," Ally says, jutting her chin out.

"You see what she did to my friend? Our friend?"

Ally opens her mouth to argue, but shuts it quickly and turns away. She hates conflict and her divided loyalties are probably tearing her apart.

My gaze connects with Sonia's. "Do you trust her?"

Her shoulders rise and fall, but she doesn't answer.

"Hell, no." Mateo gets up and walks over to the door. "Not even a little. But the truth is, we wouldn't be where we are right now if it wasn't for her. I don't believe a damn thing that came outta her mouth, but it isn't in her best interest to turn us in, so I think we can trust she'll do what's good for her, which is to stick to the plan."

"Who's in the Southern Province? Who's this person we can supposedly trust?"

"A doctor," Bryce says. "You remember Dr. Martinez?"

I nod. Like I could forget the man who removed a bullet from my shoulder.

"I asked him for a recommendation for my burns. Someone who wouldn't ask too many questions. He gave me three names — one in the Western Province, one in the Southern, and one in the Eastern. The one in the South is closest."

"We don't know what to expect when we get there," Colin says. "If the hospitals are still open or the doctor will even be there when we arrive. The whole damn Union could be torn apart by now."

Sonia opens a small backpack and hands everyone a snack bar and bottle of water. "Parting gifts from Draya."

I take small bites of mine and wash it down with the water. When I finish, I lean back and close my eyes. Behind my eyelids, the events of the past few days fill my semi-conscious mind. My eyes fly open and my head swivels around, searching the car. "Where's Rainey?"

"She went to find Simon," Mateo says, turning his attention away from the crack in the door. He peers back out through the narrow opening. "We have another couple of hours at least."

I give up the struggle to keep my eyes open. "I'm gonna to take a nap then."

Mateo takes the spot on the floor on my other side and stretches out his legs. He pats his thigh as invitation to use him as a pillow again. I lie down, resting my head on him and slip away.

A warm hand brushes my hair from my forehead, pulling me back to consciousness. Contentment flows through me, and I turn to snuggle into Cyrus only to be met by sharp pain radiating through my torso. I let out a low moan and the hand shifts to help me to a seated position. Mateo. Not Cyrus.

"Thought you were never gonna wake up," Mateo says.

Colin is manning the door and glances over at us. "Time to go. You ready for this?"

I nod and push to standing, but as soon as I'm upright, the edges of my vision darken. Mateo reaches out a hand to steady me, then lifts me with ease, cradling me in his arms. The car rocks as he walks toward the door, but that's the only movement I can discern. The train is no longer moving. The others jump down, one by one. Mateo squats and hands me to Marcus, who doesn't even bother trying to set me down.

Bryce takes point and guides us from the cargo tunnels into the corridors of the Southern Province. We emerge into darkness where warm, humid air slams into me like a wave. The footsteps of my friends are quiet but sure as we navigate the sidewalk. Bryce pauses and motions us back. Mateo ducks around the corner of a building into the shadows, everyone else trailing behind him. After a few tense moments, Bryce signals for us to follow.

When we reach the doors to the commuter terminal, Marcus whispers in my ear, "Can you walk?"

"I think so."

He sets me down, gripping my hand in his as we enter the bustling hub of travelers. I avoid eye contact with other passengers, trying to blend in as we make our way across the polished concrete floor. Marcus guides me onto the train and into the first open seat before sliding in next to me. Ally and Colin drop onto the bench across from us. I lean my cheek against the cool window and watch the tunnel walls zipping past as we pick up speed.

On the other side of the aisle, Bryce is on high alert, his head pivoting, watching everyone and everything until we get to the back wall. Mateo helps me stand and I trail after him to the high-speed elevator where we ride up, stopping a couple levels below the top. Bryce exits first and returns a moment later with a head nod, letting us know it's all clear. He leads the way through the borough, pausing outside the hospital.

"Wait here," he whispers, then he and Mateo disappear through the emergency room doors.

I lean my head back against the wall and my eyelids are drooping by the time the guys return.

Bryce gives me a strained smile. "Okay, Evansville, Dr. Albertson is going to see you. You can trust her. She's friends with Dr. Martinez and she knows your uncle." He takes my hand and guides me forward. "Just a few more steps."

"Mm-kay," I murmur.

The doctor greets us at the doors. She's young. Freckles dot her face and soft brown eyes scan me from head to toe. She nods at a woman on her right, making her shimmery ponytail bounce, and the room snaps into action. A big guy lifts me onto a gurney before pushing me down a hall, the overhead lights passing like scenery outside a moving train.

"I'm Jericho," the guy says with a smile that crinkles the corners of his dark green eyes. He makes a sharp right into a tiny exam room and hands me a gown. "Can you change on your own, or would you like me to send someone in to help you?"

"I've got it."

"Okay. Everything off, the ties go in the back. The doctor will be in shortly."

Sitting up, I swing my legs over the edge of the gurney and peel off my clothes. Everything aches, but I manage to undress by myself and put the gown on. I'm just tying the strings around my neck when someone knocks on the door.

"Come in."

I tense as the door opens and Dr. Albertson enters followed by Jericho and a middle-aged woman in scrubs. Before the door closes, Sonia slips into the small room, filling it to capacity, and picks up my hand. Having my friend at my side among all these strangers puts me at ease and my muscles begin to unwind, like a rubber band being slowly released.

Dr. Albertson pulls a tablet out of her lab coat and attaches a scanner. "Okay, Evan, I'm just going to start off by examining you." She places the device on my wrist and stares at the screen as my vitals scroll across. "Your blood pressure is low, and that's concerning." She retrieves a penlight from her pocket and shines it in my eyes, has me track her finger, then asks for permission to examine my body.

I close my eyes and nod.

She shifts behind me, and opens my gown. "What—"

Jericho joins Dr. Albertson at my back. "Oh my god."

"She was tortured. By soldiers." Sonia's voice is dripping with anger.

Dr. A takes my hand from Sonia. "Lie down, please." She guides me back, then her fingers slide along the multi-colored skin covering my ribs.

A cry escapes my lips when she presses too hard. The door flies open and Mateo's head appears, ever my bodyguard. Sonia shoots him a look, and he puts his hands up before backing out.

Sonia shakes her head. "Sorry. He's a little protective of her."

After more poking, pushing, and probing, Dr. A sighs. "I'm ordering some scans to find out the full extent of your injuries." She turns toward Sonia. "You'll have to wait out in the front with the others...and take your protector with you."

Sonia leans down and kisses my forehead. "We'll be here." She squeezes my hand and watches as they wheel me out of the room.

Jericho wheels me to another room with more bright lights that bounce off stark white walls, a huge display filling one of them. "I need you to remain still during the scans, so I'm going to give you something to help you relax. On three. One, two, three... deep breath in..."

A sharp pinch in my neck fades as warmth spreads through my body, my eyes slipping closed and I float on soft feathers as the medical team goes to work. Only bits and pieces of conversation make it into my drug-addled mind, but a few words filter through: massive internal injuries.

Tears fill my eyes.

"Everything will be fine, Evan." Jericho squeezes my hand. "Dr. Albertson's the best surgeon in the province. She'll have you back on your feet in no time."

I nod, but that's not what I'm worried about. We need to find Cyrus before the Uprising does. Before they do this to him.

13

THE LATEST

Cyrus

When we finally make it back to the Southern Province, I'm ready for some time to myself. After six days with Valencia, I'm done being social. I'm also looking forward to a fresh-cooked meal and sleeping on a comfy cot back in the staff quarters.

When the train slows, I toss our bags off and jump down, turning to help Valencia, but she doesn't need it. I escort her to the commuter terminal and wait with her, but when she moves to board, I say, "I'm sick of sitting on my ass. I'm gonna walk. You're welcome to join me."

She eyes me sideways. "Uh, no thanks. That's like twenty miles. I'll ride."

"You'll be fine. They aren't looking for you."

I watch her hop on, and she waves as it pulls out, then I turn and hike through the corridors toward the coast. This is the first time I've been alone in almost a week, and tension pours out of me like sweat on a hot, dry summer day. With nothing but time, I spend the walk strategizing our next move. Hopefully they did some significant recruiting while we were gone. When we amass enough bodies, we'll need to start training. I could really use Rainey and Mateo.

Halfway back to camp, I stop at a café, bells ringing as I push through the door. The smell of yeast and tomato sauce hits me and my stomach responds with a low rumble. I order a slice of pepperoni and take it to a table where I can keep an eye on the door. Pizza in the Union is nothing like what we had out in the Ruins. This is a gooey, cheesy mess. The amount of milk necessary to make cheese meant we didn't have much, and what we had wasn't used to bury our pizza with.

I haven't seen the news in a while, so after finishing my meal, I head to the nearest bar to catch up.

———

When I arrive at camp with my load, I'm exhausted but too keyed up to sleep. Walker, fucker who had my brother killed, is running the Union. I knew he was knee-deep in the Uprising, but I never thought he was that high up. Anger and hatred ripped through me when I saw his face on the screen, followed by a chill that froze me to the core. He's out for Evan. Since I don't know where she is or how to find her, I have to stop him.

I dump my bags in the staff quarters, securing the guns and ammo in my foot locker before going by the mess tent to grab dinner. Selma is eating with the other admins. She glances up and nods before excusing herself and approaching me.

"Hey, Cyrus. Did you find your family?"

I hated lying to her, but it was all I could think of to justify the time off. Pressing my lips together, I shake my head, not needing to fake concern for Eddie and the kids.

She places a hand on my shoulder. "I'm so sorry."

One of the porters hovers behind her, dancing on his feet like he needs to find a bathroom. "Um, Selma?"

She turns her attention to him, and I mumble, "See you later," before taking my food out to a bonfire to eat in peace.

Soon people I barely know are asking how things went and wanting to talk about what happened while I was away. Valencia takes the spot beside me, and relief washes over me at seeing her back safely. After she took off on her own, I felt guilty. She might be a native, but this is no longer the Union she grew up in.

She nudges me with her shoulder. "So, how was the walk back?"

"Long."

Dom, Nate, and at least a dozen others join us. The new faces are mostly guys, various ages, all with eager smiles directed at me. My hot dog sits in my gut like a rock. I take a swig of beer and wonder if I'm leading them to certain death.

They discuss a resistance and bringing down the Uprising as if they're planning a party. I let them go on for a little longer before speaking up.

"We're a long way from being able to do anything. We're not organized, no one is trained, and we don't have nearly the numbers we need. Doing something before we're ready would be a suicide mission."

"This is our land, our country," says a blond dude. He's a year or two younger than me, tall and broad, but being large isn't enough.

"It is, but the Uprising planned their attack long before they executed it."

A dark-haired girl pins me with a penetrating stare. "I heard you were with them, is that true?"

I cut my gaze to Dominic and Nate, and they both quickly glance away. It'd be best if that wasn't common knowledge. With a sigh, I turn back to the girl. "I was. I joined up to find out what they were up to so we could stop them. My friends and I did what we could. We trained, planned, and executed a well-constructed mission, but it wasn't enough. That's how I know what needs to be done."

"Where are we going to train? And where will the weapons come from?"

"I'm still working on that."

The long days of travel have taken their toll. I say my good-nights and head to the staff quarters for my first decent nights sleep in a week.

Routine is the new normal. Starting before sunrise, I labor around camp, doing whatever Selma directs me to. Long after it sets the horizon ablaze and disappears into the ocean, I park myself at a bonfire, joining the swelling number of people who say they want to fight back.

Today is payday and most are planning a night of fun at a local nightclub, but I'm in no mood to party. Plus, I'm saving my pay to buy weapons, once I figure out how best to do that.

As soon as I'm done for the day, I leave the beach and head to a bar on one of the lower levels to catch the news. The first place I come to is a pub packed with refugees and a handful of harried staff trying to keep up with orders. The screens around the bar are all displaying various news programs. One reporter says things will be different now, better for everyone. No way is that Walker's end game, which makes me think it's propaganda. Hell, even the gossip that spreads through camp like blackberry bushes holds more truth than that. A lot of the stories making the rounds are about Unis being held captive and brutally beaten for information.

This is a total waste of my time. I drain the rest of my beer and turn in early. In the morning, I get to work while it's still dark, opting for a late breakfast. I'm on edge and need to exert some physical energy. Chopping firewood is the perfect cure. By mid-morning, the sun is plenty high, and mixed with the ever-present humidity has me yanking my shirt over my head and tucking it in my waistband.

Back in the zone of cutting and piling wood, I don't hear anyone come up behind me and I startle at Valencia's voice.

"Did you eat yet?"

She holds a plate of eggs and bacon and I can't fight the smile overtaking my face. The heavenly aroma invades my senses, punching me in my famished gut. After driving the ax into a log, I join her on the bench.

"Thanks."

"I figured you'd be hungry. What time did you get out here?"

I stuff a forkful of fluffy eggs in my mouth and swallow. "Early. Been at it a couple hours."

"Couldn't sleep?"

I shrug and take a bite of bacon. Damn, Unis have the best bacon. "Too much energy, I guess." When I'm finished, I lean forward and place my plate on the ground by my feet and gulp the rest of my coffee.

"What does all this mean?" she asks, staring at my back.

Maybe if I ignore her question she'll drop it. Her eyes are glued to my tattooed shoulder, so it's doubtful. "When you join the Uprising, they brand you as one of theirs. After four weeks of basic, they ink the circle around the U, signifying you've completed training. With each increase in rank, they let you add whatever you want. Usually personal stuff. When I was promoted to leader, I included the names of the people who meant the most to me, the ones I lost, the reason I was there. The barbed wire came when I made second in command."

"Why did you choose that?"

"As a symbol of protection around them."

"What about the sun?"

"I added that when I became commander to symbolize a new day, hope for a better future, even without the people I loved."

She's quiet for a moment, then says softly, "Benjamin?"

"My dad."

"Calliope...your mom?"

I nod, my jaw clenching as she gets to my brothers and sister.

"Lucien, Bartholomew, Penelope—"

"Siblings," I grind out before she can go on.

"Evan..."

I tug my shirt back on and reach down to grab my plate before heading back to the mess tent. "Thanks for breakfast."

Evan may not be dead, but sometimes she feels lost to me just the same.

———

Sitting around the campfire after a long day, I study our newest members. Only two tonight. A middle-aged mother and her teenage son.

The woman turns toward me and shoves her sleeves up to her elbows. "Did you hear the rumors about the Uprising raiding beach camps?"

I nod, having heard that particular one just this morning, and it's not sitting well with me.

"They're after specific people, though," her son says, long dark strands of hair swinging into his eyes.

"Could be," I say. "But we all should be extra cautious. I've got the next two days off. I plan on spending it looking for someplace better to meet. The fire ring was fine in the beginning, but we need somewhere more discreet."

"Like where?" asks a guy in his twenties. He was one of the first to join us. I think his name is Gunther or Grayson or something.

"I'm not sure yet, but if they really are raiding beach camps, our days here may be numbered."

"This is turning out to be harder than we thought."

The mother turns her steel-gray eyes on Gunther/Grayson. "Some people are fine with what's going on as long as they have enough to eat and somewhere to sleep."

"This guy, Walker, isn't who he wants you to think he is," I say.

"Who is he?" Gunther/Grayson asks.

I shrug. "A smuggler, kidnapper, murderer, among other things. Whatever he's doing is not for the reasons he's telling us."

"So, what do you think he's really after?" The teen boy peers at me between his long bangs.

I scratch a hand through my hair and blow out a breath. "I don't know, but I'm going to stop him."

"How?" pipes up a girl with too much makeup, sitting dangerously close to the teen boy. My eyes are drawn to his hand on her thigh, hers under his shirt.

I lift my gaze to meet hers. "That's one of the many things I'm still working on."

After wandering up the beach for a couple of miles, I head back toward camp. I don't have any brilliant ideas for locating a resistance headquarters. There's nothing except ever-expanding camp-grounds as each one adds tents as fast as they can. My mind wanders along with my feet. A memory flashes. When we came back after hitting the Uprising camps, Sonia and I stumbled upon a bunch of abandoned warehouses in the deepest parts of the Union near the back wall. That was in the Western Province, but maybe there's something like that here.

I turn inland and cross the boardwalk, heading into the busy, populated lower level. Seaside restaurants, bars, and nightclubs that don't appear to be lacking customers despite the Invasion and occupation. Bistros give way to train terminals and the business district the farther back I go. Because of the Union's architecture, like those old-fashioned building blocks, where they just kept building up and out, most of what's here is underneath the structure. Only apartments and businesses that deal with retail and entertainment get to see the light of day.

I traverse the brightly illuminated hallways, passing one locked door after another, uniformed workers, and automated cleaning machines that keep every inch spotless, even the underbelly. I hike up several flights of stairs and wander back into a dimly lit corridor with more grunge than I've seen anywhere in the Union. It's like no one has been here recently, not even the auto cleaners. Most areas with high traffic are also well illuminated, but here lights flicker, as if they're sleepy toddlers, struggling to stay awake.

After trying every door I pass, I work my way back toward the beach. Zigzagging through corridors, up and down stairs, I finally find an unlocked door. I reach into my waistband for my gun before pushing the door open with my shoulder. The room is dark and I pause, listening for any movement as I wait for my eyes to adjust to the darkness. My hand runs along the wall in search of a light switch, hitting cobwebs before passing over a sensor.

Overhead lights provide a dingy glow that builds in intensity over time until the room is bright. The space is huge, maybe five thousand square feet, covered in at least a half-inch of dust and grime. Spider webs are rooted to every corner, and strings of broken web dangle from busted ceiling panels. It's perfect. I step outside and close the door behind me, carefully examining the surrounding space. My eyes sweep the walls and ceilings for cameras, motion sensors, or any other evidence the area is being monitored. After scouting a little further out, I'm convinced this place has seen little to no foot traffic in months if not years. I make my way back to camp feeling lighter than I have in weeks.

"Hey, Cyrus..." Valencia says the moment my feet hit the sand.

"Hey, Val."

"Um, I was wondering if we could talk."

I lift an eyebrow, but her features give nothing away. "Sure. What's up?"

She turns toward the roaring surf and leads the way down to the water's edge in silence before stopping and turning toward me. "I know you're still not over your ex yet, but I also know there is something between us. I can feel it. Call it physical attraction if nothing else. I'm not asking for your heart, but maybe we can take things slow, see where they go."

I blow out a frustrated breath. Here I thought she finally gave up on me. No way do I want or need a relationship, but I'd be lying if I said I wasn't lonely. Tilting my head, I study her, looking for hope or anything to indicate she wants more from me than she's asking. Maybe I'm crazy or just in a great mood because of the warehouse I found, but I nod. "Okay, but I'm not promising you anything."

"Of course not." Her mouth tips up in a smile.

"And we're taking it super slow. I'm not going to use you."

She snorts. "Yeah, I've figured that out by now."

"Alright. We can start by going out tonight. Not on a one-on-one date, but with the group. We actually have something to celebrate."

"We do?" Her eyes widen and her smile broadens.

"Yep. Come on, let's go find the others and I'll fill you in."

14

MAIMED, TORTURED, & ABUSED

Evan

*A*n ache starts deep inside and crawls its tentacles into every part of me. I groan and attempt to roll to my side, but that only makes it worse.

A warm, rough hand brushes hair from my face. "Hey."

I open my eyes and turn toward the voice, not sure where I am. After blinking a few times, my eyes focus, first on Mateo, then shift to Marcus standing near a door. A smile pulls at his lips before he leaves the room. On the other side of me a beep draws my attention to several screens displaying my vital signs. Right. I'm in a hospital. My eyes close again.

The door creaks as it opens and low voices converse somewhere nearby. I crack my eyelids and find Dr. Albertson behind Mateo, Sonia, and Marcus.

She pushes past the bodies in her way and pastes on a forced smile. "Hello, Miss Taylor. How do you feel?"

"Maimed, tortured, abused...." My voice is still gravelly.

Dr. A swipes across her screen, and within seconds the pain drifts away on feathery wings.

"Thank you," I croak.

She leans against my bed and pulls out a tablet. "We had to remove your spleen, I'm sorry. Frankly, I'm shocked it hadn't ruptured yet. You're very lucky."

A laugh bubbles up. Lucky is not what I'm feeling. Nope, I'm floaty and weightless.

"We also had to fabricate a new kidney and three ribs," Dr. A goes on, explaining about DNA infusion and the low rate of rejection, but I'm finding it hard to focus on her words and instead watch as the muscles in her face contract and move with each word.

When she's done, she pats my shin. "Do you have any questions?"

"How long have I been here?"

"A little over two days."

Sonia's brow creases and I'm mesmerized by the lines on her normally flawless skin. "They're looking for you. Well, for all of us. We have to get you out of here."

Dr. A nods. "It's only a matter of time before one of the staff lets something slip to the wrong person."

"How soon can we take her?" Mateo asks.

"Now that she's awake and stable, you can leave any time. Check into a nearby hotel. I'll give you my number and you can call me if you need anything. I can come there if needed."

As they talk, my eyes flutter closed, and the next thing I'm aware of is being lifted out of my bed. I wake enough to wrap my arms around Mateo before succumbing to the drugs.

A velvety blanket brushes against my cheek, and I sink deeper into a pleasant dream. At least until a sharp pain in my neck jolts me awake.

"Sorry," Sonia whispers. "I didn't mean to wake you."

"You stabbed me. How was that not going to wake me."

Darkness engulfs us, but I can still detect a smirk. "You slept through the last two times I injected you."

"With what?"

"Antibiotics. Dr. Albertson sent them with us. Without a spleen, you're more susceptible to infection."

"Oh." I'm too tired to think of anything more to say and drift away again.

The next thing I'm aware of is a warm hand squeezing mine. "Cyrus," I croak, but when I open my eyes, instead I find my best friend. "Lisa. Oh, my god, I am *so* glad you're okay." A wave of love bubbles up from my toes. She helps me to a seated position and I drape one arm around her neck in a weak hug. "When did you get here?"

"Bryce contacted us from the hospital. We got here as fast as we could." Her dark eyes fill with tears. "Oh, Ev, I'm so sorry we weren't here for you."

A knock at the door interrupts us, and Rainey pokes her head in. "Hey." Her eyes narrow. "You look like shit."

"Um...thanks?" I let go of Lisa and settle back against the head-board, Lisa propping a pillow behind my back. "Did you find Simon?"

Simon peeks over Rainey's shoulder, a broad smile on his face, his blue eyes crinkling. "Yup. We found another friend of yours."

My heart jolts in my chest, pounding a crazy rhythm as I search beyond Simon for Cyrus, only to dive into my stomach when the hulking figure appears. But my disappointment quickly gives way to relief again. "Chase! Did they hurt you?"

He shakes his head. "Not much. They knocked me around a bit until they figured out I didn't really know you. Then they sent Simon, here, to talk to me and when he couldn't get anything more out of me, they finally gave up and let me go."

"They let you go? Then why are you here?"

"I knew they still had you, so I didn't go far. When I saw these two sneaking out..." He jerks his thumb toward Simon and Rainey, "I followed them."

Rainey smirks. "I knew he was back there. Stealthy, he is not. I let him tail us out of the compound before I cornered him."

"For a little thing, she's damn tough." Chase grins down at her.

She rolls her eyes. "Anyway...I asked why he was following us and he said he was looking for you. When I asked why, he said he wanted to make sure you were okay."

Chase shrugs. "I was worried about you."

"He joined us on the train," Rainey says, "but I kept my eye on him."

"And your gun," Chase mumbles, glancing around the room. His face scrunches up. "This place is a dump."

Rainey cuts her eyes to him. "It's a palace compared to where we're from."

Chases cheeks redden and he steps back, leaning against the wall.

The door opens again and Sonia drags Marcus in behind her. "Okay, everyone else out. She needs to eat something and rest."

Lisa levels her with a stony stare. "Even me?"

Sonia's gaze goes back and forth between us. "Yeah, for now. I think it would be best."

Lisa nods, but her mouth is pulled tight. She leans over to give me a gentle hug. "I'll see you soon, Ev. Get some sleep."

I squeeze her hand. "Thanks, Lis. Love you."

"I love you, too."

Marcus thrusts a paper bag at me, disrupting my melancholy. The scent of fried food hits my nose and my stomach recoils.

"You don't have to eat a lot," Sonia says. "Just a couple bites."

"Okay, but that's all I'm promising." Once I munch on a few french fries and take a bite of burger, though, my natural hunger kicks in, and I end up eating half the sandwich and most of the fries.

Sonia drags a chair over to the side of my bed and sits while I eat. "Dr. A thinks you'll be fine. There's no sign of infection and that was the biggest thing she told me to watch for."

"Good. So as soon as I get my strength back, we can look for Cyrus, right?"

She sighs. I already asked her this at least a dozen times. "Yes, but—"

"I need to find him, Sonia."

"I know. I want to find him, too. You need to let someone else handle it, though. It could be awhile before you're strong enough."

"I don't want us to split up again."

"I get that, I do, especially after what you went through." She glances down at her hands. "Let's talk about it later, okay?"

Which means they'll discuss it while I'm sleeping and let me know what they decide.

Dr. A places her scanner on my back. "Can you take a deep breath for me?"

I breathe in as much as I can before a hacking cough rips through my chest, making my side scream in agony.

"Again."

I'm beginning to believe she's the devil, but I do as instructed. This one is better and doesn't result in me heaving my body in half.

"You're healing nicely. I'll remove your disk port and give you oral antibiotics and pain killers if you need them."

"Thanks. Ummm...why didn't I get a new spleen?"

She studies her screen. "They take more time than kidneys and bones, and we needed to move you before you were found." She glances up, her eyes meeting mine. "Don't worry, you can live without a spleen."

"I can survive with only one kidney, too."

"True." She pats my shoulder. "But if something happened to your remaining kidney, you wouldn't last long. Kidneys are common enough we have a fabricator dedicated to them." She hands me a small jar. "Apply this serum to your burns. Eventually they'll fade some, and when this is all over, you can come back for skin fabrication."

I nod. "Thanks. For everything you did for me. I realize it was a risk."

She presses her lips together and shakes her head. "Good luck. To all of you."

Sonia escorts her out and twists the lock before resting her forehead against the door. She sighs and squares her shoulders before turning to face me. "Let's get you out of bed. Lisa will take you to the park. Some fresh air will do you good."

Lisa arrives shortly, wearing a huge grin and carrying a shopping bag. "Hey, I got you some things." She pulls out a pair of sweat-pants, flipflops, new undergarments, and a soft white T-shirt. "I thought these would be more comfortable. They shouldn't press on any of your sore spots."

I give her a genuine smile and take the bag from her. "Thanks, Lis." She always seems to know whatever anyone needs at any given moment. The overhead light in the bathroom sheds a yellow-tinged hue over the small room. A handful of fading bruises are all that mars my face, but I'm not sure if the lack of color is due to the creepy lighting or the fact that I've been cooped up inside for weeks. My cheekbones jut out of a narrow face, my eyes sunken. God, I look like a skeleton with skin. After a quick shower, I dress and find a jar of hair product in the bag as well. I apply some to my curls and rejoin the others in the bedroom, thoroughly worn out from the effort.

Lisa nods. "Much better."

Sonia begins opening windows as Lisa pulls me out the door. "Let's head to the coast." She hooks her arm through mine and leads me toward the express elevators. "You should wear these." She hands me a pair of sunglasses and a black ballcap.

"I thought we were going to a park?"

"I think the sea air will do you good, plus you really need some good-old fashioned vitamin D, girl."

I glance at my pale arms. Yeah, not just the bathroom lighting. "Okay."

The sun is bright when we arrive at the other end of the commuter line and warms my skin on the final two-block walk. We make it to the boardwalk before I'm forced to park myself on the first bench I find to rest.

The briny air and the waves crashing in the distance remind me of Cyrus. "We have to find him."

Lisa rubs my arm. "I know. Jack and Bryce are out looking for him."

My head whips toward her. "What?"

"Bryce had an idea of where he might be."

"Where? I mean, how?"

She shrugs. "He just said he had some ideas. They took off while you were in the hospital, after we knew you'd be okay."

"Where are they?"

"They were in the Eastern Province, but that didn't pan out, so they're on their way back here. If he's in the Union and on the grid, they'll find him. It just might take longer."

"And if he's off the grid or out in the Ruins?"

"Then it'll take longer, but no one's giving up."

"What if something happened to him?"

"Ev..." She blows out a breath. "Let's not go to the worst case yet. Okay?"

I force myself to think positively. "Okay."

"What were you doing on that train?" she asks after a long stretch of silence.

"I was on my way to see Tony."

"Tony? Why?"

Leaning back against the seat, I close my eyes and let the rays of the sun strike my face, absorbing as much vitamin D as possible. "It was so hard, Lis. I just...I had so much guilt. About Bryce, about what we did, the kids we killed, and I hated that he died for nothing because no one knew what he sacrificed for. I wanted everyone to know that he gave his life to save them." I crack open an eye to Lisa's gaping face. "I called Tony and we agreed we were going to tell the story of the century. All of it, including the Ruins, the Uprising, what we did."

Lisa reaches out and takes my hand, squeezing gently. We sit quietly beside each other for a few moments.

"Did Bryce tell you he's going to be a father?"

Her hand tightens around mine, until I'm sure my bones will be crushed. I snatch it back and shake it out.

"Sorry, but...what? I mean are you serious?"

"Yeah. He met some girl in the Ruins."

Her mouth falls open and she stares at me. "You *are* serious. Oh my god, oh my god, oh my god. I don't know what to say."

"So that's a no then?" I smile. "He didn't tell you?"

She slaps my shoulder, making me wince inside. "Shut up! Wow."

"I know."

"What's he going to do?"

"Have a baby, I guess."

"No I mean...where's he going to live?"

"He said he was going to go out there and get her, but that was before all this happened. Everything's totally messed up, Lis. He said he doesn't love her and she's in love with someone else."

She blows out a breath. "Look, I get you have your parental issues, but things will work out. Somehow. They don't have to get married to be good parents. We know plenty of kids from divorced homes and they're perfectly normal." She waves her hand at me. "You had extenuating circumstances."

"I think I'm ready to head back," I say, pushing up.

"I can't believe one of us is going to be a parent."

"I know. It feels way too grown up."

Colin takes another oversized bite of hamburger and wipes his mouth with a napkin before sitting back and patting his belly. "The burgers here are the best ever."

Lisa eyes him. "The best?"

His cheeks redden. "Well other than yours, but let's face it, Kendall, you haven't cooked for me in a long time and haven't made me a burger in like a year." He tips his chair onto the back legs, his head resting against the wall of my hotel room.

Lisa rolls her eyes and smiles. "These are pretty good, though."

I only eat about a third of mine before I'm full.

Colin stares at my food. "You gonna finish that?"

"It's all yours." I push my wrapper with the rest of my burger across the small table to him.

"Mateo's talking about putting together some sort of organized effort to take on the Uprising," Lisa says. "He's furious about what happened to you."

"Everyone is," Ally says, anger lacing her words.

My gaze flickers to the hardness in her face before turning back to Lisa. "What kinda organized effort?"

"Like a militia or something. He spends a lot of time planning and stuff. He's got some ideas."

"Who's got ideas?" Sonia asks, entering the room with Marcus in tow, carrying a plain paper bag. She reaches in and pulls out an ice cream bar, handing it to me before distributing the rest.

"Mateo," Lisa says.

"I hadn't really thought about what was next beyond finding Cyrus and my family." I take a bite of the bar, the chocolate coating crunching between my teeth before the cold, creamy vanilla ice cream hits my tongue.

"That's understandable," Sonia says. "To completely change the subject, some of us are going out tonight. Just to get away from this place for a couple of hours. You should come."

I'm tired, but this drab hotel is starting to eat away at me, too. "Okay, but only for a bit."

She smiles. "Good, and whenever you're ready to go, let me know and I'll walk you back. I promise. Also, no alcohol for you."

"Fine by me."

An hour later, showered and in more new clothes Lisa brought me, I meet the others in the hotel lobby, feeling almost human. This gets me a nod of approval from Mateo and a wide grin from Marcus. I nudge Mateo. "Any day you don't have to carry me somewhere is a good day, eh?"

He grins and ruffles my hair.

Once Rainey, Simon, and Chase exit the elevator we head outside. I glance past the others to Chase. "What are you still doing hanging around here?"

He shrugs. "I don't really have any better place to be."

"What about your family and friends?"

"My family's fine. I called them. They're still at home. My friends are all displaced, though, so I may as well make sure you guys are okay. It sounds like your friends have some ideas I might want to be a part of."

Lisa velcros herself to my side as we walk and asks me how I'm doing every few minutes until she grates on my nerves.

"Where's Jack?" I ask, trying to distract her.

"He and Bryce are following up on something. They'll meet us at the bar."

Marcus stops in front of a wood door with a frosted glass panel, muffling the clinking of glasses and the low thrum of a bass behind it. He pulls it open, allowing me to enter first. The place is dark, with only candles providing any light, but it's bustling with activity. Waitresses lift their trays high, squeezing between tables, and voices rise, trying to be heard over the roar.

My eyes scan the room, hoping to find an empty table. What I find instead stops my heart. Cyrus is sitting at a table no more than ten yards away. My feet refuse to move. It's like my shoes are glued to the floor. My heart restarts, slamming into my rib cage, attempting to break free, to close the distance between us, wrap itself in his embrace.

Two guys I don't recognize are on his left, the chair to his right, empty. I drink in every inch of him after being apart for so long.

He's clean shaven, and his hair is longer than I've ever seen it, the way guys here wear it.

Someone grabs my arm from behind, startling me. That movement draws Cyrus's attention. He starts, his gaze locking onto mine. Butterflies the size of small cats scramble in my belly and a smile tugs at my mouth. My feet unlock and I take a step forward.

"Cyrus!" Ally screams and pushes her way through the crowd toward him just as a tall, beautiful dark-haired girl takes the empty chair next to him, setting four beers on the table before wrapping her hand possessively around his biceps.

My gaze shifts from Cyrus's face to the girl's hand, my body going rigid. Rigidness gives way to fluid disgust. After everything I went through, what I endured to keep the Uprising from getting their hands on him, and he's been involved with someone else?

Every cell inside me vibrates with anger, threatening to ignite an inferno of jealousy and pain. But mostly royally pissed-off furious indignation. I feel as if I'm one of those lottery games with the ping pong balls bouncing off the sides until one pops out the top. Each ball has one horrific emotion written on it, and it's only a matter of time before the one that gets released unleashes something ugly.

I need to get out of here. Turning, I push my way through my friends, grabbing Lisa's arm as I go. "I'm done."

"Okay." She eyes Cyrus over my shoulder before walking me back to the hotel in silence.

15

EVAN TAYLOR

Cyrus

My gaze sweeps Evan's body as she barrels out of the bar, and fear shoots straight through me. She looks like a skeleton. What happened to her? And where's the tool who was supposed to be protecting her?

I shove back from the table and start after her, only to have Mateo block my way. Where did he come from? Mateo, Rainey, Simon, Sonia, Marcus, Ally, Colin. All eyes on me, but I only have one thing on my mind. I try to push past Mateo, but he puts out an arm to stop me.

"Get out of my way," I growl, my hands fisting as I'm this close to decking him.

"Not happening."

The red haze in front of my eyes snaps, and I glance at Mateo. There's a hard edge to his face, his eyes dangerous. "What happened to her?"

"Have a seat," Mateo directs.

I cross my arms and stare at the door over Mateo's shoulder, calculating my next move.

"Sit," Mateo orders again.

My attention shifts to Marcus. "What the fuck happened to her?"

Marcus takes a step back, confusion briefly coloring his expression. He opens his mouth to say something, but a sharp glare from Mateo shuts him down.

"Where have you been?" Marcus asks. "We've been looking for you everywhere."

"What's wrong with her?"

"Where've you been?"

For the first time in my life, I give serious thought to pounding the crap out of my best friend. We stare each other down, me refusing to respond until I'm sure Evan's okay. *Shit...* Realization slams into me like a bag of wet cement, and I stumble to the side. Marcus is used to seeing her like that, no wonder he looked confused. Hell, maybe she even looks better to him than she once did. I take a step forward until our faces are inches apart. "Tell me what happened to her, or so help me I'll beat it out of you."

Marcus pushes back. He's bigger and taller and he knows it. Something flashes across his eyes, and he glances away before turning back to me, all fight gone out of him. "She was on one of the trains."

I shake my head. "What does that mean? What train?"

"One of the ones boarded by the Uprising."

"Shit," I breathe out, my legs suddenly like jelly, and I have to grab the nearest chair. "What was she doing on a train?"

"Where've you been?" Marcus's words are tighter this time. "I answered your question, now answer mine."

"Here for the most part. I met some locals and we're putting together a resistance of sorts. I went to Eddie's and gathered up the leftover weapons, but it's not enough." I run a hand through my hair and let out a breath. "Look, I need to see Evan."

Mateo shakes his head. "Tomorrow."

"What the fuck, man?"

Mateo glances beyond me to Nate, Dominic, and Valencia. "She's been through a lot."

"Yeah, I get that. What?"

"Not my tale to tell."

Frustration burns through me and my fists clench tighter.

Sonia steps between us and places a hand on my chest. "Cy, it's good to see you. We've *all* been worried about you."

"What's going on, Sonia?"

"It's a long story. We'll fill you in, but Evan needs...some time."

Of course she does. She's with dickweed and, based on what she saw, probably thinks I'm hooking up with Valencia. I turn to the group I came here with. Now's as good a time as any to make introductions, so I incline my head at my companions. "C'mon, there's a few people you should meet."

Ally slides up to hug me and I wrap her in my arms, smelling her scent, a little bit of straw and a whole lot of berry. Colin glares at me and gives Valencia a once-over.

"We need to talk," Rainey stretches up to whisper in my ear.

Yeah, I don't need another Rainey pep talk now. Or ever.

"So..." I gesture toward the table, "this is Dominic, Valencia, Nate, Gunther, Jenna." I introduce the rest, although I doubt anyone will remember all their names. I can barely keep them straight. Chairs are dragged to the table as people sit, Ally on Colin's lap, Sonia on Marcus's.

Mateo turns his chair around backwards and straddles it. "Whaddya got so far?"

"I located a warehouse today that should serve as a decent headquarters."

"Can I check it out?" The wound-up muscles bunching beneath Mateo's shirt have relaxed over the past few minutes, allowing me to unwind some myself.

"Yeah. I'll take you by in the morning. I want to surveil it for a couple days, just to make sure, but it looks like no one's been there for a long time."

Over the next hour, we discuss options for building a resistance. Having my friends back is the inspiration I needed.

"I'm going back to camp," Valencia leans over to whisper in my ear. "Are you coming?"

"Not now. I'll see you later."

After Val leaves, the others relax more and spend some time bringing me up to speed on what they've been up to since we parted ways after attacking the Uprising camps. The details are sketchy, though, as if they're holding something back.

It's getting late so we make plans to meet after breakfast before a few start heading back toward camp, including Nate and Dom. I make my way up to the bar and order a scotch, turning when a loud ruckus over my shoulder draws my attention.

Jack and Bryce enter the pub to what appears to be a heroes' welcome, based on all the hugging and backslapping going on. Bryce's eyes sweep the room, no doubt looking for Evan, before they land on me. His expression is guarded, but not surprised. While everyone else appeared shocked to see me, this douche doesn't. Then again, he knew I was around since my fist got familiar with his face. The door pops open again and Lisa reenters. Her eyes drag across me, her mouth pulled down, until she locates Jack.

She skips through the room and wraps her arms around him before pulling Bryce into a tight hug. "Oh, my god! Bryce, Evan told me. Congratulations. I can't believe you're going to be a father! I'm so happy for you."

Hot air scorches my lungs before engulfing my chest. I down my drink, letting the scotch work its magic. Evan's pregnant? Things fall into place. That's why no one wanted to tell me what was wrong with her. That's why she turned and ran when she saw me. *Fuck.*

My head drops into my hands and my fingers run over my scalp. It's really over this time. For good. No matter what she might still feel for me, she'd never leave the baby's father. Not after Eddie bailed on her before she was even born. I down the scotch and signal for another drink, gulping that one, too. Pushing my glass across the bar, I toss a few bills down and shove back from the counter, someone calling after me as I head outside.

My head swims from too much anger and booze on the way back to the beach. I stumble through dry sand and right myself, my gaze fixed on a bonfire — an unmoving target. It sways a couple of times as I stagger toward it and drop to the ground before its orange and yellow glory. With a deep breath, I lean back against the log, letting my head rest on top of it, staring at the stars.

"Why didn't you tell me your ex-girlfriend is Evan Taylor?" Valencia's voice comes out tight.

I lift my head and turn to gaze at her. "I didn't realize you knew her."

"I don't *know* her, but I know who she is. I mean everyone does."

I shrug. "I didn't think it mattered."

"So...when we went to the Western Province, to her dad's place...that was Eddie McIntyre's apartment?"

"You know him?"

She huffs out a loud breath. "Dammit, Cyrus, no, I don't know him. But he's the lead singer of Epic Vinyl. What the hell is wrong with you?" Anger is carved into the soft planes of her face, making her appear harsh. "Do you still love her?"

I'm not sure why we're having this conversation after we agreed to take things slow, but the alcohol interferes with my ability to form an argument. "Yeah, I do, but it's over, so what fucking difference does it make?"

Valencia turns her gaze to the fire and my eyes slip closed as I listen to the snapping and cracking of burning wood.

"I'm going to bed," she announces, startling me from near sleep.

"G'night," I manage to slur before closing my eyes again.

16

LEADERSHIP

Evan

*H*ow can a person break my heart and infuriate me at the same time? I simultaneously want to rip out his spleen through his belly button and beg him to tell me what's going on. On top of that, I'm relieved he's okay. I'm happy we found him and he's safe, but how dare he be *so* okay. How could he just give up on us like that? The day he left, I didn't say much to him, but he *did* say he was coming back.

Sleep didn't come for me last night, but at least there weren't any more dreams. The shadowy, twisted nightmares that follow me when I close my eyes were kept at bay by my tossing and turning and pillow punching. After a quick shower, I dig through the bags Lisa brought me yesterday and find another outfit. I apply a small amount of makeup to cover the dark circles under my eyes, but it's a lost cause.

With shaking hands, I let myself out of my room and pad down the hall to knock on Sonia and Marcus's door. Sonia appears as tired as I feel, making me wonder what went down in the bar after

I ditched them. Marcus exits the bathroom and gives me a tight smile that doesn't reach his eyes.

With a sigh, I fall back onto their bed. "Um, did you tell Cyrus what happened to me?"

They exchange a look before Marcus takes a deep breath. "Not exactly. I only told him you were on a train that was boarded."

"Please don't tell him anything more."

Sonia's eyes widen. "Are you sure?"

"Yeah. Positive. I don't know what's up with him and that brunette chick, but I do not need his guilt, and I especially don't want his pity."

"Evan, this is—"

"Sonia."

She blows out a breath and shakes her head before locking eyes with Marcus. "Okay. If you're sure..."

"I am."

We meet the others for breakfast in a nearby café where the air is somehow both heavier and lighter than recent days. I've been singularly focused on finding Cyrus for weeks, and now that I have, I switch my focus to finding my family.

Colin scoots into the booth beside me, smashing me into Lisa until I can't move my arms. "Um, guys..." I try to gesture that I need more space, but my hands only flap like tiny bird wings.

Our waiter arrives with another chair and places it at the end, allowing Chase to slip out and take that seat, giving the rest of us a little, albeit not much, breathing room.

Mateo drains his coffee and sets it down, leveling me with a harsh stare. "Cyrus is putting together a resistance. He's got a basic organization, but his freedom fighters leave a lot to be desired. We should consider joining forces."

I swallow hard. "What kind of organization?"

"Rudimentary at best." Colin reaches across the table for the bowl with the butter in it.

Mateo nods. "I'm going with Cyrus to check out a warehouse he located after breakfast."

Things are moving too fast, and a lump lodges itself in my throat. "Are you looking to me for an answer?" I shake my head, this can't all be on me.

Lisa twists to face me. "We won't do this if you're not comfortable with it."

No one else says anything and an uncomfortable silence settles over our table. Chase is the only one who doesn't understand what's going on, but I'm not about to clue him in. I feel the weight of Mateo's stare and turn to meet it. "The fate of the world can't rest on my love life."

"That's not what I meant," Lisa says. "We need to decide if we work with or without him. Are you going to be okay seeing him every day, working with him?"

I reach for the salt and sprinkle some on my eggs, to give me a few extra seconds to respond. "I guess I'll have to be."

Mateo's face is tight, but he smiles a little as he rubs his jaw.

While Mateo meets with Cyrus, I wear a pattern into the dingy orange carpet of my hotel room. I understand why he thought a one-on-one meeting would be better, but the anticipation of not seeing Cyrus until later might just kill me. My emotions are all over the place. Part of me wants to see him again, make him look me in the eye and tell me he doesn't love me. Another part doesn't want to even deal with any of this, just go find my family and get them somewhere safe. Unfortunately, this resistance thing is key to having a safe place for them to go. So, I'm stuck waiting and wondering and building up the inevitable meeting between us.

Tears prick my eyes when I try to figure out what went wrong for about the thousandth time. He gave me no indication when he left that things were over. Just the opposite. Maybe he fell in love with this girl and decided not to go back to the Ruins. Maybe something happened in the Ruins that kept him from getting home. Sonia and Marcus said he never showed up out there, and that girl is definitely from here.

Seeing him with Bridget was bad enough, but at that point he was with me, and Bridgett was just a girl from his past. Now I'm the girl from his past. Lucy warned me he doesn't settle down, that he's too wild, too free, but I refused to listen.

It doesn't matter how much I time I spend obsessing about it, I still don't know what he's thinking. I only know my own thoughts and feelings, and they nearly eviscerate me. The pain drives me to change three times and do my hair and makeup before meeting the others in the lobby.

The elevator doors open, and Colin lets out a low wolf whistle. "If you're trying to show him what he's missing, you're doing a hell of a job." He bends down to kiss my cheek.

As more of our friends assemble and the hour of reckoning nears, butterflies scramble in my belly. I can't decide if it would be better to never see Cyrus again or see him with that girl draped all over him. Definitely not see him. I should go back to my room.

"This way." Marcus grabs my arm before I get far and drags me along.

The knots in my stomach tighten. Mateo meets us on the sidewalk outside and leads us up a couple of levels, then back into an abandoned part of the Union. We were told that every square inch is maximized to its potential. So many lies. We turn down a hall with grimy walls, dripping with rust stains. Cobwebs dangle from the low ceiling.

Colin reaches down to grasp my hand and gives it a squeeze. He's the one person who really understands what I'm going through. How many times did his heart die a little when he saw Lisa and Jack together? I find a small smile for him and squeeze back.

Mateo knocks on a door in a pattern of four then two then three, Jack and Bryce flanking him with guns drawn. The door cracks open, revealing one wide blue eye topped with a bushy pale eyebrow.

"We're here to meet with Cyrus," Mateo says, his voice full of authority.

The door opens and a kid about my age pokes his blond head out, peering both ways before inviting us in. I squeeze Colin's hand tighter as I glance around the huge open space. There are maybe twenty other people in the room, including Cyrus and his new girl-friend. Her dark, velvety gaze bores into me and I force myself to look away before she steals my soul.

My attention swings to Cyrus who is staring at my shirt. I resist the urge to glance down. I'm just wearing a plain blue top and I'm pretty sure I'm not showing off any cleavage, although his eyes are focused south of my chest.

We move away from the door and across the warehouse toward Cyrus and the group he was with last night. Yellow lights dangling from the ceiling by frayed cords provide eerie light that does nothing to lighten the mood around here. I stick close to Mateo on one side and Rainey on the other, asserting my right to be here. Jack and Bryce stay near the door, their eyes on a constant sweep of the room. Bryce catches my eye and gives me a tight smile.

By the time I turn back, we've reached a scowling Cyrus and the others. Mateo and Cyrus shake hands before Cyrus makes introductions. He indicates the girl. "This is Valencia, her brother, Dominic, and their friend Nate."

The guys give me a curt nod, but Valencia continues to glare at me. Her hand is wrapped around his arm, as if I'll reach out and snatch him from her if she doesn't hang on for all she's worth.

Marcus clears his throat. "I like what you've done with the place."

Cyrus's shoulders drop a fraction and some of the stress lines in his face relax. "I think it'll suit our needs for now."

I gnaw on my lip as they talk and look around. The rest of the people in here appear to be Unionites. Probably displaced resi-dents. My attention returns to the conversation at hand.

"We need to select leaders who can work together to make decisions," Mateo says.

Cyrus grunts an agreement. "We should limit the number to four or nothing'll get done."

Mateo nods. "Agreed. We—"

"Cyrus should be one." Valencia shoves her chest out, crossing her arms underneath. "He's already accomplished a lot and everyone respects him."

Mateo's eyes narrow and he blows a breath out his nose. "Fair enough." He turns to Cyrus. "You pick the next leader, who'll pick the third, and the third picks the fourth."

My stomach drops. Great, Cyrus will choose his girlfriend.

Cyrus's gaze travels the warehouse before resting on Valencia. I come close to chewing a hole through my lip before he says, "Mateo."

Valencia's eyes widen in disbelief, and I swallow a smile of satisfaction. I'm so caught up in my internal gloating, I miss Mateo's choice, but it doesn't escape me for long that everyone is staring at me.

"What?"

The corner of Mateo's mouth quirks up. "Who's your pick?"

"My pick?"

"Yes, you're up."

Mateo chose me and I missed it. I whip around and grab Rainey's sleeve. "Rainey."

Just like that, the leadership is set and Valencia isn't one of them, but I am. She's no longer glaring at me, but has moved to throwing miniature daggers with her eyes. I almost feel satisfied. Except for the part where she's with the boy I love.

After the selection of leaders yesterday, I couldn't get out of the warehouse fast enough. We're meeting again this evening after Cyrus gets off work. He's got some gig at the campground and is the only one of us with a job.

"He needs to quit," Mateo mumbles.

I pick at my blueberry muffin and sip my coffee as I watch the café door. A couple people pass by out front, but no one bothers to look in.

"You gonna finish that?" Colin points at my half-eaten muffin.

I shove it across the white tile tabletop. "All yours."

He stuffs the other half in his mouth in a single bite, grinning as crumbs spill out the sides.

"Pig." Ally swats his arm with an affectionate smile.

Colin shrugs and washes the rest of it down with coffee. "I'm a growing boy."

Mateo leans forward, resting his forearms on the table. "We can't accomplish anything if Cyrus is only available a few hours a night." He turns to study me. "How much money can you access?"

"I don't know, I haven't tried in a while. Colin, have you used your card recently?"

"Yeah. Last week."

"Are we certain they're still safe to use?"

Jack reaches out his hand and Colin hands him the card. He swipes it along a device connected to his tablet, his eyes narrowed at the screen. "It still generates a random code so no one can track its use."

"What about when it's reloaded?"

Jack stuffs the tablet into his pocket and hands Colin his card. "I don't know. Depends on how talented their techs are. If they've got someone who can hack the banking system, it's possible. But that's only one half. They'll be able to see money going into the account, but they still can't track where it's being used."

"Then no one needs a job," Mateo says.

My breakfast balls in my stomach. "Did you make me leader because I've got the funds?"

He narrows his eyes and shakes his head, "You're too smart to ask that question."

That wasn't an answer, but I know him well enough to know

it's the only one I'm getting. "Look, if you want Cyrus to quit his job, you need to be the one to convince him. Any money has to come from you. He won't take it from me."

"He'll know though," Ally says.

Mateo nods and purses his lips. "We don't have a choice. He's gonna have to accept he has a new job and it's being financed by Evan. Whether he likes it or not."

"Before tonight's meeting, let's decide what we want to accomplish," Jack says, leaning forward, resting his chin on his propped fingers.

"What if what we want to do isn't the same as them?" Lisa asks.

"We're all in this together now," Rainey says. "The four leaders can iron out any differences in goals."

I take another sip of coffee, licking the foam from my upper lip. "So, what do we want to take on first?"

"Cy's talking about weapons and training," Marcus says.

"Where to train is going to be an issue. It can't be here. We're too visible. But we may be able to get supplies in the Northern Territories or the Ruins." Mateo cuts his eyes to Rainey. "Since Mexico is probably off the table."

"I want to find my family," I say. "I know it's not Resistance-worthy, but I have to make sure they're okay or I'm going to be completely useless."

"We all want to find our families," Lisa says.

"I know. It's selfish, but I can't help worrying they might be targeted because of me."

Rainey narrows her gaze on us. "We need as many recruits as possible. You can recruit your families."

I'm not sure if she's serious, or just giving us cover. In either case, I'm grateful for her support. The rest of the day passes with us compiling a growing list of things to accomplish while we wait for Cyrus to finish his shift. When it's time to meet him, I follow Mateo and Rainey out to the beach.

The sun dips behind the clouds, chilling the moist air around us. My eyes scan the area until they spot a familiar silhouette in front of a bonfire, my breath catching in my throat, my body aching to be in his arms. His usual crew is huddled with him.

"Hey," Mateo says.

Cyrus's eyes sweep over us and the tension is so thick, I'm beginning to wonder if merging our two groups is a good idea. He moves away from the fire, leaving his friends behind, and heads toward the jetty. We follow him as he climbs up to take a seat.

Mateo clears his throat and turns to Cyrus. "So where do we stand?"

"My group is dedicated, but they're green and don't fully understand the scope of what they're in for. They can be trained, but I'm not sure they can really be prepared for what we're up against."

"Lisa, Colin, and I were no different," I say.

Cyrus studies me, and for a split second the hard edges to his face give way to a softness. "You and Colin trained with Mateo."

"And Mateo can work with them. Plus, you and Rainey, and Sonia and Marcus. Hell, even Colin and I can help. Everyone in our group has had some training. Well, except Chase."

"Who's Chase?" Cyrus asks, directing his question to Mateo.

"He was on the train with Evan. He's been tagging along after us."

Cyrus's jaw clenches. "Are you sure you can trust him?"

"No, but he doesn't appear to have any love for the Uprising."

His double-standard grates on my nerves and before I can stop myself, I snap. "What about *your* merry band of misfits? Can *they* be trusted?"

His shoulders lift and drop as if he's letting out a deep, silent sigh. "I know enough. They're in this for the right reasons."

"Why do you think Chase isn't, then? I mean you don't even know him."

"You aren't necessarily the best judge of character."

My face ignites and I shove to standing, my hands flying to my hips. "Well, you'd know, wouldn't you?"

He fiddles with a piece of drift wood. "I guess I'm no better then, am I?"

"What the hell, Cyrus?" I yell, trying to get a reaction out of him. His demeanor is so calm, detached, but his words cut me to the bone. "What's that supposed to mean?"

He tosses the wood into the sand. "It means what you think it does."

"God you're an ass. What is your problem?"

Betrayal cuts across his features and he opens his mouth to say something, but before he can get a word out, Mateo is in front of me.

He slings an arm around my waist and yanks me off the jetty, setting me down a few feet away. His large hands come to rest on my shoulders, anchoring me in place. "Calm down, Evan. This isn't helpful."

My breathing is a raspy mess. "How dare he? Who does he think he is?"

"You need to settle down. Right now." Mateo's face is so close I can see the darker ring around his nearly black eyes. They're flashing anger, but also something else. A warning of sorts.

"Fine," I huff out between my teeth. My hands are still shaking, but my heart rate is returning to something less stratospheric. "Maybe I should step down. It's not like I'm not going to fund this operation."

"Do you honestly think that's the reason I chose you?" There's an unfamiliar edge to his voice. "I selected you because you're the best candidate for the position."

My mouth drops open to protest.

"You have solid instincts and people trust and respect you. But you do some stupid ass shit when it comes to Cyrus."

"Well, what about him?" My anger is building again.

"I don't know what went down between you two, and I don't need to, but you belong here. So, fix things with him. He's not gonna take the first step, so you'll have to."

I glance back up into his chocolate brown eyes in the dying light and note the pleading in them.

"Okay." I sigh. "But not now. I'll do it in the morning."

He lets out a long breath. "I'll walk you back to the hotel."

17

COEXISTING

Evan

$\mathcal{I}$ march down to the beach on a mission before I lose my nerve. My hands are steady although my insides are a quaking disaster. I couldn't even choke down a piece of toast this morning, but I promised Mateo I'd smooth things over, so here I am. After scanning all the outside tables at the campground, I duck into the mess tent. The smell of greasy food and hot coffee makes my stomach heave.

My eyes sweep the large canvas-created room and find Cyrus at a table with Valencia, Dominic, and Nate. Pain sears my heart until there's nothing left but ashes. Swallowing hard, I stand up straight and make my way across the fake grass carpet.

I halt next to their table and wait for him to glance up. He doesn't. "Cyrus, can I talk to you?"

He looks up, blinking, as if I'm a stranger. Valencia, on the other hand, doesn't attempt to mask her contempt for me. I turn and walk away, refusing to watch them together, my guts twisting with agony and heartbreak. Tears betray me as I make my way down to the water's edge. Dammit, I don't want him to see me crying over him. With a quick check over my shoulder to make sure he's not looking, I wipe my eyes with my sleeves and blink hard until my emotions are under control.

"What do you want?" His deep voice startles me and I jump.

After reminding myself what I'm here to do, I close my eyes and get centered before turning to face him. "Look, I'm...sorry...for whatever it is I did to make you *so* angry with me." I have absolutely no idea what I'm apologizing for, but he's clearly pissed. His anger is too intense, too consuming to be just about my meltdown after we thought Bryce died.

"You can't just apologize for 'whatever'."

"Well, I don't know why you're so torqued off at me. When you left, I thought it was for the best—"

"I went to find you because I *loved* you. Instead I found Bryce. In your bed."

The past tense of love is not lost on me, nor is the delivery, as powerful as a slap across the face. I spent one night with Bryce in that hotel. What are the odds that he'd show up when Bryce was there? The betrayal flaring in his eyes for a fleeting moment before he shuts me out tells me it's the truth. My heart constricts at the pain I caused him, but it's all a huge misunderstanding. I reach my hand out, my fingers lightly brushing the soft cotton of his shirt sleeve. "Cy...listen, it's not what—"

He jerks away from me. "Save it."

"No. Not this time. It's not what you think."

He spins and pins me with an intense glare that melts my insides, and not in the good way. "It's not what I think? I think Bryce answered your door half naked after getting out of a rumpled bed for two. It's pretty clear what I saw."

His anger fuels my own because the conclusions he jumped to are something I thought we were beyond. "So, you just assumed if some guy was in my room I must've slept with him. I mean, how could I *possibly* resist the temptation."

He stares me down with murderous rage. I look away first, dammit. "Not my first conclusion, but your boyfriend was only too happy to fill in the missing pieces until the whole picture became clear."

"M-my, my what?"

"You should talk to him, I'm sure he'll explain it to you."

"Oh I will, but we're not done here yet."

"We are. You and I need to get along, and I'm willing to put it in the past for the sake of the Resistance. But when this is over, I don't ever want to see you again." He turns and stalks back to the mess tent, fracturing my heart a little more with each step he takes away from me.

I will not cry, I will not cry, shit, I'm crying. His words shake me until I crumble. I don't understand what's going on, but one thing is clear, he hates me. Bryce has some explaining to do, but the fact that Cyrus was so quick to discard what we once had without finding out what happened means he never loved me the way I thought he did. The way I loved him. The way I still love him.

Things between Cyrus and me are...better, I guess, now that we came to an understanding. The understanding that he believes I slept with Bryce and I'm the devil's spawn. We don't interact except at our meetings, and even then he mostly talks to Mateo and Rainey. He won't look me in the eye, instead staring below my breasts, like he doesn't want to be caught looking at them either.

My energy and strength grow a little with each passing day, but I still need a nap most afternoons. Cyrus can't conceal his irritation when my fatigue interferes with planning. Mateo always has my back, though.

The warehouse headquarters is taking shape. Everyone worked together to acquire tables and chairs, shelving for supplies, and some makeshift dividers to create the illusion of office spaces for meetings. Cyrus, Mateo, Rainey, and I make our way to the back corner, which has become our spot.

We take seats around the table and Cyrus gets right to business. "We need weapons. I inventoried everything I grabbed from Eddie's but it's nowhere near enough."

My head whips up, my heart pounding in my chest. "Wait, you went to Eddie's? When?"

His eyes meet mine for the first time in days. "Yes."

"How is he? What about the kids?"

"I didn't see any sign of them. Uprising soldiers were squatting in the apartment."

A shudder rolls through me as hope seeps from my pores. I close my eyes and whisper, "Where are they?"

"I don't know." Cyrus's voice is softer this time, compassionate. "Based on what we learned, they're only booting people out of their homes on the top levels. He might be at one of the camps in that area."

I open my eyes and meet his stare, the contempt from earlier is gone, but he offers nothing else. I disappear into my own thoughts, wondering how soon I can go look for my dad and siblings. A sudden silence draws me out of my head and I realize everyone is staring at me.

"Uhh...sorry, what?"

"No objections?" Rainey smirks at me. "To me and Mateo heading down to Mexico?"

"What happened to going out to the Ruins?"

"We talked about it." Mateo cuts his eyes to Cyrus. "That's an unknown quantity at the moment. We don't know what we'll find out there now, but Mexico is a sure bet."

"Isn't taking Rainey risky?"

His gaze slides to her and he rubs his chin. "She'll be fine. We're heading to my hometown. She speaks the language and no one there should recognize her."

"When are you leaving?"

"Tomorrow."

Once again, two of my best friends are headed into danger.

After dinner, the Resistance converges on the warehouse to

talk. Like the past couple of nights, too many bodies and not enough ventilation makes it stifling. Cyrus and I will be the only leaders remaining once Rainey and Mateo leave tomorrow. I'm not sure if we're going to continue to meet, or awkwardly avoid each other, but I don't do well with uncertainty. At least if I know what to expect, I can prepare for it.

I find him on the other side of the room talking to Valencia and head over. When I reach him, I dig down deep for my calm voice. "Cyrus?"

He turns toward me, eyebrow raised in silent question.

"So, I just...with the others leaving tomorrow, I figured we should work out some more plans tonight. Before they go." The silence that follows grows louder, and I shove my hands in my pockets to keep from gnawing on my thumbnail while I wait for him to answer.

"Okay," he finally says.

We walk to toward the door where Rainey and Mateo are speaking with Bryce and Chase. When we get closer, I overhear talk about logistics with the trip to Mexico. Rainey glances up, looking beyond me at Cyrus, before returning to the conversation.

"Alright, so we'll meet you in the lobby in the morning." Chase grabs Bryce's sleeve and tugs him out the door.

After it closes, I steal a glance at Cyrus, wondering if he's going to challenge her on the whole "Chase can't be trusted thing," but his jaw is clamped shut, his face a mask.

"We can work on recruiting while you're gone," I say.

"How are you gonna do that?" Mateo asks.

"It won't be easy. Not that anyone's happy about the Invasion, but people here are different. Everyone's still grappling with the fact that people live in the Ruins. Some of them probably won't even have a problem with the Uprising. They'll think what the Union did was wrong and what's happening is fair. But those will be the ones who aren't kicked out of their homes. Anyone whose life most resembles the pre-Invasion days will be more difficult to get onboard."

I take a deep breath while I try to figure out how to explain the rest in a way they'll understand. "The other problem is a big one. One a lot harder to overcome. People here value life differently. Taking a life, any life, isn't something easily done."

"It's not easy for any of us." Rainey's voice has a hard edge to it.

"I know. I'm not saying it is." I stare into her dark eyes before my gaze shifts to the scar running from the corner of her eye down to her jaw. "Where you come from killing someone might be the only thing that saves your life, but that's not the same for us. All I'm saying is it'll be hard to find people willing to kill, even for a cause they embrace. They may be willing to die for it, but not necessarily take another life." Mateo wears a thoughtful expression, giving me hope. I dive into something I've been thinking about for the past couple of days. "Maybe we can pick up Uprising members. Many of the kids I trained with didn't want to be there. They hated everything the Uprising was preparing them to do. If we can convince some of them to join us, they're already trained."

Mateo smiles. "I like the way you think, Taylor."

That's encouraging, so I launch into my last bit while I'm still riding my wave of success. "I was also thinking while you guys are in Mexico, I can hit some of the camps on the beach, try to recruit more."

"I don't like it." Mateo shakes his head, his gaze flicking to Cyrus for a second. "That's a lot of walking...and—"

"I'm fine." I cut him off, not wanting to even hint at my condition in front of Cyrus.

Cyrus eyes the two of us before rubbing the back of his neck. "It's a good idea. I'll find some locals to go with you. They might know some of the campers."

"Thanks," I mumble and turn toward Mateo again. "I'll see you tomorrow before you leave, but I'm tired." Then I head back to the hotel to find Bryce for a long overdue confrontation.

I find him talking with Jack and Lisa in the dingy lobby when I arrive. I grab Bryce's sleeve. "We need to talk."

His eyes search my face and he must see some of the anger

burning in them because he swallows hard, nods, and gestures toward the front door. We take the meandering paths down to the beach. Seagulls screech overhead, searching for leftovers on the picnic tables. Two of them stand atop a trashcan, fighting over a crumpled bag.

"What's up?" Bryce asks.

As much as I want to get to the bottom of what happened between him and Cyrus, I start with the easier topic. "Why are you going to Mexico?"

"Why not?"

"I don't know, how about you don't speak the language, you're still recovering, this is like a seriously dangerous assignment, and you're going to be a father. You have big responsibilities now."

His expression hardens. "I know, and those responsibilities include ensuring the world he's born into is a safe one."

I raise an eyebrow. "He?"

"I gotta call him something."

"What about the baby's mother? Have you seen her at all since you came back here?"

He shakes his head. "Her name's Miranda. I don't want her delivering in the Ruins, so when we get back from Mexico, I'm going to bring her here. I was just talking to Jack and Simon about that yesterday."

"Sounds like you have it all worked out."

He cocks his head and studies me. "Is that what you wanted to talk to me about."

I nod, gnawing on my lip. "Yes, and..."

"And?"

"Cyrus said something the other day about seeing you in my hotel room. I'm not sure what he was referring to, but I suspect you do."

His slate gray eyes fall away from mine and he stares at his feet like they're suddenly the most interesting thing around.

"What did you do?"

"Okay, so first, you need to understand—"

"What. Did. You. Do?"

"I thought you were in the room, I didn't realize you were gone."

"Bryce," I grind out, my arms crossed so firmly over my chest, I'm losing the feeling in my hands.

"Cyrus showed up at the hotel the morning after you left. Like I said, I thought you were still there. I might have let him think we slept together—"

I reach out and slap the back of Bryce's head so hard, my hand stings.

"Ow!" He reaches up to rub the spot. "I thought you were in the bathroom. I figured you'd pop out and, sure, he'd be pissed, but you'd explain how things were. I had no idea he was going to deck me and storm off."

I lift a brow, the corner of my mouth joining it. "He punched you?"

"Yeah. And it fucking hurt."

"Good! Why would you do that, Bryce?" I sink onto one of the benches along the boardwalk, gripping the seat with my hands. "No wonder he hates me."

"The guy's an idiot if he really believes you'd sleep with me."

I turn to glare at him. "*You* believed I'd sleep with you when you showed up at my door."

He shrugs and gives me a sheepish smile. "Yeah, well, I think we've established that I *am* an idiot."

I shake my head, refusing to let him blow this off like it's some big joke, although he has a point. While Bryce led Cyrus to believe something happened that didn't, Cyrus didn't question it. I'd *never* cheat on him. When I slept with Bryce, it was because Cyrus sent me away with no hope of ever finding him, or any indication he wanted me to. We weren't together at the time.

Shit, maybe that's why he hooked up with Valencia. Maybe she's revenge. Or maybe he's just done with me and moving on. Our relationship's always been tumultuous, maybe it was too much for him. What doesn't make any sense, though, is why he stuck around after he left the hotel room that morning. Why didn't he go back to the Ruins? I have too many questions, and the only person who can answer them isn't speaking to me unless it's required.

I drop my head into my hands and groan. The thing is, I'm in no mood to play stupid games with him right now. I risked my life to save him and he let one comment, one unfortunate scene, dictate his feelings for me. He didn't trust me and that hurts the most. I'm not sure I can forgive him for throwing us away based on assumptions.

"You're too quiet over there, Evansville, you're starting to scare me."

I glare up at him. "You're not off the hook either."

"Do you want me to talk to him?"

"Good god, no. You've done enough. I just…I don't know what to do about any of this. I need some time." Lots of time. The one thing we don't really have.

After a quick breakfast, we gather at the warehouse for a short meeting before the team heads to Mexico. At only seven-thirty in the morning, the temperature is already a balmy eight-five, making the loose top I'm wearing stick to me. I'd kill for some air conditioning in here. Cyrus's recruits were busy over the past few days installing soundproof panels on the walls and purchasing some large fans that move the stagnant air around, so at least the air moves.

My eyes find Cyrus across the room where he's talking with Dominic. Now that Bryce clued me in on what went down, I waffle between wanting to clear things up with Cyrus and wanting to pummel him. No doubt a little fear is mixed in there as well. Even if I explained everything to him, he might tell me it's too late. For now, the ball is in my court. Once I give it up, I may never get it back.

After the leader meeting where we discuss plans for an extraction mission if they aren't back in two weeks, Mateo pulls me aside. "You need to alter your appearance before you head out."

"I'm going to stick to recruiting from the camps at the beaches. There aren't any Uprising soldiers there."

He places his hands on my shoulders. "They're looking for you, Evan. Just because there aren't soldiers down there now, doesn't mean there won't ever be, or that others aren't searching for you." He stares at me for several long seconds. "Humor me."

I roll my eyes. "Fine."

He pulls my forehead to his lips for a brief kiss, then hugs me tight, like the morning we split up to attack the Uprising.

"Keep your eyes open, and don't do anything stupid," I say.

"Mateo," Cyrus calls from across the room.

Mateo tears his gaze from mine and nods at Cyrus. With a quick pat of the side of my head, he's gone, and I go in search of Sonia and Marcus. I still need to find traveling buddies for my recruiting trip.

18

MISSIONS

Cyrus

*T*he Mexico team gathers near the door. I wish I was going with them, although that's beyond stupid. It's probably not even a good idea for Rainey to head back there, but at least she speaks the language.

My eyes are glued to Evan as she says her goodbyes, careful to keep from getting caught staring. The way she parts ways with Bryce is tense. Over the past week their interactions have been sparse and stiff, which is strange considering they're going to be raising a baby together. Rainey pulls open the door to leave, and Mateo grabs Evan's arm, pulling her around to face him. The way he's looking at her is pissing me the hell off. He takes her face in his hands and I come close to losing my cool.

"Mateo." I don't know what I'm going to say, but he needs to get his damn hands off her.

He approaches me with a scowl. "Yeah?"

I scratch the back of my neck and stare at my shoes, unsure what to say, but the words fly out of my mouth against my will. "What's up with you and Evan?"

Mateo glances over my shoulder, likely at Valencia, before returning his attention to me. "I don't see how that's any of your business."

My fists clench at my sides.

His gaze drops to my hands and he smirks. "I'm not the one screwing things up between you two. That's all on you..." He takes a measured breath. "Out of respect for our friendship, I haven't pursued anything with her, but if she shows interest, I won't push her away." He pivots and joins his team, the door closing behind him without a backward glance.

What the hell? My attention returns to Evan talking with Marcus and Sonia. She doesn't seem the least bit interested in either Bryce or Mateo leaving. I shake my head and turn around to find Valencia watching me, her face twisted up in concentration. This situation, if that's what you can call it, is totally fucked up.

Valencia makes her way over to me and hooks her hands around my forearm. "I want to suggest something, and I don't want you to be mad, okay?"

This can't be good and the best I can offer her in response is a grunt that is neither a promise nor a refusal of her request.

"I want to go with Evan on her recruiting trip."

Before I can tell her just how bad that idea that is, she throws her arms up in front of me. "Hear me out. It's not what you think. Well, not exactly. My mom's family is from here, from this province, we used to spend all our summers here. I might know some of the people in the area. Personal relationships can go a long way toward building trust. Besides, we won't be the only two going. It's not like it's going to be just your ex-girlfriend and your new girlfriend." The moment the words exit her mouth, her face flushes bright red.

My confrontation with Mateo is still fresh, and I'm in no mood to argue that she is not my girlfriend. After the night we ran into Evan in the bar, whatever we thought we were going to explore, slowly or otherwise, has been put on hold. But I'm well aware everyone assumes Valencia and I are together, and I haven't done anything to clear that up.

If I take all emotion out of the situation, it's not the worst idea, but it's not a good one either, because too much emotion is involved. Not just mine, but Evan's a complete unknown. She's got a wicked temper and I never know what's going to set her off. Add to that pregnancy hormones and it could be explosive.

I open my mouth to tell Val that, but I guess I took too long to mull it over, because she's kissing my cheek and bouncing away. "Good. I'll find a few more volunteers. See you before we go."

"Hey…Valencia…wait." I call after her, but she's already reached Evan. All I can do is watch as Val breaks the news. Evan's gaze drifts in my direction, her expressive eyes wide before turning her attention back to Val. They talk a little longer while I hide like a total chickenshit on the other side of the warehouse, trying hard to appear busy.

When Evan turns toward Sonia and Marcus, Val pivots to me, flashing a brilliant smile and a thumbs-up before heading to a group in the corner, presumably to enlist more help.

19

RECRUITING

Evan

As Sonia, Marcus, and I walk down to the beach, I tell them about the weird conversation I had with Valencia. "What do you think she really wants?"

"Honestly?" Sonia shrugs. "She's sizing up the competition."

Marcus lets out a half laugh. "Sleep with one eye open."

Sonia rolls her eyes. "She doesn't need to go with you. You're a leader, don't let her push you into it."

I shrug. "But if I don't, then it's like I'm afraid of her. What kind of leader is afraid of a teenage girl?"

"I understand, but make sure *you* pick the rest of the team."

"Yeah, I'm thinking about dragging Ally and Colin with me."

Marcus and Sonia exchange a loaded glance.

"What?"

"We've been talking about getting the boys," Sonia says. "Plus, we could use more experienced help if Zak, Ilona, and Alexander are interested in joining us."

"Oh...when would you leave?"

"Coupla days," Marcus says.

"Makes sense. Maybe I shouldn't do this whole recruiting thing. I could let Valencia put together a group and do it without me, then I can go in search of my family."

"You're not going alone." Sonia shakes her head. "Who'll go with you?"

"Lisa and Jack."

We stare at the boats bobbing up and down on the waves as the sun rises high overhead.

"Not a bad choice," Marcus says. "Are you up for a long trip like that?"

"No, and that's probably why I'm not pushing too hard to go. At least with this recruiting mission, the camps are all close by."

Sonia places a hand on my shoulder. "We'll go with you to find your family when we get back."

"Thanks." A larger boat cuts across the water, making waves that the smaller boats rock and roll across, one tiny sailboat nearly ending up on its side.

"So, we need to talk to you about something else."

This can't be good. I steel myself and turn to face Sonia.

"Mateo said Cyrus wants us to move down to the beach with them. He thinks us being in the hotel sets us apart or something, I forget the words he used, but that we think we're special or above them."

I return my attention to the horizon. "You guys can go if you want, but I'm staying here."

"It's safe, Evan. At least as safe as here."

"That is *so* not what I'm worried about."

"Then what?"

My eyes meet her pale brown ones. "Sorry, Son, it's just...I'm trying, I am, but...

She shakes her head. "I don't understand. Trying what?"

"Sonia..." Marcus's tone is soft, and she turns toward him. He's doing all kinds of facial exercises to communicate something without words and I can't help laughing.

"I don't want to spend any more time with the happy couple

than required. Sitting across from them all cuddled up at the fire pit at night or watching them walk hand in hand to their love nest, or worse, hearing the sounds coming from their tent." I shudder. "I can only take so much."

"Ohhhhhhh..." She draws the word out, her lips forming an O. "I didn't think about that. For what it's worth, I think you're handling it way better than I would. If Marcus was with someone else, he'd be castrated by now."

Marcus presses his thighs a little tighter together, but wisely keeps his mouth shut.

"I appreciate the effort, Sonia, but that would never happen. For one, Marcus would never be with anyone but you."

"True statement," Marcus says, grinning.

"And for another, you'd never let him leave you when you needed him the most."

She squeezes my hands. "Time to stop beating yourself up over that. He's a big boy and he made a choice. After that, I don't know what got into his head."

I let out a deep sigh. "Ugh, I do." Then I proceed to tell them what Bryce did.

"I'm gonna kill that boy." Sonia's voice is tight, her facial features so screwed up, I swear her skin is going to crack.

"Get in line," I say.

"What are you going to do? You have to tell Cyrus."

"No way, and neither are you. He chose his response, regardless of what Bryce said or did. He chose to believe the worst about me. I really thought we were beyond all that, Sonia. After everything with Bridget and what happened with Bryce before...I thought we moved beyond petty jealousy."

"This is a little more than petty jealousy," Marcus mumbles.

I spin to face him. "If you came upon that scene, what would your reaction be?"

He runs a hand over the top of his head and shifts on his feet. "I don't know. I mean, I'd want answers, but—"

"But you'd give Sonia the benefit of the doubt."

"Come on, Evan, give him a break."

"I might if he had just stomped off and had a tantrum. But he didn't. He moved on to someone else. He *gave up* on us without talking to me first. That hurts..." My voice breaks and I'm done with the conversation.

"Okay, okay." Sonia puts a hand on my arm and glares at Marcus. "We'll stay at the hotel with you, right Marcus?"

Marcus blows out a long breath, "Yeah, sure."

"Everyone else can go, though. I think Cyrus has a point with the whole us versus them thing." I let out a short laugh. "When did Cyrus become the voice of the Union?"

Sonia giggles. "No clue, but it's a bit ironic, eh?"

Just a bit.

I cross my arms and narrow my gaze at Valencia. "I promised Mateo."

She squints at me from different angles. "Well, it's going to delay our departure."

"I don't care if it delays it by a week," Lisa says. "She can't go out on a recruiting mission looking like herself. The Uprising is looking for her, you know that, right? Or maybe that's your plan."

Valencia's mouth drops open and her normally huge doe eyes are even bigger. "What's that supposed to mean?"

I blow out a frustrated breath. "That's enough. I need a disguise. Period. You don't have to come with us, Valencia. I can find someone else, but if you're coming, get yourself ready."

Valencia glances between me and Lisa before storming out of my hotel room. When I'm sure she's out of earshot, I snort.

"She's the definition of high maintenance. Other than the fact that she's pretty, I don't know what Cyrus sees in her." Lisa's head whips toward me. "Oh, Ev, I'm sorry."

"Don't be. She *is* pretty. I still can't believe I agreed to this."

Lisa and I resume sorting clothes and are in the middle of

making piles when someone knocks on the door. We both freeze then turn toward each other. Jack would've used the secret knock. Hell, anyone in our group would.

"What do we do?" Lisa mouths.

I shrug. All the guns are in the warehouse. If the Uprising has tracked us down, we're pretty much sitting ducks.

"Well they were here twenty minutes ago." Valencia's voice comes from the other side.

Seriously, why didn't Cyrus bother to teach his recruits the proper way to knock?

Lisa pulls open the door and Valencia is standing with another girl I've seen around. Long brown hair with highlights, long nails, always made up.

"This is Jenna." Valencia leads the way into the room. "She used to be a stylist before the Invasion."

Jenna follows her in pulling a wheeled cart. "I'm still a stylist, but I don't get many clients at the campgrounds. She studies my face longer than socially acceptable, and I'm about to go into the bathroom to escape her scrutiny when she says, "I've got the perfect look for you. No one, not even your own parents, will recognize you."

Four hours later, I stare at the stranger before me, my own hazel eyes stare back, but they're the only part that looks like me. Jenna dyed my red locks a brown so dark, they're almost black. Then she flat-ironed the curls so my hair hangs straight. The difference is remarkable. She cut bangs that frame my eyes, making them look as if they're glowing and my face even paler than normal. Cat-eye makeup and some contouring completes the effect, and she's right, my parents wouldn't know me.

She dug through her clothes as well as mine, Lisa's, and Valencia's and pulled together a very retro-boho outfit with leggings, a short flowy skirt, combat boots, and a slouch hat.

"Wow..." is the only word I can find, and it comes out as a whisper.

"I'm good." Jenna nods with a satisfied smile. "I always wanted to work in the film industry doing special effects makeup. Then this stupid Invasion happened."

"You'd be great at that." I'm unable to take my eyes off the girl in the mirror. I move my head and watch as her head moves the same way. I understand she's me, but only on a purely logical level.

Jenna rubs her hands together. "It's getting late. I'm ready to unveil my creation. C'mon, let's get you to the warehouse."

I pick up my duffel bag and follow her out, making sure the room is securely locked behind us. We traipse through humid hallways, our bags slung over our shoulders. We're traveling light, but in this weather, they're somehow heavier. I'm beginning to wish my new style didn't require quite so many layers. Jenna reaches out and gives the secret knock, so apparently Cyrus *does* teach it to his people, but only some feel the need to use it.

The door cracks and Gunther, a blond kid I've seen around, peeks out and smiles at Jenna before scowling at me. "New recruit?" I can't hide my smirk as his eyes widen so much, they eat up half his face. "No way!" He flings the door open to let us in and follows us across the warehouse without a word, likely to catch everyone else's reaction when they figure it out.

My eyes instinctively find Cyrus on the other side of the room. He glances at us briefly, narrowing his eyes at me, then returns to work for only a second before his head jerks up, his jaw hinging open. A murmur goes up as people pause whatever they're doing to stare.

Jenna takes a dramatic bow. "What do you think of my masterpiece?"

Marcus lets out a wolf whistle and a couple of the other guys do, too, and I can't stop my cheeks from turning bright red. I take a quick glance back at Cyrus and he's staring at me, even as Valencia wraps her arms around him.

No longer in the mood to smile, I turn to the rest of my travel companions. "You ready to go?"

"I'm coming, too." Jenna grabs her bag and slings it over her shoulder. "Might know some folks, former clients or whatever, plus you'll need touch-ups."

"Fine by me. We leave in five."

I hug Marcus, Sonia, Ally, Colin, and Will goodbye, making them promise to be careful and hurry back with the boys. By the time I'm done, Jenna, Valencia, Lisa, and Jack are clustered around the door. Without another look back, I yank it open and lead the way out.

Sweat drips down my back, drenching my bra. The air is so thick, it feels heavy in my lungs. "I need to stop again," I announce, dropping onto the closest bench.

"How you holding up?" Lisa asks.

"The days are long and I don't feel like we're doing nearly as well as I'd hoped."

"In what way?" Valencia asks, taking the spot next to me.

After a week with her, it turns out she's not completely awful. She's clearly got it bad for Cyrus, but then again, so do I. But she hasn't said one unpleasant thing to me, nor has she asked me anything about Cyrus or how I feel about him. If I was her, I'd be trying to find out as much about my competition as possible. Although, Cyrus hates me, so she may not see me as a threat.

"I don't know, just more enthusiasm, I guess."

Valencia rolls her eyes. And just like that, I'm not so fond of her.

"You know what it's like," Lisa says.

We've talked about this many times now, particularly when we first got back. That people in the Union are basically peaceful, but we believed they'd want to do something if they knew people lived in the Ruins.

I throw my hands up. "It's different now. That was before they were attacked and kicked out of their homes."

"They're still getting three squares a day and a place to sleep at night," Jack says. "For some people, it takes more."

I know he's right, still, I turn toward Valencia. "You guys didn't have such a tough time recruiting, and you only looked in your own camp."

She shrugs and a small smile plays at the corners of her mouth. "We had Cyrus." She eyes me from the side, like she's afraid to look at me straight on. "You know how he can be."

And just like that, the knife twists in my gut. Lisa grabs my hand and squeezes. Either to comfort me or to keep me from decking Valencia. She smiles sweetly at Valencia. "Yes, we've known him for a long time, but we also know he's not the pied piper. What is he saying to them?"

Valencia shrugs. "I don't know. Just how he was born in the Ruins and Walker isn't being honest with us and it's only going to get worse. Stuff like that."

"That would have been useful to know a week ago," I grumble, yanking my hand back from Lisa, not sure I'm not going to flatten the bitch. "Why are you even here if you're not doing what you already know works?" I ask her.

Her cheeks redden and she turns away, her fingers flying to her hair, twisting her long locks. "You're the leader. I didn't want to step on your toes, you know?"

Now it's my turn to roll my eyes, but she has a point. I haven't been leading much, mostly deferring to Jack on stuff. I'm just sort of used to it with his law enforcement background. Even so, she's taking the easy way out. She could have offered that up at any time. Which makes me believe she's on this trip for another reason, one she'll never admit to me. "Look, Valencia, from now on, please share any and all ideas you have, okay?"

"Sure."

"We've haven't been doing horribly," Jenna says. "I mean, we're getting at least a couple every day."

"Yeah," I say on a sigh. "I was hoping for dozens, though. This is going to be harder than I thought."

"We still have another week," Lisa says. "We just need to up our game."

I hike my bag up higher on my shoulder, and step past Jack, assuming the lead as we make our way down the beach to the next camp.

20

STAGING

Cyrus

"Throw me that stack, will you?" I call to Dom.

He flings a pack of shrink-wrapped blankets to me and I shove them on the top shelf. We've spent the last week buying non-perishable food, cots, clothing, tents, bedding, cookware, and other basics. We're bursting at the seams, but as I take it all in, I realize I've been preparing for a move out to the Ruins. This warehouse isn't a long-term solution, but a good place to stage for our next destination.

No doubt that talk will meet with lots of resistance, but if I can convince all the leaders along with Dom, Nate, and Valencia, it may go better than expected. I'm fairly certain I can get Dom and Nate to agree, but Val is an unknown, and likely a lot of it depends on me. With the way she looks at me, this isn't a casual thing for her, and it's not even a thing. We hang out and she's affectionate, but nothing more is going on. In fact, with Val and Evan both gone, the tension usually engulfing the warehouse has vanished.

Bryce, Sonia, and Marcus still haven't moved down to the beach. Maybe the baby is the reason why, but if so, no one is talking about it, making me wonder if the pregnancy isn't going well. My gut tightens at the thought. I hate everything about Evan and that toolbag having a kid together, but the baby is half her, which means, dammit, I fucking care about it, too. Something hits the back of my head and I whip around to find Dom, a pair of socks in his hand, cocked and ready to throw. "What the hell, asshole?"

"You daydreaming about my sister over there? Wait, never mind. I don't want to know."

"No. Something else. Grab Nate and meet me at the bonfire after dinner. I need to talk to you two about something."

After grabbing a quick bite in the mess tent, I take my beer to a fire pit near the perimeter of camp and wait for Nate and Dom to join me. Resting my head back against the log, I close my eyes and listen to the gentle lapping of the low tide as the cooler air drifts across my skin.

Laughter ebbs and flows as campers pass on their way back to their quarters for the night. Over the past several weeks, dozens of tents of all sizes were staked in the sand, expanding the size of the campsite and stretching resources. My history with Selma helped me finagle a small private tent, which is nice. The thin canvas doesn't block the night sounds, but I like having my own space.

The recruits Evan's team are sending this way are further swelling the population. Not a lot, but enough that I feel guilty enough to volunteer around here again. Selma and her crew are harried on their best days.

Although I'm not sure where everyone would sleep, I'm disappointed in the numbers so far. Maybe I overestimated the level of support for a Resistance. It might be time to consider Evan's idea and start picking off reluctant Uprising soldiers. Evan...shit, things with her are so fucked up. Maybe we joined forces, but there's a division that runs right down the center. If we can't bridge it, we're doomed to fail.

I need to find a way to work with Evan without all the animosity, and that's on me. She came to me that morning on the beach to try to patch things over, and instead of meeting her halfway, I was more interested in getting in whatever digs I could. Now it's up to me to figure out how to fix things.

"Hey, there you are." Dom stumbles through the sand, a bottle in each hand, Nate on his heels. "You couldn't find anyplace farther away?"

I glance up and drain my beer. "I tried, but nothing was available."

They do some sort of stupid Uni fist bump thing with me and drop down to sit on the ground, Dom handing me the second beer. "So, what'd you want to talk about?"

"Thanks," I say, taking the bottle. "I think it's time to move out to the Ruins, and I could use your help convincing the others."

I'm just getting ready to head off to dinner when someone knocks on the warehouse door. Nate cracks the door before opening it wider to admit Mateo, Rainey, Bryce, and Chase, loaded down with overstuffed bags. My gaze meets Mateo's and locks for a second, neither of us blinking before Rainey tosses her duffels on one of the tables with a hard thunk.

"Well?" I ask.

She gives me a sly smile and nods. "Helps when I have a partner who doesn't go rogue on me."

I clench my jaw at her reference to our trip down there when I almost got us killed. Bryce's smirk tells me he already knows the story. My only response is to narrow my eyes at Rainey and shake my head, which makes her smile grow broader.

The others line up their bags on the table and unzip them, revealing guns and ammo. More than enough to arm our small, but growing resistance for now. We aren't going to be able to teach them how to shoot in this warehouse. Good thing most of them are at least open to the idea of training in the Ruins.

We have a lot to catch up on, so after we inventory and load everything into the locking cabinets I installed the other day, we head to the mess tent for dinner, taking it to a fire ring to eat, Chase staying behind to talk to some girl.

Rainey crosses her ankles and leans back, resting her arm on the log. "The hardest part was getting to the Southwestern Province to hire a boat. We were almost caught twice on the trains heading west, but we managed to dodge them. The Uprising is in some sort of intensive search mode for someone or something." She cuts her eyes over to Mateo before taking a long pull on her beer.

He leans forward, picking up the story. "Once we got to the Southwest, things went smoothly. We went to a small town southeast of Ensenada where I still have family. They knew some people who could help us, no questions asked. They said they could get us more if we ever need them."

"You have any issues on the way back?"

"Nothing we couldn't handle," Douchebag says.

"What does that mean?"

Rainey takes another sip and swallows. "We ran into some Uprising trouble a few boroughs over. Someone recognized Mateo. We had to run for it, ducking into the tunnels and running like hell, which is no easy feat weighed down by bags full of weapons."

Mateo wads up the wrapper from his burrito and tosses it into the fire. "We were prepared to use them if necessary."

Bryce shakes his head. "I'm just glad we didn't have to. That's more trouble than we need right now."

"Who made you?" I ask Mateo. "Anyone you recognized?"

"No, but now they know I'm here."

"That may or may not matter. It depends on what they want with you." Mateo wasn't a recruit and isn't a deserter. He was there as a mercenary. Paid to do a job he walked away from. Still, they're aware he's in the province. I fill them in on what's been going on here while they were gone and my idea of moving into the Ruins.

"You hear from the others?" Bryce asks.

I let him squirm for a long moment before turning toward him and giving my head a short shake.

Rainey's gaze shifts between me and Bryce. "When are they due back?"

"Any day now. They're sending recruits our way, so they're making progress, although it's been a few days since anyone new has arrived."

Bryce's shoulders tense. "If they don't show in the next couple of days, I'll go look for them."

My fist grabs my bottle a little tighter. I'll be damned if this tool is going to tell me how we're running things. "If they're not back in forty-eight hours, we'll organize a team. If you wanna be part of it, let one of the leaders know."

Rainey smirks next to me and I might or might not deliberately let my elbow jab her in the biceps.

21

HOME

Evan

"My feet are killing me," Jenna whines.

"We're almost home." Lisa pauses, a wistful expression crossing her face. "I can't believe I'm calling that campground 'home' these days. Who would have thought a year ago?"

A year ago, we were aboard a luxury train on our way to the Western Province before I was kidnapped and taken out into the Ruins. That innocent time seems like another lifetime.

Jenna groans. "Ugh, I have blisters on my blisters."

We've been walking for two weeks, and yeah, my feet hurt, too, but talking about it doesn't make it any better. I'm close to snapping at her to keep it to herself when Valencia says, "Jenna, please...can we talk about something besides your feet?"

I resist the urge to laugh, but mentally high-five Valencia.

The sun is drifting toward the horizon, piercing our eyes as we make the final trek west before turning north and into the tunnels of the Union. I'm sticky, sore, tired, and cranky by the time we reach the warehouse door. Jack steps forward and knocks three times quickly, followed by two short raps, a pause and four more.

We wait only a few seconds before the door cracks and a kid whose name I can never remember peers out.

Inside, the fans move air and I'm instantly at ease in a way I wasn't during the weeks we were gone. On the other side of the room, Cyrus is bent over a tablet, a hand running through his hair, his nervous tell. He glances up, his eyes going directly to Valencia before finding me. Our gazes collide for a moment longer than necessary. For a split second, I swear I see relief in his eyes before they mask over.

Cyrus comes across the warehouse to greet us, shaking hands with Jack first before nodding at the rest of us and pulling Valencia aside, making me bristle with further irritation. I'm not sure why I expected anything else from him. The relief I thought I saw was obviously for her sake, not mine. As soon as Valencia's hands slides around his waist, I turn away and come face to face with a smiling Mateo.

"Welcome back to the hive." He wraps his arms around me and lifts me up so my feet dangle.

I laugh and slap him on the shoulder until he puts me down. "How'd it go?"

He nods. "Good. C'mon, I'll show you." He leads the way to the far corner where two new cabinets sit, and presses his finger to the scanner. The doors open, revealing an unfathomable number of guns. Every shelf is filled.

I stare at him, lifting an eyebrow. "How did you get all this back here?"

"We all carried a lot of shit." Rainey's raspy voice comes from behind me.

I spin around and hug her.

"Wanna try one on for size?" One side of Mateo's mouth lifts.

"Not now." To me, they're still a necessary evil, especially since the last time I held one, I shot and killed three kids in an Uprising camp. Out of the corner of my eye, I notice Cyrus and Valencia in what appears to be an intimate conversation. That's more than I can handle and I turn away in disgust. "I'm gross. I'm going back to my room to get cleaned up."

"Catch you at dinner later?" Bryce asks.

"Maybe." I'm glad he's back safely, but I still haven't forgiven him for his part in the devolution of my relationship with Cyrus. Plus, I'm not sure I can stand to be around Cyrus and Valencia any more than absolutely necessary.

I stomp to the hotel, trying not to cry. Until now, I didn't really accept that we were over for good. There was always a glimmer of hope in the back of my mind that we'd eventually figure it out. That he'd tell me he still loves me, and I'd forgive him. We always find a way back to each other. Standing in that warehouse watching him with Valencia, barely acknowledging me, tore a hole through my heart that may never mend. I could be pissed at him for moving on when I thought it was temporary. Anger I know how to deal with, but this pain in my chest is worse than anything the Uprising did to me, and I don't know how to heal from it.

When I get to my room, I unlock the door and yank it open. Tossing the key on the table, I kick the door closed and head into the bathroom to turn on the water. A hot shower and a good, long, ugly cry are on the agenda. My bed calls to me. After two weeks sleeping in tents, I think maybe I'll order room service for dinner and crawl under my blankets.

After pulling off my shoes, I peel off my sweaty T-shirt. A breeze flutters across my back and I whip around. Cyrus is at the door, his eyes wide, mouth gaping. *Shit.* The burns on my back. I grab my shirt, covering my bra and scream at him. "What are you doing!"

His eyes darken and his hands ball into fists. His voice is dangerously low. "What happened to you?"

My heart pounds in my chest. "Get out!"

"I'm not leaving until you tell me what happened."

"Get out. Now!" I use my free arm to shove him, but he doesn't budge.

He turns around, giving me some privacy. "I-I came here to

clear the air. Your door was ajar. You should be more security conscious."

I choke back a sob, not knowing how to respond. Instead I whisper, "Please leave."

With a soft sigh, he leaves my room, closing the door firmly behind him.

22

SPINNING

Cyrus

My steps are sluggish as I return to the warehouse, my head spinning. I pass a few recruits on their way back to the beach for the night and we nod hellos, but that's all I can muster. The image of those scars on Evan's back are seared into my brain. Who the fuck did that to her and why? Rage builds with each step. Marcus said she'd been on one of the trains that was boarded, but so were lots of people. My best friend lied to me.

The population is dwindling when I arrive, but three little people who've never been here before make my heart lighter in a way I wouldn't have believed possible just moments before. Ben, Connor, and Ty spot me and run across the room, dodging tables on their way. I haven't seen them in months, and I swear they've grown several inches each.

Six arms wrap around me and if I could pick all three up at once I would. Tears choke the back of my throat. Damn, I missed them. They start talking at the same time, but we'll have to catch up later tonight.

I glance up at Ally and give her a quick smile. "Glad you're back. Hey, can you take the boys to camp and get them some dinner? I need to talk to Marcus and Sonia."

She nods, hugs me long and tight, then turns to the boys. "C'mon, let's go eat."

They cheer and chase after her, Colin bringing up the rear, only giving me a curt nod as he passes.

Marcus and Sonia eye me warily, but Sonia approaches and gives me a squeeze while Marcus stands back, seemingly unsure. No doubt my body language is radiating my emotions. "What the hell happened to her? I saw her back. I know what causes those burns."

Sonia opens her mouth to say something.

"Sonia," Marcus warns.

My eyes narrow. "What the fuck, Marcus?"

"It doesn't matter."

"It sure as hell matters to me."

Marcus's jaw clenches. "Really? You've got a strange way of showing it."

I push him against the wall, my forearm across his chest. "I swear—"

"I'll give you one second to take your hands off me," he growls.

Sonia grabs my arm. "Cy, stop this."

When I step back, Marcus storms out of the warehouse, and I'm left wondering how things got so screwed up. Sonia's brow is furrowed as she watches the door slam behind Marcus, then she twists back to face me. "When they were out in the Ruins together attacking the Uprising camps, they bonded. Marcus is protective of her."

"Fine, I get that. But what does he think I'm going to do to her?"

Sonia blinks. "Break her heart again."

Break *her* heart? What the hell? I study the cracks and stains in the concrete, trying to put everything into perspective. Nothing's adding up. She's so thin, I could see her ribs. Those scars. The distance she and Bryce maintain. Mateo's odd statement. Something clicks and it all makes sense.

I lift my head and lock my gaze with Sonia's watching for any reaction to my question. "Did she lose the baby?"

Sonia's eyebrows pull together before she slowly shakes her head. "What baby? What are you talking about?"

"But..." Both confusion and clarity fight against each other inside my head. "Then who's Bryce having a baby with?"

"Oh." Sonia's mouth makes a frozen O for a second before I can see the pieces falling into place for her. "That's kind of a long story, and if you hadn't been such an ass lately, you'd already know. He met a girl out in the Ruins after the accident. It's Miranda. You remember her, right?"

All the residual anger that had built up in me since the morning I found Bryce in Evan's hotel room releases at once, and I take a step back, searching for something to support my weight. My hand finds a table just in time. I had everything so wrong. Well, maybe not everything. He was in her room, in her bed, but beyond that, I don't know anything anymore. Maybe she didn't sleep with him. She was so pissed when I confronted her on the beach. That's not the reaction of a guilty person. I run a hand through my hair. Sonia's right, I've been a total ass.

I let out a cleansing breath. "What happened to her?"

Sonia eyes me. "I promised her I wouldn't tell you. We all did."

"I don't understand."

"Look, Cy, I love you like a brother, but lately, I've had a hard time liking you. Not just because of how things are with Evan. There's obviously more to what went on between you two than I'm aware of. She asked me not to tell you and I won't."

"Is she okay? Can you at least tell me that much?"

Sonia tilts her head and studies me as if weighing whether telling me more violates her promise. "I think so. There was a time I wasn't sure, but we got her help in time."

"Fuck. I had no idea."

Sonia opens her mouth and shuts it again, remaining silent for a few long moments. "Valencia was looking for you about ten minutes before you came back. She said she'd be waiting for you in your tent."

I nod. "Thanks."

After taking a quick look around, I escort Sonia back to the hotel before heading to the beach. We only talk about the Ruins and things back home instead of heavier stuff we'll need to discuss soon, but for now, it's a refreshing return to better times.

I'm so wrapped up in my head, I hit the sand before I realize it. Too much shit is on my mind, and I struggle to compartmentalize it all. Individually, I can deal with the thoughts, but together they're overwhelming. My boots drag on the way to my tent, my mind turning to Valencia. I don't know why she's waiting there rather than at the warehouse. Unless she's planning on seducing me, in which case things are going to turn awkward fast.

When I enter, she's sitting on the chair in fresh clothes, hair still wet from a shower.

"I missed you." She rises and meets me at the opening. "Where did you go? You said you'd be right back, but you just disappeared."

Oh right. "I had to take care of something and when I got back, Marcus and the others had returned, so... I didn't know you were waiting to talk to me. Sonia forgot to mention it until we were locking up."

She examines my face, her eyes squinting, as if she's trying to read something there. "Cyrus..." She stands and drops her head to the side. "You still love her." It's not a question.

"Val..."

She lets out a stifled sob.

Hell, I have no clue what to do at this point. Whatever we had was a maybe thing at the most, but she's acting like it was more.

She wipes her eyes and turns back to face me, her lower lip trembling. "You warned me, but I fell in love with you anyway. I can't blame anyone but myself." She pushes past me and grabs an overstuffed duffel bag near the opening.

"Val, what are you doing?"

She slings the bag over her shoulder without responding. I reach out and grab her arm. Her gaze drops to my hand and I let her go. When she lifts her dark eyes to mine, they're spilling with tears. "For what it's worth, I think she still loves you, too."

Damn, I don't want her to leave, but I can't ask her not to go. I have no right to, and I can't say the words it would take to make her stay.

She reaches a hand behind my neck and pulls my face down to hers, pressing her lips against mine. The kiss is slow and full of goodbyes. Her tears are salty as they stream down her face and onto my tongue. She abruptly draws back and turns to leave. I try one more time, reaching out to take her hand, but she yanks it back.

"I went on the recruiting trip hoping you'd miss me while I was gone. Realize you care for me." She lets out a choked laugh. "Absence makes the heart grow fonder and all that jazz. I guess not, though. It hurts too much being around you."

She disappears outside, and I duck out after her, but my feet remain rooted in the sand as I watch her walk away. When Valencia is out of sight, I head back inside and sit on my bed, my hands clasped between my knees.

Nothing's felt right for a long time. Not since the day when we came back after attacking the Uprising. The last time I was happy was standing in the park, holding Evan, planning our future. Together. Everything turned to shit after that, and every fucking time I think things might actually be getting back on track, something happens to turn them to shit again.

Valencia's words clang against my skull. Does Evan still love me? Did she cheat on me? Does it even matter if she did? I fall back and rub my face. Dammit, I need to get out of this tent.

The warm night air is thick, and the distant rumble of thunder reminds me of the desert, although the incoming rainstorm does nothing to dissipate the stifling humidity the way it does out there.

I make my way to the mess tent to grab a couple of beers and take them down to the water's edge, sipping one as I walk, attempting to clear my mind of girls, guns, and fighting back. Dropping to the ground, I push my feet into the wet sand, forearms resting on my knees as the waves crawl slowly to shore.

When my beer's gone, I'm empty, numb, and ready for bed.

23

EMOTIONS

EVAN

*W*hen morning dawns, I'm even more confused than last night. I still don't understand what Cyrus was doing here, and what the hell I'm going to tell him about my scars. His hard expression carried the weight of his position, as if he believes he has a right to know. He doesn't deserve an answer. He's with someone else now, and after spending two weeks with her, it's clear she loves him. A lot. Like moony-eyed love. If I love him as much as I claim to, I should be happy for him, but I'm not. I don't want him to be happy with anyone but me.

In the bathroom, I examine my reflection. My hair is curly again, but not quite back to my natural red. The temporary hair color is stubbornly hanging around longer than promised. I'm glad I listened to Mateo, though. The Uprising is heavier east of here, and they're looking for me. A shiver tore through me when I heard my name. I glance back in the mirror and wonder at the wisdom of being so quick to rinse out the dye.

Sonia and Marcus are at the restaurant waiting for me when I arrive for breakfast. Marcus stands and smiles, pulling me into a bear hug. "Good to see you."

I nod against his chest, a lump caught in my throat. Sonia shoves Marcus out of the way and hugs me longer and harder than necessary.

She releases me and I stare at her face, then Marcus's. "What? You two are acting weird."

Sonia glances at Marcus. "Nothing, I'm just really glad to see you."

I grab the menu and order pancakes and bacon. My appetite is coming back, bit by bit. The long trip took a toll on me, though, and I'm working on eating a little more to compensate. After breakfast, we head to the beach, where we fill each other in on the past two weeks.

We hit the boardwalk, and I'm cornered by two of our newest recruits, a couple who knew Valencia from before the Invasion. The girl, Bianca, pushes into my personal space. "Have you seen Val this morning? I didn't see her at camp. I need to ask her something."

"Um, no, not yet. Maybe she's at the warehouse. We're heading there in a bit."

"We're still getting settled in. If you see her, can you tell her I'm looking for her?"

"Sure."

We stop by Ally and Colin's tent, but they're not there, or at the mess tent, so we head to the warehouse. As anxious as I am to see the boys, my stomach is a churning wreck at the thought of running into Cyrus.

We continue our discussion on the walk. I want to bring up Cyrus, try to understand what the hell last night was all about, but I'm not sure how to broach the subject. Headquarters is a hive of activity when we arrive. Most of the recruits we sent ahead of us are here. Tables are organized into groups with recruits filling the chairs around them. Ally and Colin are conducting some sort of orientation, and Lisa, Jack, and Bryce are talking to a few of the longer-term members.

My eyes travel around the large space searching for Valencia, but I don't see her anywhere. Dominic and Nate are in the corner, and I work my way toward them to ask when Mateo grabs my arm and spins me to face him. "We didn't get a chance to talk yesterday. How did it go?"

"Pretty good. You were right, though, they're looking for me."

His mouth pulls tight. "I wish I'd been wrong, but you're such a high-profile prisoner, they're not going to just let you go."

"Guess not."

Before I can ask about Valencia, Rainey enters the warehouse. Eyeing her, Mateo pats my shoulder. "I'll see you later, okay?"

"Yeah, sure. Lunch?"

"Sounds good." He strides across the room and calls out to Rainey.

So much for avoiding Cyrus. He's sitting at a table studying a tablet and glances up when I approach. Something flashes in his eyes for a fraction of a second before he schools his features.

"Hey," I say.

"Hey." He doesn't bother to look up from his stupid tablet, and my irritation with him notches up another level.

I sigh and try to keep the snark out of my voice. "Do you know where Valencia is? A couple of the latest recruits are looking for her."

His focus stays squarely on his screen. "She left."

"When will she be back?"

His fingers run through his hair, then he finally turns his attention to me. He didn't shave this morning, something that would have been normal months ago, but now is out of the ordinary for him. "She's not."

"She's not what?"

"Coming back."

"What? Why? Is she okay?"

He stands and grabs his tablet in one hand. "She's fine. She just left...me."

A weird sensation flutters in my chest and I realize I don't know what to say. "Oh...umm, wow, I..."

He seems to be evaluating what to say next, his eyes blazing with emotion. But instead, he just turns and walks away.

Lisa and I have dinner at a restaurant near the ocean. After finishing our meal, I move to the bar on the balcony and stare out at the water, trying to make sense of the last twenty-four hours. I've done a decent job of pushing everything to the background as we worked today, but now I can't avoid it. Valencia is really gone and no one knows why she left.

Lisa walks up behind me, a bottle of beer in one hand and an iced tea in the other. She hands me the glass. "What're you thinking about?"

"Everything and nothing, I guess. Sounds crazy, right?"

She laughs. "Coming from you? No."

I take a sip of my drink and set it down on the wood railing. Cyrus walks past on his way to the beach. We haven't spoken since this morning; I think we're both avoiding each other. He passes without noticing us, but Lisa spots him and catches me watching him. He stops and takes a seat on the sand about twenty feet from the boardwalk and stares at the horizon. The sun is just starting its descent over his shoulder, illuminating the right side of his face, throwing the left half into shadow.

"Do you think there's any chance he still loves me?" Maybe with Valencia gone, we stand a chance.

Lisa turns to study me, but doesn't say anything until I meet her gaze. "Of course, he does. I doubt he's spent a single day not being in love with you any more than you've spent even an hour not being in love with him. Regardless of what you tell yourself, and what you try to tell me, I know you. You might be confused sometimes, and you both do things I can't pretend to understand, but you love him. Always."

I return my attention to Cyrus. He looks so alone. "I don't know what to do."

"Go talk to him."

"It's not that simple."

"Yes, Ev, it is. You love him. It's so obvious. And he adores you. He still looks like he'd die if anything happened to you. He doesn't want to be with anyone else. You're both human, and you've both made mistakes. Be honest with him and let him be honest with you without judging him."

I let out a soft sigh. "I'm not the same girl he fell in love with."

"Everyone's been shaped by the events over the past year. You're not the only one."

"Lis...I've done terrible things."

She sets her beer on the railing and turns to stare at me. "Why? Because you wanted to or because you had to?"

"You know why."

"And yet I still love you. Do you think he's more flawed than I am that he can't love you despite everything we've done?"

My gaze returns to Cyrus, and I wonder if there's anything he could do to make me stop loving him. He's treated me horribly over the last month, but my feelings for him are as strong as ever. I push off, handing my glass to Lisa and rush toward the beach.

At first I run down the sidewalk, but as I near Cyrus, I slow, beginning to second-guess what I'm doing. I glance over my shoulder, and Lisa waves me on. Steeling myself, I step on to the sand. When I reach his side, I take a seat beside him.

He doesn't turn to look at me, nor does he say anything or give me any indication he's aware I'm here. I sit cross-legged next to him and watch the calm surf, wondering what he's thinking about.

My mouth opens and closes several times before I blurt out, "I didn't sleep with Bryce."

His jaw ticks, but he doesn't respond, his eyes remaining fixed on the horizon.

"Yes, he spent the night in my hotel room, but he was on top of the blankets and I was underneath."

He drags his gaze away from the beach and turns to face me, his eyes overflowing with raw emotion. His chest rises and falls with deep breaths, as if he's attempting to keep himself under control.

"Maybe I should have kicked him out, made him get his own room, but—"

"Evan. Stop."

He doesn't care. It's too late. My throat clogs with tears. I took a chance with my heart and I lost.

24

HELPLESS

Cyrus

*S*he's killing me. After the way I treated her, she's explaining herself to me. I can't let her go on. There's so much I need to say, but I don't trust myself to speak. My hand lifts, reaching for her, but I have no right to touch her, so it falls back to my knee.

I swallow hard and try out my voice. "I never should've doubted you."

"No, you shouldn't have." Her voice cracks and I feel like an even bigger ass.

"Shit, Ev...I..." I run a hand through my hair, struggling with how to explain my frame of mind at the time. "You were so torn up over Bryce's death, I couldn't reach you. I left to give you some space to heal without worrying about me, but I didn't know where things stood with us. When I saw him in your room...he said you told him we split up, and he had that stupid smirk..." I shake my head. "He can offer you more than I can. I lost it. Dude didn't even defend himself, so I thought that meant..." My back teeth grind against each other as I fight against my emotions.

She scoots over and places her head on my shoulder. My whole body goes rigid before relaxing. Having her so near makes it difficult to focus on anything except wanting her even closer.

"I *was* sad Bryce died, and I missed him, but it was more than that. I...god...I thought it was my fault he was dead. It was too much, and I wasn't any good for you, but I didn't know how to change that, to change anything. I was helpless to find my way back."

I lean over and kiss the top of her head, inhaling her scent of grapefruit and fresh linen. God, I've missed the way she smells. "You're always good for me, but I didn't know how to help you."

"I'm sorry I made you feel that way," she whispers.

"You don't need to apologize to me, okay?"

"Okay."

We sit in silence for a few long moments before I take my turn. "I never slept with Valencia."

She turns to face me, her eyes searching mine. "I'm—"

I put my finger to her lips. "No apologizing."

She nods and sits back, staring off into the distance. "I killed people. *Kids,* Cyrus."

My chest squeezes, but I don't have any words to fix this. Nothing I can say will ease the guilt she feels. I know, because I feel it, too. Maybe not to the same extent, but it's still there, haunting me.

I stretch out my legs in front of me, and she pivots, straddling my lap and taking my face in her hands. My heart pummels my insides, and my gaze travels from her eyes to her perfect lips, then back to her eyes. I need to kiss her more than I need to breathe, which I'm not even doing at the moment, but I let her take the lead.

She inches her face closer until her mouth rests soft against mine. My arms wrap around her waist and I drag her tight against me, her chest pressing into mine. Tears slip down her cheeks and drop onto my face, her body trembling. I part my lips, inviting her in.

Her tongue glides over mine, and I lose the tenuous hold I had on my self-control. I roll her onto her back and my mouth explores hers as my hands roam down her hips. She's so thin, her ribs are prominent, even through her clothes, and her hip bones jut out. My fingers slip beneath her shirt and over the soft skin of her sides, brushing against the angry scars on her back. We both freeze. Anger pulses through me again that someone would do that to her.

Evan pushes me back and pulls down the hem of her top. I push up and sit beside her, dragging her closer. Her head rests against my chest as I cling to her, never wanting to let go. We're too out in the open, too public, and I want her to myself. I stand and reach for her hand, pulling her to her feet before leading her to my tent.

25

SOOTHING WORDS

Evan

*C*yrus takes my hand, threading our fingers together and leads me along the beach. I use my free hand to work the sand out of my hair, but it's going to take a lot more than that to get it all out.

"How did you score your own tent?" I ask as he lifts the flap for me.

"I help Selma out when I can."

"Selma?"

"The camp manager. I'm not officially employed anymore, but I still stop by most evenings to see if she needs a hand with anything. This is her way of paying me."

Even though it's one of the temporary tents set up after the Invasion, it's nice. Tall enough for both of us to stand in and wide enough to hold a double bed and small wooden table, plus room on either side. Small white lights illuminate the interior, giving it a soft, welcoming glow. My eyes shift from the bed to his duffel bag.

"I'm going to take a shower." I need an excuse to be alone as much as to clean up.

Grabbing one of his T-shirts from his open bag, I duck outside the tent and head to the showers. My hands are shaking as I step into the stall, trying to calm my nerves. Cyrus and I haven't been together in a long time.

I towel off and pull on Cyrus's shirt. It smells like him, and I lift it to my nose, breathing in his scent. A flood of emotions rocks me until I'm fighting back tears. I grab my sandy clothes and walk slowly back to the tent. Cyrus is sitting on the end of the mattress, his hands resting on his knees. He glances up as I approach, but I can't read his expression. I set my soiled shirt and shorts next to his bag and take a tentative step toward him.

When I'm in front of him, he wraps his arms around my waist and tugs me closer. This isn't like the last time we were alone in a tent together. So much has happened since then. I run my fingers through his hair, and he closes his eyes, tilting his head back. He tightens his hold and draws me with him as he lies back on the bed.

He tucks my head under his chin, and I can hear his strong heartbeat through his chest, steady, although a bit faster than normal. Soon his rhythmic breathing lulls me to sleep.

My eyes open to complete darkness and I have no idea where I am. Soft lips press against my temple, whiskers brushing my cheek and it all comes back to me.

I reach up and kiss the hollow of his throat. "I love you," I whisper.

His embrace tightens and something warm and wet drips onto my face, but I'm dozing off just as I register them as his tears.

A scream rips me from a vivid nightmare. Arms wrap around me and tug me against a solid chest while lips murmur soothing words against my hair. When my heart stops pounding, I sit up and pull my knees to my chest, wrapping my arms around them. Cyrus lies on his side next to me, head propped up on his hand. We stare at each other in the dark for several long moments.

His fingers skim across the skin of my back until he reaches one of my scars. "What did they do to you?" This time his voice is softer, less angry than when he saw them the other day, but I know better.

But I also know it's time to tell him everything.

26

EVERYTHING

Cyrus

*E*very ounce of effort goes into controlling my voice when I ask her what happened, because I will kill the fucker responsible. But if she knew that, she'd never tell me. I *will* find them, though, and when I do, their death will be prolonged and painful.

She starts, her voice soft and low. "Bryce showed up at my hotel, I already had a ticket to the Western Province to meet Tony. We were going to tell the world what Bryce died for. I think I needed to reassure myself that what we did, what *I* did, was for the greater good."

I pull her closer, but she shrugs out of my grasp and gets out of bed, pacing the little patch of space beside the bed.

"I left while Bryce was sleeping so I could catch my train. Tony and I still had a story to tell." She shakes her hands, like she's trying to get something off them. "I dozed off at some point during the trip and woke when we slowed, but we were nowhere near a station..."

She trails off and I struggle to remain silent so she'll go on.

"Chase was sitting across the aisle, staring at his tablet. He said the news was reporting that the Uprising was boarding trains. I knew I had to get off. It was the only thing I could think about. Chase and a few others decided to join me. We created a rope from blankets and climbed down. One of the people who jumped down with us was a young teen girl. She was cold, so I gave her my outer shirt to wear. My tattoo was visible on my shoulder and one of the soldiers spotted it."

My heart slams into my ribs. I asked for this, multiple times, but I'm so on edge, I'm not sure I'll be able to keep it under control. My fists clench at my sides as she continues.

"They took me into custody. At first...they left me alone, but then..." She stops and glances up at me, gnawing on that bottom lip. "But then..." she whispers and pauses again. "Someone high up in the Uprising came to question me." Her eyes close and she swallows hard.

I want more than anything to pull her back to me, wrap my arms around her, and protect her from whatever she's about to say, but she's wound too tight to let me.

"She asked where I trained, and when I didn't answer she had them hit and kick me."

Anger burns through me, scorching my veins, my throat. My head buzzes and the tent is suddenly too hot. I can't stay still any longer and push up, forcing myself not to punch something. Someone beat her. I will fucking kill them.

"The questions kept coming, but I refused to answer, and eventually I couldn't take it anymore and I guess I blacked out."

"Fuck!" My fingernails dig into my palms hard enough I'm probably drawing blood. "Why? Why not tell them?" My tone is too accusatory, and she flinches. I soften it so she'll know it's not directed at her. "It was over at that point."

She glances at the ground, then back at me. "I was sure they'd kill me as soon as I gave up the information they wanted. I was buying time..." She pauses and stares at her hands. "And a part of me believed I deserved it."

"Ev—" I growl.

"I killed kids!"

For the first time, I'm beginning to fully understand how much what we did ripped her apart. To the point that she let soldiers beat the shit out of her as punishment she felt she earned. "Baby..."

She ignores me and continues. "They moved me to another location and starved me in addition to beating me, hoping to break me, I guess. Finally, I told them some stuff to make it stop. I just couldn't take it anymore. I admitted to a lot. Stuff we did plus some we didn't do, but I made sure they thought I did it all. I didn't want anyone else to be at risk. Then she told me what she really wanted, and...when I wouldn't tell her, she had them burn me."

Blood rushes through my ears like a roar and I'm on the other side of the bed, pulling her to me before I realize it. She tries to push me away, but I won't let her. My arms pin her against my chest.

"I was terrified..." she whispers, "that I wouldn't be able to resist, and I'd tell her everything."

"Ev..." My words choke off, and I'm doing my best to hold it together for a few more minutes. "Why? Why not just tell her?"

"Because..." Her voice is thick with unshed tears. "She wanted to know where you were."

"But you didn't know."

"I knew where you said you were going, and I believed you were there. There was no doubt in my mind she'd hunt you down." She lets out a sob, tears soaking through the front of my T-shirt. She lifts her head and her eyes connect with mine. "Cyrus, it was Draya."

My legs give out and I stumble, falling against the bed, nearly toppling her in the process. A chill breaks out across my skin and my stomach pulls tight until I'm close to puking. I'm torn between needing to lose my dinner and comforting Evan. She wins, although I'm still not sure I won't hurl all over her. I reach out a hand and pull her to me. As soon as she's in my embrace, she releases a fresh sob, followed by another, until she's barely breathing through her tears, huge hiccupping sobs that threaten to tear her chest open.

I can't comprehend what happened and who's responsible. Knowing Draya did this to her sends a new wave of bile bouncing through my guts. I swore to kill whoever did this to her, make them pay, but Draya?

I can't understand how she could do this to anyone, least of all to the girl I love. We grew up together, I've known Draya my whole life. She always played tough, but inside, underneath all the bravado, was a warm and caring girl. It was one of the things Lucien loved most about her.

Evan's cries subside, but her body continues to tremble with emotion. I lie back, tucking her into my side. My own tears begin to fall as hers dry up. The whole time I was twisted up in anger and heartbreak, she was enduring unimaginable physical pain. God, I don't deserve her. That's the only thing I can focus on as I struggle with my thoughts, wrapped around her, doing my best to protect her, even though I failed her over and over.

My eyes open to exhaustion and confusion. I'm in a tent, but a warm body is next to mine. The body takes a deep breath and everything from last night comes crashing back. I roll over, a wave of happiness mixed with grief engulfing me.

I watch the gentle rise and fall of her shoulder as she gets much-needed sleep. I'm paying such close attention, that I notice the slightest change in her breathing, indicating she's waking. With a stretch, she rolls over, her mouth curling up into the most beautiful smile. My heart melts and I'm completely useless. She's always had this effect on me, but after having lost her for so long, coming so close to losing her forever, it slams me harder than normal.

Ev reaches up and takes my face in her hands, pulling my mouth to hers. She kisses me with soft, but deliberate movements, and there is no part of me that isn't responding. My hands have their own agenda as they grip her waist and pull her in tight. I sigh heavily and my brain goes fuzzy with a growing need.

Her stomach lets out a long, loud rumble, and she turns away, but not before I see the blush creeping up her cheeks. "Sorry. I'm hungry, I guess."

My forehead drops against hers. "Then let's get you fed." I roll out of bed and dress. When I turn around, she's still in my T-shirt, tucking the bottom into her shorts. The sight of her in my clothes nearly steals my breath. I draw her into my arms and place a gentle kiss on her soft lips before taking her hand and leading her outside.

She pulls away as soon as the tent flap falls back into place.

"Is something wrong?"

She turns to glance up at me, the morning sun making her squint. "It's just...well, the others, they don't know our history. To them, I'll be the boyfriend stealer who drove Valencia away. I need them to respect me as a leader, not hate me as a home wrecker."

"First, she wasn't my girlfriend. I told you we never slept together, hell, I barely kissed her."

She lifts her left eyebrow as if she's calling me out on my bullshit.

I put up my hands. "Truth. Yeah, she wanted more, but I didn't. I wasn't ready. Then you showed up, and I thought you were with Bryce. I took advantage of the situation to let you think I'd moved on, too."

"Well you fooled me and probably everyone else. And if they believe it to be true, it might as well be."

"Look, Ev, I don't give a shit what anyone thinks. I don't want to be away from you for even one minute." She sighs and glances away. I didn't fight for her last time, but I'm never making that mistake again. "I spent the last two months pretending I don't love you. I'm not going back there. I don't care who knows, in fact I want everyone to know. Look, you're sleeping in my tent, they'll figure it out sooner or later...wait, you *are* sleeping in my tent, aren't you?"

She smiles and drops her gaze to her toes, wiggling them in her flip flops. "Yes." Then she takes my hand and we walk to the mess tent for breakfast.

Over our meal, we talk about nothing important, just enjoying being together. When I'm done with my eggs, I set my fork down and wrap my arms around her waist, putting my forehead to her temple as she finishes her coffee. I can't seem to keep my hands off her. She turns to face me, her hazel eyes locking with mine before she reaches over and rests her warm lips against my mouth in a too brief kiss. I could sit here like this all morning. She pulls back too soon, grabs her dishes, and heads to the conveyor belt with them.

I follow her and take her hand, weaving our fingers together. We enter the warehouse and dozens of pairs of eyes are trained on us and our entwined hands. I'm beginning to understand her earlier concerns with our relationship. Dominic catches my eye, a frown forming. I may not owe anyone else, but I owe Dominic. When Evan goes over to talk to Lisa, I head to Dom.

Dominic inclines his head toward Evan. "So, is that the reason my sister left?"

My fists ball and I have to unclench my jaw to speak, forcing my voice to remain steady. "Her name is Evan and she's a leader here. If you don't like that, you're free to leave, too."

Dominic blinks before his eyes widen. "No, no, I mean...no."

Watching him squirm is kind of fun, but I came here to give him the explanation he deserves. "Evan's the reason I was in the Eastern Province, the reason I met you all. We weren't together at the time, and I didn't get involved with her again until after Valencia left."

"Did Val know that?"

"She knew everything."

Dominic nods. "Yeah, I can see that. I knew she was interested the day she saw you in the bar. I told her I thought it was a bad idea, you were putting off a vibe. Val told me she knew what she was doing. She was always hooking up with the wrong guys."

"So, we're good?" I ask.

"Yeah. Yeah. I'm staying."

"Good." I pat his shoulder and hope things really are okay between us. Dom's a trusted member of the team and the other recruits look up to him.

Mateo's watching me as I cross the warehouse. Something else to deal with. Better to get it over with now. I nod at a few people as I work my way down the length of the tables.

"Are we cool?" I ask.

"Yeah."

I'm not so sure I believe him. "Are your feelings for her going to be an issue?"

"No, and we're done talking about this."

We've known each other too long and we have too much to do to not take him at his word. "Okay. Then we should work on finding a place out in the Ruins, not too far from here, where we can train the recruits."

Mateo nods. "Been thinking the same thing. I'll take a team out later today to scout the area."

We discuss details before Mateo moves to start gathering people for his scouting mission. He stops and turns back toward me, his face stoic. "You hurt her again and I will end you." He stalks off without waiting for a response.

My gaze naturally seeks and finds Evan in the corner with a handful of the new people. She's animated, but there's a weariness in her actions I noticed all along, but attributed to her pregnancy. Something I now know never existed.

Sonia sits at one of the tables, studying a tablet. We haven't spoken much since the other night, and now that I know what happened, I need someone who can help me understand Draya's involvement in all this.

Sonia tracks me, her eyes searching mine when I approach.

"Can we talk?"

She nods and I take the seat opposite her.

"Evan and I talked last night. She told me everything. I...How much did you witness?"

"I didn't see anything happen to her, only...the results."

"How could Draya do that? She's not the girl I knew." I let out a sigh. "But I'm not the guy she knew either."

Sonia puts a hand on my shoulder. "It was like she was dead inside. Her eyes were so cold."

Marcus walks up and places his hands her shoulders. "Chase needs to ask you something about the medical supplies."

"Okay." Her eyes lock with mine, something long and unsaid passing between us. "I need to take care of something, Cy. I'll talk to you later."

Marcus watches her walk away, his eyes glued to her ass, then sits in her chair. "So, you guys are back together?"

We've been best friends for as long as I can remember, but my relationship with Evan is none of his business. Still, what Sonia said the other night hits me hard. I appreciate that he cares about my girl. "We're sorting it out."

"She's not as tough as she seems."

I raise an eyebrow. "You think I don't know that?"

"Sometimes I think maybe you forget." His words are measured and precise.

I glare at Marcus. That was uncalled for. "I've made my share of mistakes, but when it comes to her, nothing is forgotten. Ever."

We stare at each other for a long time, then Marcus smiles wide, his white teeth glowing against his dark skin. He stands, scraping his chair across the floor and walks around to hug me. "Man, it's good to have you back but you do that to her again, I won't be responsible for my actions."

Last night after dinner, Selma showed a movie for the campers. Evan wanted to go, but she only lasted twenty minutes before she dozed off. It was some thriller set during the Second Civil War, so I stuck around for about half of it before wondering why anyone in the campground found it entertaining. The movie was dark, violent, and a lot like our lives these days. I always thought Unis watched movies for entertainment, to escape life, not relive it on a large display.

Ev barely woke when I carried her to bed, and now she's sleeping soundly beside me. Where she belongs. Pulling her back against my chest, I wrap my arm around her waist and drift off.

Something flutters along my neck, like a bug, or maybe a spider. It takes me a moment to realize that something is a beautiful girl. I smile before rolling over and wrapping my arms around soft skin. This is a pleasant surprise and my grin broadens. My gaze drifts down from mischievous eyes to curls of red hair fanning out across the pillow. Further down I pause at three small scars on her side. My fingers trace them, and she stills. They're unusual, like narrow slits, as if they were intentionally cut.

"Where did these come from?"

She presses her lips together and pulls the sheet up. "I...Three of my ribs were crushed, so they had to fabricate new ones and put them in through those incisions."

The extent of the damage done to her once perfect body makes my guts clench. I hate that she ever endured any pain, but her scars are a part of her now, and I bend down to kiss each one. She trembles beneath my lips and gooseflesh rises across her stomach. With a sigh, she pulls back, lying face down with her back exposed to me.

My breath stalls in my chest and soon the tent is spinning as I stare at the burn marks covering more than half her back. They may be smooth and silvery now, but at the time she got them, they would've been angry, red, crusted. I try and fail to smother my feelings. My fists flex and relax as I work to regain control. My eyes trail lower to two more scars, similar to the ones on her side. Two fingers reach out, shaking, to trace the smooth pink lines.

"They had to make me a new kidney, too, and remove my spleen, but there wasn't time to fabricate a spleen."

I never should have left her, but I let Eddie talk me into leaving. Never again. When my lungs are under control, I bend down and press my lips to each scar on her back, tracing them with the pads of my fingers.

I kiss the last burn, the one near her shoulder blade, and she rolls over, wrapping her arms around my neck. "I love you."

Only three small words, but they light my heart like a torch that spreads like a wildfire through my body. My mouth finds hers with renewed determination, her desperation soon matches mine until waves of emotion build to near tsunami proportions.

"Cyrus, hey, you in there?" Colin calls from outside.

"Fuck." I drop my forehead to Ev's. Doing my best to remain quiet, I lean forward and kiss her again, forgetting about Colin for a moment.

"Cyrus..." His voice is louder this time. "Are you in there?"

"Maybe if we ignore him he'll go away," Ev says, smiling against my lips.

I gently tug on her bottom lip with my teeth and she sighs, resuming the kiss.

"Is Evan with you? We've got company out here. And not the good kind."

Shit. My already pounding heart picks up another notch, but this time from fear. "Yeah. Hang on a sec."

Evan rolls out from under me and fumbles on the floor next to the bed for her clothes. She's clothed and moving toward the tent flap by the time I finish dressing. Her eyes are wide as she glances at me before admitting Colin.

"Hey, EvTay." Colin bends down to kiss her head. Worry lines etch his face as his gaze travels from me to Ev and back again, seeming to weigh his options.

I nod. No more secrets.

"A group of Uprising soldiers are searching tents in camp for someone."

Running a hand through my hair, I glance at Evan. The tenseness of her features tells me she knows how serious this is. I reach into my bag and grab a gun. After checking the chamber for a round, I stuff it into my waistband and pull my shirt out to cover it. "Stay here," I say to Ev, stuffing my feet into my flip flops. "I'll be back."

"What if you're not?"

"I will. I promise." I kiss her forehead before turning to follow Colin out.

"But what if you don't come back?" Her voice rises with irritation. "I know you intend to, but stuff happens. We usually run into the most trouble when we don't make plans for things to go wrong."

She's got a point. I dig around in my bag for another handgun, making sure it's loaded. "Here, use this if you need to, but I don't plan on letting anyone in here, so you shouldn't need it."

"Okay." She takes the weapon in her shaking hands. "And if you don't come back?"

"I'm coming back, Ev."

"What if you don't?"

I let out a long, loud sigh. "Fine, if I don't come back, meet me at the warehouse. I'll find you. And if I don't someone else will. Okay?"

She nods and I brush my lips against hers before following Colin outside. When we're out of earshot, I ask, "What's the scoop?"

"They showed up looking for someone about ten minutes ago. They haven't said who yet, but I'll give you one guess."

Yeah, I can almost guarantee it. The soldiers are still a few tents over. I rub my hands over my face, trying to formulate a plan. I count six of them so far. We can't shoot them all before one of them fires on us, but I can't let them inside the tent either. "Where're Mateo and Rainey?"

"They left for the warehouse already."

"Are you armed?"

"Yep."

"We're gonna need to figure something out. Who's still here?"

"Ally, me, some of the newer recruits. Maybe Bryce."

"Okay, round them up and meet back here. But fast. We don't have much time."

Colin turns and moves away from me, walking so slow it grates on my nerves, but running would draw too much attention. My teeth grind into one another as I alternate between watching Colin and the steady approach of the soldiers only two tents away now. I inch closer to the opening, flexing my hands at my sides to keep from reaching for my piece.

They exit the tent next to mine and I move closer, my left hand on my hip, ready to grab my gun if necessary. My next step puts me between the soldiers and my tent. My body is too tense, they're going to sense something's up.

They're nearly in front of me and I take a deep breath before opening my mouth to say something when the first soldier shifts his gaze beyond me. I glance over my shoulder to find Colin, Bryce, Jack, Lisa, and Ally trudging through the dry sand toward us.

"Hey, there you are." Colin inclines his head in the direction of the mess tent. "We're going to go to breakfast. Wanna come?"

"Uh yeah, just a minute." I'm not sure what he's up to, but I'm not about to leave now.

Colin goes rigid and he glances at the water before looking back at me.

I don't have time to play this game. The soldier before me has my full attention. "Can I help you?"

"You can get out of our way."

The guy's bigger than me in every way, but I'm more motivated. These punks would've been under my command not that long ago.

"What are you looking for?" I ask, keeping my voice light.

"Someone. It's of no concern to you."

The woman behind him pushes forward and points her rifle at me. "We have our orders."

This isn't going to go off without a fight. Before pulling my weapon, I glance over my shoulder one last time to make sure the others are ready, and Colin is bouncing his head on his neck like a crazed bird, his eyes wide. Movement to my right in the direction Colin's nodding catches my attention. A drifter stumbles across the beach, mismatched sweats three sizes too large, hood pulled up over his...no...her head. The way she moves is as familiar as the lines on my own palm. She lifts her head and turns toward me for only a second before dropping her gaze back to the sand and stumbling on.

My gray sweatpants are bunched at her ankles, and my favorite blue hoodie covers all her hair, the sleeves hanging down past the tips of her fingers as she trudges south toward the jetty.

I swallow a smile and step aside, gesturing to my tent. "Help yourself. I'm the only one assigned, and I'm out here. Okay if I eat breakfast with my friends?"

"Wait here." The woman stands guard over us with the big dude, while the other four duck inside, returning moments later, shaking their heads.

When they move on, we head to the mess tent under the pretense of getting food.

I turn to Colin. "Are they looking for her?"

"I think so. They're definitely looking for a female. I heard them say, 'she' a few times."

I scratch a hand through my hair and glance back down the beach, watching as Ev makes her way closer to the jetty.

"Hey, gotta second?" Dominic asks with Nate in tow.

Not really. "Uh, what's up?"

"I need to tell you something." He pauses and glances around the area. "I'm *really* sorry."

27

BACKUP PLAN

Evan

*A*fter climbing over the rocky jetty, I walk a little farther south along the beach before heading inland. I'm glad Cyrus agreed to a backup plan, because there wasn't any way he could have prevented those soldiers from entering the tent.

Ducking into the first narrow hall I come to, I peel off the sweats but leave on the ballcap, my hair still tucked underneath it. It's not an adequate disguise, so before meeting Cyrus at our rendezvous spot, I take a detour to the shopping district and enter the first boutique I come across, buying myself some mirrored sunglasses. I wander down a few more shops and pick up a pair of decent track shoes, because if someone's after me, I'd better be able to run.

Working my way deeper into the bowels of the Union, I take the stairs down to the ground level to get my bearings, then head toward the warehouse. As soon as I arrive, I know something's wrong. Everyone is packing up the equipment and supplies and rushing in a dozen different directions. Cyrus is here and the moment he spots me, the hard edges of his face give way to relief as he rushes to my side.

"You okay?"

"I'm fine. What's going on?"

Mateo approaches, his eyes searching mine. I nod, letting him know I'm good.

"I'm getting her out of here. Now," Cyrus says. "Can you finish up and meet us out there?"

Mateo grunts. "I think the spot we talked about is too close. Let's rendezvous there, but we need to settle somewhere else."

The gravity of the situation hits me. We're leaving the Union. I'm good with that, but what about the others? How much do they know about life in the Ruins? I doubt any of them are prepared for what they're about to experience. Although they weren't prepared to be invaded and thrown out of their homes either. It's more important than ever for me to find my family once we get settled.

"Come on." Cyrus takes my hand and pulls me from the warehouse.

He leads me deeper into the underbelly of the Union and I blindly follow him at first until I realize he's planning on walking all the way to the back wall. It's more than twenty miles from here and I'm not sure I can make it without a break, especially with his much longer legs going at warp speed. Eventually, I'm forced to pause.

"Why are you stopping?" he asks, his voice is gruff.

"Sorry," I say between labored breaths. "I can't walk as fast as you."

"Oh." His determined scowl morphs into understanding. "We can slow down."

"It's more than that. I can't go that far without frequent rests, and you can't carry me all that way. Let's take the commuter."

"That's a bad idea, Ev. They're looking for you. Spotters will be on the trains."

"You don't know that for sure, and if they're on there, we can get off. We'll spot them before they spot us. But in here, if they see us, we have nowhere else to go. We're trapped."

He rubs his chin with his hand, his whiskers scraping against his palm. He hasn't shaved in days, but Sonia cut his hair yesterday. He's starting to look more like my Cyrus and less like Valencia's.

"Okay, but stay by my side. Don't let go of my hand, and for god's sake, make sure your gun is loaded."

I pat the weapon he gave me earlier where it's tucked into my waistband.

He takes my hand and pulls me down a hallway in the direction of the terminal. We're less than a mile away, but I'm still exhausted by the time Cyrus leaves me on a bench to go get us tickets. The firm arch of his shoulders tells me this is the worst part for him, being separated from me. He returns quickly and grasps my hand, hauling me to my feet.

We wave our tickets in front of the sensor and hop on when the doors slide open with a hiss. Cyrus chooses a seat in the back where he can watch all the entry points without needing to turn his head. I enter first and he sits next to me, on the aisle, ready to bolt. We pull out of the station, and he's so taut, his breathing is the only indication he's a living human being and not a marble statue.

Exhaustion eats away at me and I lean my head on his shoulder, surveying my side of the car, but soon, my eyes are slipping shut. I don't even realize I've dozed off until a hand grabs mine, and I startle, my eyes flying open. Up ahead two Uprising soldiers are boarding, and my heart kicks into high gear.

Beside me, Cyrus leans forward and reaches behind his back. There are too many people for us to shoot our way out of this. Too many innocent people.

I place my hand on his arm. "Wait."

Without taking his eyes off the soldiers he nods, but doesn't drop his hand. I nudge his shoulder with mine. Another stop is coming up and he pivots in his seat before standing. His body is wound so tight, if he was a rubber band, he'd snap. He stays behind me as he guides me toward the door. When we're in position, he wraps his left arm around my waist, gun in hand.

Leaning down, he whispers in my ear, "When I tell you to, run. No questions asked, no looking back."

He's going to sacrifice himself for me. "No," I whisper. "We stay together, no matter what."

As we slow, he glides his lips up the side of my neck, as if we're nothing more than a happy couple in love, not two people ready to run for our lives. "I'm not leaving you, but you need to do what I say."

"Then tell me the plan."

His lips turn inward against my skin and I can only imagine his expression. The moment we stop, I press the button to open the doors. Several people jostle for position behind us, and I take advantage of it, joining the flow of passengers.

"Wait!" Someone yells from the front of the car.

I pause, but Cyrus pushes my back, whispering in my ear, "Go, and laugh like I said something funny. Act as if you're so wrapped up in me you didn't hear him."

I let out a weak laugh that sounds more like a strangled snort and no doubt Cyrus is glaring. He guides me forward, his hand still around my waist. My heart pounds in my ears as we climb down, the soldier still yelling for us to stop. Cyrus nudges me, my other foot landing on the bottom step. His movements are casual, but his body is tense. We move away from the car as the other passengers block the soldier's path off by obeying his command.

Cyrus reaches for my hand and pulls me into a run as the train pulls out. I chance a look over my shoulder as we barrel out of the station. The train is already slowing, two soldiers waiting by the doors for them to open.

We dash through the crowd and down a narrow hall. Cyrus leads me up two flights of stairs and down another corridor before dodging into an alcove, both of us gasping for air. He presses me up against the wall, his back to me, his gun trained straight ahead, waiting for anyone to come around the corner.

I wrap my arms around Cyrus's waist and press my cheek against his back while my lungs burn with the need to refill themselves. He covers my right hand with his, lacing our fingers together and gently squeezing.

When my breath returns, I ask, "What's the plan?"

He doesn't answer and I duck out from behind him so I can peer down the corridor. There are so many hallways here, I'm not sure they could have easily followed us. Although that doesn't mean they won't do a thorough search of the area.

"Cyrus?"

He glances at me, his eyes intense.

"Are we going to shoot our way out of this?"

He scratches a hand through his hair. "If we're forced to."

"You realize that's not the best idea, right?"

He sighs. "Yes. It's not Plan A, but I will if necessary. I'll do whatever it takes to protect you."

"Okay, so what's Plan A?"

"I'm working on it."

I sigh and lean back against the wall while he "works on it," giving plenty of thought to my own plan. The concrete is cool and hard against my back, and I close my eyes, running scenarios over in my head. An idea comes to mind and I open one eye, glancing at the boy next to me, jaw ticking like mad. Yeah, he's not going to like it.

"Uh...you got anything yet?"

"No." Irritation laces that one short word.

"Well, I've got something, but you're gonna hate it."

He eyes me, his mouth set. "What?"

"We need to split up—"

"No."

"Cyrus..."

"Ev, no."

"Wait...just hear me out. They're searching for two of us, as in a couple. If we split up, change our appearances, then meet up again, maybe ten levels up, they won't be looking for us up there yet." I rush on before he can interrupt, but his jaw is already releasing some. "They don't have enough soldiers to do a massive search, so they'll be going level by level. It'll take a while before they reach level twenty-five."

He studies me, then shakes his head. "They'll be watching the stairs and elevators though."

"They can't watch all the stairwells, there are too many to post a soldier at every one."

While he's quietly processing that, I take the opportunity to open the backpack and grab his sweats, handing them to him. Then I strip the ballcap off my head and place it on his before pulling on his hoodie, yanking the hood up to cover my hair.

"I know it's not perfect, so I'll stop somewhere and buy a change of clothes. You do the same. We'll meet on level twenty-five at First and A. I don't know what's there, but if you don't see me, I'll be nearby watching for you."

He sighs, his mouth pulled in a tight line. "I don't like this."

"I know. I don't either, but it's the only way." I reach up on my tiptoes and give him a quick kiss, then I take off before he can change his mind. Gun in hand, I dash down the hall and peek around the corner before heading to the nearest staircase.

Leaning against the wall in the stairwell, I gasp for air. Perhaps running up three flights of stairs wasn't such a good idea. The whole reason I wanted to take the train is because my stamina sucks right now. After catching my breath, I pace myself and head up two more flights, rest, and climb again, before poking my head out of the door to make sure no one is waiting for me.

The coast is clear and I ease out the door, disappearing into the throngs of people in a busy retail district. I pop into the first clothing shop I come to and grab a pair of jeans, top, and a hat. After checking out, I duck into the closest café and lock myself in the bathroom to change. Freshly changed, I stuff my other clothes into the shopping bag and trash the backpack. I order a coffee and make my way outside. No one pays any attention to me as I move about between hallways and stairwells up to level twenty-five.

The map display shows I'm a few blocks from where Cyrus and I are supposed to meet. I take my time, peering in windows, which make excellent mirrors, attempting to appear like a lazy shopper rather than someone surveying my surroundings. Convinced no one is any more interested in me than anyone else, I continue on and spot a familiar figure up ahead sitting at a table at an outdoor café, sipping coffee.

His back is to me, so he doesn't see me coming. Nor does he see the soldiers that just turned onto the walkway from between two buildings, their eyes scanning the area. My heart pounds and I can feel it from my toes all the way up to my scalp. I push through the door of the shop I'm in front of before they spot me.

"Can I help you?" A voice asks from behind me.

I turn to find a young woman glancing at my belly, then back at my face. My eyes scan the store...cribs, tiny little outfits, strollers. "Oh...I uh...I'm looking...for something...for my sister. She's having a baby. But we don't know of it's a boy or a girl yet. She just found out."

"Oh, that's nice. You must be excited to become an aunt."

"Yes." I force a smile and step closer to the window, peering out. The soldiers I spotted are no longer in sight, and Cyrus is still sitting at the same table, although his body is much tenser than earlier. I return my attention to the clerk who's now smiling at me with both confusion and expectation. Suddenly, I get an idea, a rather brilliant one if I do say so myself. "You know, it's probably kinda early to get a baby gift, but maybe I can get my sister something. Is there a maternity store nearby?"

"Yes, two blocks south."

"Thank you," I toss over my shoulder as I hurry from her shop.

I head south, scanning the storefronts until I find the one I'm looking for. Five minutes later, I'm wearing a new shirt and a little something extra I found in the changing stall. I planned to wad up the hoodie and tie it around my waist, but it turns out they have these little strap-on pillows to simulate different pregnancy sizes. Under the maternity top, I look very pregnant. The woman in the baby store glanced at my stomach before she bothered to look at my face. My mom used to complain when she was carrying my sisters that no one ever looked her in the eye anymore. They couldn't get past her enormous belly.

Mimicking the actions of pregnant women I've seen, I waddle back to the café where Cyrus is now shifting in his chair, glancing around. His eyes lock on me for a second, or rather my stomach, then he continues his scan. Twenty seconds later he's back to me, this time his gaze rising to meet mine. His eyes widen, and the color drains from his face before he chokes on the sip of coffee he just took.

I start laughing and can't stop. When I reach his side, I suck in a breath and place a hand on his shoulder before bending down to kiss him. "Don't worry, it's yours, I promise." If he didn't look so freaked out, I'd be laughing again. "It's only a pregnancy pillow; you can unswallow your tongue."

The color returns in full force, bringing all the blood with it until his face looks like it's going to combust.

Once I'm assured he's still breathing, I grin. "They're not looking for a pregnant girl. This is perfect."

A slow smile spreads across his face and he leans forward to kiss my fake belly. "I may have underestimated your brilliance."

He pushes up and takes my hand, leading me to the nearest stairs. Two soldiers approach from the north and Cyrus's grip tightens around my hand. One of them glances at my stomach with disinterest before looking away. And as easy as that, we blend into the crowd, nearly invisible.

28

INVISIBLE

Cyrus

She's trying to hide it, but I know Ev's exhausted. We already covered close to ten miles, and we're still at least five miles away from the Ruins. I offered to carry her a few times, but the last time she snapped at me, so I've backed off. In fact, we're not talking much at all. The heat is getting to me, too, but I'm not healing from a near-fatal beating.

We enter the Ruins by late afternoon and I'm slammed by glaring sunlight. I pull down the cheap sunglasses I bought to shade my eyes. If the others exited here, they didn't leave any evidence. I squat, searching for footprints, matted grass, or disturbed rocks, but come up empty. No one has been through this door in a while. Confident we're safe for now, I reach back for Evan's hand and guide her into the Ruins.

We walk in silence, the sun beating down on us, for a couple hours before we take a break. I hand her the canteen and she takes it with a small smile. She guzzles a healthy amount and wipes her mouth with the back of her hand. "I'm sorry for being so bitchy. I'm exhausted."

Although I probably shouldn't be agreeing with her, I nod, not wanting to patronize her either. "Hand me that, why don't you?" I point at her stomach.

"Oh, yeah." She reaches under her shirt and strips off the over-sized curved pillow.

We hike on until dusk settles upon us and voices up ahead indicate we're close to reaching the others. Ev picks up the pace with renewed energy, likely forgetting we're not staying here. We still need to put some distance between us and the Union before we set up camp.

I pull her to a stop and turn her to face me. "There's something I need to tell you. I should've said something earlier, but we were both a little preoccupied."

Her eyes widen and unease spreads across her face in the growing twilight.

"Dominic cornered me on the beach this morning. He's Valencia's brother." She nods. "He's pretty sure she's the one who turned you in to the Uprising."

She shakes her head, the curls that escaped her hat dance in the breeze. "No, I don't think so. I spent two weeks with her, and although I'm not thrilled about it, she really loves you. She'd never do anything to put you in danger."

"Ev, she didn't turn me in. Or anyone else. Only...you."

"Oh."

Several moments pass without her saying anything more, but no doubt she's putting the pieces together. I had a hard time accepting it, too, but Dom was sure. He said it was her signature move — getting the competition out of the way.

"Thanks for telling me," she finally says.

There's way more going on in her head than those four words, but we can save the rest of this discussion for another day. I pick up her hand and we hike through the brush to our friends.

BOOK 3 :: THE RUINS

"Three things cannot be long hidden: the sun, the moon, and the truth."
    – Buddha

29

SETTLING IN

Evan

*M*id afternoon sun strikes the side of the tent when I wake. I reach over for Cyrus, my hand finding nothing but sleeping bag. Still wearing the same clothes I hiked in yesterday, I head outside to find him and hopefully a place to clean up. Trees stretch tall, filtering sunlight through fat leaves, while weeds carpet the ground beneath them. The constant buzz of insects hums in the background, becoming white noise.

My gaze sweeps the area until I find Cyrus a few dozen yards away, talking to Mateo and Rainey. We arrived long after midnight and only bothered with pitching tents to sleep in before turning in. But it appears everyone has spent the morning setting up camp while I slept through it. A pathway lined with rocks and cleared of plants and other debris winds between the tents, creating a sort of makeshift town. Recruits are busy staking more tents farther out. A delicious aroma draws my attention to a kitchen on the outer edge of camp near another path. Judging by the dozen or so people carrying buckets of water along said path, I'm guessing it leads to water.

Cyrus catches my eye and smiles. I wander over to the three of them, and he wraps his arms around me, kissing my temple.

"Why didn't you wake me? Everyone else is up and working."

"Because you needed sleep."

"Everyone needs sleep. Yesterday was a long day."

"No one else here is recovering the way you are," Mateo says with a grunt.

"Fine." I don't want to fight about it, but I hate that it makes me appear weak.

"Hungry?" Cyrus asks next to my ear.

Before I can answer, my stomach lets loose a loud grumble. "Is there anything left?"

Mateo gives me one of his signature almost smiles. "Plenty. Good stuff, too. Lisa is a goddess."

"I'll catch up with you later then." I kiss Cyrus's scruffy cheek and walk to what is now the mess area. Grabbing a plate, I dish myself up some stew, a piece of pan toast, and a cup of coffee. An upended log alongside a slab of stone functions as a table, and I take a seat, Lisa parking herself beside me.

"How's things?" I ask.

She smiles. "Good. I'm going to have so much fun coming up with new meals out here. Sonia knows which plants are edible. Did you know that?"

I nod, smiling around a mouthful of steaming hot stew, the rich gravy coating my tongue. "This is great, thanks."

"I don't mind. It's good to see you with an appetite again." She glances around our little corner. "Mateo's going to have some of the recruits build actual picnic tables tomorrow."

The area is beautiful in a different way than the desert Southwest where I met Cyrus and the Northwest where I trained in the Uprising. "How far is the water?"

"Not far. It's a big freshwater lake with a spot reserved for bathing. Bryce and Rainey hung some sheets from a tree limb and staked them down. Men on one side, women on the other."

"Do you know how many people are in camp?"

She scrunches up her nose. "Maybe a couple hundred."

Nowhere near enough, but it's a start.

After lunch, we find Sonia and the three of us walk along a loose dirt patch to an inlet where water laps the shore in gentle waves. Taught white sheets billow in the soft breeze, which brings scents of fresh grass, magnolia, and gardenia. Someone even constructed a rack made of horizontal branches mounted in larger vertical branches, and thatched together with vines.

I strip out of my dirty clothes, draping my clean ones along with a towel on the rack, and wade into the lake. The bottom drops off rapidly, and soon I'm treading water. What was close to bath temperature near shore cools dramatically farther out.

While I wash up, Lisa fills me in on the latest camp gossip. "They sent scouts back to the Union this morning to see what's going on." She pauses and chews on her top lip. "Did Cyrus tell you they think Valencia turned you in?"

"Yeah." I dunk my head to rinse my hair and avoid discussing Valencia further.

"One group stuck around last night and reported back. The Uprising doesn't seem to be aware we left the Union yet. They're still looking for you there. But even if they figure we're in the Ruins, I doubt they'll find us. At least not without us knowing well ahead of time they're coming. Jack and Bryce spent the day setting up a solid perimeter system."

Although Lisa has seen my scars, she still inhales sharply when I step out of the water to grab my towel.

"They look better than they used to, Lis, ask Sonia."

Sonia nods. "A lot better."

"Just before you got up," Lisa says eyeing me, "Jack, Bryce, Colin, and Ally left to get Miranda."

"Good."

Lisa continues to scrutinize me with her dark stare. "Will you be okay with her here?"

"Of course."

"What about Cyrus?" She eyes Sonia. "My understanding is she's from the valley where you guys lived."

"She isn't one of the girls he used to mess around with, if that's what you mean," Sonia says. "At least I don't think so."

"I think Bryce being here is the issue for him, not Miranda." Although it hadn't occurred to me until now that she might be another girl from his past.

Sonia squeezes the water from her long braids with a thick towel I'm pretty sure she took from the hotel. "Everything will work out fine. We're all grown-ups now with bigger problems than who slept with whom."

"Good point," Lisa says.

"When will they be back?" I ask.

"A week, tops."

"Okay." I'll wait for them to return, but then I'm leaving to find my family.

Over the last week, we've been busy building up the camp, setting up training zones, and planning. Daily missions to the Union ensure we have all the supplies we need. Lisa organized her mess area with sections dedicated for prep, cooking, storage, and cleanup, rivaling anything in the Union. The only thing she's missing is high-tech gadgetry, which she doesn't appear to mind. She was actually using a rock to crush nuts for her pizza crusts last night. Fresh game is plentiful around here, including wild hog and crocodile in addition to fish, fruit, and greens. Sonia and I started a garden yesterday, but it'll be awhile before it produces anything we can eat.

This afternoon, Mateo and I put the finishing touches on the area where Colin and I will teach knife throwing. I grab a large rock, my calf screaming in protest. "Your workout this morning was hardcore."

Mateo turns toward me, a slight grin pulling at the corners of his mouth.

"That was way harder than what we did in the Uprising."

"If we want to succeed, we must be stronger and better trained than them."

I place the rock where I want it, swiping my brow with my shoulder. "I was in pretty damn good shape before I got shot."

He paces off the distance from a target and places a stone to mark the spot. "The Uprising trains their recruits with the basics necessary to achieve their objective. Nothing more. We need to go beyond that."

"Yeah, doesn't mean I have to like it," I mumble.

"What?"

"Nothing. I'll finish up here if you want to go."

"No. You go on. I got this."

I watch him lug four large stones back from the wooded area. I can only carry one at a time. Maybe I'm better off using my time elsewhere. "Thanks."

He nods and I hike off in search of Lisa.

I find her with Marcus and Simon doing laundry with a few of the recruits. Marcus hangs a rope between a couple of trees. I love the way my clothes smell when they dry outside, clean with a hint of sunshine.

"How's the stabbing area coming along?" Simon asks with a grin.

I laugh. "Almost done. We'll be ready for stabbing in no time."

Voices approaching the camp grow louder and closer. I reach into the back of my waistband for my gun, which is always on me these days. Lisa reaches out and touches my arm.

Laughter echoes off the boulders, and I recognize it as Jack's. Lisa drops the shirt she's holding and runs up the path, disappearing into the thick bushes. I pick up the wet piece of clothing from the ground and toss it back into the wash bin before following her. Jack, Bryce, Ally, and Colin hike through the center of camp with an obviously pregnant girl.

The girl eyes Lisa and then me with pale blue eyes.

"Miranda, this is Jack's girlfriend, Lisa, and another friend of ours, Evan."

I paste on a smile. "Hey. Welcome. How was your trip?"

She shrugs. "Long, but not too bad. It's humid here."

Bryce throws an arm over her shoulder and grins. He appears... happy. "Yeah, the humidity takes some getting used to. Come on, I'll get you settled."

Colin and Ally stick around to help with laundry and fill us in on their trip. Colin shakes out a sheet and clips it to the line. "We took Miranda to the beach in the Southwestern Province before we boarded the cargo trains. Bryce figured she'd want to see that."

"Did you run into any trouble?"

"Not a bit," Ally says. "How are the boys?"

"Having the time of their lives."

Ally crosses her arms and narrows her eyes. "Did they even miss me?"

"Of course." I suddenly find myself needing to backtrack. "But come on, this is like boy heaven out here."

I hang the last towel and turn to Colin. "Come on. Let me show you where we're going to be working." My smile is evident in my voice and Colin's eyes light up in response. I drag him over to the training area.

He glances around the clearing, his jaw slack. "This is...*awesome*."

Instead of a basic circle and a tree with a target like we had in the Uprising, Mateo and I created zones for working on different skills, including moving targets.

"Check this out." I press a button on a remote and a stuffed dummy glides forward across a pulley system. "And this one moves it side to side." I push a lever and the dummy veers off to the left.

Colin's mouth drops open. "No way."

"Way. And we cordoned off an area inside the trees to practice throwing on the run. I'm excited about teaching but also learning.

Mateo's gonna teach us how to throw while spinning, jumping, and even around obstacles."

"When do we start?"

I shrug. "Soon. But first we need to find the closest trading post and buy a butt-load of knives."

Colin and I spend a few minutes discussing training objectives and logistics before heading back to camp. I hop over a fallen log, my thighs burning from this morning's workout. "How are things with you and Ally?"

"I wrote her a song."

I laugh. "You what?"

His face is dark crimson. "I wrote her a song. Do you think she'll like it?"

It's the most adorable thing Colin's ever done. To my knowledge, he never did that for Lisa. Although maybe he's got a secret stash of them in his room back home. "I'm sure she'll love it. Your songs are good. And the fact that you wrote it for her? She'll think it's perfect."

"Yeah?"

I've never seen Colin this unsure. "Wait...do you love her?"

"Yeah. You know I do."

"No, I mean, like are you *in* love with her. Like mushy, head over heels and all."

"I'm not a girl, Ev. But yeah, I'm in love with her."

"Oh, my god, that's so cute."

"Shut up," he mumbles.

We arrive at the center of camp in time to help with cooking. With everyone back, the atmosphere is celebratory. We make a bonfire after dinner and gather around. Colin disappears for a few minutes, returning with an acoustic guitar. I raise my eyebrow in silent question. He shrugs and gives me his crooked smile. He must have picked it up before they left the Union.

Colin resumes his spot next to Ally and strums a quiet melody. Cyrus leans back against a log beside me, one leg outstretched in front of him. I lean over and put my head on his shoulder, contentment spilling through me like an over-filled glass of water. I'm as close to happy as I can be with the Union in turmoil and the whereabouts of my family unknown. But in this moment, my friends and I are safe, and the guy I love is warm and solid by my side.

The gentle serenade from Colin's guitar provides background music as we talk late into the night. First about the day's events, then about tomorrow's training, and finally about life before the Invasion. As the crickets join Colin and the stars become a brilliant blanket against the blackening sky, most of the recruits head into their tents for the night.

Bryce and Miranda sit across the fire from us, Bryce's arms are around her, rubbing her belly in gentle circles. He looks at her with such devotion, my heart warms further. He glances at me and smiles and I return it. I still haven't completely forgiven him for his role in my breakup with Cyrus, but I'm truly happy for him.

Colin's voice joins his fingers in making music, distracting me with a song that was popular a few years ago. He seamlessly moves into the one of Eddie's he played up in the bar near the border last year when he first met Ally, and then he begins picking a melody I don't recognize, the lyrics are brand new and there's no doubt who they're about.

When he strums the last note, Ally takes his face in her hands and kisses him while the rest of us clap. Colin grabs her hand and pulls her to her feet, leading her back to their tent.

Soon Cyrus and I are the only ones left at the fire, and it's the first time we've been alone while I'm awake since we arrived out here. So, did you and Miranda ever hook up?"

"Why, are you jealous?" I can hear the smile in his voice.

I shove his shoulder. "No. I was...curious if you had a history and if that affects how you feel about Bryce being with her now."

"I never 'hooked up' with her as you call it. She was a girl I saw around, but contrary to popular belief, I didn't sleep with everyone in town." He kisses the side of my neck and his whiskers tickle the sensitive spot under my ear, sending chills racing across my skin.

"You decided to stop shaving?"

He rubs his jaw, making a scratching sound. "I was never a big fan of shaving every day. Does it bother you?"

"If by bother you mean turns me into a puddle of goo, then yes, it bothers me greatly."

He shifts behind me and lets out a groan.

"I like you better this way."

"Why's that?"

I twist and take his face in my hands, kissing him softly, letting my lips trail over his scruff when I'm done. "Because it feels like you." I turn back and lean against his chest. Thinking about his smooth face, the way he looked when we were apart, brings up reminders of something else. "Cyrus?"

He clears his throat. "Yeah?"

"Why do you think she did it? Valencia turning me in, I mean. I don't understand her angle. It's not something I would do to someone I love, so I'm worried there's more to it."

He's silent for few moments before taking in a deep breath and blowing it back out. "I don't know. She always knew I was still in love with you, and like I said, we were never a couple. I don't think she expected to come face to face with you, but I really don't know what she was thinking."

"She loved you, that was obvious. Maybe she blamed me because you didn't reciprocate her feelings. Maybe she didn't want to hurt you, but me."

He sighs. "Maybe. The truth is, I didn't really know her. She hid a lot of herself from me, but I also never took the time to get to know her. I knew more about you a week after meeting you than I know about Val after spending two months with her."

My stomach does a crazy flip-flop.

"I love you, Ev. You're it for me. Always. I think I've been in love with you my whole life, it just took me eighteen years to find you."

A tear trails down my cheek, and I pivot, straddling his lap. I kiss him hard, letting him know without words what his declaration means. The kiss is long, languid, deep, and soulful, making my entire body turn to mush. This boy is everything. Strike that, this man is everything. His love for me, his devotion to the cause, his need to do the right thing.

He breaks the kiss and presses his forehead to mine. "Did Sonia tell you I thought you were pregnant?"

My mouth drops open, and I squeak, "Wh-what?"

"When you walked into the bar that night, you looked so..." he shrugs. "And I overheard Lisa saying something to Bryce about being a father and after catching him in your bed, I just..."

"Oh." My mind blanks out for a few seconds before another word comes tumbling out. "Wow."

"Given your history...I thought I'd lost you forever. It nearly destroyed me, and I wanted to make Bryce pay. That might've been Val's motivation." He lets out a long sigh. "I kept hoping to see evidence you were further along, so maybe the baby would be mine. Your stomach was so flat, though, I knew it couldn't be. But I couldn't leave you either. Even though it wasn't my baby, it *was* yours."

He lifts his hands from my hips and runs them through his hair, swallowing hard. "I never should have left you." He lets that hang there for a minute and then he shifts under me before clearing his voice and wrapping both arms around my waist, pulling me closer.

I lean my head on his shoulder, nestling my nose into the crook of his neck.

He places a soft kiss on my cheek. "I know when you're worried, pissed, nervous, happy. I know all your tells because I want to know *everything* about you."

"Cyrus—"

"Shh," he interrupts me. "I know you, and yet I don't know what you're going to say next."

I lift my head and stare into his amber eyes, confused.

"You're my one and only..." he pauses and presses his lips into a tight line. "I want to spend the rest of my life with you. After this is all over, I want to make it official. I don't care if we have a Union wedding or a Ruins commitment ceremony, I only care that we're together. I've lost you too many times, and I don't ever want to lose you again."

My mouth hangs open and my brain struggles to form a response.

He smiles. "I didn't know what you were going to say, but I thought you might at least say *something*." Although there is a lightness to his words, there is an underlying tension as he waits for my answer.

He's asking me to marry him, and I don't know what to say. I'm still a teen. Who the hell gets married at eighteen? Right, people in the Ruins do, which is where I'm currently sitting and where Cyrus is from. He's not saying now, but when this is over, which may be months or years. Assuming nothing happens to either one of us. There's only one answer.

I nod.

His body unwinds beneath me and he cradles my face in his hands. "So, tell me again how much my whiskers bother you." His voice is deep, dangerous, exciting.

"They bother me so much I almost can't stand it," I whisper.

He gives me a sexy grin that melts my heart and curls my toes. "Then I guess we'd better do something about that." He stands, and pulls me to my feet, leading me back to our tent.

30

SAYING YES

Cyrus

*M*y world is perfect even though we're about to wage war. How fucked up is that? But the girl beside me, the only girl I've ever wanted, said yes. I stare at her in the darkness, her hair obscuring her face, one curl fluttering with each deep breath. A smile takes over my face as I watch her sleep.

I know I should leave her alone, let her rest, but I can't seem to help myself. Reaching out, I move a lock of hair away from her neck before bending down and trailing kisses along the length until her thick lashes flutter against her now fuller cheeks. She rolls over and opens her eyes, giving me a drowsy smile.

"Hey." Her voice is thick with sleep.

"Hey."

"Can't sleep?"

I shake my head.

Her gaze sweeps across my face before she leans in, eyes closing, her lips resting on mine. The kiss is soft and filled with promise. I roll onto my back, bringing her with me.

Her full lips blaze a path from my ear to my throat and I'm lost to her. She props her chin on her fist in the center of my chest. "I love you."

My heart stops, then picks up again, my chest tight with emotion.

31

ENGAGED

Evan

*M*y eyes flutter open to find Cyrus watching me. He smiles when he realizes he's caught. "You're beautiful when you sleep."

"That's not creepy at all."

His grin broadens as he leans down to place a soft kiss on my lips. "Nope."

The events of last night come flooding back — the proposal, my acceptance. "Are we really engaged?"

His jaw tightens. "Are you having second thoughts?"

"No. Of course not." I reach up and stroke the scruff on his cheek. "But this feels...surreal. Kids my age don't get married."

"We don't need to tell anyone if you'd rather not." His face is an emotionless mask.

"I'm not embarrassed or anything, but can we keep it to ourselves? Just for a little while."

"We can keep it to ourselves forever if you want. You and I are the only ones who need to know."

"Thanks. It's just, well, I should tell my parents first, and I don't even know where they are."

His features soften. "We'll find them."

"I hope so," I whisper.

My stomach rumbles and I roll over to grab my clothes and dress.

"I'm late meeting Mateo," he says, "but I'll catch up with you later." He walks up to me as I attempt to detangle my hair with my fingers and pulls me into a hug. "I love you."

I place my hands behind his neck and pull his face down to kiss him. We part ways and I head to the mess area for breakfast, grabbing a cup of coffee and a piece of Lisa's famous cinnamon breakfast cake. I park myself at one of the newly constructed picnic tables with Jack, Bryce, and Miranda. Miranda's expression darkens and her gaze drops. My eyes flicker to Bryce, wondering if he's told her about our history. His sheepish grin and slight shoulder shrug says he did.

Miranda pushes back her plate before whispering something to Bryce and leaving the table.

I watch her go before turning back to Bryce. "Really? What the hell possessed you to tell her about us? She didn't need to ever know."

"I didn't want to have any secrets. And it's not like no one else here knows. She was bound to hear it eventually."

I roll my eyes. "Suddenly honesty is your thing?"

He shrugs. "Well, hiding the truth didn't work out so well last time. Figured I'd try something new."

I don't know whether to be insulted that he couldn't bother with me, or grateful he's trying. I decide grateful is the way to go. "So how are you doing with impending fatherhood?"

"Scared. Excited." A smile lights up his face before falling away.

I can understand feeling that under normal circumstances, but given the world we live in now, that's like scared and excited squared, or cubed, or quaded, or whatever the fourth power is called.

"I was hoping you could help Miranda get to know everyone here. I think she feels out of place. She might take a little work to come around completely. The pregnancy's been rough, but she's feeling better now that her morning sickness is over. Still, she gets moody sometimes for no reason."

"And now you've given her a reason to dislike me."

"She doesn't dislike you. She's just...insecure."

"I'll try."

His smile is back. "Thanks, Evansville. I knew I could count on you."

32

FULLY COMMITTED

Cyrus

*T*he past two weeks have exceeded my expectations. The recruits are picking up skills faster than the kids I trained in the Uprising. Perhaps because they're fully committed to the cause rather than being reluctant, but no matter the reason, for the first time since we started this whole thing, I'm hopeful for success.

Lisa magically transforms the available food into mouthwatering meals, somehow managing to make crocodile and rice delicious. She sends shopping lists with the scouts for herbs and spices and made something called jambalaya, which tastes way better than it looks.

After lunch, the leaders convene at the lake to assess how things are going. A breeze blows across the water, keeping the heat from being unbearable. I lean back against the trunk of a tree and cross my feet.

"Colin and I are happy with the results we're getting," Ev starts. "Everyone is working hard and seems motivated."

Rainey snorts. "Wish I could say the same. They're learning to shoot, and shoot straight at that, but I wouldn't say they're excited about it."

Ev wasn't bullshitting me when she said Unis don't like guns.

"How would you rate our chances?" Ev asks.

"I'm impressed with the workouts, but we just don't have the numbers we need yet," Mateo says.

Ev nods. "But if we get them? I mean, they're eager, willing, and they work hard."

"I was expecting them to be whiny and lazy, but they keep surprising me," Rainey says. "I actually thought you and Colin were the exception to the Uni rule, but I've never been so glad to be so wrong."

"I'm still worried about the reality of the Resistance," Ev says. "I still have nightmares. I know you guys hear me screaming. What you may not know is that the worst ones aren't about what was done to me, but about the things I did. I'm not sure how ready they are to deal with the over- whelming guilt that comes with what we're training them to do."

I scratch a hand through my hair. "I've put some thought into that. We can't win this on manpower alone, but maybe we can go about it a different way."

Rainey scowls. "What do you mean?"

"I mean we can't outgun them, but we can outsmart them. We came close before, but made the fatal mistake of not having all the necessary information. We thought we knew enough. This time we do it right, we do what we know we're good at."

Mateo blows out a breath. "We still don't know what went wrong."

"We knew we were missing a piece of the puzzle all along, we just didn't think it mattered. Now it's clear they had a backup plan."

"That sounds good in theory," Rainey says.

"Not everything's worked out yet, but we stand a better chance at small, individual well-planned missions than an all-out bloody war. Even if we had enough troops, what kind of society would that leave?"

Rainey shakes her head. "I don't understand. What do we do with the intelligence if not attack?"

Mateo nods with a hint of a smile. "We aim for the top. The Uprising is so loosely organized that if we take out the leader, it'll wither up and die like a snake without a head."

"We have another problem." Rainey gives me a hard look. "We're running out of ammo. Teaching them to shoot is using a lot. Mateo and I are gonna have to go back to Mexico soon."

"You shouldn't both go," I say. "Mateo's family is there, he can take someone else. We should institute a policy that for now, the leaders don't team up on missions. If things go south, we could wipe out half the leadership at once."

"I can find someone to go with me," Mateo says.

Ev's head swivels around to Mateo. "What if you don't need to go? To Mexico, I mean. What if there was another option?"

"To be honest, I think we're pushing our luck down there," Rainy says, blowing out a breath. "What option?"

"When Colin and I were gathering information on the Uprising, we located a warehouse Walker was using. That's where we found the tablet and downloaded the camp locations. In the back of the warehouse was a boatload of ammo. I'm talking millions of rounds. We told Jack's dad about it before we left to attack the camps, but I don't know what happened after that."

"Last I heard, they came up empty when they searched the warehouse," I say.

Evan sighs and leans back. "It's probably in the hands of the Uprising then." She taps her lips with her pointer finger. "But if it's not...maybe we can get it, and even if they have it, they must be storing it somewhere."

"Ev, if the Uprising has it, it'll be well guarded. Mexico is a safer option."

"But if it's not?"

I rub my jaw. "It might work."

"We're going to need Tony's help."

It suddenly occurs to me what she's suggesting, and I don't like it. I put up my hand and open my mouth to protest.

"Cyrus, I have to be the one who goes."

"No, you don't," I grind out.

"Tony knows me and we work well together. I know the borough, how to move around there, and how to use the news site's search engines."

Mateo shakes his head. "They're looking for you, Evan."

"I need to find Eddie and the kids. I've already put it off for too long. I can accomplish two things while I'm there."

"Ev, no. Look, the plan has merit, but if it requires you to go, we're better off sending Mateo back to Mexico."

"Why? Because it's okay for him to risk his life but not me? I thought we were all leaders."

I clench my jaw, doing my best to remain calm. "We are, but you're still recovering."

"They're looking for you, Evan," Mateo says.

Rainey stops twisting a piece of grass between her fingers and flips it to the side. "They've got wanted displays up in the Union with your picture."

Ev's head whips toward Rainey, her face paling. "What?"

"The scouts've been reporting seeing more and more of them."

"And you decided to keep this from me?"

"There was no reason for you to know before now," I answer for Rainey since it was my decision not to tell her.

"This is what I'm talking about. You act like there's something wrong with me, like I'm not an equal. You make decisions without me. That's bullshit."

Mateo leans his head back against the tree and closes his eyes. This is probably better as a private conversation. I walk over to her and reach down a hand. She glares at me through narrow slits but takes my offered hand and lets me pull her to her feet.

Once we're out of earshot of the others, I start. "You can't go to the Union. Not now." I place my hands on the back of her neck and skim my thumbs along her jaw.

"Would you say the same thing if it was Rainey or Mateo?"

I drop my hand to my side. "No, of course not, but I'm not in love with them."

"You treat me like I'm less of a leader than the rest of you. I know you didn't choose me, Mateo did, but—"

"I'm not the only one who thinks this is a bad idea."

"Rainey didn't say jack about it and Mateo's only comment is that they're looking for me. I'll disguise myself. You saw what Jenna was able to do."

She was nearly unrecognizable, I'll give her that, but it's still not sitting well with me. I don't have a valid counterargument, though. The truth is, she's right that it has nothing to do with her abilities and everything to do with the fact that I can't stand the thought of losing her. I'll never be comfortable with her being in danger.

"I know you're thinking something. Just say it." Her arms are crossed, nostrils flaring. "Half of our communication problems are because you're afraid to tell me what's on your mind."

My response flies out before I have a chance to soften it. "Fine. I think it's a crazy idea, and you haven't thought this through."

"No, it's logical but you're reacting emotionally."

I may be emotional, but she *hasn't* planned this out. She'll figure it out along the way. She talks to me about planning all the time, but when it comes to her, she's always flying by the seat of her pants.

"What?" The word drips like acid.

"You're going to go no matter what I say or think." As soon as I say it, I want to snatch the words back, but she doesn't give me the chance.

Her face is like a boiled beet, her chest heaving. She locks eyes with me before turning and marching away.

I totally screwed that up. Again.

33

INSUFFERABLE

Evan

I love that boy more than I ever thought possible, but sometimes he's insufferable. We need to talk, but we both need to cool off first. Heading toward the lake, I kick off my boots and rip my socks from my feet before walking fully-clothed straight into the cold water. I dive down, letting the soothing wetness wash over me, penetrate me, wick away the angry heat. Only then am I able to view our conversation from another angle.

Rainey, Mateo, and Cyrus treat me differently, but maybe that has nothing to do with my condition and everything to do with the fact that I'm from the Union. It's probably so ingrained in them, they don't even realize they're doing it.

Regardless of what he says, I don't know if Cyrus believes I can take care of myself, and not because I'm a girl. He obviously thinks Rainey can do anything, so it must be the whole Uni thing. No matter how dedicated the recruits are, how hard they work, there are still some long-held prejudices about how we live our lives and therefore what we're capable of. After swimming around a little while longer, I'm much calmer and a lot cooler.

My shirt and shorts cling to me as I wade to shore, water dripping down my legs. I reach down to grab my stuff and head back toward where the others were gathered, but Cyrus and Mateo are gone. Rainey sits cross-legged in front of the tree, head back, eyes closed.

"Where'd the guys go?" I ask.

Her eyes pop open. "Back to camp. Cyrus needed to have his hand looked at."

"Why? What happened?"

"He punched a tree."

"He what?"

She shrugs and smiles. "You have your way of dealing with anger, he has his. It must suck to be a slave to testosterone."

I can't help but laugh as I sit beside her. "Speaking of testosterone, whatever happened with you and Simon?"

She sighs. "Nothing ever really happened. I know he's interested in me, but I never thought of him that way. He's more like a brother. He finally made a move and I let him know it wasn't gonna happen. We're still friends. I like him a lot, just not like that."

"Oh." I've never seen anything go on between them. It was always more one sided now that I think about it.

"The only guy in camp more popular than Simon right now is Mateo, so I don't think he minds."

I smile. Apparently, I missed out on all the best gossip. "Mateo is breaking Union girls' hearts?"

"No." She gives me a sideways glance. "They'd be clawing each other's eyes out over him if he showed interest in any of them."

He's smart enough not to get involved with anyone under his command. I always thought he'd go for Rainey, though. She seems like his type.

When my feet are dry, I put my socks and shoes back on, and we walk to camp, my stomach knotted preparing for the conversation I need to have with Cyrus.

Cyrus has kept his distance since our fight. He didn't sleep in the tent with me last night. In fact, I have no idea where he slept. I was so pissed at him for that, I've been avoiding him today. Rainey told me one of the reasons Cyrus was so frustrated is because he's the one who instituted the one leader per mission policy. Meaning he can't go with me by his own edict.

Instead, Colin's coming with me and he suggested we bring a third. That way, if something happens to one of us, the other one won't be alone. I invited Will and he jumped at the chance. Then I had Jenna bleach and straighten my hair.

We're leaving in the morning, so after everyone turns in for the night, I search for Cyrus. He can slink off to Mexico in the middle of a fight and leave me fuming, but I won't do that to him.

Marcus and Ally built a spring house on one of the streams that comes off the lake where a small quantity of beer is currently being stored. The scouts brought a couple of cases back with them on their last trip. I snag one of the bottles as a peace offering.

I find Cyrus sitting alone at the campfire, his back against the log, his knees up. I climb up and sit behind him, resting my chin on his head as I hand him the beer.

He reaches out and grabs it with his right hand. "Thanks." He takes a long pull and sets it down.

His left hand is bandaged, but I resist the urge to say anything. We're both quiet for a few minutes, the sounds of crickets and frogs serenading us before I break the silence. "You need to be able to talk to me or this isn't going to work. *We're* not going to work. You close yourself off from me. You didn't even come to bed last night."

"I didn't sleep with anyone else."

I bite my lip to keep from laughing. "I didn't think you did."

"I'm just putting it out there for the record."

A snicker escapes before I can stop it.

He sighs and reaches out to take my hand, pulling it to his lips.

I slide down and sit next to him. "What's bothering you the most about this?"

He takes several long moments to respond. "I think you don't care if you die."

"What are you talking about?"

"It's like you're not afraid of dying."

I roll his words around in my head for a moment. "No, I guess I'm not. Not anymore. But not being afraid to die and not caring if I do are two separate things."

He wraps his arm around me, and I lean into his shoulder. "I think you can do anything. You know that, right?"

I pivot and climb on his lap, taking his beer and setting it on the ground beside him. "That's incredibly romantic."

His hands slide up my back, my favorite smile lighting up his face. "Does that bother you?"

I smile back. "Mmm, yes. It bothers me greatly. In fact, it might bother me more than anything else." Wrapping my hands around his neck, I lean in to kiss him, showing him just how much it bothers me.

Cyrus sits so close to me I can feel him watching me eat breakfast. Colin and Will finished and are in their tents packing. My bag is sitting beside the table, ready to go. I drain the last of my coffee and turn to the man next to me who owns my heart. The thought of leaving him, even for a week, is tearing me apart. We've been away from each other far too much.

"I'm gonna miss you," he says softly.

I tip my face up to kiss him, my lips lingering on his. "I'll miss you too."

"I won't tell you to be careful, because I know you will." He pulls me to my feet, grabs my bag, and leads me to where Will and Colin are saying their goodbyes near the edge of camp. When we're only a few yards away, Cyrus tugs me against him and I burrow my head into his chest.

He lifts my chin and gives me a soft kiss. "I love you, Ev. Always."

With a quick squeeze of his hand, I grab my bag and rush to meet up with the others. Cyrus gathers Ally from Colin's arms and the two of them watch us go.

We decided the safest approach is to parallel the Union for a dozen miles before heading inside and hopping the cargo trains. The farther we are from camp when we enter and leave the Union, the safer everyone will be. The hike is long, hot, and humid, and we're all drenched in sweat by the time we stop for lunch, swatting at bugs, and snapping at one another. We resume our hike, and to lighten the mood, Colin initiates word games until we're even bored with those and lapse back into silence.

It takes me awhile to figure out Will is watching me like a kid who needs to use the bathroom but doesn't want to go. He clearly wants to ask me something.

"Just spit it out, Will." Any pretense at civility gone with reasonable temperatures.

He smiles and blushes, shoving his fists into his pockets. "What's it mean if a girl's always looking at you?"

"Usually it means she likes you."

"Or you've got corn stuck in your teeth," Colin offers.

I slap Colin's shoulder. "Don't listen to him, Will. I used to stare at Bryce all the time when we were in school."

"Well, what if she looks away whenever you look back?"

"It's a good sign. Do you like her?"

He blushes a deeper hue and kicks a rock, sending it skittering across the ground. "Yeah."

Colin nudges him. "Who is it?"

Will only shakes his head.

"Come on," Colin begs. "Tell us. Who is she?"

Will studies the path in front of him as he walks, his toes scuffing in the dirt. Finally, he glances up at me. "Charlotte Wells."

Colin grins. "No way."

Charlotte Wells is one of the girls who came to camp with her whole family. She's very pretty with light brown hair with golden streaks. I'm not surprised Will's taken notice. Her wide-spaced blue eyes and freckles make her appear younger than her fifteen years. She's also painfully shy.

"Way to go, Will." Colin reaches out to fist-bump him.

"What should I do?" Will asks, a hint of desperation in his voice.

"Start by letting her know you're interested, but take it slow," I say. "Ask her about herself and her family and friends. Tell her about your life. If she likes you, she wants to learn more about you."

Colin rolls his eyes, like he's some kind of expert on fifteen-year-old girls. "Watch out for her dad, though. Union dads are very protective of their daughters."

Will blushes so darkly that I swear he no longer appears human. "Yeah, so are some Ruins dads."

"Uh, something you want to share, buddy?"

Will shrugs. "When we went back home after the attacks, I went to see this girl I like from work, Julia. After Bryce and every-thing, I thought maybe I shouldn't wait anymore to tell her I liked her. So, I told her, and we were kissing and...doing other stuff...in her room..."

"Other stuff?" I wonder aloud before I can stop myself. How experienced can he be if he's this nervous about Charlotte?

He shrugs again. "Yeah, you know, like touching and stuff, but we had all our clothes on. Still, her dad was super pissed and started yelling. He left and came back with a gun, said if he ever saw me again, anywhere, he'd shoot me. I ran home as fast as I could and quit my job the next day."

Colin laughs so hard, I'm not sure he's breathing. "So..." he gasps between fits of laughter, "that's what happened...the day you came home...and locked yourself in your room?"

"What else was I supposed to do?"

"Oh man, that's great. I wish I'd have known."

"You guys are unbelievable. Colin, knock it off, and Will, I doubt he would've actually shot you. Let Charlotte's dad know you respect her, and for god's sake, don't do anything in her tent. Go somewhere else."

Will sighs before lifting his bright pink face. "Thanks. Probably should've talked to you about this a while ago."

I just shake my head and smile. *Boys.*

34

FIGHTING BACK

Evan

*W*e arrive at the Union's back wall close to sunset, tired, sweaty, and gritty. We're forced to walk another several miles before we locate a door. There doesn't seem to be any pattern to their spacing, making me wonder if these openings were all an afterthought.

Inside, I pause long enough to grab the pregnancy pillow and maternity top from my bag and put them on.

"I know we talked about the cargo trains," Colin says, "but I'm thinking your disguise is nearly foolproof. Maybe we can take the A-Train instead. The sooner we get out of here, the better."

I don't disagree, but I'm not sure I'm invisible to the right people. Facial recognition will still tag me. "We need to stay off cameras."

"We'll be careful, but what we don't have a lot of these days is time to waste."

He's right, and other than a general feeling of unease, I can't come up with a valid reason to disagree. "If we're going to take public transportation, we all need to clean up. You both smell. Bad."

No doubt I reek, too, and we don't want to draw attention, especially the wrinkled-nose type. The key to survival is blending in.

"Over here." Colin points his chin at the express elevators that will take us up to a hotel where we can take quick showers.

We traverse a sparsely populated neighborhood in an average part of an average borough. Between the blond hair and the pregnancy pillow, most people glance at my stomach first and lose interest, but I keep my head down anyway, a ballcap pulled low.

My attention is drawn to a projection screen on the side of a building. My face is prominently displayed along with the words "wanted" and "substantial reward." It's from the night I was taken into custody in all my red-haired glory. At least they want me alive. My guts churn until I'm close to hurling. Colin grabs my arm and pulls me toward a hotel, but I can't stop the building nausea.

"Hey," Colin says, "Check it out."

I glance up and my mouth falls open. All around us are people with red hair in every shade. Long, short, curly, straight, and people of every age from toddlers to an adorable elderly couple peering in a shop window.

"What does this all mean?" I whisper.

"The Uprising has made you the face of the enemy and people are standing up."

I spin, taking it all in. These people may not know why the Uprising wants me, but it seems that if they're against me, my fellow citizens are for me.

Something burns deep down inside, pushing out the nausea, building into something more. Something hopeful. The people of the Union are fighting back.

We race across the Southwest on an A-Train. Since Cyrus said Eddie's not in his apartment, I'm hanging my hopes on finding Tony and having him help me locate my family.

It's the middle of the night by the time we reach the Western Province. Will gets us a room, and Colin and I duck in unseen. Colin and I take one bed, Will the other, and I'm asleep before the words "good night" leave my mouth.

I'm the first to wake in the morning, and take the opportunity to shower. The girl in the mirror with her pale hair, pale eyes, and pale skin is foreign to me. Maybe we can pull this off after all. I do up my makeup the way Jenna taught me, and use the flat iron she gave me to keep my curls at bay. Both boys are still sleeping when I'm finished in the bathroom. I decide to let them sleep, although I yank the drapes open so when the sun comes up in a little over an hour, hopefully they'll wake.

After jotting a quick note letting them know where I'm going, I slip out the door and head downstairs. The hotel staff is preparing the common area for the breakfast buffet. One of the servers glances at my swollen belly, nods and smiles, never looking at my face. Apparently pregnant women are nothing more than a host to the next generation, without faces or identities of their own. For now, this works in my favor. I pour myself a cup of coffee and locate the locked business center with a sign indicating it opens at six.

With nothing better to do, I return to the lobby and relax in one of the comfy chairs next to a potted plant to sip my drink. The low whine of a robovac invades the silence as it works its way around the space. A girl a couple of years older than me approaches and sets a tablet on the table in front of me loaded with the morning news. She turns and uses a giant feather duster on the long shiny green leaves to my left.

I glance up and take in her bright curly red hair that is in contrast to her olive complexion and coal black eyes. The way she's staring at my face sends a shiver down my spine. My gaze rises to meet hers and I know she recognizes me. She places a finger to her lips before dropping her hand and continuing her task, but makes an exaggerated attempt at small talk.

"Have you seen today's headline?" She shoves the tablet closer to me.

I pick it up and stare at the words — "Manhunt on for Evan Taylor." My heart stops and a light sheen of sweat turns into beads that run down my back and chest. The headline is accompanied by a surveillance photo of me taken around six months ago. I scroll past the picture and read the story. They're accusing me of dozens of horrific crimes from killing kids, which I did, to plotting to blow up the Union, which isn't true. There's even a bit about how I planted a bomb on an A-Train. My uncle is listed as a co-conspirator, although he hasn't been seen since the Invasion.

"No one believes it," she whispers as I read.

The article doesn't mention my capture and torture nor my escape. I guess they can't release details of what they did to me, but why not at least report that I escaped from custody? There's got to be more going on, I just have no idea what it is.

When I finish reading, my blood pulses through my veins like slush, making my hands shake violently. I glance back at the girl, taking note of her name tag. "Becca, can you get me into the business center early?"

She nods and inclines her head in that direction. Using her fingerprint, she pops the lock and opens the door for me, turning on the overhead lights. My pulse pounds as I sit at one of the monitors and turn it on. I type up a quick text to Tony. *Sorry I missed our meeting — I was detained. Let me know when you have some time to get together.* Short and cryptic and won't mean anything to anyone but Tony.

While I wait for him to respond, I search for more news stories about me, finding plenty, some going back several weeks. All on a similar theme about how I shot and killed the kids out in the Ruins, and how I'm working with my uncle to keep the existence of the Ruins a secret from the Union. Another story talks about how I'm leading a group of others like me who will do everything to conceal the truth in order to retain our wealth. I don't recognize the names of any of the journalists who wrote these articles, none of the usual writers from before the Invasion. It reads like pure propaganda. If Becca doesn't believe it and says no one else does either, maybe everyone can see through it.

But what if this girl changes her mind and decides I am guilty of something? She can point them in the direction of a blond pregnant girl. By six o'clock, I still haven't heard from Tony and slip back into our room where Colin and Will are starting to stir.

Will rubs his face with his hands. "What time is it?"

"A little after six. Um, I have some news."

Colin bolts up, eyes wide, hair crazy. "What happened?"

"Nothing. Well, not exactly nothing, but... I woke early and went to the lobby for coffee and to check the news. They're setting me up. For what I'm not sure, but it's bad. I sent a text to Tony, but didn't get a response."

"Wait, wait, slow down," Colin says. "Tell me everything from the beginning."

With a sigh, I fall back onto the bed and hand him my cup. He drains the rest of my coffee while I recount my morning.

Colin's slack-jawed when I'm done. "We need to get you out of here. This was a colossally stupid idea."

I drop my head into my hands. "I'm beginning to think I agree with you, but before we go, I want to stop by Western Provincial and see Stevie. She can pass on a message to Tony for us."

"Are you crazy?" Colin's eyebrows shoot up into his messy hairline. "After what you just told us?"

"If what Becca from the lobby said is true, it should be okay. It won't take long. We'll just pop in, talk to Stevie and get the hell out of here."

"And if she's lying?"

I shake my head, a ball of fatigue rolling through me. "Then it's already too late. She'll have alerted the Uprising and someone is on their way here for me now."

Colin narrows his eyes and studies me in that way he does when he's processing my crazy schemes, weighing his options. If we go back now, this whole trip was wasted, but if we can trust the people of the Union, our fellow citizens, and do what we came here for, perhaps we'll get some answers.

His shoulders drop. "Okay."

Once they shower, we head to breakfast at a nearby café where no one pays any attention to us, then make our way to the news site where I worked for all of three weeks last year. Technically I still work for them — on assignment with a pair of undercover detectives.

We park ourselves at a table across the plaza from the office and observe the entry. I turn to Will sitting beside me, a jittery mess of nervous energy. "You go first."

Colin and I scan our surroundings as Will crosses the walkway toward the front doors. He reaches the entrance and disappears behind the darkened glass. Less than ten minutes later, he returns, his smile nearly as wide as one of Marcus's famous grins.

He saunters over to our table and drops down between us. "She's in there. She'll be over as soon as she finds someone to cover the phones." He glances briefly at Colin. "Have you met Stevie?"

Colin laughs and his slow, crooked grin spreads into a full smile. "Oh yeah."

I punch Colin harder than I intended. "Knock it off, you two."

Colin rubs his shoulder, but his smile never falters. We don't wait long before Stevie glides out, but it's not her graceful movements that catch my attention. Her once-platinum blond hair is now redder than mine has ever been, a stunning contrast to her porcelain features. She still wears it long and pulled into a high, elegant ponytail, but she's even more striking somehow. Everyone on the plaza turns to watch her make her way over to us.

Stevie doesn't appear to recognize me at first, but as her gaze flickers from Will to me, her eyes widen and she smiles broadly, sitting down on my other side and placing her hand over mine. "Wow, you look so different."

"So do you."

"Oh, yeah, what do you think?"

"It's striking on you. But...why?"

Her smile shifts to one of nonchalance. "Well, when I read the articles about you, I knew they weren't true. I figured if they're looking for a redhead, let them look. After I did it, some of the other girls in the office did, too. Then my friends joined and soon it just kind of took off. The barista at my local coffee shop, the girl I bought these shoes from…" She twists her ankles to show off her new footwear. "Even the guy at the music store down the street from where I live."

"Wow." The word falls out on a stunned whisper. "Aren't you afraid they'll mistake you for me? Isn't anyone?"

She shakes her head, her ponytail whipping in the air, Will and Colin staring at it mesmerized. "Not really. Other than the hair, I don't look anything like you."

"Um, so, I need to talk to Tony. I sent him a message this morning, but didn't hear back. Usually he's super prompt."

Her gaze drops to the table, the corners of her mouth dropping for the first time. "When you didn't show up here after the Invasion, he figured something happened to you. He went to see your dad and no one's heard from him since." She lifts her head and our eyes lock, concern pooling in her pretty blue eyes.

My stomach twists with dread. Where the hell are they?

35

EARLY RETURN

Cyrus

With Evan and Colin both gone, Mateo added knife training to his physical fitness routines, while Rainey and I continue to work on marksmanship practice. Between that and hunting and fishing with Marcus, I can almost keep my mind occupied during the day. Nights are a different story. The tent is too large without Ev's warm body curled up next to mine, and the ache in my chest isn't eased with sleep, especially since the pillows smell like her.

Vivid dreams of the girl I miss invade my subconscious until I can practically feel her smooth skin against mine. My eyes fly open and I shove the blonde beside me off my sleeping bag.

Her eyes widen in shock as her mouth goes slack.

A lazy grin spreads across my face, and I shake my head. "Sorry. I have a girlfriend. She wouldn't like you being in here while she's gone."

"Oh, really?" She draws the word out, arching one eyebrow.

I laugh and pull her into my arms. "God, I missed you."

She shoves me back hard. "What was that all about?"

"Nothing. I wasn't expecting you to be back yet. Plus, the hair. Wait, what are you doing back so soon? Is everyone okay?"

"Yeah, it's a long story. I'll tell you later. Do girls crawl into your tent while you're sleeping on a regular basis?"

"Only once. I'll tell you about it another time. Right now, I have a dream to get back to." I reach out and tug her closer and this time she doesn't resist. My lips find hers and I kiss her softly, still hazy with sleep, but getting warmer and more alert by the second. This girl will possess me forever, and I'm not even sure I care anymore.

When I wake, Ev is still sleeping soundly. I dress without waking her before slipping out to find Mateo and Rainey. They're sitting around the morning campfire eating something that smells like heaven on a plate.

Over at the cooking area, Lisa is dishing up breakfast.

"Hey, Cyrus," she calls. "Want a crepe?"

"Crape? Like fancy crap?"

She glares at me. "You're spending way too much time with Colin."

That gets a laugh out of me, and I take a tray with something that resembles thin pancakes filled with fruit and topped with syrup. After grabbing a coffee, I head back to the fire to join the other two.

"They're back," I say greeting them.

Mateo's eyebrows notch up as he stuffs another bite of crepe into his mouth, washing it down with coffee. "Evan, Colin, and Will?"

"Yeah," I get out between bites, savoring each morsel. "Last night."

"She say why they're back so soon? Something happen?"

"Just that it was a long story and she'd fill us in later."

I'm finishing the last of my breakfast and thinking about going back for seconds when Evan drops down next to me, eyeing my empty tray.

"I'll be right back." I push up and grab a plate for Ev along with a coffee for her and a refill for me.

When I return to the fire, Evan's talking to Rainey and Mateo, and I only catch the tail end of it.

"It was weird, all those people with red hair, but also hopeful. Like a silent yet very visual protest of what's happening. I'm not entirely comfortable with being the symbol for resistance, but there's nothing I can do about it."

She glances up and gives me a grateful smile when I hand her the plate. Leaning back against the log, she digs into her breakfast.

"How many were there?" I ask.

"A lot. They were everywhere. It was surreal. In my whole life, Quinn is the only other person I've ever seen with hair as red as mine, but there were tons of them."

Mateo mops up the last of his syrup with his remaining piece of pancake, until it drips off. "Who's Stevie, again?"

"She's the receptionist where I used to work with Tony. Oh, I need to tell you about the news stories." She takes a sip of coffee before sharing what she read about herself.

My guts twist with anger and fear. "They're setting you up," I growl.

"I know." She turns and locks eyes with me. "But for what?"

I shake my head, not sure, but there's a reason. What can they hope to gain by blaming Evan? If they wanted to turn the Union population against her, it backfired.

Will joins us, plate in hand, followed by Marcus, Sonia, Colin and Ally. My brain churns out possible scenarios while Evan brings Sonia and Marcus up to speed.

Ev nudges me in the ribs with her elbow. "Are you paying attention?"

"Yeah, sorry."

"No one's seen or heard from Tony since," Colin says.

"Stevie said he was on his way to Eddie's when he disappeared." Evan turns toward me. "What did you see at my dad's?"

I scratch a hand through my hair, trying to remember details from that trip. "We stopped across from Eddie's. I was on my way over when I spotted a couple of soldiers. They went into his apartment like they owned the place. I needed the guns, so I waited until they left, hopped the back wall, and entered the through the sliding door. There was no sign of your dad or the kids."

She's quiet for a long time, her head back, eyes closed. "I need to find them. All of them. My mom, Joe, Katie, Rachel, and my uncle, too. I already put it off too long." She opens her eyes. "I know we're doing something else here, but I *have* to do this."

Sighing, I glance at Rainey and Mateo, who are keeping their thoughts to themselves. "I know." I take her hand and lace our fingers together. "We'll figure it out."

The dwindling fire snaps, sending a lone spark skyward. The evening air is warm and moist, so the campfire was mostly so the kids could roast marshmallows earlier. Evan sits beside me making plans with Lisa and Jack to return to the Union, and there's not a damn thing I can do to stop her from going. The last time I tried to talk her out of something she wanted to do, we ended up in a fight. I hate that I can't go with her because of the policy I instated. If I wasn't determined to lead the search for her mom, I'd resign my leadership position.

Bryce and Rainey are planning the East Coast mission. I haven't told anyone yet that I'm taking Rainey's spot. Since I can't be with Ev, the next best thing is finding the rest of her family and bringing them here.

A conversation on the other side heats up until Colin yells, "Why not?"

Lisa's hands fly out. "Because our team is set. Jack's a detective; if anyone can help track down someone who doesn't want to leave a trail, it's him."

Colin leans roughly back against the log, crossing his arms over his chest. Ally whispers something in his ear, but he shrugs her off.

"Fine, but I'm not taking any shit over my cooking while you're gone."

A ripple of laughter spreads through the group, easing some of the tension. I'm still lost in my own thoughts, trying to figure out how best to break the news about my plans when the others start saying their good nights. Evan pushes up and reaches for me, the perfect opportunity to talk to Bryce and Rainey alone presents itself.

"I'll be there in a bit."

She eyes me for a second before turning and heading toward our tent. I gather my thoughts before interrupting their conversation.

"I'm going with you."

"Like hell you are," Rainey says. "You're the one who came up with the no two leaders policy, and for the record, I agree with it."

"I'm aware of the rule. I'm going and you're not."

"Fuck that, Cyrus. Who died and made you king?"

"She's my girlfriend. They're her family. I need to do this."

"This isn't some sort of pissing contest," Bryce says. "Are you worried if I bring them back she's going to dump you for me?"

My anger flares, but that hits closer to the mark than I care to admit. "No, but I'm responsible for their safety. I'm going."

We stare each other down and asshat blinks first. "Alright, but if Rainey's no longer coming, you're in charge of finding our third."

Rainey swears under her breath and stomps off, but I already know who to ask. I get up to find Colin.

"We're leaving day after tomorrow," Bryce calls after me. "You going to be ready by then?"

"Yeah." We'll have more to talk about before we go, but I can't handle any more of pretty boy tonight.

Ev's hair is splayed across my chest, her head using my arm as a pillow, while I struggle with how to tell her where I'm going and who I'm going with. The third time I open and close my mouth without saying anything, she says, "If you don't tell me whatever it is, your head's going to explode."

I lean forward and kiss her forehead, stalling for time before spitting it out. "I'm going to find your family."

She pushes back, pinning me with an intense stare. "I'm sorry, you're what?"

I prop my head up on my hand. "I'm going back east. With Bryce. And now Colin."

"Why? I mean, why you? I thought it was all set with Rainey and Bryce."

A lot of reasons factored into my decision, but only one is a reason I can tell her. "They're gonna be my family, too, and I feel responsible for ensuring their safety. Next to going with you, it's the most important thing I can do."

She studies me as if she's trying to solve a riddle.

"I told you I'd never leave you again and I meant it. This feels like I'm doing just that. But I also know if we're going into the Union, we're probably both safer if we're not together. I have to trust Jack and Lisa to do as good a job as I would protecting you." I sigh, wondering how bad I'm screwing this up. "I didn't want you to think I was keeping it from you."

"Okay, but why the sudden need to go? What prompted this change after everything was settled?"

I've tried everything else, might as well go for total honesty. "I don't want you feeling like you owe Bryce anything. If I go with him, then it won't be him doing this for you, it's us doing it."

A slow smile breaks across her face like the dawning sun. The kind of smile that says she knows how damn jealous I am. "I love you." She leans forward, planting a gentle kiss in the center of my chest.

I was expecting anger since I basically manipulated the situation and then wasn't completely forthcoming with my reasons. "Just when I think I have you figured out..."

She shakes her head and gazes up at me. "I think that's the first truly honest thing you've ever said about how you feel about Bryce. It means a lot that you shared it with me."

I kiss her briefly then murmur, "I'll find your family and get them here safely. I promise."

"Just make sure you come back safely, too. I can't lose you."

36

PROMISES

Evan

*T*he clanking of dinnerware around us sets my teeth on edge. The door to the café opens, rattling the bells hung above. Jack's head snaps up before dropping back to his tablet, secure that whoever walked in isn't worth his concern.

Lisa returns from the bathroom and drops down next to Jack. "Any luck?"

His focus remains fixed on the screen before him. "So far so good."

We're all aware it's only a matter of time before someone notices an unauthorized tablet on the police network and boots him off again. That just means we'll be moving to a new location and hacking in with a new randomized device ID until we're found again.

"Okay, hang on..." Jack pushes his bangs out of his eyes with his left hand. "Tony got on a commuter the morning he disappeared. The camera picked him up here." He points to a shot of Tony, head down, boarding a southbound train.

"Then what?" I ask.

A window pops up warning us that we're not authorized and subject to prosecution.

"Crap." Jack unplugs his wireless connector and packs up so we can head to another café.

"This is taking forever," Lisa says.

"Police work is a lot more boring than it looks in the movies." After spending time with Jack and Bryce as an embedded reporter last year, I found that out the hard way.

We move south to the next neighborhood and set up again. Jack hacks back in and gets right to it. "Look, here he is leaving the commuter station near Eddie's place. See, he's going up the stairs."

My heart beats faster as I realize we're close to finding out what happened that morning. Lisa groans and I glance down to see we've been kicked off again. The only upside is that they can't trace back who we are. They can only detect the access, but Jack has us so well masked they don't know if we're logging on from the Northeastern Province, or right outside their doors.

"It's been a long day," Lis says. "Can we go back to the hotel?"

Jack rubs her arm. "Sure, babe."

Back in our room, I get cleaned up while Jack and Lisa go get takeout. The hot water soothes the aching muscles in my shoulders after the second day in a row spent hunched over a tablet. After my shower, I pull open the bathroom door and a cloud of steam precedes me. It clears to reveal Lisa pulling Chinese food out of a bag.

She hands me a bowl of something and a pair of chopsticks.

"Thanks." I take my dinner and sit on the bed, cross-legged and dig in to my Mongolian beef while Lisa takes her shower. "What's the plan for tomorrow?" I ask Jack.

He glances over his dinner at me. "More of the same. We try to find out what happened to Tony after he left Eddie's, if he made it that far. On the upside, from what you told me about your interrogation timeline, they probably weren't watching Eddie at that point. If they were focused on you before the Invasion, they would've known exactly which train you were on. Based on your experience, though, it sounds like they didn't know who they had in custody. At least initially."

I nod and take another bite. A piece of rice falls on the blanket and I flick it off. I'm frustrated by how long this process is taking. "What do you know about your dad?"

Jack swallows and wipes his mouth with a napkin. "I texted him yesterday. He's still hiding out. I want to meet up with him while I'm here, if possible. My mom's been evacuated to one of the camps and I guess my sister and her husband are fine, still in their own place."

Lisa pokes her head out of the bathroom and zeroes in on Jack. "Your turn."

He swallows the last of his moo shu pork before sauntering in to take his shower, giving Lisa a quick kiss as they cross paths.

"Have you heard from your family?" I ask Lisa as she takes Jack's spot in the chair and picks up her dinner.

"As far as I know, they're fine, but I have no way to check on them."

"Maybe Colin will find them when he's there. He's going to try to see his family."

She glances up at me, her dark eyes hooded. The events of the past year are etched deep into her face, and I'm just now noticing. I suck as a best friend.

"I'm so sorry, Lis..."

"What for?" Her face screws up in genuine confusion.

"For making this all about me all the time. For relegating you to supporting cast in the Evan Taylor show."

"Oh, Ev." She laughs, shaking her head. "You're crazy, you know that? I don't know how you've been able to think about anyone but yourself lately. Honestly, if I'd gone through what you did, I don't think I'd be holding up nearly as well as you are."

"Lis, come on—"

"I'm serious. What you went through...I'm surprised you find a way outside your own head sometimes. With your uncle being who he is and your dad missing, the wanted posters, it makes sense that you're focused on your family. No one is hunting my loved ones."

"But they're still *your* family," I whisper. "And you love them as much as I love mine."

"I know. And I'll find them. I will, but I almost think they're safer if I leave them alone for now."

"I love you, you know."

"I know."

When Jack's showered and dressed, we set up shop in a new café and watch Jack as he tracks Tony and Eddie out of the Western Province on commuter trains heading south, then east. It looks like Tony found Eddie after all. The trail goes cold once they leave the terminal in the Southwestern Province.

"What were they doing there?" I ask.

"Don't know," Jack says, "but I think we need to go there if we have any hope of finding out."

My head is down, my ballcap pulled down low on my head as we traverse the A-Train station. Cameras are everywhere. I'm surprised Tony and my dad allowed themselves to be recorded so many times, but then I guess they aren't in the habit of being hunted by the Uprising.

The ride is short, and we arrive in the Southwest before lunch, catching a commuter east several boroughs to the last known location of my dad and former boss. As heavy as the Uprising presence was in the Southern and Western Provinces, I don't see any evidence of them here.

"So now what?" Lisa asks as we thread our way out of the busy terminal.

"We look for clues." Jack points to a sign that says SW-B1. "We saw them get off here."

"What kind of clues?"

"Your dad's a rock star. Someone must have seen him in the area. He can't go far without being recognized."

"I'm not sure if that makes me feel better or worse," I mumble. If the Uprising or Walker are looking for him, he'll be easy for them to track down, too.

We enter a nearby café, the early afternoon sun casting hard shadows against the terracotta tiled walkways and heating the air around us. Jack parks at a table and we sit next to him, watching the sidewalk and doors while he logs on.

I glance over his shoulder and watch him swiping rapidly from one screen to the next. "What are you doing?"

"Creating a search grid for any mention of Eddie McIntyre in the Southwestern Province." His brows pull together and his lips pucker.

"What is it?" Lisa asks.

"Someone's looking for Evan."

"That's not necessarily news."

"No, but there's a digital fingerprint all over the grid of searches. Someone is desperately trying to find you. It could be the Uprising or Walker. Although this is a more aggressive means than giant wanted displays." He reaches back and scratches his neck. "This looks more like a targeted search based on your last publicly known location." He lifts his head, his dark blue eyes connecting with mine. "It could be Tony and Eddie."

Lisa walks around the table to study the tablet over Jack's shoulder. "When was the last time they searched for her?"

"A few hours ago."

"Can you tell where the search is coming from?" I ask.

"No. Whoever it is, is as skilled as I am." He glances at me, his half smile indicating how skilled he feels he is.

I return his smile and pat his arm.

"What if we plant some information to draw them out?" Lisa suggests.

I turn to stare at her with genuine awe. "That's a brilliant idea, Lis."

She grins broadly. "I know."

I gnaw on my thumbnail as we stare at the tablet. Jack entered clues into the grid that show me entering the Southwestern Province, but if the Uprising is also searching, they might find me before Eddie and Tony do.

"The way I input the information, it won't be obvious to anyone who didn't enter the original search string," Jack says.

"I don't understand. It says I'm here."

"They left a trail when they searched for you. All I did was nudge breadcrumbs into their path. Trust me, Evan, this is what I do."

"I know you know how to enter clues. I also get you know how to look for them. But how do you know the Uprising isn't looking for me here right now?"

"I don't, but if they happen to stumble upon what I just did, it'll be pure luck, and they may not even realize what they're looking at." He shakes his head. "But I'm almost positive it was Tony searching for you. The work is too meticulous to not be that of an investigative reporter. Much cleaner than a detective. He'll spot the data I inserted and know immediately what it means."

"Okay, well, what if the Uprising hired a journalist or offered detectives freedom in exchange for finding me? We could be walking into a trap."

Jack rubs his fingers along his jaw. "Is that a risk you're willing to take?"

He knows it is, but I nod anyway.

"You won't be going in blind," he reminds me. "The clues lead to an open-air market. If anyone other than Tony or Eddie shows up, we bug out."

"Okay..."

Jack checks the time. "Let's go."

As edgy as I am, I'm relieved the waiting part of this is over.

Jack hands me my ballcap and I smash it down and push my sunglasses up my nose. I decided to forgo the pregnancy pillow for this stage of our mission. We walk to the market and approach the back side. Young and old, displaced upper level residents as well as lower level locals pack the place, looking for deals on necessities or a little something extra to make life feel normal for a short while. Before the Invasion, there would have been a waiting list with vendors lined up to get into a market like this one, but it's only at about seventy-five percent of capacity. The Invasion hasn't been good to the economy on the lower levels, except for the camp-grounds, which have more business than they can handle.

I slide under the table in one of the unused market stalls and lay on my belly, pulling my gun from my waistband. I lift the drape that covers the table and peer out underneath it. We're at the base of the U-shaped market and a bottleneck forms, allowing us to view anyone approaching this end. It also allows us easy escape if it comes to that.

The information Jack planted will lead Eddie and Tony straight here if they got it. Hopefully they've been paying attention, but Jack warned me it could take a few days before they show up. Morning passes into afternoon, and Lisa slips out to get us lunch, returning with sandwiches. We take turns keeping watch and eating. Shadows stretch longer, their edges becoming softer as evening arrives and neither Tony nor Eddie has shown up. Disappointed and emotionally exhausted, we retreat to the hotel for the night.

Yesterday looked a lot like the day before. This morning we retrace our steps, ready for another long day of waiting without results. My arms are beginning to ache from propping up my head when I see Tony walking slowly through the crowd, his eyes sweeping the market, presumably for me. I nudge Lisa and Jack and incline my head toward Tony.

Jack's head swivels. "Where?"

"Over there. The guy with the dark hair and in desperate need of a shave." I point to Tony, who is now blocked by a group of people trying to make their way down to this end.

"We have to make sure he's not being followed."

"I'll go," Lisa volunteers.

"Lisa, no," Jack and I say in unison.

"You can't go, Ev, and no one will suspect me of anything." Before we can stop her, she ducks out and enters the swelling crowd.

Beside me, Jack's grip on his gun tightens, his body taut, ready to act at the first sign of trouble. I hold my breath as Lisa moves around Tony before doubling back to follow him. No one appears to be paying any attention to her or Tony. Tony's body is tensed as he continues to scan the market.

Lisa circles around him again, and when Tony doesn't react, she returns to us. "I think he's alone. I didn't see Eddie anywhere."

My eyes still search the crowd for Eddie. If he's hiding and observing Tony, he would've recognized Lisa. Tony and Lisa barely interacted at Bryce's funeral, so I doubt he'd remember her.

Lisa grabs a napkin from her pocket. "Do you have a pen?" Jack hands one to her. "I'll write him a note and slip it to him. Where should I tell him to meet us?"

Jack glances at Tony, then back to me before scratching the back of his head. "There's a café on level twenty-five at the corner of Ninth and C. Say two hours. That'll give us time to get there, scope it out, and make sure he's not followed."

"I don't think he is," Lisa says.

"Maybe. Maybe not. If they're looking for Evan, they may wait until they see her before making a move."

Lisa scribbles the information before dodging back into the crowd as Tony spins around with a frustrated scowl. Lisa bumps into him intentionally. I can't hear what she says to him, but his body goes rigid. She slips him the napkin and keeps walking. He stares at her as she disappears into the throng, and glances around the market again, stuffing the note into his pocket unread.

Lisa pops in behind us. "Okay, let's go."

I jump, my heart pounding. "Geez, Lis, you scared the crap out of me."

She shrugs and crawls out with me and Jack on her heels.

37

TENSION

Cyrus

𝒰prising soldiers swarm through the neighborhoods with authority. Their presence is heavier here than anywhere else I've been in the Union. Bryce and Colin are both tense, eyes darting around, likely drawing the same conclusions I have.

"This isn't good," I say.

Bryce grunts, the tension between us thicker than ever before. He doesn't appear to want me here any more than I want him. We've been doing our best to keep our distance from one another, with Colin acting as a buffer, but being cooped up on a cargo train together over the past few days hasn't helped.

I take point and we move through the crowd, avoiding soldiers, toward the nearest camp as dusk settles. The first one we come to is less than a mile, but it's another mile until we reach the check-in tent. The camps just keep growing.

"Got anything for a night?" I say to the kid behind the desk.

"I have a couple of small tents," he says, eyeing the three of us.

"One will be sufficient."

"Suit yourself." He shrugs and shows me the location on the map.

After dropping our bags in the tent, we head to dinner. Once again, our meal is eaten in silence, and without a word Bryce gets up and wanders off.

Colin turns to me. "Want a beer?"

"Yeah, thanks."

He returns a few minutes later with two ice cold bottles and inclines his head toward the campfire. We walk over, and I collapse in the sand, propping myself against a log before draining half my bottle. "Damn, that's good."

"Yeah." Colin tears his eyes away from the flames and directs his narrowed gaze at me. "You're sweating animosity and hatred. Knock it off."

My back teeth lock down and I take another swig of beer. "I'm trying really hard not to hate him, but it's not as easy as it sounds."

"I get it." His tone tells me he really does. "I know what it's like when someone else loves the same girl you do. It sucks. But, I also know what it's like to be the one that loses that girl to the other guy. Don't get me wrong, I love Ally, and I'm happier now than I thought possible." He turns back to the fire and takes a sip of his beer. "But back then..." He shrugs. "You won, man. You need to get over it."

I take in a deep breath. "Did you know he asked her if they still had a chance after he got Miranda pregnant? He asked Ev that shit knowing her family situation, the stuff with her dad. What kind of asshole does that?"

Colin raises his eyebrows. "Seriously? You're telling me if Valencia was pregnant, you'd have walked away from Evan?"

"No, but that's different because it wouldn't have been my baby."

Colin pulls his chin down to his chest, clearly not believing me.

"Honest." I put my hands up. "But, let's pretend I slept with her and she *was* pregnant, it wouldn't matter. Evan wouldn't have given me a choice, and I would've known better than to even ask."

"Bullshit."

"I'm not saying I'd be happy, just that it'd be over between us, and there wouldn't be anything I could do about it. Asking her to be in the middle of that would be selfish of me and unfair to her."

Colin takes another sip of beer and is quiet, no doubt the word "bullshit" on repeat inside his head.

"She was on that train because of him."

"No. Sure, she was on her way to see Tony. And, yeah, maybe because of Bryce, but even if he hadn't shown up at her hotel, she still would've been on the train. She still would've been gone by the time you got there."

I run a hand through my hair and finish my beer. He may be right. I've been trying to blame Bryce for what happened to Evan. "Okay, I'll talk to him tomorrow."

"Thanks, man." Colin stands and pats me on the shoulder. "She's my best friend and if I thought you were wrong for her, I wouldn't hesitate to tell you."

I don't need his approval, but Ev might, so instead of cussing him out, I give him a curt nod. After Colin disappears from sight, I turn back and stare at the fire and imagine how things would have turned out if I hadn't listened to Eddie and never left her in the first place.

I'm the first one up in the morning and my stomach draws me to the mess tent before the other two stir. The omelet looks less appealing than Lisa's, but I choose it over the breakfast burrito dripping with grease. Even the coffee smells like it was made last night. The acrid odor hits my nostrils and I reach for tea instead.

The first bite of food is on my fork when Colin drops into the seat across from me, his tray piled high with eggs and a burrito.

"Hey."

I nod in response, not in a mood to talk.

Five minutes later Bryce arrives with a plate of scrambled eggs and takes the spot next to Colin. My throat suddenly narrows and I take a sip of still too-hot tea, burning the roof of my mouth. Might as well get this over with.

Clearing my throat, I glance up at Bryce. "Sorry I punched you in the hotel that morning."

Bryce's eyes widen for a moment, and Colin cuts me a look. Maybe not the apology Colin had in mind, or maybe he was hoping he wouldn't have to witness it.

Bryce studies me across the table with his cool gray eyes. "No, you're not."

He's right, I'm not. Well, maybe sorry I didn't kick the shit out of him when I had the chance.

"I don't know what she sees in you," Bryce says, calmly taking another bite of eggs. "A scruffy illiterate who sticks his dick into anything that moves."

My back teeth grind against each other and I push up, ready to end this. Colin chokes on his coffee and his face is screwed up like he just swallowed dog piss. I blow out a slow breath through pursed lips until I'm sure I won't pound the crap out of douchebag.

"Do you have any idea what she went through while you were banging the brunette?" Bryce asks, his voice rising in volume. "Do you know what they did to her? She let them do it. To protect *you*."

"It's none of your damn business, and I don't give a shit if you believe me or not, but I did *not* 'bang' Valencia. But to answer your question, yes, I know what they did to her. I know a hell of a lot more about it than you do."

"Doubtful. She probably only told you what she wanted you to hear, and even then, she didn't want you to know. Because that's how she is. She didn't want you to feel guilty."

Fuck. I hate him for knowing that about her.

"They used her like a punching bag. Her torso, shit man, they crushed three of her ribs. And her face..." his voice is strained as he trails off, like he can't bear to think about it.

I cut my eyes to Colin. He never told me how bad it was, no

one did. He turns a dark shade of red and he drops his gaze to his food, but no longer eats.

I swear loudly and slam my fork on the table. I may not hit Bryce, but he's not getting off the hook either. "Do you know what she was going through while you were knocking up Miranda? She was a mess. Her injuries might not have been physical, but they were still deep and ugly. She blamed herself for your death. Did you know that?"

His slack-jawed expression tells me this is news to him.

"You could've come back sooner. If you had, she wouldn't have been on that goddamn train."

Bryce swallows hard and opens his mouth to say something, but closes it again, his eyes narrow slits.

"Your burns were healed over by then. You coulda come back a *lot* sooner."

Bryce sighs and drops his head. "You're right. I wasn't going to come back at all. Why would I? She made it clear she chose you."

"Because she loved you, dammit," I say, surprising myself. "You had to know what losing you would do to her."

Bryce turns away and I know I got to him, but I don't feel the satisfaction I thought I would. Instead, unexpected guilt settles in my gut. He shakes his head and sighs. "I only came to make sure she was okay."

There may be a small part I don't want to acknowledge that feels for him. I was in his position when I thought the tables were turned, I know what that's like.

Neither one of us says anything, but some of the tension dissipates as an unspoken agreement grows that we won't be pummeling each other over Evan. We're not friends and never will be, but I suppose we can work together. For now.

Colin lets out an audible sigh, then digs into his breakfast like he hasn't eaten for a month.

After our big blowup the other morning, things are less tense. While I'll never admit it, Colin was right about clearing the air with Bryce. I still can't stand the guy, but at least I can tolerate being around him.

We hike another long day before arriving in the Eastern Province, then turn inland and head to the back wall. Keeping my head down, my ballcap shielding my eyes, we ride up to the top level. Colin leads the way to where Evan lived with her mom. He nods toward an apartment on our left, but doesn't slow as we pass, instead heading to a nearby park where we can scope it out.

The parks here are more heavily vegetated and denser than the ones in the West, making this province feel older and more established. Bryce walks along a path to a clearing and sits on the ground with his back against a tree. He plucks a piece of grass and strips off pieces, tossing them aside. "I doubt they're in there. It looks like it's just Uprising here."

"We need to take another pass by before we give up completely," Colin says.

I run a hand through my hair and glance at Bryce. Investigation is his area of expertise. He'd never survive a week in the Ruins on his own, but this is his world. As much as I hate to, I defer to him.

He leans his head back and closes his eyes. "We should stake out the place to be safe."

We set up surveillance across from the Minellis' inside a neglected greenhouse. Weeds roam freely and rotting fruits and vegetables pepper the ground.

After several hours, there's been no activity. No one walking in or out. Dusk settles over the province, and I'm readjusting my position to get some blood flowing into my limbs when two soldiers exit the front door. They're approached by three others carrying a bag of takeout. They exchange words before the three enter the apartment, and the other two disappear down the sidewalk and around the corner.

"Well, that's interesting," Bryce says.

Colin tears his eyes away from the sidewalks to stare at Bryce. "How so?"

"It's possible the soldiers are holding them inside, but it's unlikely."

I lift an eyebrow. "You got all that from a shift change?"

"Yes and no. There are four family members, so if they're all in there and alive, they would've brought more food. Plus, the relaxed body language suggests they're not concerned with much. If they had high-value targets inside, there'd be more guards and they would've been much more aware of their surroundings when they left."

"If they're in custody, they'll have them in a facility with fewer windows and doors."

Bryce nods. "Right. This is the end of this lead."

"What now?" Colin asks.

"Now, we search the refugee camps, see if they managed to escape," I say.

The afternoon sun beats down on me with overwhelming strength as I trudge up the boardwalk to the next camp. The briny ocean air I used to love is pungent now. A couple of boys race by on their way to the water to cool off. My gaze follows them, wishing I could do the same.

We spent the past two days searching all the camps in the area, but there's no trace of the Minellis. People know who they are because of their relationship to Evan's uncle, the governor of the province, but no one has seen any of them.

I tear my eyes away from the surf and head for the registration desk. Just like the last dozen camps, Bryce asks if the Minellis are here, and again we're told no one with that name is registered. Again, we scour the camp for any sign of them, in case they checked in under a different name. I take the mess tent and Colin and Bryce split up, one heading north, the other south.

"Colin!?"

All three of us turn toward the voice, then Colin is off, stumbling through the loose sand toward a woman, frantically waving her arm. When he reaches her, he throws his arms around her shoulders, bending down to hug her. Bryce and I walk over to join them.

Colin pats the crying woman. "It's okay, Mom. I'm okay. Everything's good."

The woman pulls back and calls out, "Josh, Christian, Zoey, come see who's here."

A dark-haired man and two kids exit the closest tent and run over to Colin. I turn away, feeling like I'm invading a private moment.

"Cyrus, Bryce." Colin grabs my sleeve and yanks me closer. "Mom, Dad, this is Evan's boyfriend, Cyrus, and our friend Bryce. This is my family, Louisa and Josh Jennings, and Christian and Zoey." He ruffles his little sister's hair.

As I shake hands with his parents, I struggle to breathe, my chest squeezing tight. Christian is about the age Bart would be now and Zoey's not much older than Penelope would have been if they'd survived the tornado.

I need some air. "I'll give you guys some time to catch up." Backing away from their reunion, I head down to the water's edge. I've seen plenty of kids that age recently and none has affected me this way. Not sure what's so different about these two, but at least I can breathe again. When my hands stop shaking, I go to the mess tent and grab a coffee, taking it to a table to sit. I stare out at the waves and contemplate our next move. How many camps are we going to search before we give up? If we check all of them, we'll be here for months instead of weeks.

"Hey, you ready to go?"

I glance up from my cup and turn to Bryce. "Yeah. Colin done with his family reunion?"

"He'll need to be. It's getting late."

We find Colin where we left him, still talking with his folks. I catch part of it, carried on the wind. "...haven't seen the Minellis at all. Not here or the last camp we were in."

I incline my head and Colin nods his understanding that we're leaving. "Mom, Dad, I gotta go, but, I want you to come with us."

His dad shakes his head. "We're staying here for now, but if we move, we'll find a way to let you know where we're going."

More hugs and tears follow before we finally leave with Colin. For a minute there, I wasn't sure he was coming with us. The next camp is another bust.

We're just walking back to the boardwalk when someone calls out, "Colin? Colin Jennings?"

The three of us spin and within moments, a woman flings herself in Colin's arms. How many families does he have? The woman is small, much smaller than Colin, and yet she seems to swallow him in her embrace. She's probably mid-forties, though it's hard to tell. Unis age well with their easy lives, good genes, and access to the best medical care on the planet. She pulls back, and it becomes clear that if she's not Lisa's mother, she's at least an aunt.

Her eyes search Colin's face, an unanswered question pouring from them.

"She's fine. She's with Jack and Evan in the West looking for Eddie."

Lisa's mom/aunt bites her lip, and with tears in her eyes, hugs Colin again. Colin turns slightly when she releases him and introduces us. "These are my friends, Bryce and Cyrus."

She reaches out a small hand to shake mine and her handshake is warm and inviting. "I'm Jessica Kendall."

"Nice to meet you."

"We're trying to track down the Minellis," Colin says.

Mrs. Kendall shakes her head. "I haven't seen them since the Invasion, but I saw your family a few weeks ago."

"I ran into them earlier today."

While Colin and Mrs. Kendall visit, Bryce drags me off to the side. "I'm concerned that no one's seen the Minellis. It's like everyone is accounted for *except* them."

I run a hand through his hair and blow out a breath. "Yeah."

"I have an idea. I'm not sure how wise it is, but it's all I've got."

"What's that?"

"As deep as Peter Benton is in all this, he might be our best bet at finding them. He may know something."

"Peter Benton?" The name is familiar.

"The mayor of this borough. The one you got your credentials from."

Yeah, that guy. Probably better than anything I could come up with.

An hour later, we park ourselves outside Benton's place, concealed behind a row of shrubs opposite the walkway. The apartment is brick and stone, with polished wood accents. A trellis scales either side of the front door, ivy curling up and around, stopping below the second-story windows. The air is heavy with jasmine and cut grass.

Several hours pass without a sign of anyone going into or coming out of the mayor's apartment. After another hour passes, Bryce motions us to move in closer and whispers, "We're gonna have to break in."

"Uh...what?" Colin asks.

Bryce presses his lips together and hunches his shoulders. "We need to get inside. There's been no activity, but that doesn't mean there isn't information there that might help us locate the Minellis."

"And if it's not deserted?"

"Then we better be ready to shoot our way out. Benton's in this thing up to his eyeballs, so no way is he displaced."

"I was more worried about, you know, armed soldiers," Colin says.

"We can't rule that out, but I know the layout of the place. We can avoid them. Dating Alivia had a couple advantages. One of them is knowing the secret way in and out, plus several hidden corridors."

"He's right." I place a hand on Colin's shoulder until he looks at me. "We're out of other options. But we wait until nightfall."

Colin rubs his hands together. "I could stand to eat. As long as we're waiting and all."

We start toward the walkway when Bryce freezes. My eyes scan our surroundings for whatever spooked Bryce, my hand instinctively reaching for my gun. A stunning girl with long dark hair approaches us from the south. She spots us and her eyes widen for a moment. She crosses thin arms over a non-existent chest and focuses on Colin.

"Colleen. Where is the rest of your lame girl band?"

Colin's shoulder's pull back and he stiffens. "Delightful to see you, too, Alivia."

The pieces begin to fall into place. The mayor's daughter. The girl who beat up Evan in a bathroom.

"I'm sure it's the highlight of your loser day." Her attention shifts to Bryce. "I haven't seen you in months. Where have you been?" Her gaze makes its way to me. "And who is this tall drink of water?"

"Never mind him," Bryce says.

Alivia steps forward and places a hand on his chest. "Do you want to come in?" My eyes are drawn to a ring on her finger. An antique that is far too unusual to be anything other than the one I used to pay her father for my Uni credentials.

"We need to talk to your father. I'm looking for the Minelli family."

Her eyes narrow and she shifts away from him. "What do you want with them?" Her mouth screws up, like she sucked on a lemon. "The whole Union is looking for her. You're not going to find her. She's probably dead anyway."

My hands curl into fists at my sides. I don't realize I've moved toward her until Bryce grabs my arm.

"Cut the crap, Alivia. I'm interested in her family. Do you know where they are?"

"No."

Bryce levels her with a gaze. "I think you do."

She stares at him with cold, hate-filled eyes. "I can't believe I ever loved you." She turns and studies me for a few moments, her finger resting on her chin. "You, on the other hand, could be a lot of fun." She glances at Bryce.

"Where's your dad, Alivia? We need to talk to him." Bryce wraps his fingers around her wrist, pulling her to him.

She cocks her free hand and slaps him hard, his face rocking to the side.

Bryce glares at her then jerks her forward, Colin and I following as Bryce heads down the back of the apartment, before stopping suddenly. With a quick glance around, he reaches out and presses a loose brick and a small door opens.

38

CATCHING UP

Evan

*T*he alley across from the café where we're supposed to meet Tony is deserted, allowing me to pace in peace. Trash cans are evenly spaced beside the back door of whichever establishment they belong to. My shoes scuff on the pavement, swept clean earlier today by an automated sweeper. One hundred steps, pivot, one hundred steps back.

Lisa is three blocks east and Jack is a couple blocks west, waiting to tail Tony as soon as he shows up in the vicinity. On my third lap, I spot Jack heading this way. He gives me a brief nod, signaling he's seen Tony and the coast is clear. That's my sign to head back to the hotel.

Back in the room I pass the time by alternating between looking out the window and through the little peephole in the door. A half hour goes by before the door clicks behind me. I spin around and freeze, tears pooling in my eyes before I launch myself across the room and into my dad's arms.

He clutches me to his chest so tightly I struggle to fill my lungs. Neither of us says anything, we just hold each other. When he finally loosens his grip, he says, "You're so thin." He leans back and pulls a lock of hair out to the side, letting it fall back. "And blond."

I laugh and pull back to study him. He's thinner than I remember, too. "You should have seen me before."

Eddie releases me and Tony stands awkwardly until I walk up and wrap my arms around him. He folds me into a monster hug. "We've been looking for you," he says.

"Thank you. Jack figured that out." I climb on the bed and lean against the wall. With the adrenaline flooding out of me, I'm suddenly exhausted.

"I got your text," Tony says, "but when you didn't show, I called Eddie. He told me he'd also heard from you, but you hadn't arrived at his place either. It didn't take us long to figure out what'd happened."

I look down at my hands resting in my lap. "I have a lot to tell you." Then we spend the next few of hours bringing them up to speed on everything we've been up to since the Invasion.

Eddie cried harder than I expected when I told him what the Uprising did to me. In some ways, it was worse than telling Cyrus. After we finished our story, Jack, Lisa, and Tony went out to pick up dinner, leaving me and Eddie in the hotel room. Neither one of us has spoken since the others left.

Eddie stands near the door studying the floor.

"Please say something, Eddie."

He shakes his head. "I don't know what to say." His voice is choked with emotion. "I...I should never have sent you to your mother's."

"This isn't your fault."

"How can it not be? I sent you away because I didn't know what else to do for you."

"Nothing you did or didn't do is responsible for the Invasion.

I've spent a lot of time blaming myself for a lot of what happened, but there's no one to blame except Walker."

He turns and stares out the window, bracing his hands on the sill. "I'm sorry I didn't warn you about Bryce. He begged me to let him surprise you. At the time, I thought it was a sweet gesture, but when Cyrus showed up the next day..."

"Oh yeah, about that..." I shove my hands into my back pockets. "Things got kind of ugly after that...but it's *not* your fault. It's mostly Bryce's fault." I give him a very brief summary of what went down with me, Bryce, and Cyrus. "In the end, it all worked out." I take a deep breath to prepare myself. "I...I have something to tell you. Cyrus asked me to marry him, and I said yes."

Eddie shakes his head and opens his mouth to say something, but stops himself.

"I'm not you or Mom and I'm not making a mistake. I know what I'm getting into." I meet his gaze. "We want to be together and we don't want to wait until we're older, because we may never be older."

Deep lines etch his face, but he doesn't respond. I want his approval or his blessing, but I don't need it. Before either of us can say more, the door opens.

I cut him a look and mouth, "No one else knows," before Lisa, Jack, and Tony enter the room with lunch.

Eddie nods his understanding, but this conversation is only delayed, not over.

Over sandwiches, we talk about what to do next.

"I want you to come with us to the Ruins," I tell Eddie. "You're a target here as long as you're my dad."

His expression is grave. "I can't leave without Liam and Quinn, and I'm not sure how to find them."

"What happened to them?"

"I left them with Ashlynn when I went looking for you."

"Where's Ashlynn?"

"I don't know." He lets out a deep sigh, both of his hands gripping his hair before he slumps against the door. "I've called her dozens of times, but there's never an answer."

"She's probably been displaced," I say. "It's not safe to go back to your place, either. Cyrus was there and said soldiers are living there now."

The color of his face builds to a dark red and his jaw ticks. I only lived there for a few short months, and it was never really my home, but the thought of them sleeping in my bed, the kids' beds, touching our stuff, makes me ill. It's such a violation.

"I can help you track her down," Jack offers.

"We can use the news site's resources as well," Tony says.

"Will Ashlynn even let you take the kids if you find her?" I ask.

Eddie shakes his head, looking defeated.

"Well, they can't stay here. Quinn looks like a mini version of me. I'll be the first to admit, living in the Ruins is no picnic. The beach camps where the refugees are going are like five-star resorts by comparison, but staying here, being related to me, that's not really an option."

Eddie's head drops. I push off the bed and walk over to him, wrapping my arms around his waist and rest my head on his shoulder. "It's going to be okay, Dad."

He sighs but doesn't say anything. It's like the weight of it all is pressing down on him so firmly he can't get a breath. When he speaks, his voice is as tired as the rest of him looks. "I need to get Talia out of here, too."

"Where is she?"

"Home last time I talked to her. We have to get Ashlynn and the kids first. She'll never come if Talia's with us."

It takes all my self-control not to roll my eyes. I hoped a lot of this stuff I'm dealing with goes away with maturity, but I guess not. My former stepmother is no more interested in spending time with her ex and his new girlfriend than I was with Cyrus and Valencia. It helps me understand her a little. She may not be the most pleasant person on Earth, but she's still human and capable of being hurt. Maybe I can try to cut her some slack.

Jack and Tony get to work, heads bent over a tablet, carrying on a quiet conversation, while Lisa and I watch Eddie pace the hotel room. As the day wears on, it becomes apparent that locating Ashlynn won't be easy. Recordkeeping went out the window weeks ago. The beaches are so overrun with families kicked out of their homes by the Uprising, they can't keep track of who's there and who isn't.

"I doubt Ashlynn would've gotten very far with two small kids," I say.

"We're starting with the ones closest to her apartment for that reason," Jack says without lifting his head. "Because their names aren't showing up anywhere, it's likely they were booted recently rather than early on when guest registries were being used religiously."

"So, what can you do?"

He shrugs. "There's not a lot to go on, but we're looking for anything that might give us a clue." He turns to Eddie and pushes his bangs out of the way with his hand. "Is there anything special Ashlynn or the kids would need that could help us? Medication or dietary needs? We can track supplies going into the camp."

"No." Eddie slams his palm against the wall. "This is getting us nowhere. We're wasting time when we could be searching the beach."

Tony stands and walks over Eddie. They carry on a hushed conversation before Eddie leans back, closing his eyes. Tony resumes his spot at the desk beside Jack and pulls the tablet closer to him.

"Why *can't* we just search the camps?" Lisa asks.

"It's a needle-in-a-haystack approach." Tony presses his lips together and stares at Jack.

"Maybe it's worth a shot." Jack stretches, rolling his shoulders.

Lisa goes over to him, gently rubbing the tight muscles in his neck with her thumb and forefinger. "We go look for them, then?"

"Yeah, I think it's time."

"I think I found something." Tony sits back, a small smile

tugging at the corner of his mouth. "There's a significant Uprising presence around one campground. It's not far from Ashlynn's place."

Jack lifts the tablet and studies it. "The sheer number of soldiers around this one is so much greater than anywhere else, it can only mean one thing."

Tony nods. "They're watching the camp."

"Because they have a high-profile camper?" I ask.

"No." Jack scratches the back of his head. "If it was someone, like an official, they would've taken them into custody. They don't have the manpower to guard a beach camp full of prisoners. They're too porous."

Tony shifts in his seat, his dark eyes penetrating mine. "More likely, they're watching for someone."

"Me." I slump onto the bed. "So, what do we do now?"

Jack lets out a long sigh and tosses the tablet on the chair. "We need to see what we're up against. Let's scope it out."

We trudge along the beach at dusk, doing our best to fit in with the homeless drifters who've become a staple in the Union since the Invasion. Soldiers surround the perimeter, just as Tony said. It's an unwelcome sight and a definite departure from every other camp we've seen.

We're able to easily walk past, but it won't be so easy getting in. Or back out again. We continue for at least a half mile without seeing a soldier before Jack stops at a bonfire so we can talk. The evenings are far cooler here in the Western Province than they are in the South, and the cold, moist air chills me to the bone.

A group of displaced Unionites stand around the fire, hands outstretched, trying to warm their fingers. They appear as if they've been homeless for months. Three men with heavy beards are drowning in torn and stained clothes, their arms and legs like sticks popping out of tents. Two young women and one child huddle nearby, eyes wide with hopelessness. This is not the Union I grew up in where no one went without their basic needs. The drifters watch us approach with wary eyes, but when we do nothing to threaten them, they ignore us.

We sit in the sand on the opposite side, drawing close to talk without having to raise our voices above a murmur.

"How are we going to get in there?" Lisa asks.

Tony's eyes drift across the fire pit, the wheels turning in his brilliant mind. He glances at me, a twinkle in his eye, and I know what he's thinking before he even opens his mouth. I smile slowly at first but then I'm grinning as I realize how incredibly ingenious his idea is. Without a word, Tony pushes up and approaches the group on the other side.

Lisa turns toward me, her eyebrows raised in silent question.

"We're about to become destitute."

"What?" Her adorable face screws up as she tries to figure out what's going on, but her features relax one by one as she puts it all together.

Tony makes his way back over to us and nods. "Give me your clothes."

Even though I knew this was coming, I'm totally unprepared to strip in front of my dad and friends. Turning my back, I peel off my shirt and jeans, handing them to Tony. I make the mistake of twisting just enough to catch a glimpse of my dad in his boxers before whipping my head around. That's not something I can ever unsee. A few minutes later, Tony returns with a pair of pants and a long-sleeve T-shirt for me that are so ripe, my lips curl back. The fact that I need to wear them makes bile rise in the back of my throat, but I shift to breathing through my mouth and pull them on.

When I'm done, I turn around and notice Tony rubbing sand on his face and into his hair. The rest of us follow suit. My new pants fit my waist fine, and I stuff my gun into the back of the waistband, but I have to roll up the cuffs so I don't trip.

"Are you two armed?" Jack asks my dad and Tony.

"No," Tony answers for both of them.

I also have my knife, which I'm much more comfortable using anyway, so I hand my gun to Eddie. "Do you know how to fire this?"

"Yeah."

That response makes me feel better, because I know he's prepared, and worse, because I live in a world where my dad needs to use a gun.

We walk back in the direction of camp, but when we reach the perimeter, the Uprising presence is heavier than earlier. Soldiers glance our way as we pass, but quickly lose interest. A group of filthy drifters with smelly, torn clothes and sand in their hair are not who they're looking for. We stumble past them and head toward the mess tent, which is the first place any homeless would go. Doing my best to keep my head down, my eyes sweep the area for any sign of Ashlynn or my siblings.

After grabbing food, Lisa and I take seats at a table and shove it into our mouths as if we haven't eaten in days while Eddie, Tony, and Jack search the camp. Bent forward, my hair covers most of my face, and I peer between the dirty strands that are beginning to curl again, on alert for anything.

"Maybe it would be better to leave them here," Lisa whispers.

"I thought of that." I stuff a muffin into my mouth, chew, and swallow. "But after what the Uprising did to me, I can't take a chance they wouldn't hurt them to get to me. If the added security is because they're hoping to catch me, then they know exactly who Liam and Quinn are."

"If so, why did they let us just waltz in here. Wouldn't they be paying extra attention to all new arrivals?"

"I don't know. They must have a profile, and we don't fit it. If I had to guess, I'd say they're watching Ashlynn and the kids, keeping an eye on everyone who interacts with them."

Tony, Eddie, and Jack join us, setting trays of food down in front of them. Jack turns to me. "We found their tent. It's the only one with posted guards. Getting in or getting them out is going to be tough. We need a solid plan."

After they finish eating as if it was their last meal, we shuffle out of camp and head back to our hotel room.

Eddie closes the door and leans back against it, his hands covering his face. "We have to get them out of there."

Jack sits on the edge of the bed, his elbows resting on his knees. "It's not going to be easy, and there will be no going back, but I think it's doable."

"How?"

"I don't have it all figured out yet, but I have something that might work."

We spend the next couple of hours discussing Jack's skeleton idea, filling in details, coming up with alternatives, and putting on the finishing touches. By the time the Union lights go out, we have a fairly decent plan.

39

ASSIGNMENT

Cyrus

*W*e exit a hidden stairway into a dim hallway. "Are there any soldiers in here?" Bryce asks Alivia. When she doesn't answer, he grips her arm and asks again.

She shakes her head, lip trembling.

Bryce guides us down the hall past a lavish entryway where an impressive light fixture with dangling crystals hangs from the second-story ceiling, nearly filling the oversized space. Dark wood furniture perches atop polished marble floors that amplify our footsteps. We enter an enormous kitchen with metal counters and shelving and a stove that takes up close to half of one wall. It smells of cleaning solution with a hint of fresh-baked bread.

Bryce escorts Alivia to a small table that sits beside the door and pushes her into one of the chairs. "Where's your father?"

A tear slips out the corner of her eye and the trembling lip becomes full on blubbering. She points upstairs in response.

Bryce turns to me. "Watch her." Then he pivots and moves to the stairs.

Alivia trains big blue eyes on me, tears pooled above her lashes. "Please don't let him hurt me."

I lean back against the wall and stare at her until she drops her head. Bryce returns a few minutes later with a man I can only assume is Alivia's father. He's tall and slightly built with dark hair and eyes the same color as his daughter's. He walks with a purpose, like a wolf, but lacks the confidence of the pack leader. Bryce directs him into the chair next to his daughter, gun pointed at his head.

"We invited you into our home," Benton spits at Bryce. "We treated you like family."

Bryce licks his lips. "Your daughter was an assignment. Nothing more."

"What are you talking about?" Alivia whispers.

Bryce takes his eyes off Benton for a moment and glances at Alivia, but when Benton shifts, Bryce pulls the slide back on his gun and steps closer to him. "I'm an undercover detective and I was assigned to investigate your father. My superiors thought it would be easier to get to him through you."

"That's not true." Her face is defiant, as if she knows she's far too pretty to have been just an assignment.

Bryce shrugs. "Believe what you want, it makes no difference to me." He leans back to Benton. "I'm only going to ask you one more time. Where are the Minellis?"

Benton sets his jaw and narrows his eyes. Bryce presses the gun against his temple and his trigger finger twitches. Alivia lets out an ear-piercing scream. He shifts his gaze to Alivia and studies her for a few beats, his face a mask of indifference. In a flash, he grabs Alivia and shoves her face-first against the wall. Pressing the barrel of the gun to the back of her head, he glares at her father. Benton's eyes are splayed open, dripping horror. His mouth gapes like a fish struggling to breathe out of water.

Alivia sobs, her knees buckling. "Bryce, why are you doing this? All I ever did was love you."

Bryce pushes his face closer to Benton's. "Where?"

"Why do you want to know? What are they to you?"

"That doesn't concern you."

Benton swallows hard. He must have figured out Bryce isn't above shooting his daughter. "Fine." His voice is low, his shoulders slumped. He drops his head like a defeated animal. "Fine. I'll tell you."

***

Colin grabs Alivia by the arm and leads her toward the door. "I'll text you both when we're set," he calls out over his shoulder.

"I love you, Daddy," Alivia yells as Colin drags her from view.

Tied to the kitchen chair, Benton struggles until Bryce places the barrel of his gun against the guy's forehead and presses hard. "Sit still and this will all be over soon."

Benton slumps back and I fight the bile rising in the back of my throat. I don't trust either of them, so why is guilt gnawing through my guts? They're both self-centered and spoiled, but I guess even selfish people can love someone. It might be their only redeeming quality.

Bryce and I take turns guarding Benton and changing into the Uprising fatigues we picked up along the way. Geared up, we go over our plans with Benton one last time, explaining in detail everything we expect from him and what will happen if he doesn't cooperate.

It's more than an hour before Colin texts that he and Alivia are safely stowed somewhere. Even Bryce and I don't know where he's taken her in case things go south.

"Time to go," Bryce announces and unties our prisoner while I train my gun on him.

"I promised to get you in," Benton says, "but you'll have to sell them on the reason you're there. It's against protocol, but not unprecedented. This group is...undisciplined."

"Yeah, well they are from the Ruins. We're nothing but a bunch of feral heathens," I say.

Bryce snorts.

We ride south until we arrive at the southern boundary of the borough. Benton's eyes dart around, as if he's looking for something or someone. The hair on the back of my neck stands on end and I shove him back into his seat.

"Hey, this is it," he says.

Bryce's face is a mask of confusion as I push Benton down into the seat.

"What aren't you telling us?" My face is inches from his.

He swallows, but stares defiantly back.

Bryce pulls out his tablet and begins typing something.

"Nothing. It's just…"

"It's just what?" I growl. He might be doing this to protect his daughter, but I have no doubt he also has a strong self-preservation mode.

We start moving again and Benton glances out the window as buildings begin to move by faster until they become a blur. I shove his shoulder back. "It's just what?" I force myself to keep my voice low but calm.

He lifts his head, his gaze finally meeting mine. "It's just… people who enter the warehouse need the proper credentials."

My blood boils in my veins and it takes all my self-control not to deck this asshole right now. "You son of a bitch. Bryce…"

Bryce types something else as beads of sweat build on Benton's forehead. A smile spreads across Bryce's face before he shows his tablet to Benton. A photo of Alivia's terrified face fills the screen. Tears well up in Benton's eyes and he blinks them back.

"Oh, and you should know that Alivia no longer has her phone, tablet, or watch," Bryce says. "You have no way to track her location."

Benton's face becomes dark. "You people are sick."

"*We're* sick? Do you know what your people did to my friend? They burned dozens of holes into her back, beat her until she was a head-to-toe bruise, crushed ribs, ruptured organs. Trust me, you're getting off easy. For now." Bryce's voice drops enough that it even chills me. Every word he said is true, and the way his voice cracks tells me how deeply it affected him to see her that way.

Benton swallows hard. "Take me back to my place, and I'll get them for you."

"That had better be the only thing you've kept from us," I say.

We get off at the next stop and take the commuter train north, retracing our steps to Benton's apartment. He leads us into his office and sits at a monitor.

Bryce pushes him aside. "Tell me what to do."

Benton instructs Bryce on how to generate the credentials. When he's finished, we clip them on our waistbands.

I turn to face Benton. "You fuck with us again, and your daughter will pay the price."

The color drains from his face and he nods his understanding.

When we arrive at the same stop from earlier, Benton's face is downcast. Whatever he was planning before is irrelevant now that he has no way of finding his daughter without us.

We walk down a narrow hall, half the yellow overhead lights burned out, then down several flights of stairs, our boots beating a rhythm against the steel steps. Benton points the way to a metal door on the right. He knocks and Bryce stiffens. The door cracks and a green eye topped by a dark bushy brow peeks out. Benton flashes his credentials and the door opens only wide enough for the three of us to file in before it closes with a thunk of finality.

My eyes sweep the room for Evan's family, but only find soldiers.

One of them, barely more than a kid, walks up to Benton. "What are you doing here?" His dark eyes dart toward Bryce, then me.

"We have orders to move the Minellis. This place has been compromised."

A sudden string of clicks, as at least a dozen guns are cocked and readied for use, sends a chill straight to my gut. I steel myself and turn to find us surrounded, muzzles pointed at us, fingers on triggers.

40

ASHLYNN

Evan

*L*isa and I stand on the outskirts of camp, our backs to the water, watching Tony, Jack, and Eddie sneak in under a half-moonlit sky. The surf behind us roars and the wind whips the strands of hair inside my hood. I palm my knife in my jacket pocket and check the time again. It's nearing one thirty. We're betting an awful lot on the soldiers being bored after weeks of nothing happening.

I peer into the darkness, searching for any signs of movement, but the campground is peacefully asleep. Ten minutes pass with no sign of anyone, not even a soldier. When another five minutes go by, my pulse quickens further, and my palms begin to sweat. I wipe my hands on my grungy pants and grip the knife handle tighter.

Loud pops from inside the camp send my heart tumbling into my stomach. Lisa and I turn toward each other, and without another thought, I propel myself toward the sound of gunfire, Lisa on my heels. The hard-packed sand gives way to the soft, loose stuff and my shoes sink down, slowing my momentum. My thumb hovers over the button, ready to release the blade.

Lisa stops behind a tent, peering around it.

"I'm going to go get Ashlynn," I say. "You find the guys."

She nods and slinks off, appearing far more confident than I feel. Crouching, I make my way through camp, my head rotating in every direction. Soldiers were everywhere earlier, particularly around Ashlynn's tent, but now they're gone. They must have taken off when the shooting started. This might be the only break I'll get. I round the corner and pull up short. A lone soldier stands beside the opening, her back to me. I take a few steps back and duck around the side.

With a guard posted out front, my only option is to go under. I crawl beneath the bottom edge and sit long enough to allow my eyes to adjust to the darkness. Either Ashlynn shares this tent with another family or I'm in the wrong one, because a man is sleeping on a cot to my right, snoring, a woman in his arms. On my left are two more cots, and I sigh with relief to find my estranged step-mother in one and Liam and Quinn in the other. Their little faces are slack and they look so peaceful, so unaffected by the Invasion. Quinn's curls are a jacked up mess and Liam's are cut super short. His pale lashes rest on his cheeks as he breathes in and out through his mouth.

I crouch beside Ashlynn and place my hand on her shoulder. She rolls over, but doesn't wake at first. I shake her with a light motion, and she bolts up. Putting my finger to my lips, I glance at the other cot. Neither the man nor the woman have moved. Ashlynn stares at me, but I'm not sure she actually sees me. Her eyes are wild, unblinking, but after a moment, recognition dawns on her sleepy face.

She opens her mouth to say something, but I shake my head, then bend down and whisper in her ear. "I'm getting you out of here. Eddie is with me."

Her straight blond hair is piled on her head in a messy bun, pieces of escaped hair framing her face. "Why are you here?" she whispers harshly.

The man stirs, but rolls over so his back is to us. "To get you out. It's dangerous for you to be here."

"You being here is what's dangerous, Evan."

"Ashlynn, your tent is surrounded by soldiers because they want me. You and the kids are a means to an end."

She gives her head a sharp shake and I know I'm going to have to show her. Let her see what they did to me. I slowly turn so my back is to her, and lift my jacket and shirt. She takes in a sudden breath.

"They did this to me. To get information from me. They'll do the same to you. Or Liam and Quinn."

Ashlynn sits up as a creaking comes from the cot on my right. The man rubs his eyes and squints through the darkness. My heart pounds as I try to figure out what to do now. If he yells, we're all dead.

Keeping my face down, I mumble, "I'm hungry. I was just looking for something to eat."

He nods, rolls over, and wraps an arm around the woman next to him, his body relaxing, unconcerned with a vagrant in search of food.

I turn back to Ashlynn. "Please."

She tears her eyes from mine and glances at the cot where her two offspring are sleeping soundly.

"I know what they're capable of." I drag out each word out to make sure she fully understands. "It's a long story, but I know because I trained with them."

Her eyes widen and her mouth drops open for a few seconds. She glances over at the kids again, then nods at me, throwing off her blanket and sitting up. Ashlynn grabs Liam and I reach for Quinn, whispering to stay quiet. We ease across the tent on silent footsteps to the front flaps. I peek out, hoping the girl I saw earlier is gone, but she's been joined by a second solider. Ashlynn turns to me, fear zipping across her features. My mind whirs with potential solutions, but we only have one option — we leave the way I came in. I take a step back and glance around, my eyes landing on the sleeping couple. Motioning the others forward, I move to the back of the tent and lift it, peering out. No one is in sight.

I indicate to Ashlynn that we're going under and she nods. Dropping to my belly, I slide out first and wait for Ashlynn to send the kids. Liam wiggles out next, followed by Quinn, and finally Ashlynn.

After assessing our surroundings, I take two small hands and start moving toward the water. Without knowing the fate of Eddie, Tony, and Jack, or where Lisa is, my only focus can be on getting these three to safety.

As we step away, a boot comes around the corner. Ashlynn sucks in air and I'm afraid she's going to scream, but instead she claps her hand over her mouth and reaches for Liam, lifting him and holding him against her chest.

I grip Quinn's hand tighter in my left hand and flick open my knife blade with my right. In one fluid motion, I fling my hand out, sending the dagger sailing through the air before embedding itself into the side of the soldier's neck. His eyes widen and he drops his weapon as his hands fly up to the gushing wound before he drops to his knees. I hit an artery, precisely where I aimed.

Quinn stares, mouth wide in horror. I pull her to me to pick her up, but she pushes me away and runs to her mother. Ashlynn glances from the soldier to me and back again, her body trembling. I move to her side where Quinn is whimpering in her arms, Liam now standing beside her. I try to take Quinn again, but she won't even look at me.

"We need to get out of here," I whisper. "Now."

Ashlynn swallows hard and takes Liam's hand in her free one while Quinn burrows into her shoulder, hiccupping.

I jog to the soldier and retrieve my knife from his neck, wiping the blood on his uniform. Then I grab his gun and slip past Ashlynn to take the lead. We reach the edge of the tent, and I peer around, making sure it's clear before motioning for her to follow.

The shadows soon swallow us as we move through the sand on our way to the boardwalk.

The continued lack of presence by any soldiers other than the one lying dead in the sand unnerves me. It doesn't bode well for Eddie and my friends. When we get to the sidewalk, I pause and turn to Ashlynn. "I have to go back for the others." I press my room card into her hand. "We're staying at the Western Palms on level sixty-three, at the corner of Third and F. Room 712. Can you remember that?" She nods, but the terror pooling in her eyes makes me doubt it. "Repeat it back to me."

"Uhh...room 712, Western Palms, level 63." Her voice shakes so much, I need to strain to hear.

"Corner of Third and F. Go there. Stay. I'll join you as soon as I can. Ashlynn, this is important, okay? Don't stop until you get there."

Quinn sobs into her mother's shoulder and I reach out to touch her before thinking better of it. Instead, I pivot and head back, refusing to let myself think about what Quinn saw me do or what it means. I move into camp, avoiding moonlit patches. My knife is back in my waistband, but the Uprising rifle is in my hands, cocked and ready to fire. I can't pass for anything other than what I am right now — a traitor to the Uprising and a threat to every soldier here. If I'm spotted, they'll shoot me on sight.

My heart beats in my throat, making it difficult to breathe as I inch my way around the next tent. I glance to my right and see the dark pool of blood in the sand next to the body of the soldier I killed. I push back the guilt, reminding myself I had to do it. For Liam and Quinn.

Inching forward, I search for any evidence of Eddie and my friends. As I approach the water, the roar of the surf gets louder, and just above that, I can detect voices. With my back to the tent, I strain to hear what they're saying. I recognize Tony's raspy baritone, but can't make out his words. Another voice answers back, a voice I don't know, but the tone is angry and frantic. A bad combination.

I close my eyes and force myself to come up with a plan. Something flutters against my arm, and I spin toward the movement, my finger trembling on the trigger. Swallowing a scream, I fight for my breath, forcing my lungs to restart. "Lis!" I whisper shout. "I almost shot you!"

Her eyes are huge as she stares down the barrel of the gun, still pointed at her.

I quickly lower it to my side. "What's going on?"

Not taking her eyes off the rifle, she says, "They have Jack, Eddie, and Tony. I don't know how, but they've got them surrounded. It's not good. Where did you get that?"

"From a solider. I sent Ashlynn and the kids to the hotel. We have to figure out how to get the others out of here."

Lisa lifts her eyes to meet mine and the fear radiating from them echoes my own. "So, what now?"

I shake my head. "The only thing we might have going for us is the element of surprise if the soldiers don't know we're here." I blow air into my cheeks trying to come up with a plan, but there isn't much to work with. "We need a distraction. Can you do something?"

"Like what?"

"I don't know. Something to occupy their attention for just a second or two. You still have your knife, right?"

She nods, her body trembling now.

She has less experience than I do with this kind of action. I put my arms around her and squeeze. "You can do this, Lis. You trained for it. Just find a way to distract them. Be a stumbling drunk, cry out in pain, anything. If they're distracted long enough, I can take out two of them. That might give Tony, Eddie, and Jack a chance to take care of a few more. Maybe that'll be enough."

"What are you going to do?"

"You don't want to know." Hell, I don't want to know either, but I do.

Lisa nods and takes a step back, squaring her shoulders. Slowly, like gelatin solidifying, she gains control of herself. I give her arm a quick squeeze before she moves away from me. I get into position and scope out the situation. There are about a dozen soldiers surrounding my dad, Jack, and Tony. The three of them are kneeling, hands behind their heads. One soldier is taunting Eddie, a shiner forming around his left eye.

"What's the matter old man? Can't take a punch? Too many days of hard partying?"

My blood boils as I watch them goad my dad. The knife handle digs into my palm as I hold it with a white-knuckled grip.

Lisa begins to stumble as she approaches the group. Bent over and holding her stomach, she cries, "ohhhh," as she zigzags her way across the beach. All heads turn toward her, Jack's eyes widening in horror.

With only seconds on my side, I flick my wrist, sending the blade on a sure course. I know it will reach its target so I don't waste time watching it impale the nearest soldier. The moment the knife leaves my hand, I pull up the rifle, aim, and fire at a second soldier.

The crack of gunfire takes their attention off Lisa, but not before Jack lunges at the soldier closest to him, his fist connecting with the man's jaw. The attack was unexpected, giving Jack the upper hand, but they still wrestle for the gun. Before I can fire again, Tony moves in front of my target. Fists fly and grunts pepper the night air. Two blasts come in rapid succession, but I can't tell who fired or if anyone was hit.

Rooted to my spot in the shadows, I keep the scope on the group, biding my time until I can safely fire. When the sea of bodies parts, Tony is holding my knife to the throat of a soldier, his hand on her shoulder, shoving her to her knees.

Lisa shoulders two rifles, each one aimed at a soldier. Man, I wish I'd seen her disarm them. That leaves just two armed guards who begin firing.

I drop to the ground as a bullet rips through the sand to my left. With fewer targets now, I aim at one of them as she lines up a shot on Lisa. Taking in a deep breath, I hold it and fire, dropping the soldier, a dark stain spreading across her chest. Jack is still wrestling with one, attempting to get his gun. A vision of Lucien fighting with Walker's henchman, Hopp, over the gun that killed him makes bile rise up. I swallow it down and it burns the back of my throat.

Jack lands a solid gut punch, doubling the guy over, then reaches for the soldier's rifle. The guy only holds it tighter though. For a split-second, I have a shot — a non-lethal one — and I take it, hitting him in the arm. He drops the weapon and Jack snags it, spinning around and freezing. I follow his line of sight and my pounding heart stalls along with my ability to think.

The last soldier standing is pressing the muzzle of a handgun against Eddie's forehead.

"No!" I scream, scrambling across the sand, leaving my rifle behind. "No, don't shoot him." I put my hands above my shoulders in surrender.

"No, Ev," Lisa yells, but I don't have a choice.

I take a few steps forward, my eyes locked onto the soldier's finger resting on the trigger. I realize he could take me and still shoot Eddie. In fact, I suspect that's his plan, but I have to find a way to prevent it. Quinn and Liam need their dad. *I* need my dad. My entire body quakes as I stumble forward, lifting my eyes from the gun to the soldier's face, silently pleading with him not to do this.

A shot rings out through the silent night, my body instinctively dropping to the ground.

41

SURROUNDED

Cyrus

*B*ryce and I have our hands above our shoulders, but Benton's are still at his sides. One of the soldiers steps forward and pushes the muzzle of his gun into Benton's chest. That makes his hands fly up way over his head. I'd laugh if this wasn't so intense. He's totally out of his element.

Another soldier removes my weapon from my waistband before taking Bryce's.

The first soldier, the one who opened the door, turns his attention to Benton. "What's going on?"

"We have orders to move the Minellis."

"Is this because they caught the girl?"

Bryce and I exchange a brief look. Do they have Evan? Engaging my training, I prevent anything from registering on my face, but my heart is hammering in my chest. "I'm a commander and we have our orders."

His gaze flies to my credentials. "Sir. Sorry, sir." He nods to the others and they drop their weapons to their sides and return our firearms. Before we go any further, I need to know that Evan's safe.

T.H. HERNANDEZ

"What've you heard about the girl?" I keep my voice low, appearing interested, but only as it pertains to my current task.

"Just a rumor, sir. That she was spotted in the Southwestern Province and was picked up. But there aren't any concrete details."

"When?"

"Yesterday, sir."

I glance at Benton. "Can you find out more? I don't want to move them if they're no longer needed."

I hope he can get the information. I shoot Bryce another look and note his barely controlled attempts to mask his concern. He might be a cop, but he's not a soldier. He needs to work on that.

A kid steps forward and hands Benton a tablet. Bryce approaches him from behind, whispering something in his ear. Benton swallows hard, a thin sheen of moisture forming on his upper lip. He taps a few things and waits as Bryce watches over his shoulder.

After a minute, Benton glances up. "It looks like it was nothing more than a rumor. There are two sightings but so far no reports of capture. They've increased security where the rest of her family is being kept. If she shows up there, they'll grab her. It's only a matter of time—"

"Let's get them moved." Bryce cuts him off. "Where are they?"

Benton's eyes dart to the back wall. Bryce steps closer to Benton while I move to get the Minellis. We may still have his daughter, but he's proved himself to be untrustworthy. My eyes sweep the surface and land on a hidden panel, or rather, a less-than-hidden panel. I push on it and it opens.

Behind it is a tiny, furnished room, although I think our little campground is nicer than this. Sitting on the floor with her back against the wall is Evan's mother, Katie and Rachel curled up on either side of her. When Christine's eyes open, they widen in surprise. Recognition colors her blue eyes, and I give my head a quick shake.

A small dog begins to bark furiously at me, snarling as he lunges forward, attempting to escape the arms of the girl holding him. "Barklyn, no!"

Two men standing in the corner stare at me. Evan's stepfather and uncle. The girl holds the yapping dog in her lap as Christine whispers something to her, then turns and whispers to the other girl. I still can't tell them apart.

"We have orders to move you," Bryce says gruffly, coming in behind me.

The uncle starts at Bryce's presence, but recovers immediately. "Where?" His eyes shift beyond Bryce. "Peter, what are you doing here?"

Benton suddenly finds the toes of his shoes fascinating. "There's reason to believe your location has been compromised."

This is taking far longer than it should, and if this was a real Uprising operation, we wouldn't be answering their questions. "You don't need to know any more than that. Let's go." It's easy to lapse back into my old role. I played it well for long enough. I turn to Bryce. "Cuff them."

"Even the girls?" Christine's voice is shaking, the only indication of her true state of mind.

I don't answer, but nod at Bryce. This needs to look legit, which means all of them should be cuffed. Bryce pulls out zip ties and secures their hands in front of them before we transfer them out of the back room. With guns drawn, we march Evan's family toward the exit, my heart still pummeling my ribs.

As we reach the door, one of the soldiers calls out, "Hold up. We'll escort you."

I freeze and cut my eyes to Bryce. This wasn't part of the plan. Technically, I outrank them, but I can't come up with a logical reason to refuse them. Bryce shifts his shoulders up a fraction of an inch letting me know he doesn't know what to do either. My gaze sweeps our group. Between me, Bryce, Joe, and David, if we can limit the entourage to two, we can overpower them.

"Sure." I incline my head at the youngest soldiers, the oldest is sixteen at the most. "You two. The rest of you stay here, secure the location, and wait for orders."

"Yes, sir!"

We move out and I glance at Bryce. We need to neutralize these two before they figure out what's going on.

"You two take the lead."

They fall in line up front, with Benton and the Minellis in the middle, and Bryce and I bringing up the rear, giving us a chance to talk without being overheard.

I lean in close. "We have to do this fast. Like in the next few minutes."

He nods and tenses beside me. I keep an eye open for the right moment. Benton is a wild card. He can sabotage anything we try to do, so we'll have to rely on David or Joe, even cuffed, to help us rein him in.

The soldiers ahead don't know our destination, providing a small window of opportunity. Once they reach the elevators, they'll look to us for direction. As long as their backs are to us, we hold the advantage.

I take a deep breath. "Now."

Bryce glances at me for a split second before moving up the left side of the group, while I go right, placing my gun at the base of the young soldier's head.

I remove his weapon. "I'll take that."

A quick glance over my shoulder confirms Bryce has done the same with the other one.

As anticipated, Benton makes a run for it. I hand my gun to Joe and point the rifle at Benton. "Stop."

He halts in his tracks.

The takeover went far smoother than I hoped, but we need to do something with these two before we meet up with Colin. I pull my knife out of my pocket and cut the zip ties from everyone's wrists while Bryce secures the hands of our Uprising friends behind their backs.

"Benton, too," I remind him.

With her hands now free, one of the twins sets the dog down, who runs to the corner and lifts a leg to pee. "Come on, Barklyn." She pats her thigh, and after thoroughly sniffing his own urine, Barklyn rejoins the family, sitting at the girl's heel. Taking that dog is a bad idea, but if I force them to leave it behind, I'll never hear the end of it.

"Carry him," I order her.

Her eyes widen and her lips part, but she reaches down to pick him up.

"Look, sorry, I didn't mean to snap at you, but we can't afford to chase after him if he runs off."

She nods and buries her face in his fur.

David, Joe, and I cover Benton and the soldiers while Bryce disappears down an intersecting hallway, returning a few minutes later.

"What's going on?" Christine asks, chewing on her lip.

"We're getting you out of here."

"I don't understand."

David opens his mouth to say something, but quickly closes it again as Bryce returns.

"There is a storage closet down there. We can stow them there for now. He pulls out his knife and cuts the T-shirt off one of them, making a gag. Following his lead, I do the same with the other.

Bryce shoves them into the closet and jogs back over to us. "We'll let Benton share their location after we're safely away. But first, I have a couple more questions."

Bryce texts Colin, telling him where to meet us, while I take Ev's family and Benton to a warehouse near the back wall where we can question Benton. It's only a matter of time before word of the prisoner transfer makes its way up the ranks and someone starts looking for us.

The space is musty and filled with folding tables and chairs. Dust clings to every surface. I grab a chair and open it up. "Sit," I order Benton.

He glares at me, but drops into it. I cut the ties around his wrists and secure his hands behind the chair, then his ankles to the metal legs. After testing he's adequately bound, I turn around.

"Where's Evan? Where's my daughter?" Christine demands.

The first time I met her was in the hospital after Evan was shot. She made it clear then she didn't approve of me. She doesn't know anything about me, but her objections were palpable. The next time I saw her was at Bryce's funeral. She was there for her daughter and her daughter was barely there. Christine went out of her way to avoid me. I have no idea what she thinks of me, but dammit, I care.

I swallow and meet her hard stare. "She's in the Western Province getting Eddie, Liam, and Quinn."

Christine collapses against a stack of tables as if whatever had been holding her up vanished. "So...she's okay then?"

That's a loaded question. "She's...she's fine. With any luck, she'll be back by the time we get there."

"Get where?" Joe asks.

Joe has been less obviously antagonistic toward me, but there's always a hint of accusation in his dark eyes.

"He's on his way," Bryce says, joining us.

Christine stands with such force the table on top clatters to the floor. "We thought you were dead. We attended your funeral."

Bryce hangs his head. "Yeah, I'm sorry about that."

"Do you have any idea what you put our daughter through?" Christine's face is bright red, anger flying from her green eyes, and I almost feel bad for Bryce.

"We can talk about all of this later," Bryce says. "I need a few answers first, then we have to go."

"I don't understand what's going on," David says.

"That's what we're all trying to figure out," Bryce says. "What can you tell us? What happened on the day of the attack?"

Christine responds first. "I got a text from Evan. Sh-she said she was okay and that she'd let me know more later. We've been so worried about her..."

Bryce shifts on his feet, glancing at his watch.

I peek at my own watch. We're running out of time. "I promise, we'll tell you what we can once we're on our way. Evan can tell you the rest when we see her, but right now, we need information."

Bryce leans over Benton. "Spill it."

Benton remains stoically silent. I grab my gun from my waistband, pull back the slide, and point it at his head. "I'm not a Uni and have no qualms about ending your life if you don't start talking."

He swallows hard and nods. "I don't know much. I had my orders. I took the Minellis into custody and moved them to a secret location."

"On whose orders?"

"Walker's."

"What's his end game? What does he want and why is he after Evan?"

"I don't know."

"Bullshit." I jam the gun into his cheek, pressing hard. Beads of sweat form on his brow as he stares at me, his eyes wide. "You were trusted with the whereabouts of the highest-ranking Union official still alive."

Snot runs from his nose, and I press harder until the muzzle is up against bone. He flinches and sniffs.

"Walker's not calling the shots. Not really. He's a figurehead. It's..."

"Who? The cartels?"

He shrugs. "Yes and no. At first, we were told a family member of someone high up in one of the cartels needed treatment only available in the Union. They tried to negotiate at first, but got nowhere. I was well-paid to arrange the necessary care. Turns out there's more to it than just that. A guy named Kearney is at the top of the pyramid. He wants access to the oil fields in the Southern Province and off the coast."

"Why?"

"The rest of the world's oil has been depleted over the past two hundred years. All that's left is in the Union. It's worth trillions."

My hand drops to my side as I stare at him in disbelief. This is about money? There are so many other sources of power. Oil is the least practical.

"What does he want the oil for?" David asks behind me.

Benton bites the inside of his lip. He glances around the room, fear etched into his face. "They'll kill me if I say anything."

"I'll kill you now if you don't." I jam the barrel of my gun against his forehead again.

"What is he going to do with it?" David asks.

Benton sighs, a dark stain spreading across the front of his khaki pants. "The jets. He needs jet fuel."

I don't understand, but David slumps against the wall. "My god."

"For what?" I ask. "What's he talking about?"

David's face is pulled tight. "He must be planning on becoming the sole military power with air capabilities. No one will be able to stop him. He'll control every country on the planet in a matter of days."

"But why?" I ask, still not following.

"For any reason he wants."

42

BREATHING

Evan

$\mathcal{M}$y dad is dead. Tears fill my eyes and I can't breathe. Sand gathers on my face as I burrow further into it, refusing to look at what I know is waiting for me.

"Evan." Lisa's voice somehow sounds both close and far away.

With shaking limbs, I push myself up, keeping my face down.

"Let's go," Tony yells from somewhere nearby.

I can't just leave Eddie here. "We need to bury him."

"What?" Lisa asks.

I lift my head and turn to her as arms wrap around me from behind, pulling me back. I jerk away. If they want me, they're going to have to kill me, too.

"Hey," Eddie's voice says in my ear.

My breathing cuts out and I spin around to face my father. Alive. Unshot. My head swivels to where he was only moments ago. The soldier who had the gun to Eddie's head lies in the sand, a gunshot to his temple, dark blood pooling around him under the moonlit sky. Lisa moves beside me, still holding a rifle smelling of spent ammunition, and my stomach lurches.

I tear my gaze away from the dead soldier to the girl beside me. "You..." Nothing else comes out as the realization of what happened sweeps over me. She shot a man to save Eddie's life. And mine.

Tony sprints toward us. "We need to go. Now!"

Choking back a sob, I walk on quivering legs, and retrace my steps to grab my rifle from where I dropped it. I blindly follow Tony out of the camp, low voices murmuring in the tents we pass. By the time we hit the boardwalk, we're running full speed into the bowels of the Union without looking back.

Jack leads us down a corridor off the main walkway to allow us to catch our breath, assess our injuries, and ensure we weren't followed. My chest feels like it's being ripped apart as air screams its way into my depleted lungs. Next to me, Eddie's bent over at the waist, hands on his knees, dragging in breaths.

Jack peers around the corner and waves us forward. I reach over and take Eddie's hand, giving it a quick squeeze, needing to make sure he's real, before we follow Jack back to the hotel. My siblings are curled up beside their mother on the bed. Ashlynn appears...frazzled, something I never would have believed she was capable of. Until this moment.

The kids stir as we stomp into the room and Liam sits up, squinting. "Daddy!" He leaps into Eddie's arms.

Quinn lifts her head, her eyes widening as she zeroes in on her dad, but one look at me and she burrows back into Ashlynn's shoulder. Eddie holds Liam for several long moments before setting him down and reaching for Quinn. She whimpers and turns away, gripping even tighter to her mother.

A look of confusion crosses Eddie's face. Her reaction has more to do with me than him, although his battered and bruised face probably isn't helping.

Remaining near the door, I watch the activity in the room play out as if I'm underwater. Like everything is muted and slightly out of focus. The only thing that's clear are my actions tonight. My gaze drifts to Lisa as she stares at her hands. She killed, too. But for her, it was the first time. For me, it was just more lives in a growing list. I'm not sure which one of us is dealing with more. It doesn't get any easier with subsequent killings; maybe it's less shocking, but no less horrifying. It's like I've accepted that I'm a killer. I'm sickened by what I've become, but no longer surprised by it.

My eyes close as I lean my head back against the door, fighting tears. The kids can't see me cry. They're already frightened enough.

"Evan, are you alright?" Tony's low voice next to my ear startles me.

I shake my head, but the word "yes" comes out.

Tony's dark eyes search mine, but I can't handle the scrutiny. I'm too raw and exposed.

"I need a shower." I push off the door, moving toward the bathroom.

"You killed Germy," Quinn says as I pass her.

"Germy?" I ask, stupidly.

"Jeremy," Liam says.

Quinn's bottom lip quivers. "He's my friend."

There is no way to explain to her what I did or why. I look to Ashlynn for help, but her eyes are filling, threatening to spill over.

"Show them," Eddie murmurs.

"What?"

He nods and it sinks in that he wants me to reveal my scars. But I can't. Quinn's only three, too young to understand, and I'm worried it will only scare her more.

Eddie approaches, wrapping his arms around my shoulders, tears running down his face.

"Whatssamatter, Daddy?" Quinn asks.

"Someone hurt Evan." Then he whispers only to me, "Show them. It's okay."

I take in a deep, shaky breath and nod before slowly exposing my back.

"Ohhhhhhh," Liam says, hopping off the bed. He moves up

behind me, reaching out his chubby hand to touch the scars on my back. "What happened?"

I drop my shirt and turn to face him, my voice unsteady. "Someone wanted me to tell them something I didn't want to share. And when I didn't, they thought if they hurt me, I would tell them. But I didn't."

His eyes are wide, his bottom lip trembling. "Who?"

I look at Quinn. "Soldiers."

"Not Germy." She crosses her arms over her chest.

"No, not Jeremy, but soldiers like him. I was afraid they would hurt you, too. You and Liam and your mom. I didn't want to have to...to do that to Jeremy. I'm sorry I did." I want to tell her not all soldiers are bad, but this situation is so complex, so messed up, it's more than she's capable of understanding. All she knows is that her friend is dead and it's my fault.

Silence fills the small room and I am still in desperate need of a shower. I grab fresh clothes from my bag and lock myself in the bathroom. The water is scalding as I attempt to scrub not just the dirt, sand, and grime from my skin, but memories of what I did. No matter how hard I rub, it won't go away. My soul is stained too deep to be reached from the outside. Quinn may not understand everything, but she understands right and wrong better than I do. I let my training turn me into something awful, someone who kills without thinking. I can tell myself that my motives were true, but it doesn't change anything.

All the lives lost over the past year flash behind closed eyes. Dead family and friends, dead soldiers. My legs give way and I crumple to the floor of the shower and curl on my knees, my back arched, hugging myself tightly. My body shakes uncontrollably, but I don't cry. There is no release of pent up emotion to leave me feeling drained but better. There is only me and my sins.

I don't know how much time passes, but a knock at the door drags me out of my nightmare. It comes again, louder, and Eddie says, "Evan, are you okay?"

I can't answer him because I'm not and I never will be again.

I hug my dad tightly. "Be careful, and hurry."

"You, too. They know you're in the area, and they'll be looking for you."

I nod and back away. After hugging Jack and Lisa, the three of them slip out of the hotel room to get Talia. As much as I'd like us to stick together, I know it's not safe for me here. In fact, we've probably been here too long as it is.

"You ready?" Tony asks.

"Yeah. Let's do this."

Checking my gun, I crack the door and peer out. Jack, Lisa, and Eddie have already blended into the shadows. The hallway outside the room is eerily silent. I ease out the door, Tony following. He waves Ashlynn forward, Liam's hand gripped in hers, Quinn clinging to her like a baby chimp.

"Where are we going?" a sleepy Quinn asks.

"Shhh," her mom answers. "We're going camping. But you need to be quiet."

"Oh." Quinn snuggles into her mother's chest, curling her hand under her chin.

Our steps only make soft scuffing sounds on the carpeted floor, except for Liam's shoes, which squeak with each step.

"Hey buddy, hop on," Tony whispers, bending down to allow Liam to climb on his back.

We exit the hotel and move into the passageways of the Union. It's a long walk to the back wall from here, close to twelve miles. Twelve miles of looking over our shoulders, making educated guesses about which tunnel to take next, and avoiding the commuter trains that crisscross this level.

I'm drenched in sweat by the time we arrive at the express elevators, but to Ashlynn's credit, she hasn't complained once. I tried to take Quinn from her a couple of times, but my sister is still refusing to have anything to do with me. When we reach the end of the hall near the elevator bank, Tony halts in front of me, his body tensing. I peer past him at the two armed soldiers guarding the elevators.

Tony eases Liam off his shoulders, and I pick him up, not wanting his noisy footwear to give us away.

"Take his shoes off," I whisper to Ashlynn.

She unties and slips them off, stuffing them in my backpack.

"Okay, buddy, you're going to walk in your socks for a bit."

We move back down the passageway until we're well out of earshot of the soldiers. "What do we do?" I ask Tony.

He shakes his head. "We have to assume they're on every level. There's no way they knew which level we were on."

"Even if we manage to get on the elevator, more will be waiting for us when we get off."

Tony runs his hand over his face and sighs. "Should we try the stairs?"

"It's worth a shot. They don't have enough troops to guard every stairwell."

"It means heading toward the commuter stations though."

We hike back the way we came and turn south when we reach an intersecting corridor. We're halfway to the end when voices echo off the concrete walls. It's impossible to tell which direction they're coming from. Tony pauses and puts up his hand. I press my back to the wall and indicate for Ashlynn to do the same.

Quinn begins to cry and Ashlynn tries to calm her, but she only cries harder. I close my eyes and suck in a breath before turning toward my little sister. "Quinn, you have to be quiet, sweetie, please."

"No!" she screams. "I want to go home."

The soft murmurs we heard a few moments ago pause briefly before someone shouts, "This way."

I'm almost positive they're ahead of us, so I grab Ashlynn's hand, pulling her behind me. We dash back the way we came, our footsteps and heavy breaths echoing through the corridors.

"I think they went that way," someone yells, a young teen boy based on the way his voice cracks.

At the end of the corridor, we turn away from the elevator bank. The stomping of boots on pavement behind us means we haven't lost them yet. Tony passes me and leads the way, zigging down one hall, then zagging down another until he reaches a stair-well. He enters the open door and runs up. I trail after him, but Ashlynn's falling behind, the weight of Quinn and trying to hold onto Liam's hand are slowing her pace.

Our pounding feet make a racket on the metal stairs. They'll be on us in no time.

"They're in there," the pubescent boy yells.

"Follow Tony," I say to Ashlynn. "I'll be along as soon as I can."

Her eyes are wide with terror.

"I'm going to buy you some time, but not much, so run as fast as you can."

She turns and rushes up the stairs after Tony.

With trembling hands, I grip my gun with both hands while releasing the door catch with my foot, letting it swing closed. Then I head down one flight and wait.

The boots and voices grow closer, and someone fumbles with the door before getting it open. "Which way?" the kid asks.

I duck back into the shadows and hold my breath, my pulse pounding, while they heave, trying to catch theirs. "Quiet," an older male says. "Up."

Dammit. I need to lead them down. Pushing off, I thunder down the metal staircase.

"No, down there."

I jump down three stairs, turn, and take the next flight two at a time. A bullet pings off the railing next to me. I swallow a scream and pick up the pace.

A second shot chips the concrete to my left, pieces falling away, the sound echoing like thunder. My toe catches on the bottom step, sending me sprawling head-first into the brick wall, my gun clattering down ahead of me.

My head pounding, ears ringing, I scramble belly first after my weapon. Pivoting, I fire up, momentarily stopping their momentum. When I stand, the stairwell spins. My back pressed against the wall, I continue moving down, firing random shots upward, sending them ducking for cover. I dodge through an open door, down the hall, and around a corner, my skull throbbing with every footfall. I reach up and feel a knot forming, but no blood.

My lungs burn until I'm forced to stop and catch my breath. I listen for anyone behind me, but all I hear is my own lungs straining to refill themselves. I'm totally turned around and need to find Tony and Ashlynn. The problem is, I don't know how far up they went, or where they disappeared to after that. I wish Jack had left me the tablet, but we thought he'd need it to track down Talia. We didn't count on our group splitting up.

Exhaustion takes over and I slump to the ground. The soldiers will search the vicinity until they're convinced I'm gone, then they'll report in for instructions. That could take at least an hour. They know I'm in this province now, which means all resources will be redirected here. We have to get out of here now. Instead of through the back wall, we can take the cargo train and spend less time hiking back to camp.

Tony will have figured all this out already, so we just need to find each other. I check my surroundings before stepping out and working my way back up to the level where we split up. I search near the train tunnels before going up to the next level and doing the same. The corridors are quiet this early in the morning, making it easier to detect the presence of anyone else. No boot-steps echo off concrete walls, only my own soft footsteps and shaky breaths.

Five levels up, I'm grimy, exhausted, and frustrated. Where on earth could they be? Voices coming from behind make me stop cold before tearing down the hall and around the corner, knowing my feet are giving away my position. I dash toward the passageway leading to the cargo trains, hoping to hide. Someone grabs my arm, yanking me into a dark warehouse.

I take a deep breath in preparation to fight when a hand clasps itself over my mouth. "Shhh," Tony whispers.

Collapsing back against him, I relax for a moment before pressing my ear against the door and listening for the soldiers pursuing me. They run past and I drop to the floor in relief.

Twenty minutes later, Tony cracks the door and peeks out. He waves us forward and I step out behind him, followed by Ashlynn and the kids. Guns drawn, Tony and I surveil our surroundings before dodging into the tunnel. Getting on a moving train with Liam and Quinn will be challenging, but I think we can do it. When the next one approaches, we wait for the engine to pass before coming out of the shadows. Tony parallels the slow-moving car and hops on first. He reaches a hand down for Liam, easily lifting him up.

Quinn cries, clinging to her mother, but Ashlynn convinces her to go to Tony. Once Ashlynn is aboard, I hop on and lie down on the bare floor, completely spent. We pick up speed, cruising east. It will take at least a day before we reach the Southern Province, so between the long day and the gentle rocking of the train, one by one, we doze off.

43

DISGUSTED

Evan

"*E*van...it's time."

My eyes open to gray light and a sore arm. Cargo train. Tony. I sit up and run a hand through my hair, my fingers finding the tender spot on my scalp. "What time is it?"

"Almost time to get off."

Wow. I slept eighteen hours. I rub the sleep from my eyes and look around the car. Ashlynn is sitting against the side, the kids curled up on either side of her.

I push up and join Tony at the door. The walls rush past us as we glide along the smooth track, before the train slows and pulls to a stop. I jump down and Tony hands Liam to me. Then Ashlynn climbs to the ground so Tony can place Quinn in her arms before he joins us. We move quickly away from the tunnel and into a hallway, working our way to the back wall where I locate a door into the Ruins.

Once I step through, my body and soul relax. I take in a lungful of fresh air and turn to Ashlynn and Tony. "It's about a half-day's walk from here, but we'll take a few breaks."

Ashlynn glances around, and it strikes me this is her first look at life outside the Union. It's a lot to take in. I lead the way through dense growth, as bugs buzz our heads and a variety of critters scamper across our path.

"Look, a bunny." Liam points to a white-tailed rabbit hopping into the underbrush.

"Where?" Quinn pushes down from her mother's arms and crouches beside me.

"Over there," I whisper.

Quinn follows my finger and her eyes widen, hands flying over her mouth. "Oh!"

As the day wears on, the kids stop to examine flowers, rocks, leaves, and more bugs. It's going to take us more than half a day to get there at this pace. The sun rises high and the humidity becomes stifling without the Union's dehumidifiers.

Tony and Ashlynn are in quiet conversation behind us as my young siblings continue to exclaim at each new discovery.

"She did what?" Ashlynn yells.

I glance back at them. Ashlynn is staring at me, venom dripping from her eyes. Tony says something to her and then she shouts, "I don't care. She's risked all of our lives!"

I have no idea what she's blaming me for now, but I'm getting tired of it. Pivoting, I walk back to them.

Ashlynn's eyes narrow as I approach. "Did you really blow up Uprising camps?"

My body tenses, but I keep eye contact. "Yes, and I'd do it again. It was the best chance we had to stop the Uprising."

"All you did was kick a hornet's nest."

I sigh. "Ashlynn, I did what I thought was right at the time. But it doesn't matter, everything I do is wrong."

She rolls her eyes. "What are you talking about?"

"The fact that you've treated me like Eddie's mistress instead of his daughter for as long as I've known you. You act like I was the other woman in your marriage. You've always hated me and nothing I do is ever right in your eyes."

She stares hard at me. "You acted like a spoiled brat, and—"

"I was twelve."

"You refused to even meet him half-way. Do you have any idea how difficult that was for him?"

"I was a kid. I didn't care that he married or that he was having a baby. I cared that he didn't give a shit about me until Liam came along."

"Hey, watch your language around my kids," she says under her breath, but with enough poison to melt steel. "He tried, but you wouldn't even see him. He was crushed."

"What the hell are you talking about? He was completely non-existent. Total deadbeat dad. My mom felt so bad for me that she lied and told me he was dead." I let out a bitter laugh. "She actually thought it'd be easier for me to think that than to know he just didn't want me."

Ashlynn halts and stares at me, her lips parted.

Quinn pulls at her mother's arm. "Up, Momma."

Ashlynn brushes her aside, too busy studying me. "Evan..." she lets my name hang there until I give up.

Disgusted, I storm through the Ruins toward camp.

The heat and humidity do nothing to improve my mood, but the closer we get to our destination, the more I focus on Cyrus, hot food, and a cool bath in the lake. I sure hope Cyrus and Bryce are back and that their mission went better than ours. I could use some friendly faces.

"I'm sorry," Ashlynn says quietly from behind me, startling me from my thoughts. "I shouldn't have said what I did. You were a kid. I keep forgetting how young you were."

I press my lips together and study her, suspicious of her motives, although she appears sincere. "Okay."

Tony has dropped back a good twenty yards, holding both Liam and Quinn by the hand. He gives me a quick nod.

"So, tell me about where we're going."

"Uh, well, it's a camp, but not like the ones in the Union. It's pretty rugged. Nothing like you're used to."

"How many people are there?"

"Maybe two hundred or so. Most of them are Unionites, but about a dozen are from the Ruins." I pause, remembering a key piece of information about a few of those Unionites. "Umm, there's something I need to tell you. My fiancé is in the Eastern Province getting my mom, stepdad, and my sisters. I should've told you earlier, I just forgot about it...with everything else."

"That's okay. While I can't say your mom is the first person I'd choose to go camping with, under the circumstances, there are bigger things to worry about."

My jaw about hits my chest. I glance back at Tony again, wondering what he said to her.

"So, fiancé, eh? How old are you, Evan?"

"Eighteen. I know what you're thinking and you can't say anything to me that Eddie hasn't already said. I get it. I'm young. But I don't care. It's my life to screw up any way I choose."

"I'm not your parent, Evan. I'm just curious, that's all. I wasn't much older than you are now when I married your dad. But...your life is very different than mine was."

I shake my head, trying to get a grasp on this mystery woman, but we've reached the outskirts of camp and I can't focus on anything except the one person I most need to see. We pass a couple of tents and a handful of people milling about. My eyes dart around, seeking and finding him. He's standing with his back to me, talking to someone. He's wearing shorts, sandals, and a navy T-shirt that loosely hugs his body, making my heart beat faster. Abandoning my travel companions, I run toward him.

He turns, my favorite smile overtaking his face. I throw my arms around his neck and he wraps me up, lifting me off the ground. When he sets me back down, he holds me tightly to him for a long time, neither of us saying a word. My face buried in his shoulder, I inhale his scent of soap, sweat, and earth. He smells like Cyrus, like home.

When he finally pulls back, he presses his forehead to mine. "Hi." His voice is low and sexy.

"Hi."

I could stand here with him like this for hours, but Quinn runs up. "Cywus!"

I step out of her way and she flings herself into his arms. I guess he's still okay in her eyes. Liam reaches us shortly after, and Cyrus bends down to scoop him up, holding one in each arm.

He smiles broadly at me, but my heart breaks in half when Quinn says, "Eban killed Germy."

Cyrus raises an eyebrow at me, but my face must tell him volumes, because he changes the subject, asking them if they're hungry.

"I'm starving," Liam says.

"Me too," Quinn chimes in.

Cyrus sets them down. "Okay, let's get you something to eat." Before he can do or say anything more, his attention is drawn behind me.

I turn to find Ashlynn and Tony finally catching up. I'd almost forgotten about them. "Cyrus, this is Ashlynn, Quinn and Liam's mom. Ashlynn, this is Cyrus."

Ashlynn appraises him as they shake hands, a smile of appreciation on her lips.

"How was your trip?" Cyrus asks her.

"Long."

Tony steps forward and they share a manly one-armed guy hug, then I push my way back into his arms. "I need to get them settled in."

"I'll take care of that. Go find your mom. She's anxious to see you."

Butterflies scramble in my stomach at the anticipation of seeing my family. "Thank you. For finding them for me."

He kisses my forehead and releases me. "Be forewarned, she's not my biggest fan."

"I'm not worried. That position has already been filled."

I take his face in my hands and kiss him softly, letting my mouth linger on his. His hands snake back around my waist and pull me against him. Warmth flushes through me and chips away at some of the stress binding me. He's like my own sweet therapy. Reluctantly, I draw back and give him a quick hug before heading off in search of my mom.

Within moments I spot her walking through the camp, seemingly taking it all in. When her gaze lands on me, she smiles and her eyes fill with tears. I jog the distance between us and throw my arms around her. We're both sobbing by the time we embrace. We cry for several minutes before she pulls back and places her hands on either side of my face, studying me. Her beautiful green eyes are overflowing as she takes in my appearance. I know I look better than I did a month ago, but nowhere near how I looked the last time she saw me.

"I'm fine, Mom, really."

She wraps an arm around my waist and we walk, my head on her shoulder. I want to ask her a million questions and tell her everything that's happened to me, but I don't even know where to begin. Before long, I realize we're headed toward the lake.

When we get to the rocky shore, we still haven't said anything. It's like we're just enjoying being with one another and that's enough for both of us for now. But before I strip down to take a bath and she sees my scars, I need to tell her *something*.

We stop by the edge of the water and I plop down on a log, patting the spot next to me. "Mom, sit with me for a minute."

She's wearing a soft gray print sundress that reaches her ankles and a pair of hiking boots that don't match. My mother, the fashion goddess, dressed like a Ruins survivor makes me smile. Mom brushes the bark off with her hand and sits.

"I have so much to tell you. How much do you already know?"

"About what?" she asks, a harsh edge to her words.

I sigh, this is going to be harder than I thought. "I don't know, Mom. About any of it? All of it. You obviously realize by now that things were never what we thought they were. But I knew a while ago. I could start at the beginning, but that would take too long. Did Colin, Bryce, or Cyrus tell you anything?"

She studies me, her eyes blinking like an owl, and it's somewhat unnerving. Like she's on information overload and I might just make her completely shut down. Finally, she shakes her head. "They told us about this Uprising and what they know about the politics surrounding it. Plus, your Uncle David filled in some blanks. But, what does any of this have to do with you?"

It might be easier to work my way backward in time rather than forward, because I've got to get this sticky, sweaty, dusty feeling off my skin. I bite the inside of my lip and think about all the lies she told me growing up. And yet, I still feel guilty for keeping so many huge secrets from her the past year.

"There's a lot to tell you, but I'm gross and need to clean up. When I undress, you're going to see something. I have to tell you about it first."

"Oh my god, you're pregnant, aren't you?" Only my mother would suddenly jump to that. "Is it Bryce's or that Cyrus guy? We really need to talk about Cyrus. I just—"

"Mom, no, I'm not pregnant. Just listen to me, okay? I was on a train that was boarded by the Uprising. They captured me."

She sucks in air and her hand immediately flies to her mouth, blinking furiously, but she remains quiet.

I close my eyes and blurt it out. "They tortured me, Mom. It was awful. I wanted to die. They brutally beat me and burned me. I'm not telling you this to hurt you or try to make you feel sorry for me, but because when I take off my shirt, you're going to see the scars. And they're bad... really bad."

I strip, eyes closed, then without looking at her I wade into the lake, leaving her alone with her thoughts and so she can compose herself before I return. Because I know that's what she needs. She won't want me to see her upset.

As I submerge into the cool waters, I'm sorry I didn't bring any shampoo or soap, but at least I can remove most of the grunge from my body. When I finish, my mom is still sitting on the log, her back to me, shoulders shaking. I take a few noisy steps, to let her know I'm coming. She sits upright, wiping her cheeks and appears more in control by the time I sit beside her to dress.

She stands without a word and walks around behind me. Her fingers glide over the healed burns on my back. "Oh, baby."

"I'm okay now, Mom. I really am. The others, they rescued me. They got me to a hospital, and took good care of me."

Mom returns to sitting beside me, taking my face in her hands, barely controlled emotions just beneath the surface. "Why?" she asks, her voice a low whisper. "Why did they do that to you? Because of David? Because of who he is?"

I take a deep breath and I start at the beginning, as I've done so many times before, and tell her what happened to me from the minute I got on the L-Train in the Eastern Province last summer up until the Invasion this past spring. The light fades as I talk, casting long shadows across the ground in front of us.

My mother has been strangely silent through most of it. Listening to me, not asking many questions, but finally she speaks. "But why did they do that to you? Abuse you like that? Because of what you and your friends did? The blowing up of their weapons?"

I shake my head. "No. They wanted information, and I didn't want to tell them." She's going to ask, and I need to tell her, but Cyrus's words come back to me — *she's not his biggest fan.*

"What information? And why wouldn't you tell them?"

With a deep sigh, I realize I'm done with secrets, lies, and half-truths. There may be very little of my life under my own control these days, but this is one of those things I can control. It's my story. I own it. I decide who I tell and what I say. "It was Draya. She was...with Cyrus's brother, Lucien. She's always been like a sister to Cyrus, but after Lucien was killed, she became different... she ...she blamed me for his death."

"Okay...but I'm still not following. What does this have to do with those..." she swallows hard, as if attempting to push down on the memory of my scars. "...with those marks on your back?"

"Draya joined the Uprising and was one of my captors. She wanted to hurt me the way she believes I hurt her." I pause as the events of that day come flooding back. "She told me she was going to kill Cyrus so that I would know the pain she lives with every day."

"I don't understand, Evan. Why would you risk your life for him?"

My mouth drops open and I swivel to face her. "You can't be serious, Mom. I love him. Have you been paying attention to anything I've said over the past two hours? My god, he's...I love him."

Mom's lips are pressed into a tight line and her hands fiddle with the buttons on her dress. She glances up at me. "You're only eighteen. He's not from...surely you don't think—"

"I don't think what? That I'm going to spend the rest of my life with him? Yes, I do. He asked me to marry him. And I said yes."

Her face darkens and her eyes narrow. I didn't get my temper from Eddie. "That's ridiculous, Evan. You're too young, and you can't marry a boy from the Ruins. What kind of future can he offer you?"

A strangled laugh escapes. "You want to talk about my future? Look around, Mom." My arms sweep the great outdoors. "We're living in the Ruins, running from people who want to kill us. We don't have a future, but I want to spend my present with the boy I love."

Her shoulders drop and the spark fades from her eyes. "How much do you really know about him?"

"Everything I need to."

"It's been a long day. Let's head back." She stands and starts back toward camp. Her movements are so sudden, I have to run to catch up to her. When I reach her side, she pauses and turns to face me. "I know you're an adult now, but you're still a role model to your sisters. Please act like it."

"What's that supposed to mean?"

"It means set an example...and maybe they don't need to know everything...about..." she flicks her hand toward me.

"You don't want me sitting around the fire tonight telling them stories about all the people I've killed?"

Her gaze narrows before she sighs and continues walking. I watch her go, realizing we don't know each other anymore. I'm not the daughter she thought I was and she can't cope with it. A wave of hopelessness washes over me — *everything* really is different now. My life, the Union, even my family.

While I was gone, someone put up solar lights, and they flicker along the pathways as I make my way to the center of camp. When I get to the mess area, dinner is winding down. A sharp yip is followed by a blur of brown and white fur, shorter than it's ever been, as my dog, Barklyn, bounds toward me. Unexpected tears clog my throat as I bend down to greet him. He launches himself at me, squirming and wriggling, his tongue lapping my face.

I pull him into my arms, and he whines in delight. "What happened to your fur, buddy?"

His only response is more dog kisses.

I set him down and glance around for my friends, locating Rainey and Mateo at a table with Lucy, but there's no sign of Cyrus. All I really want is something to eat before I drag Cyrus to bed with me.

Mateo smiles broadly and stands when he spots me. He crosses the short distance between us with a few long steps, and envelopes me in his giant arms. "You're back. How'd it go?"

I shrug. "It...went. I'll fill everyone in tomorrow. I need dinner and sleep."

He glances at my feet where Barklyn is sitting and lifts an eyebrow.

"This is Barklyn. Barklyn, this is Mateo."

"We've met, although he's usually plastered to the side of one of your sisters."

"Well, we haven't seen each other since...well...since just before the Invasion. But he was always my dog when I lived at home."

The corner of his mouth lifts in a sort-of smile, the kind Mateo is famous for. "It's good to see you back in one piece."

"Ha, thanks for the confidence." I pat him on the back. My gaze drifts past him to Rainey and Miranda, my brain finally making a connection. "Where's Bryce?"

Mateo scratches the back of his head. "Cyrus said they got a lead on where to find Draya as they were leaving. Colin and Bryce stayed behind to look for her."

"What? They're bringing her here? Why?"

"She has information we need."

I try to understand what the grand plan is, but I'm too tired to process it. Instead I switch gears. "Have you seen Marcus and Sonia? I want Sonia to check on Quinn and Liam. They're kind of traumatized. Maybe give them something to help them sleep."

"Yeah. By the campfire. I'll fetch Sonia, you get something to eat."

I scoop some rice, fruit, and weird-looking boiled meat onto my plate and sigh. We really take Lisa for granted when she's here. There's an empty spot on the end of a picnic table beside Rainey and I snag it, digging into my food.

We make small talk before she and Miranda leave. Miranda is beginning to do that waddling thing that pregnant women do.

I finish my meal and I'm about to go looking for Cyrus when a voice I recognize says, "Is this seat taken?"

A grin spreads across my face and the fatigue that was weighing me down suddenly dissipates. I turn and throw myself into Joe's arms, closing my eyes and letting him hold me. A throat clearing interrupts us and I open my eyes to find my Uncle David behind his brother, flanked by my half-sisters, Katie and Rachel. I was so worried I'd never see him again, that he'd been killed with the rest of the governors. Joe releases me and I rush to the others, who pull me into a group hug of laughter and tears, Barklyn bouncing up and down about our ankles.

"I'm starving," Katie says when our embrace has lingered long beyond what is probably normal.

I wipe a tear. "Then go get something to eat, you goof."

While they go in search of dinner, I resume my spot at the

table, eager to talk to them. They return with food piled high, plunking down their metal plates around me. Voices rise and fall with animated discussion as they recount their adventures of being rescued by Bryce and Cyrus. My sisters chatter non-stop, with Joe and David filling in some of the finer details. It becomes clear my sisters are awestruck by their rescuers and Katie can't stop talking about how hot Cyrus is.

I want to spend some time with my uncle, but I can barely keep my eyes open. So, when Joe and the girls offer their goodbyes and my uncle's expression indicates he's ready for an extended conversation, I say, "I'm sorry, Uncle David, I know we have a lot to talk about, but I've been walking since before the sun came up this morning. Can we do this tomorrow?"

He gives me a lazy smile. "Of course. It's good to see you, kiddo."

I kiss him on the cheek. "It's so good to see you, too. I was sure you...well, that..."

His eyes crinkle. "I know. We'll talk in the morning."

I give him a quick wave and head off in search of Cyrus. He's at one of the fires with my family, Rainey, and Mateo, discussing life in the Ruins, but there's a palpable level of tension. Cyrus is leaning back against a log, one leg bent, his forearm draped across his knee. My body relaxes with each step toward him. He glances up and smiles as I approach. I nod to my family as I take the spot beside Cyrus, putting my head on his shoulder. Barklyn plops down next to me, resting his chin on my foot. I wait for Cyrus to tug me close and push away the rest of the ugliness trying to drag me under, but he doesn't. Instead, he rests his arm across the back of the log, only making minimal contact.

He stares at my mom and Rainey, who are deep in conversation, as if I'm not even here. I recognize the behavior is not normal, but I'm too tired to figure out what it means. Between the fire's warmth and the sultry evening air, my eyelids become too heavy to keep open.

The next thing I'm aware of is whiskers tickling my neck and a soft sexy voice murmuring in my ear, "Time for bed."

"Mmmm," I say, "Bout time."

WRONG

Cyrus

*A*fter Ev's parents go to bed, I wake her. Christine's words are still ringing loud inside my head. She expects us to set an example for the girls. Her meaning was clear — no messing around. I would have laughed if she hadn't been dead serious. Her husband giving me a bone-crushing glare didn't help either. While I have no intention of abiding by her request forever, I think a couple of nights wouldn't hurt. Maybe Ev can smooth things over with her.

I stand and reach down for her hands, pulling her to her feet. Without a disapproving audience, I wrap my arm around her waist, and she rests her head in the crook of my shoulder as we walk, the dog following. I halt in front of our tent and take her in my arms. My kiss is soft and gentle, lingering, but I'm careful not to cross any lines. She pulls back and stares up at me, questions etched into her features. I don't know how to tell her without setting up her mother as the bad guy.

She takes my hand and drags me toward the tent, but I dig in my heels.

"Ev..." When she looks up at me with searching eyes, I nearly lose my resolve. "Go to bed, baby. I'm gonna sleep in Will's tent tonight."

"What?"

Something between a groan and a sigh escapes my lips. "With your parents here...I just think it would be best."

"You can't be serious."

"We can talk more about it tomorrow."

"Cyrus, they're not going anywhere. For a really long time. Are you saying what I think you're saying?"

"No...but...just for a coupla days." I squeeze her hand. "I'll see you in the morning."

"I can't believe you." She shakes her head, her voice thick with emotion and not the good kind.

Things are about to get ugly, so I pivot and start walking before that happens.

"God, you are such a coward."

My eyes close and I let out a sigh, my shoulders tensing. "Evan, don't." She's looking to pick a fight, but I refuse to play along.

"Don't what? Don't tell you that you're afraid of my mother, of all people? Honestly? After everything we've been through, you're going to let *her* decide who I can and can't sleep with?"

I turn back and level her with a stare. "Aren't you overreacting just a little? Let's just wait until everyone gets settled into camp before we start riling up your parents."

Even in the moonlight I can see the interior war she's waging. I'm betting that's due in part to a similar conversation she had with her mom.

"You know what, just go. I don't want you here with me anyway."

"Evan, stop it."

"Or what? Or you're going to go stomp off and sleep in Will's tent?"

I run a hand through my hair and shake my head. "Goodnight, Evan." I move quickly away from her, but before I've gone far, something hits me squarely between the shoulders. I whip around and stare at her. She fucking threw something at me. I can't decide if I'm more annoyed or amused. Her face is dark with anger and her breath is coming in short puffs, like a pissed off mule. To keep from laughing, I clench my fists. "Dammit, Evan, just let it go. Please."

"Or what?"

"You're being obtuse."

She lets out a nasty, almost hateful laugh. "Learn a new word, did you? Well you used it wrong."

No longer wanting to be around her, it's easy for me to turn away and cover the short distance to Will's tent.

45

DEMONS

Evan

*T*he expression in Cyrus's eyes lets me know I hit a mark. The pain is evident, but then he quickly masks it. He shakes his head, turns, and walks away without another word. I stomp into the tent and fling myself down onto the sleeping bags, letting out a frustrated yell. Barklyn follows me and sits at my feet, looking up at me.

"What the hell is wrong with me?"

He tilts his head, but offers no answers. I grab Cyrus's pillow and hug it to my chest, breathing in. It smells like him, like warmth, and love, and home, and I was just a total bitch to him. Exactly what I accused my mother of. I took the one thing I know he's self-conscious about, his lack of a formal education, and threw it in his face.

How could I say those things to him? It's like I wanted to hurt him. Maybe I did. Maybe I needed him to see me for who I really am — the girl who killed Quinn's friend, the monster I've become. I couldn't find the words to tell him, but I sure found a way to show him.

I should go to Will's tent right now and apologize to him, and I would if my limbs weren't filled with sand. Maybe after I rest for a few minutes. Just a short nap, then I'll go find him and tell him he's too good for me. Except he already knows that. No wonder he doesn't want to sleep with me.

My eyes slip shut and darkness consumes me.

"We have to go. Get up," Lisa screams at me.

"Lis, you're back? Where's Eddie?"

"Come on, Ev, get up."

But I can't. My arms and legs are too heavy. I roll over and see soldiers running down the path. I need to get up. Pulling myself to my knees, I reach into my bag for my gun, but it's not there. My knife is under my pillow, and I grab it, flicking open the blade. The Uprising swamps the camp, killing everyone they see. Bodies are falling around me. I throw the knife at the closest soldier, but I know it's not enough. There are too many of them.

I spin around, looking to Lisa to help, but she's gone. "I need backup," I yell, but no one comes. Squatting, I approach the downed soldier to retrieve my knife and find Quinn beside me crying hysterically.

"You killed Daddy," she says.

"No, I didn't, he's a solider, see. We have to go. Come on, Quinn."

"No," she screams. "You killed Daddy."

I glance down and see the handle protruding from Eddie's neck, blood streaming from the gash I inflicted. Somehow in my sleep-induced stupor, I didn't realize it was my father and not a soldier. Blood pours from the gaping wound and washes over me like a wave. Quinn's high-pitched howls fill my ears, and soon I join her, screaming until nothing more comes out. I double over into heaving sobs as what I've done devours me the way a hungry animal does its latest kill.

Warm arms surround me. Someone has come to get me, but I don't want to go.

"Shhhh, baby, it's okay. You're dreaming," says a voice.

My eyes open, soaked with my tears, my throat raw. The arms holding me are strong and secure. I grab Cyrus with both hands and bury my face in his shirt, trying to catch my breath and convince myself it wasn't real. He wraps me up in an iron grip, whispering soothing words that don't register.

"What's going on?" Mom asks.

I lift my head and glance up. Mom, Joe, Tony, and David are squished into our tent and stare at me with wild-eyed fear and confusion.

"She had a nightmare," Cyrus said.

Mom stoops next to me and tucks a curl behind my ear. "It's okay, Evie. You're okay."

I turn away and burrow deeper into Cyrus's shoulder. "Stay with me. Please don't leave me." I beg, my voice muffled by his cotton T.

He presses his lips against the side of my head. "I'm never leaving you again. I promise."

He says something quietly to the others, and soon I realize we're alone. Even Barklyn left. Cyrus rubs my back until my breathing normalizes.

"Do you want to talk about it?" he asks.

I shake my head. I can't. It was too real. "Not right now."

We don't move for a long time. He holds me, stroking my hair, my back, my arm, kissing my forehead, my cheek, my shoulder until I'm no longer shaking. I pull back so I can see his face. My eyes are swollen from crying and I'm sure my face is blotchy. Although I know I look like a disaster, I need to see his eyes. "I'm so sorry, Cyrus. About what I said before. I didn't mean any of those things."

"I know you didn't." He kisses my temple. "I love you, Ev."

"Why? How can you love me after the way I treated you?"

He smiles, his beautiful soft lips pulling tight. "You're everything to me. I don't want a life you're not a part of." His face is full of deep emotion, but I don't understand any of it. It makes no sense.

"I'm a monster."

"You're not." He tucks a wild curl behind my ear. "You're complex as hell, but genuine. You own my heart. I can't stop loving you any more than I can stop breathing."

My eyes fill with tears at his words. They're so beautiful and so moving and I don't know how to respond. My lip trembles and I bite it. He bends down and lets his mouth brush against mine, stilling my lips with his.

"I know you, Ev. I know that whatever that was before, that wasn't you. Whatever's wrong, I know you'll tell me when you're ready. You are...amazing and caring, but god help me, you've got a temper like a Tasmanian devil, and when that flares, I gotta learn to duck." He grins and brushes the few tears that have escaped away with his thumb.

I remember throwing the dirt clod at him. "Oh, my god, I'm so sorry. I don't know what's wrong with me. I'm scared, Cyrus. I'm terrified of what I'm becoming. The things I did...I did them without even thinking. The demons are taking over. I'm losing myself."

He holds me tighter, but he doesn't say anything. I wonder if he's worried I'm disappearing, too. I reach up and kiss him hard, with a deep ache. "I need you," I whisper, kissing him more aggressively.

He kisses me back with enough heat that tells me he knows what I mean.

46

ABANDONED

CYRUS

*E*van breathes softly beside me, her shoulder rising and falling. Her screaming probably woke half the camp last night if not the whole damn place. Instead of doing the right thing and standing up to Christine, once again I abandoned Ev when she needed me most.

After allowing myself to watch her sleep for a few minutes more, I dress and duck out into the gray morning light. Several others are up and moving about camp. I walk in the general direction of food. Gunther's working mess duty this week, and I say a quick hello as I grab a cup of coffee.

"Good morning," Tony says.

I nod a greeting. "Morning."

"How is she?"

"Still sleeping." This man knows more about what's bothering her than I do. We take a seat across from one another. "What happened out there?

He folds his hands on the table in front of him. "Things didn't go according to plan."

"Do they ever?"

He smirks. "Not in my experience. Evan and Lisa went to get Ashlynn, but the rest of us were surrounded almost immediately. Next thing I knew, Evan was there, shooting soldiers. Everything happened so fast. They used Eddie to get Evan to surrender. Lisa saved all our asses." He stares over the top of his cup into the distance before returning his attention to me. "Evan's dealing with a lot of guilt."

I take in a deep breath and nod.

"The kids...don't understand." He rubs his face with his hands. "Apparently, she killed a soldier that Quinn was fond of. Evan took it pretty hard. I wasn't surprised to hear her screaming last night. Do you have any psychologists or anything in this camp?"

I shake my head. "I don't think so. But we can ask around."

"I'll do that. You just take care of her. I'll let you know what I find out."

"Thanks."

When Tony wanders off, I refill my coffee and head back to the tent where Evan is dressed and tying up her boots.

She glances up and smiles. "Hey."

I give her a quick kiss. "Hey. You hungry?"

She shakes her head. "I need to find my uncle."

"Okay. I'll see you later?"

"Can you come with me?"

"You want me there?"

She weaves her fingers through mine. "I do."

After last night, I can't refuse her anything. We head out to the mess area, figuring it's as good a place as any to start.

David is eating breakfast at a table with the rest of the family. Ev exchanges an awkward greeting with her mother, who stares me down.

"You up for a walk?" Ev asks David.

"Sure." He pushes up and brushes off the seat of his shorts before joining us. "Cyrus." He nods at me.

Evan leads the way to the lake, not bothering to make small

talk. Her shoulders are tense, her hand stiff in mine. When we get to the shore, she drops my hand and sits on a log. David and I find spots on the ground across from her.

Her mouth twists as if she's waging some sort of internal struggle. "So...a ton of stuff's happened since the last time I saw you."

She spends the next hour telling her story of the past few months, sparing few details as she describes the Uprising interrogation of her. The gnawing in my gut is as bad as it was the first time I heard it.

When she's finished, David raises an eyebrow. "Are there others being kept there?"

She nods. "I'm sure of it."

He rubs the side of his face. "The day of the Invasion I was in my office having coffee and preparing for a meeting when my chief of staff came in and turned up the volume on the monitor."

He sighs and stares beyond Ev at the lake. "We were all transfixed by the news as stories poured in about what was going on. They had just finished airing a piece about the Prime Minister's execution when soldiers stormed my apartment. I figured I was next, but instead they dumped me in a room that sounds a lot like the one where they were holding you."

Their gazes connect momentarily before he returns to studying the water. "Not long after, they brought in your dad, mom, and sisters. They never said what they wanted with us. I assumed it was me they were after, but as word trickled in that every other governor had been executed, I began to wonder if this wasn't about something else."

"Like what?"

David shifts his gaze to me. "Have you told her anything yet?"

I shake my head.

"We found out who's behind this whole thing. Does the name of Chuck Kearney mean anything to you?"

"The K-Tech guy?"

David nods.

Ev shakes her head, as if she's trying to make pieces to fall into the proper slots.

David spends some time filling her in on what he explained to the rest of us back at Benton's apartment. Evan gnaws on her lip as he tells her about the jets and the oil fields. "I've had time to think this through after that day, and it's starting to make more sense. Kearney lobbied hard to expand overseas trade. He didn't think his market in the Union was big enough. When negotiations with other countries broke off, he became furious, even ran for office so he'd have more power to get the changes he wanted."

"I remember that," Ev says. "But he lost out to Benton. Some scandal or something."

David nods. "We thought that was the end of it, but I suspect he's been selling products in the Ruins. He's been working with the cartels as well, so my guess is a lot has been promised in exchange for their help."

Evan shudders despite the heat.

Evan stands on the path, her back to me, the wind whipping her curls. Her body is stiff, as if she's been frozen. My gaze travels beyond her to catch a glimpse of Bryce, Colin...and Draya.

The air leaves my lungs and my feet tangle with one another, forcing me to take a sudden step to the side to avoid landing on my ass. Draya's blue eyes lock onto mine. My chest burns and I drag in a ragged breath. When my jaw aches from grinding my teeth, I realize how long we've been staring at each other. This is too much, too real. I pivot and hike back to the lake in need of some solitude.

Blood buzzes through my ears as I stand on the shore with no memory of how I got here. Something curls around my arm, and I spin, ready for a fight. Evan is beside me, her hand on my arm. I sigh and pull her against me, wrapping her in a tight hug. My feelings about what Draya did to her are jumbled up with everything else. She's a part of this, but I can't talk to her about any of it. Hell, I can't fucking talk about it at all.

"I need to be alone right now," I grind out, my throat raw with emotion.

"I know." She stands on her toes and kisses my cheek. "I just needed to make sure you were okay." She gives me a sad smile before turning and heading back toward camp.

My gaze returns to the lake, but I don't see anything beyond my own shit. My usual process for sorting everything is failing me. Draya belongs in too many compartments. One is my childhood friend. The girl who chased me under the house with a snake, the one who locked me in the storm cellar when I was six and pounded on the door while I screamed, just to see if I would. She's also the one I played tag and baseball with until our parents made us come in at night.

Another is the teenage girl who my brother fell in love with. She could be tender and sweet and loved Lucien with all her heart. That girl left her family behind when ours was torn apart because she felt Lucien and I needed her more than they did. Compartment three is the anguished girl who lost the love of her life.

The last Draya is the one who takes all the others and destroys them. She's the one who tortured Evan. The one who broke and nearly killed the girl I love. I don't know that Draya. She devoured the other versions of herself that I knew and once loved, and I hate her for that.

What she did to Evan is unforgivable, but what she did to some of my happiest memories by becoming a beast is what finally breaks me. My legs give way and I sink to the ground, shoving my head into my hands as I fight the urge to punch something.

It's past sunset by the time Evan calls my name. "Cyrus? Are you still out here?"

Darkness has filled in the shadows around me and I lift my head to find her silhouette approaching. "Yeah. Sorry, didn't realize how late it was."

She takes a seat beside me without another word. Even though she makes no move to reach for me, having her near me is comforting. I take her hand and weave our fingers together. For a few silent moments, I don't think about anything except the warmness of the girl next to me.

"Let's go get dinner," I say.

She stands and waits for me to get up, then wraps her arm around my waist as we walk back.

DRAYA

Evan

*T*he afternoon heat radiates moisture and tension as the four leaders plus Bryce and Colin sit on the lake shore brainstorming what to do about Draya. I haven't seen her since bumping into her yesterday. Cyrus wouldn't talk about her last night. I didn't get much sleep, and based on the lack of deep breathing coming from beside me, I don't think he did either.

She's being guarded in a tent on the far side of camp. Word has gotten around that she's here, and I'm worried what Joe or my mom will do if they get near her. The guards are as much for Draya's safety as they are to ensure she doesn't escape.

"How'd you find her?" I ask Bryce.

"As we were leaving, Benton got a message from a commander asking about the prisoner move we'd just conducted. Her photo popped up next to it and I recognized her. We volunteered to track her down while Cyrus brought your family back."

Colin's hands are clasped, the only indication he isn't his usual laid-back self. "We used Benton to bait her into a trap. She was spitting mad." He shakes his head and laughs. "I actually know what that expression means now."

"Once she calmed down, she wasn't so bad," Bryce says. "She didn't say more than a dozen words on the walk out here. I don't know how cooperative she'll be..."

Cyrus is rigid beside me, a palpable level of energy rolling off him. "Okay. You guys head back to camp," he says to Colin and Bryce. "We need to talk." Once they're gone, he leans forward, arms resting on his knees. "With everything we now know about Kearney's involvement, the first order of business is to locate where he's holed up, determine his timetable, troop levels and locations. Draya's our best chance to find all that out."

"Once they figure out she's been taken, they'll adjust accordingly," Mateo says. "Not sure how much value it'll be."

"This operation is too big for them to be making huge adjustments. And who's to say she was taken and didn't merely walk off like the two of us?"

"Colin said she's not talking," I offer. It doesn't much matter what the Uprising thinks if she doesn't tell us anything.

"She just needs the proper motivation," Rainey says.

I glance at her, wondering what she has in mind. She doesn't know Draya like I do. "Like what?"

"Uprising techniques are fairly effective."

My heart stops and the creeping sensation of blood draining from my head makes the world swirl around me. My hands reach for the ground to steady me. "No, no, no..." I whisper. "We can't."

With clenched jaw, Cyrus stares out across the lake.

"There has to be another way." My breaths come rapid and I search for the right thing to say so they'll understand. They *have* to understand.

"Let's take a vote," Cyrus says, his voice devoid of any emotion.

His words are a slap across my face and I jerk back.

"All in favor of using enhanced interrogation methods, raise your hand," Rainey says.

Three hands shoot up and my chest tightens. My eyes search my friends' faces, but only Rainey will meet my gaze.

Swallowing back thick tears, I turn to Cyrus, desperate for him to see reason. "Cy, please. You can't do this."

He turns toward me, myriad emotions rushing through his eyes.

"What the hell, Evan!" Rainey shouts.

Mateo's eyes flash dark and dangerous. "Look, this is a leadership council, Evan. You can't have two votes by manipulating your boyfriend."

"I'm not manipulating him, but you guys are like the Ruins bloc, always thinking and voting together. I'm the only one from the Union, and it's like my opinions don't count because of my 'socialist' upbringing."

"Cyrus is going to do whatever you tell him," Rainey says.

Cyrus narrows his eyes at her, his tone menacing. "Rainey..."

"You two were broken up when we put this council together, but now..." She shakes her head. "She has you whipped. We all know it. You might be the only one who doesn't."

Cyrus's jaw is working hard, and I'll be surprised if he has any back teeth left after today.

Mateo sighs, his shoulders dropping and his voice calmer than the rest. "I think that's an exaggeration, but it wouldn't hurt for us to add a fifth to the council. Not just for perceived purposes but to break up a tie during votes, which is bound to happen."

"Yeah, I doubt it," I mumble under my breath. "I want someone from the Union, then. You three are not only from the Ruins, but with your history with the Uprising, I feel like I'm the fourth wheel."

Mateo unfolds his arms. "Fair enough."

"What about Lisa or Colin?" I ask.

"No way," Rainey says, thrusting her chin forward, making her more formidable than her tiny five-foot frame might indicate. "That's just another vote with you."

"That's ridiculous. Cyrus doesn't even vote with me. Clearly.

And Colin and Lisa aren't going to side with me just because we're friends."

"I don't have a problem with a Uni," Cyrus says quietly. "But it has to be someone other than those two. And for obvious reasons, Bryce is out."

"What about Jack?" Rainey offers. "With his background in law enforcement, he could be an asset."

"I'm okay with that," I mumble.

Surprisingly, Mateo and Cyrus nod in agreement. But the damage has been done. I'm pissed at Cyrus, he's pissed at me, and Rainey and I glare at each other. Only Mateo managed to avoid the animosity circle. I stalk off into the trees to be alone while Rainey and Mateo go find Jack and ask him to join us.

Frustration and anger surge through my veins. There must be a way to get them to understand we can't torture Draya, no matter what words they use to label it. I need to convince them, because if I can't, I have to leave. There's no way I can stay here and be a party to what they're planning, nor can I remain in camp as a non-participating bystander.

The thought of leaving rips a hole straight through me. Resting my head on my forearms, I fight back threatening tears. I can't compromise on this and pretend it's okay. Cicada songs rise and fall, interspersed with the calls of birds. A thin sheen of sweat constantly coats my skin, but a warm breeze provides a moment of cooling.

"Hey." Cyrus's low voice comes from behind, startling me.

I quickly wipe my eyes and stand, turning to face him, my body tensed for an argument. But when my gaze meets his, I'm surprised to find only softness, all evidence of his earlier anger gone. Leaning back against a tree, I cross my arms and study him, waiting for him to speak.

He runs a hand through his hair, keeping his distance. "Ev, I love you. You will always be my first priority, but..." His gaze falls from mine and he studies his boots.

"You think I don't want you to torture Draya because of my upbringing, but that's only part of it."

"I know I grew up differently than you did, but that doesn't make me heartless."

"I never said that. I don't think you're all some sort of cold-blooded killers who aren't tormented by what we've done. It's just..." I let out a long sigh, knowing I'm not making myself clear. "I understand her. Draya. She loved Lucien and he's dead. I'm not sure what I would be capable of in her shoes."

He shakes his head. "That doesn't make what she did okay."

"Of course not, but that's not what I mean. All four of us get a vote, we're all equal, but from my perspective, mine's the only vote that should count."

"I thought you were all about equality and democracy."

"Not when it comes to this. Because unless someone else around here has a back full of burn scars, I'm the only one who's been tortured. Doing that to someone...it tears away at our humanity and it doesn't result in anything."

"You said you told them what they wanted to know."

"No. I said I told them what I thought they wanted to hear. Some of it was the truth, but a lot of it wasn't. Eventually I confessed everything I did, plus a bunch of stuff I didn't. I would have said *anything* to make it to stop. If we do this, we're no better than they are, and that's not something I can be a part of."

Voices cut through the trees as Mateo and Rainey return with Jack. Mateo glances between me and Cyrus, then back at me, a flicker of something passing across his features before it's gone. "We talked on the way back here. How else can we get the information we need?"

I close my eyes and let the relief spread through my body. We take our usual seats on various upended logs and get to work.

Rainey stares hard at me. "How do we get her to talk?"

"Just because I'm against torturing doesn't mean I have all the answers."

Mateo shrugs. "Withhold food?"

"Won't work," Cyrus says. "Not with her. Standard motivation isn't going to sway Draya."

"What about if we offer her something she wants?" Jack asks.

I stare at Cyrus as he examines the ground between his knees. "The only thing she wants is the one thing no one can give her."

While they discuss ideas, I replay my time in captivity. I didn't confess everything I knew. I believed I knew where Cyrus was, but I never told them. Draya never got me to divulge that, because I had something to protect, something more important to me than my own pain. Someone I cared about more than myself. Does Draya even have anyone she cares about? She's destroyed all the relationships with the people in her life who mattered.

Except... "I might have an idea."

48

ANOTHER WAY

CYRUS

$\mathcal{E}$v glances my way as we approach the holding tent. Her face reveals nothing, though I have no doubt she's still processing a lot. I'm worried how she'll cope with facing Draya.

Jason, a young kid with close-cropped snow-white hair, lets out a frustrated breath. "She's had lunch, but is in a generally foul mood."

I expect nothing else. Pulling back the flap, I enter to find Draya sitting on the floor, her face twisted into a hateful scowl. She startles for only a second when she registers our presence and pushes herself to standing. We stare at each other for a few moments before her gaze flicks to Evan, then returns to me.

Crossing her arms over her chest, she looks like the girl Lucien loved, and I steel myself to keep from being sucked into old patterns of relating to her. When it becomes clear she won't be speaking first, I shake my head. "I loved you like a sister."

Her blue eyes never waver from mine. "I was protecting her."

My hands curl into tight fists, my fingernails digging into my palms. "Protecting her?"

A sharp intake of breath behind me reminds me Evan is still here.

"I know it doesn't seem like it, but I really was trying to save her life. They figured out who she was. The Uprising tattoo, the red hair, it didn't take a fancy Uni education to put it all together. Walker wants her dead. They were gonna kill her right there on the spot, but I convinced them she was more valuable to us alive. As long as I could get some information out of her, prove her worth, they'd keep her alive. Long enough for me to figure out a way to get her out. I was the one who sent the troops out to locate her friends, because I knew I couldn't do it alone."

I sigh and run a hand through my hair, not knowing what to believe. What Draya says makes sense, but she has every reason to lie.

Draya directs her next words to Evan. "I knew you loved him and wouldn't give up his location. That's why I pressed you so hard. I needed you to believe it though, which is why I threatened his life. If you believed I'd kill him, you'd never give him up." She pauses and rolls her head on her neck. "It was the last piece of information I could use as a bargaining chip. I was counting on your friends arriving in time. I know it was bad, but it could've been so much worse."

"Worse?" Evan asks through clenched teeth.

"You're alive, aren't you?"

Evan turns and stalks out. I shoot Draya a warning glance before going after Ev. She's shaking all over, and it isn't until I get closer that I realize she's not crying. She's wound so tight, she's about to snap in two like a brittle twig. She lifts her head and pivots toward me. The next thing I know she lunges at me, throwing her arms fiercely around me. Still no tears fall, but her body is wracked with silent convulsive spasms. I lift her off the ground and pull her against me until she calms. Her vise-like grip relaxes some and I set her down, my eyes searching hers.

"I can't do this," she says. "I'm sorry. I believe her, but I can't... go back in there."

"I'll find you later."

She heads toward the center of camp, and I take a deep breath, returning to finish things with Draya.

"I'm telling the truth," she says.

God, I want to believe her, and Ev says she does, but I'm not sure. "Why'd you join up?"

"What the hell else was I gonna do?" Her eyes blaze, full of pain, anger, and hatred.

"You really think this is what Lucien would want for you?"

Her head snaps back as if I'd hit her, and tears well up in her eyes. My body deflates at the sight. I've never known Draya to cry. Ever. Not even when Lucien died. She quickly blinks them back and thrusts out her chin. "Well, he's not here to ask."

"He'd never want you to do this. He would've wanted you to be with the people who love you. To be with your family. To move on with your life and not continually mourn him, throwing your future away."

She drops her head, but not before I see her bottom lip tremble. "All I want is Lucien back. I'm so damn tired of hurting *all the time*. Every morning I wake not knowing how I'm gonna make it through another day without him."

I cross the tent, and for the first time since my brother died, I take the girl he adored into my arms and hold her. She wraps her arms around my back and lets me.

"Do you think she'll ever forgive me?" Draya asks.

"I don't know," I answer honestly. "She forgave me an awful lot, so it's possible. Give her some time." I sigh and lean back, propping myself up on my hands. "You know she doesn't trust easily, and once that trust is broken, I'm not sure how you get it back. The only reason she forgave me is because I didn't lie to her. If you're serious about repairing that relationship, you have to be completely honest."

Her gaze narrows. "I haven't lied about anything."

"Why are you still with them, then? You said you joined up because you felt like you had nowhere else to go, but do you really believe in what they're doing?"

She squares her shoulders. "Of course. I'm seeking justice."

"You know that's not what this is about."

"Just because I think the cartels have a warped idea of what's important, doesn't mean I don't want justice for the Ruins."

"So, the ends justify the means?"

Draya's hands shake, the only indication she's not as okay with this as she'd like me to believe. "I didn't know all of that when I signed up. I only knew I needed to move on, and...I thought Lucien would want me to do something. We talked about joining."

"That was to find out what was going on to try and stop it."

"The more I thought about what it really meant to the Ruins, the more I believed I could be a part of something good. Make a difference for once in my lousy life."

"You can't support what they're doing now, and if you knew what this was really about—"

She folds her arms over her chest. "What is this *really* about then, Cy? You seem to know so much more than I do."

"It's about power and greed and nothing more. Not social justice or even the cartels having access to the Northern Territories. It's about some guy named Kearney who wants the oil fields off the southern coast. Nothing good can come from that."

"I don't know anything about that."

"Maybe not, but you have inside information on how the organization is run. We can use that to figure out a way to stop him before it's too late."

"I don't know."

"I don't care what Walker promised you—" My eyes narrow. "Walker's crew is responsible for Lucien. You know that, right?"

Sadness and anger war in her eyes, but no surprise. Before she can offer an explanation for what she's still doing with them or why she's so reluctant to tell me anything, the flap opens, and Mateo joins us.

I begin to make introductions.

"We've met," Draya snaps.

Mateo leans in and whispers, "Are you ready?"

I nod and Mateo slips out, returning with Ty, Conner, and Ben. The boys huddle together near the opening as their eyes adjust to the darker light. They haven't seen Draya since Lucien died, and we didn't tell them about her being in the Uprising.

Ty's eyes widen with recognition. "Draya," he cries, rushing forward, but I put a hand on his chest to stop him.

I turn back to Draya. "Dray, when this is over, things won't be like they were before. Everything's gonna change, but it'll be for the worst if we don't end this now."

Draya glances from me to Ty, then beyond us to Ben and Conner. "What do you want to know?"

I cross my arms. "Everything."

Draya takes center stage while the rest of us take positions in the small holding tent. Evan stands near the opening, appearing small but defiant.

"I don't know anything about this Kearney guy," Draya says. "Walker's calling the shots from the Western Province, but I haven't seen him since the Invasion. This business with the oil is news to me, so someone else must be managing that. Walker is overseeing the relocation effort, bringing in soldiers to secure the top levels. He plans to establish a base of operations up there so they can surveil the entire Union. After that, they're going to open the Union to Mexico and the Ruins. They want to control the flow so it doesn't overwhelm the infrastructure, but that's causing problems. The cartels want the Mexican population given priority, but the Uprising soldiers want their families to be first in line."

Mateo grunts and steps toward Draya. His eyes sweep the tent.

"We don't know where Walker or Kearney are, but we know where the oil fields are, so if we're going to do anything, securing those is our best bet for stopping them."

I grin. "Sounds easy, doesn't it?"

The corner of his mouth lifts in a half smile, but there's a gleam in his eye that's been missing lately. He's itching as much as I am to do something, and now that we've identified a target, he's going to be singularly focused. "We've got a lot of planning to do, and this time there can't be any mistakes."

Draya spends a couple of hours filling us in on the hierarchy of the Uprising in the Union, where their headquarters are located, and how they communicate.

49

ONE OF THESE DAYS

Evan

A warm body is curled up behind me when I wake. Cyrus came to bed long after I did last night. I never even felt him come in. Scooting carefully away to avoid waking him, I dress in clean shorts and a T-shirt.

I'm tying my boots when a deep voice, heavy with sleep asks, "Hey, where are you going?"

I finish with my laces and turn toward him. He's lying on his back, hands behind his head, hair adorably mussed. "I'm meeting my mom for coffee. Want me to bring you back some?"

He gives me a wicked grin. "I want you to come back over here."

"I'm already dressed."

He notches up an eyebrow. "And?"

I laugh, and crawl over to him, leaning in for a quick kiss. "I'm late. I need to go."

He grunts something about my mom I can't make out, then says, "I miss you. We've barely had time to ourselves lately. One of these days, I'm just going to keep you in here all day with me."

I smile. "One of these days, I'm going to let you." As I back out of the tent, I admire the way his biceps flex, wishing today could be that day. I turn and walk out before I change my mind.

Mom is sitting at a table in the mess area, an empty plate in front of her as she nurses a chipped mug of coffee. I grab my own coffee and take a seat across from her.

"Morning."

She glances up, her eyes meeting mine. "We need to talk about you and Cyrus."

Wow, no pretenses. Straight to the point. "No, we don't."

"You're rushing into this...marriage. What's the hurry? You're only eighteen."

"What difference will waiting make? Oh...you're hoping I won't go through with it if we wait."

She takes a sip of coffee. "I thought you had some kind of an infection up in the Northwestern Province. But now, I find out you were shot? And you joined the Uprising? I'm sorry, but if he cared for you the way you seem to think he does, he wouldn't have allowed any of that to happen."

I let out a sharp laugh. "Do you hear yourself? You want a man to control me?" I shake my head. "Besides, none of this is his fault."

"Right, so you just happened to get shot while you were with him and you just happened to join the Uprising with him?"

"No, I joined the Uprising with Colin. Cyrus being there was coincidence. He saved my life. I wouldn't be sitting here talking to you right now if it wasn't for him."

Mom glances away, refusing to acknowledge my last words.

"I'm going to marry him, or be committed to him, with or without your approval. You can continue to judge him and estrange yourself, making family gatherings a nightmare, or you can accept that I love him."

"Lust isn't love, Evan. You think I'm too old to appreciate how he looks?"

"Oh, my god, you think I'm just hot for him?" This whole

conversation is a joke. I take my coffee and stand. "I'm serious, Mom. This is in your court. I love him, not his body, not his handsome face, but him. I love him for all the things he is and all the things he's not. I don't care where he was born, or that he's still learning how to read and write. He is brilliant and amazing and he loves me. I don't need anything else."

We stare at each other for a few long moments before I tear my gaze away and stomp back to the tent. Only when I get halfway there do I realize I forgot to get coffee for Cyrus.

Two days later, Cyrus gets his wish. The rain beats down on our tent before running off and carving rivers through the campground. It's impossible to go outside without getting drenched. I peer out the opening, needing to pee more than I care to think about. The rain's not helping either, and the latrines are at least a hundred yards away.

I grab my galoshes from the back corner and tug them on, but I don't have a raincoat. My eyes search the tent, landing on a plastic tarp. I drape it over my head and dash out into the downpour. Running all the way, I don't spot another person out in this monsoon. After quickly doing my business, I contemplate grabbing some coffee, but it occurs to me with this rain, there may not be any made. I wouldn't blame Lisa one bit for staying put today.

When I get back, drenched despite my best attempts at remaining dry, Cyrus is awake, both mischief and amusement coloring his golden eyes.

"What?"

He pats the spot next to him. "C'mere."

"Cyrus, I'm soaked."

As if to punctuate my statement, water trails down my cheek, dripping onto the ground beside me. I slip off the boots, leaving them near the opening, and drape the tarp over top to dry.

He's still smiling when I turn around, making heat blossom across my face.

I know what he had in mind when he said he wanted to spend the day with me, but there's so much we really need to talk about, and today seems like the perfect opportunity. I peel off my wet clothes and throw on a dry tank top and pair of sweats before sitting cross-legged beside him. He leans up on one elbow and presses a kiss to my arm.

"We should talk," I say.

He sighs and rolls onto his back. "I know."

Leaning back on my hands, I start, finally telling him everything that happened when Marcus and I blew up the camps. We take a break to eat some jerky and granola bars, then he shares his story. I want to tell him I wish he'd never gone away, but that won't change anything, and we both have enough regret for dozens of lifetimes.

Morning turns to afternoon as we continue to share the events of our time apart. He says he nearly slept with a girl the night he discovered Bryce in my room but didn't go through with it. We lay out the ugly emotions and pain we've caused each other. It's by far one of the most difficult things I've ever done and yet it's uplifting. With every hour that passes and with everything we share, I feel a little less burdened.

Finally, I get to the night we rescued Ashlynn and the kids. It's the last thing I've kept from him. Not deliberately, but because I couldn't face it myself. I'm learning that not facing the horror doesn't make it disappear, instead it eats away at my subconscious, waking me at night with hoarse screams that rip from my soul.

Evening falls before we're done talking and the hush that fills the tent when we're finished is stifling. After all we've said today, raw emotions hang heavy like the moisture in the air on a humid day.

I sit on my sleeping bag staring at my socked feet. It gets chilly here now after sunset, and my feet are the first to feel the cold. I count the alternating blue and green stripes from my toes up to the cuffs as the silence grows louder. I chance a peek at Cyrus to find him watching me. His chest rises and falls with what appears to be a huge breath before he scoots closer to me.

Without a word, he picks up my hand and rests it on his palm. I stare at our hands, his darkened by time spent in the sun making mine appear pale in comparison. Suddenly his lips meet mine, frantic, seeking, and demanding as his hands pull me against him until there is no space between us. He kisses me with equal amounts of pain, heartache, longing, fear, and desire — everything we shared today. His love rolls over me like a wave on the beach, pressing me down into the depths of the ocean, washing both of us clean of everything that tore us apart.

I cling to him, because the only way I can survive is to hang on.

The earlier downpour has tapered off to a gentle rain that helps soothe the kaleidoscope of emotions tumbling through me as I lie next to Cyrus. Clearing the air was as frustrating as it was freeing. Too many misunderstandings separated us for so long. I've never found it easy to express myself with words. Today has taught me that as terrifying as it can be to put yourself out there, it can also be rewarding.

Underlying all these feelings is something more, something enduring, and solid. These small moments when we let our guards down and allow ourselves to just be... us... together... are the best thing I've ever known.

My mind wanders over our conversation from the other day when we were fighting about Draya. Something deep in the earthy layers of my memory struggles to worm its way out. When it finally manages to free itself, I gasp.

"What's wrong?" Cyrus asks, his voice heavy with near sleep.

"Cyrus..."

He pushes up, his peaceful expression giving way to concern as he studies my face.

"The other day, when I was telling you about being tortured. I said I confessed to some things we didn't even do."

"Yeah..."

"Well, they were specific things Draya asked about. Attacks on supply trucks and missing weapons and stuff. Stuff *we* didn't do. It didn't strike me at the time. I mean, I only wanted it to stop..."

He nods, his face twisted with confusion and worry.

"If we didn't do it, who did?"

His features morph again as he struggles to shake the sleepiness from his brain and focus on my words. He sits up and runs a hand through his hair. A smile spreads across his face, slow and sure.

I match his grin with one of my own. "If we didn't do it, someone else did. There are others out there. We just need to find them."

He grabs me by the shoulders and pushes me back down, hovering over me, smiling broadly. Then he bends his head, claiming my mouth with his and smiles into the kiss.

I kiss him back, tension easing from me. What seemed impossible hours ago, suddenly feels not only possible, but maybe even likely.

We can do this.

We are not alone.

DEAR READERS

I know it's been a long time since you finished reading THE UPRISING. Thank you for sticking with me.

Last January, the day after I pressed publish on THE UPRISING, I was diagnosed with a rare and very aggressive form of breast cancer. I went through six rounds of chemotherapy, surgery, and over five weeks of daily radiation treatments. While I'll probably never be told that I'm cancer free, at this point in my life, there is no evidence of the disease.

I owe my life to my fantastic medical team, including Dr. Melissa Torrey, who recognized my particular case as inflammatory breast cancer and took an aggressive treatment route, Dr. Ray Lin, who calmed me when I needed it, Dr. Pamela Kurtzhals, who removed all the cancer, and Dr. Salvatore Pacella, who's crafting me an amazing new boob.

I heard from a number of readers over this past year, and I thank you all for your support.

ACKNOWLEDGMENTS

Thanks to my amazing family, the best support team anyone could ask for. Especially my husband, Ernie, who read countless drafts, helping me fix plot holes and find typos.

To my ever-patient editor, Barb, for polishing my manuscript to ensure it's ready for the world.

Thanks to my critique partner, Jen, this book would suck without you.

Thanks to my amazing beta readers for your invaluable feedback. You'll probably see how many changes I made from the beta version thanks to your constructive criticism.

ABOUT THE AUTHOR

T.H. Hernandez is the author of young adult books. THE UNION, a futuristic dystopian adventure, was a finalist in the 2015 San Diego book awards in the Young Adult Fiction category.

She loves pumpkin spice lattes, Comic-Con, Doctor Who marathons and Bad Lip Reading videos. T.H. adores all things young adult, particularly the three young adults who share her home.

When not visiting the imaginary worlds inside her head, she lives in sunny San Diego with her husband, three children, a couple of cats, and a dog who thinks he's a cat, affectionately referred to as "the puppycat."

For more information:
thhernandez.com
thhernandezauthor@gmail.com

ALSO BY T.H. HERNANDEZ

THE UNION - Book 1 in The Union series

THE RUINS - Book 2 in The Union series

THE UPRISING - Book 3 in The Union series

SUPERHERO HIGH - coming from Soul Mate Publishing in 2018

www.ingramcontent.com/pod-product-compliance
Lightning Source LLC
Chambersburg PA
CBHW051316250626
47155CB00007B/2350